The Condo Papers

Dick Lavine

Bloomington, IN   authorHOUSE™   Milton Keynes, UK

AuthorHouse™
1663 Liberty Drive, Suite 200
Bloomington, IN 47403
www.authorhouse.com
Phone: 1-800-839-8640

AuthorHouse™ UK Ltd.
500 Avebury Boulevard
Central Milton Keynes, MK9 2BE
www.authorhouse.co.uk
Phone: 08001974150

This book is a work of fiction. People, places, events, and situations are the product of the author's imagination. Any resemblance to actual persons, living or dead, or historical events, is purely coincidental.

First published by AuthorHouse 2/21/2006

ISBN: 1-4259-0361-4 (sc)

Printed in the United States of America
Bloomington, Indiana

This book is printed on acid-free paper.

To Eileen, whose love and

support are unwavering

and who is as young as she was fifty

years ago

Give me a young man in whom there is something of the old,
and an old man with something of the young:
guided so, a man may grow old in body,
but never in mind.

Marcus Tullius Cicero,
[106 – 43 B.C.]
De Senectute, XI

Carl set out for the restaurant at a brisk pace, despite the limp. After a few minutes the heat caught up with him and he slowed down, took off his blue blazer, and slung it over his right shoulder.

He pulled back his shoulders and picked up his step, showing a bit of the swagger he felt made his limp less noticeable. People were always telling him he looked ten years younger than he was. And although the gray hair was winning the battle with the brown, it was still there. The body was trim, energy intact, and mind keen. He knew the secret, though it wasn't what others might suspect. Keep the libido happy.

It wasn't completely dark yet and he glanced at a family of four dogwoods in full bloom standing sentinel in somebody's front yard. He sighed. Carl was aware of his reputation throughout the Oasis as an old guy who was spry, still big on sex, and indiscreet about his conquests and everything else. Some of his neighbors, he knew, thought he wasn't too bright.

But he was sly as well as spry. When they used him to broadcast information they wanted to spread around, he fell right in with their plan. He was happy to play the dupe when it helped him attain his own ends.

In the next block, in front of a large pseudo-plantation style house, he caught sight of a squadron of azaleas forming an "S." First letter of a family name, he thought. Tasteless, but then he smiled. The "S" brought to mind that "stud" status he treasured.

He was surprised but pleased to be invited tonight. Maybe the president, who must have approved the guest list, had forgiven him for shooting his mouth off. Maybe he wanted him there for old times sake. In any case, Carl was looking forward to the celebration.

*

Hiding behind a van in the parking lot before the party got underway, Gus and the boss watched the old guy with the limp enter the restaurant. Gus, who had his own limp, asked the boss who this old guy was, and the boss said, don't worry about that, just stick close to me and be there when I need you. Gus didn't press the point.

When the boss told him to do tonight's job by himself, he had begged off, saying he'd done enough rough stuff to last a lifetime. The boss got pissed, but Gus stuck to his guns. Finally, when the boss said, okay, but you gotta come with me, Gus felt he had to go. He knew he was already on shaky ground ever since falling asleep in San Juan, when he was supposed to be guarding the boss.

Besides, the boss paid him well. Which meant he could dress like a prince. Tonight he was wearing the dark grey, almost black, Ralph Lauren "Purple Label" suit he had picked up for $3500, the starched white shirt with the wide, red-flowered tie. His ex-wife had hated that tie. That alone was reason to ditch the bitch. He smiled to himself.

Now he was playing the field, and the ladies loved the tie. He shaved once a week, sometimes twice, and wore his black hair shoulder-length because he knew what turned them on. A well-dressed tough sonofabitch with a stubble. When something special came along, he put his hair back in a ponytail. Nine times out of ten that did the trick.

So Gus figured he'd be cool with the boss. He ran his hand through his hair and shut up on this one.

Gus knew something bad was going to happen, and it was going to happen to the guy whose fingers Gus had almost broken and to the guy's girlfriend. He wanted to tell the boss that messing around in the parking lot was the wrong way to do this job. Too risky. But Gus had seen a few of the boss's tantrums. He was afraid, but he wasn't about to say a single damn word and risk the dough the boss was paying him.

When the green Mustang drove into the darkened lot, the boss said, "Get ready," and ten seconds later, "Shit," because an SUV with oversized

x

headlights came gliding in, lighting up the entire place, and it was too late to do anything.

The boss said they would take care of their business later, inside the restaurant. This time Gus could not restrain himself. Doing something inside the restaurant, he said, was a hundred times more risky than doing it outside. The boss said, "Shut the fuck up and do what I tell you."

*

Gus and Carl had never met, had nothing in common except a limp. Nothing offered the slightest clue that on this hot, humid August night these two strangers would be bonded in an intimate, terrible experience.

PART ONE

It is a man's own fault,
It is from want of use,
If his mind grows torpid in old age

From Boswell, Life of Johnson
April 9, 1778

Chapter 1

When I was talked into running for condo President, I had no idea I would become embroiled in deceit and murder. My job was to help the Board undertake routine maintenance, supervise management activity, adjust the budget, and arbitrate petty disputes among the residents. As it turned out, the job description was incomplete.

Comfortable in my autumnal years, I thought I knew myself. In the course of these events, I discovered what I was capable of doing in the name of pride and retribution. Some of what I did was commendable, some was inappropriate, some was illegal. All of it was traceable to the smell of lavender.

Sarah's lavender scent clung to every particle of air in that house, every piece of furniture. The scent was my lifeline as I wandered around the house, sniffing to recapture a piece of her magic.

My son, Brad, called me once a week. A few months after Sarah's death, he urged me to sell the house and move into an apartment. "You need people around you."

At one point, Brad said, "Hold on, Skip wants to speak to you." My hearing was still sharp, and I overheard the admonition to his sixteen-year-old son, my grandson, Skip. "Talk to him, and for God's sake, be nice."

"Hi, grandpa," Skip said. "We think you should sell the house and move into an apartment. Here's Dad.

"Wait a minute," I said. "Tell me how you've been, what's happening with you."

"Same old, same old. I'm fine. Here's Dad." Excessive verbosity had never been an element of my relationship with my grandson.

In spite of the wisdom I saw in Brad's advice, I couldn't bring myself to sell the house. Brad lived three thousand miles away in California. He didn't understand about the lavender scent. Nor could he comprehend the osmosis that made Sarah and me as one, yet different. Even if he listened to Basie's "April in Paris," Brad could not have a remote idea of the shared excitement Sarah and I had re-experienced every time we heard it.

Saturated with memories, I knew I had to *do* something. I wouldn't sell the house, but I had to get out of it during the day. I had to get back to work and apply my energy to the business. The same energy I'd been using to bring back every tiny moment of satisfaction and serenity Sarah had given me.

I went at my construction business with newfound ferocity. Working fourteen-hour days, we began to make some real money. Still, I grew bored and restless. After four years, it was time to get out of the rat race and reap the fruits of fifty years of work, time to catch up on my reading, listen to CDs, make new friends.

In other words, I needed to begin a new life, and, once and for all, leave the house that Sarah's spirit haunted. I was ready.

In October I found a real estate agent. She asked what was important to me so she could help me find something where I'd be "comfortable." For the first time since Sarah died I talked about myself.

In the course of our search, I learned a trick or two about the real estate trade. Sometimes, what seemed nice could be trouble down the road, and what looked uninviting could have possibilities. It was good to be dealing with new challenges.

There were annoyances, though. Once, looking through a duplex, we got to the stairway leading to the bedrooms upstairs. The young owner said, "If it's hard for you to climb these stairs, you could install one of those small elevators." My agent turned her back on the smart-ass yuppie and whispered in my ear, "Chill out, Sid. We're not buying this place even if he offers to carry you up the stairs five times a day."

She called that one right. I have thick skin, but can't tolerate being patronized.

In November we began to focus on a two-bedroom apartment in a condominium on Connecticut Avenue called the Oasis. Built twenty-five years earlier, it had a solid look about it, and lacked the cold sterile appearance of many newer condos. The two buildings and the grounds seemed to be in good shape.

The apartment itself had most of what I wanted - a spacious kitchen, bright living room, cozy den with built-in oak bookcases, a guest bedroom, and a master bedroom with an adjoining bathroom large enough to accommodate my six-foot frame, where I could read the newspaper in the morning free from claustrophobia.

A small ground level management office nestled between two resident buildings. Each building had ten floors and nine units per floor - not too big, not too small. The unit I was considering was in Building One.

The agent smelled a closing. "This one is made to order for you, Sid. Dignified, unpretentious, lovely residents. A ten-minute walk to quality restaurants."

The by-laws and rules and regulations looked reasonable, but I exercised what the lawyers called "due diligence." The financial statements gave me pause. The reserves were at $110,000 which seemed low for an opulent condo with 180 units.

I went back to the place several times on my own. Hanging around with my ears open, I learned that the Board of Directors had voted not to raise the condo fees for each of the past several years. Most of the residents had been delighted, but a few of them, including two Board members, had expressed concern that this was a false saving and would deplete the already low reserves. These "worrywarts," as they were called, had wanted to raise fees modestly each year, but a majority of the Board clung to their position.

Each unit had recently been assessed an average of $5,000 toward the cost of roof replacements on the two buildings. When the special assessment was announced for an expense that should have been anticipated, the Board, previously regarded as sagacious, was now looked upon as irresponsible and shortsighted. Overnight, the worrywarts were now regarded as "prudent" and "insightful."

I weighed my reservations about investing in what might be a financially troubled property. "If there are financial problems," my agent said, "they can be addressed. Maybe the Board needs some fresh blood to take a more realistic view of their fiscal situation. Come to think of it, you could run for the Board. You're probably just what they need."

I grimaced.

Efficiency Management, I discovered, was the Oasis' management company. They were a division of Efficiency Management of America - EMA - a nationwide company. My agent said, "They operate a lot of properties, and they do a good job." I vaguely recalled from my business days that Efficiency Management - EM - was a well-known firm with a good reputation in the greater Washington area.

The Oasis appeared to be well-maintained, the apartment met my needs, and the location was excellent. After looking at seven or eight places, this one seemed best for me.

In late December I sold my share of the business and the house, and in early February, four years after Sarah died, moved into the Oasis. I was financially comfortable, and I settled down to take it easy. I could sleep late, take a walk, read some, and get to talk to my neighbors. My goal was to relax, take on nothing demanding, and coast.

The handful of friends Sarah and I used to see had moved away or died. But I had little interest in cultivating new friends.

Most of the women in the Oasis were unattached - widows and divorcees - and some of them interrogated me. Was I a widower? Divorced? What were my interests? Somebody named Elsie Turner asked if I'd like to come over for a tuna casserole. I came to think of them as the "Casserole Brigade." They were eager for companionship and meant no harm, but they didn't interest me. After only a month of the so-called good life, I was becoming, once again, bored and restless. The TV and pizza were not enough.

One of the men, Carl Harrison, had a coarse charm about him. Rough around the edges, even to my jaundiced ear, he was unlike the Oasis residents I had met. I saw that the Casserole Brigade besieged him, too.

Harrison told me if I wanted action, I should attend a meeting of the condo's Board of Directors. I held off for a while, but on a blustery

March night, I walked grudgingly over to the meeting room. Officially, it's the "Board room," and the residents call it the "Bored room," but it sure as hell wasn't boring that night.

When I hear "board of directors," I think back to the Board of my company, Silva Construction. There were disagreements, but we seldom raised our voices and never engaged in personal attacks. I walked into the Oasis Board meeting five minutes late, and it was a far cry from the Silva Board "discourse," as Maurice, our lawyer, once characterized one of our more heated discussions.

Over the years I'd developed an eye for observing people and situations. When I came into a room, I would size up the scene, check out the players - appearance, body language, how they related to one another. I began to do just that, beginning with the twenty-plus people seated against the walls. Sitting around a table in the middle of the room were four women and three men with nameplates in front of them.

The man sitting ramrod straight at the head of the table had a nameplate reading "Francis Travail, President." Travail and a short, stocky woman, shifting from one foot to another, standing in front of her chair, were exchanging views. Travail, fifty pounds too heavy, was staring at the woman who had short gray-trying-to-be-blonde hair and was dressed in a purple tracksuit with white stripes on the outside of each leg. She was wearing sneakers with "Air Jordan" logos.

As I sat down, Travail, shaking his head of thick, flaming-red hair, said in a low tone, "Sheila, we're only following the recommendations from our management."

Without hesitating, Sheila came back at him. "They don't know their ass from their elbow. Rhododendrons don't belong up against a brick wall. You might as well put up a urinal in the middle of the garden. Why don't you . . ."

Her voice had a grating sound, slightly hoarse, and the more she talked the more interesting I found her. I figured her for early-sixties on a good day. The Liza Minelli haircut had her looking like grandma trying to do Leslie Caron.

Emblazoned on the scruffy T-shirt hanging loosely over the tracksuit were the faded words, "**Make love, not war.**" She must have acquired that T-shirt thirty years earlier. Bottom line: a little the worse for wear but some good mileage left. And quirky. She reminded me of me.

Travail's face was now fire-engine red, matching the color of his hair. "Sheila, you're out of order," he barked.

Sheila responded, "What's out of order is rhododendrons hugging a brick wall. It's like me hugging you - too absurd to contemplate."

At this point, "Lars Rehnberg, Treasurer," broke into the discussion. About my age, he looked like a professional wrestler. His upper arms were bulging through his plaid sport shirt, and his chest muscles were like those of Johnny Weissmuller - well, Arnold Schwarzenegger. A mass of blonde-turning-gray hair sat on top of his large head.

Rehnberg was soft spoken. "Sheila has a point. If we move the rhododendrons away from the wall, they'll get breathing space. They'll look better and be healthier. The cost won't be all *that* much. We'll get it back because the rhododendrons will last longer."

Travail wiped his forehead with a handkerchief. "Lars, you're always complaining that we spend too much money. Now you want to throw it away over some perfectly nice bushes that are begging to be left alone."

The perspiration returned and Travail wiped his forehead once more. Sheila began to speak again, and got as far as, "That's the dumbest thing . . ."

Travail broke in with, "We'll take a ten-minute break so we can all calm down."

The soft murmur of conversation bubbled up, and I walked over to the large coffee dispenser and got in line. I picked up a plastic cup, hesitated, and turned to the person standing in line behind me. It was the aging hippie I'd been observing, Sheila.

"Excuse me," I said with a smile.

"What?"

"Do you happen to know if this coffee is decaf?"

"Of course it's decaf. Old farts *only* drink decaf," she said. "How come I haven't seen you around?"

"I've been hibernating for the winter."

"And this is your debut?"

An impulse seized me. "Yes, and my timing was good, because I've seen those rhododendrons and you're right. They're cramped and hideous against that brick wall."

"What's your name?"

"Sid Silva."

"Well, Sid Silva," she said, "I tell you what you do. You call me tomorrow after lunch and we'll talk. Sheila Marcuse. I'm in the directory."

I said I would and walked away, wondering how I was going to find out which rhododendrons and which brick wall they were talking about. As I sat down with my coffee, I noticed one of the Board members looking me over. Her nameplate said "Anna Carroll, Secretary."

The meeting droned on. They argued about the need, or lack of need, for redecorating the lobbies, and about the excellence, or inadequacy, of Oasis security.

I gave the Board members a quick tour. Sitting between Rehnberg and Travail was a dyed blonde bedecked with jewelry whose nameplate read "Bunny Slack." Making eye contact with everybody including me, she struck me as someone who had dedicated herself to resisting the ravages of age. I gave her a salacious sixty.

On the other side of Travail was a clear-eyed woman with dark brown hair down to her shoulders. Mid-forties, I guessed. Her nameplate read, "Nikki Bullett, General Manager." A stack of files was on the table in front of her and her function seemed to be assisting the President. Occasionally, she would whisper something to Travail, but she spoke aloud infrequently and never altered her noncommittal expression. Travail sometimes asked her for one of the files and she'd hand it to him.

Next to her sat "Dr. Morton Moody," the oldest Board member - maybe eighty. For almost the whole time I was there, he read papers from a file in front of him, but every once in a while he'd look up and say something like, "We can't do this," or "We tried that five years ago, didn't work then, won't work now."

After Moody came "Jane Fountain." She was elegantly dressed in contrast to the other members who were in casual clothes. Maybe forty, she was the youngest one there. Then there was "Audrey Weeks, Vice

President," a mousy little thing with big hazel eyes and a smile permanently in place.

The seventh Board member was "Anna Carroll, Secretary" who'd been checking me out earlier. A few strands of gray lined her amber hair tied in a knot on top, accentuating her cheek bones. She wore dark frame wide glasses and might have been in her late-fifties, but could have been hiding five years. She made me think of the junior high school librarian I'd once lusted after.

When the meeting ended, I watched Sheila Marcuse leave with most of the others.

I approached the President, who was putting his papers away, and said, "Excuse me, Mr. Travail. My name is Sid Silva. I've only been here a short time, but I want to say, you do a good job running the meeting. They sure gave you a hard time."

The sweat was creeping back on his forehead, and he wiped at it. As we talked, he was polite but kept a certain distance. I didn't know a rhododendron from a daisy, but on occasion I liked to stir things up. I said, "I don't see what the fuss is about. I never met a rhododendron I didn't like."

Finally, I got a smile out of him. "I feel the same way," he said.

"Let me ask you something," I said. "Which stand of rhododendrons are we talking about?"

I knew "stand" couldn't be the right designation, but I took a chance that Travail didn't know any more about horticulture than I did. Which is to say, nothing. I hoped there was more than one stand or clump or school, whatever the word, of rhododendrons.

"The one near the brick wall just behind the Fitness Center on the south side," he said. "Eight of them."

"Oh, I know that one," I said. "It's stunning and in harmony with the surrounding environment."

How could I tell Sheila Marcuse one thing and Francis Travail the opposite? It may have had something to do with the fact that I didn't make all that money in my business worrying about ethical consistency.

Travail looked up sharply and asked, "What line are you in, Sid?"

"I was in construction. Now I'm retired."

"What was the name of your company?" he asked.

"Silva Construction & Maintenance Company. We put up commercial buildings, hotels, malls, office buildings all over the country. Managed some of the properties, but building them was more fun."

"I hope we'll see more of you," he said.

I called Sheila Marcuse at one o'clock sharp the next day and she asked me to come over in half an hour. "Building Two, Apartment 802." Her voice had the same gravelly sound as the night before.

A garden separated the two buildings and the management office. I had heard the residents call the garden our "greenspace." I lived in Building One so I had to cross the greenspace to get to Building Two. I left my apartment early to look at the shrubs and trees. When I got to the eight rhododendrons crouched behind the Fitness Center, I studied them. They did seem crowded and too close to the wall. But what did I know? Still, I was pleased that I knew which plants were rhododendrons.

Sheila's overheated apartment was a mess. Every inch of floor space seemed to be occupied, with chairs, sofas, and tables nudging each other, paperbacks overflowing the bookcases, and still other books standing in shaky stacks wherever I looked.

She was wearing an off-white shirt falling over her jeans, and loafers without socks. We sat down in the kitchen and she brought out coffee and semi-stale Danish.

"How come you know so much about plants?" she asked.

"Well," I said, "my father was in the wholesale gardening business. He sold to garden shops in five states. When I was a kid I hung around a lot and got to know a few things about the business. It stuck."

This was a total lie. My father had been an accountant with a utility company.

"You went into that business?" she asked.

"No. I tried different things and ended up in construction."

"So tell me more about yourself," she said, "aside from the fact that if I saw you in the middle of a snow storm, I'd swear you were Burt Lancaster."

As I would discover, exaggeration was as much a part of her makeup as the rough, acerbic quality of her speech. On the other hand, I had been told a few times that there was "a touch" of Lancaster in my appearance.

"Born in Baltimore. My father was from Spain and my mother was second generation Italian. They argued a lot, most of the time she won. I got a BA from Georgetown, taught school, then the construction business, married forty years, lived in Cleveland Park, son and grandson in San Diego, my wife died four years ago, and I'm sixty-nine."

"Give me a break," she said, "you're not over sixty."

"Flattery will get you every place. What about you?"

She put a chunk of Danish into her mouth, chewed and talked. "Buffalo. After I graduated from Syracuse, I followed a rock-and-roll band. Married the drummer. Ten years later he said he was bored so we got dismarried. I never did understand that. I'm a lot of things but boring ain't one of them. We're still friends, sort of. My two daughters live in Buffalo, but we're not close. I *am* sixty-six. Have some more Danish."

"Thanks, I'm kind of full. There's no way you're fifty."

She smiled for the first time and said, "Never shit a shitter."

"How did you get to Washington?" I asked.

"After Rick and I split, I moved around the country, and had a few flings that proved to be nothing. In the mid-70s my sister asked me to come live with her in Washington. I watched them build this place, waited for the kinks to get ironed out, and three years later I bought this apartment."

I made the quick calculation. "You've been here over twenty years."

"'Fraid so."

"You must like it."

"The location is great and the amenities are nice. There are some problems, though. I'll tell you about it sometime. How about you? Short while, no?"

"Month and a half."

"So tell me, Burt, looking back at your life, what are your unfulfilled dreams? What did you want that didn't happen?"

I thought a moment. "I know this sounds like a cop-out. The answer is nothing. My life with Sarah was beautiful, my work was satisfying, and I've had a pretty good time all around."

"What about your son and grandson? Do they give you joy?"

"Mixed bag, goes with the territory. What about you? What do you want that you don't have?"

"Thought you'd never ask. Television. Can't act, can't sing, can't dance for shit. But I'd shine on TV. The Buffalo high schools get to run a local TV station one day a year. When I was a junior, they asked me to be weather girl. Bleached my hair blonde, and knocked them out. I still get a color job once in a while, but it's not up to the old days."

"Looks good to me."

"Anyway, I keep trying out on TV, anything and everything. They turn me down. The masses out there would love me . . . one of these days."

"Good luck. Speaking of the masses, what are they like here? Nice? Interesting?"

"Most of the people here are pretty much like you and me. Old farts drinking decaf and trying to stay active. There's a friend of mine I want you to meet. Anna Carroll."

"Isn't she a member of the Board? I saw her last night at the meeting."

"Yup, that was Anna. You'll like her."

Sheila's reverse image, Sarah, had been a gentle person. On those rare occasions when I was in a grumpy mood - roughly twice a day - she would come up with that defusing smile and kill in its infancy whatever argument I was about to launch. For more than forty years Sarah had been my navigating star, my anchor of stability without which my equilibrium would have faltered, and my very dreams would not have existed.

Yet when I came upon this tough-talking termagant, I was intrigued. I thought the unthinkable. Had there been an undercurrent of boredom in all my years with Sarah? Was my ear cocked for a whisper of excitement to animate the placid autumn of my life?

Or was my attraction to Sheila less complicated? Had I simply sensed that her cavalier façade concealed a core of kindness, that in her perverse way she was extending a hand of friendship? She had no romantic interest in me. She pointedly brought up her friend, Anna. *You'll like her.* I certainly had no romantic interest in Sheila Marcuse or Anna Carroll or anybody else. Could this Sheila be the friend I didn't know I needed?

A few days later, I ran into Carl Harrison, the target of the Cas-serole Brigade, while I was loading up on frozen dinners at the nearby supermarket.

"Let me ask you a question," he said. "You play poker?"

"I used to play in college, and then when I was in Korea. '50, '51. Non-combat zone. Been years since I played."

He picked up a frozen pasta from my cart, looked it over, and put it back. "We've got a monthly game going. We aim for six or seven players but sometimes we're short. Dealer's choice - seven-card stud, five-card stud, draw. Nothing wild, no high-low, no check and raise. A dollar, two dollars, three-raise max. We rotate. Next game is my place a week from today, 7:30. Why don't you give it a try?"

Carl's apartment was spare and functional - sturdy furniture and not much there that he didn't use every day. I spotted a set of Britannica on the far wall and a photograph of Carl and a young girl he told me was his granddaughter, Karen.

When I arrived the players were seated around the poker table, trad-ing pre-game banter. Carl introduced me all around. There was a bald guy from Building One named Ron Sterling, and a kind-of-gruff type named Charlie - I never did get his last name - who was actually wearing a tie.

When I shook hands with Lars Rehnberg, the Board member, he said, "Didn't I see you at the last Board meeting?"

I said, "Thought I'd educate myself on what's happening here."

"Well, I'm glad you came. We can use some new blood."

The sixth player was the President himself, Francis Travail. He greeted me with a thin smile on his thick lips. In the old days I used to think of myself as a student of the game. I would observe, surrepti-tiously, the individuals' styles of play, and apply what I learned to my strategy. I found myself doing it again.

Travail's play was super-conservative, demonstrating under confi-dence. If his first few cards were unpromising, he threw in his hand. If he stayed in, you knew he had something going. He underbet, and playing "on-the-come" - speculatively - was beyond his ken. He sulked when he lost and gloated when he won.

In the course of the game, I came to like Lars. Behind the muscles he was considerate, and his style of playing was I'm-here-to-win-straight-ahead. On a number of occasions, though, he waded into situations his cards didn't seem to warrant.

Carl Harrison wore an enigmatic smile some of the time, as though he knew something the others didn't know. He played erratically. Sometimes his cards didn't warrant his aggressiveness, and on other occasions when he spread his cards at the end of a deal, I wondered why he hadn't been more assertive with such a good hand.

Ron and Charlie were competent if uninspired players. After a while I figured I could hold my own in this crowd despite the time gap since I had last played.

Overall, the game was competitive but friendly, and we drank some beer, munched on chips, and swapped corny stories. When somebody won a big pot, he'd say something he thought was funny, and the one losing a bundle would recite the old saw, "The winners tell jokes and the losers yell 'deal.'"

When we quit at midnight, I had lost about $35. As we helped Carl clean up, he looked at me and said, "So tell me. You want to become a regular?"

"I'd like that," I said. It was the best time I'd had in five years.

Chapter 2

A week later Sheila invited me to dinner. When I arrived at her apartment a few minutes late, Anna Carroll was already there, sipping what looked like sherry. Sheila introduced me and asked me what I'd like.

"Vodka on the rocks, please," I said.

"Is Absolut okay?"

"Beautiful."

Ten minutes later a man named Clarence Mark arrived. With his scraggly beard he looked like a tough truck driver in his fifties, but his diction was that of an English professor. He was not an Oasis resident, but seemed to know Sheila well, and Anna, too, greeted him as a friend. While Sheila was in the kitchen the three of us talked casually.

It turned out that Clarence did in fact teach English literature at a nearby high school. It wasn't the same one where I had been on the staff in earlier days, but he knew some of the teachers, now retired, whom I had known.

Ron Sterling from the poker game showed up with his wife, Kathy. They were all pleasant company and the conversation, mostly about condo politics and movies, was lively. We observed, of course, the obligatory recitations of geriatric ailments. Organ recitals, Maurice used to call them.

At one point I went into the kitchen to replenish my vodka. Sheila was pouring salt onto mixed vegetables sautéing in a frying pan. Raising my eyebrows, I pointed to the bottle of Absolut. "Go for it, Burt," she said. "We don't stint in this house."

As I dropped some ice cubes into my glass, I glanced at the small TV set perched on the shelf over the stove. A local moderator, repeatedly honored for her civic activities, was hosting a weekly talk show.

"Look at that dumb-ass blonde," Sheila said. "She's got two things going for her. Tits and ass. Every question she asks is s-t-u-p-i-d, and the program is b-o-r-i-n-g. I could give that show pizzazz. *My* questions would piss them off, have them yelling at each other. The audience would double in two weeks." She was still pouring the salt. "Oh well."

After an hour, Sheila announced, "Soup's on," and we sat down in the dining room. I'm not sure what I was expecting, but it wasn't what we got. The roast beef was like shoe leather, the mashed potatoes were choking in butter, and the string beans had crawled out of some moldy can from the Depression years. But at least she served ice cream instead of stale Danish for dessert.

I could see that Sheila, bless her, was one of the great bad cooks, and I had a hunch they all shared my view. But we complimented her on the meal.

Anna lived in my building, and I walked her home through the illuminated garden. When we passed the rhododendrons, she smiled, and said, "Sheila's project."

It was a beautiful evening and I suggested we sit down on the bench looking out on the greenspace, and take in the early buds in the glow of three floodlights. The forsythia were bathed in yellow bells and our stand - stand? - of six dogwoods was eager to make its debut. It was refreshing to look at plants, shrubs, and trees pleasing to the eye instead of obstacles to be removed on a construction site.

Forming a backdrop to the horticulture was a mass of equipment encircling Sheila's building. The residents had been talking nonstop about installation of a new roof on Building Two. They weren't happy about the noise and mess we'd have for a month or so, and they were still seething about the special assessment the Board voted to pay for this roof and the new roof to come on Building One. And in the past few days there had been talk about problems with the elevators.

A tall crane loomed over Building Two. Carl had told me this was there to replace the aging air conditioning compressors on the roof. We surveyed the paraphernalia that included a tunnel-like tube extending from the roof into a dumpster sitting on the ground. I knew this was to dispose of the debris from the old roof. Next to the building were stacked crates and cartons of miscellaneous material, some of them marked "asphalt."

For some reason I found something ominous, menacing, about the scene. Pointing toward the crane, the tube, and the crates staring at us, I said they were unsightly.

Anna smiled. "I'm afraid you're right. And nobody's happy about the special assessment." She paused. "I wish that appearance and cost were the only concerns."

"What do you mean?"

She looked at me for a few moments. "It's a long story, Sid. I'll tell you about it, but not tonight. Let's not spoil a lovely evening."

I had forgotten how satisfying it can be just spending time with amiable people. We walked back to our building. The elevator got to my floor first, and I shook hands with her. She looked straight at me, and said, "I enjoyed talking to you, Sid. I look forward to seeing you again."

Another thing I had forgotten. Forthrightness.

A couple of days later, Sheila called and asked if I'd like to go to a movie with her and Anna. We spent ten minutes trying to find a movie on which we could agree. Sheila favored "a story about contemporary people working out their problems." Anna, she said, liked costume dramas faithful to history. I went for suspense and intrigue.

When we reached an impasse, she said, "Oh, hell, why don't the two of you just come over here and I'll cook up one of my blue plate specials."

I shuddered, and said, "That's really nice of you, but we were just there. How about I take you both to dinner?"

"Thought you'd never ask."

I took them to what I thought of as my personal restaurant, Buona Sera. Sarah and I had had dinner there once or twice a month for more than twenty years. The owners were Stefano, the chef, and Maria who handled the business end and supplemented the small waiter-waitress staff when the place was full - which was most of the time.

Maria and Stefano met after both their families came here from Sicily in the early sixties. They were married in 1963, when Maria was twenty and Stefano was twenty-seven. Borrowing money, they opened the restaurant in a small building just outside the commercial center of downtown Washington.

Ten years later, they had built a following and were coming out of debt. Their lease was up for renewal, and the landlord saw their success as a warrant for an obscene increase in their monthly rental fee. Sarah and I persuaded them that it made sense to buy the building, even at the landlord's inflated price. We came up with the cash they needed to do this, and they repaid us over the next twelve years.

When its lease expired a few months after they bought the building, the travel agency occupying the office adjoining the restaurant moved away, and Maria and Stefano took over that space, doubling their capacity from forty to eighty. With their nine remaining commercial tenants, they earned a more-than-comfortable living.

Reservations were made weeks in advance, but Maria would accommodate Sarah and me on an hour's notice. They treated us like family. After we had loaned them the money - unsolicited - Maria had wanted to change "Buona Sera" to "Buona Sarah." We talked her out of it.

When their oldest daughter graduated from Harvard in 1987, Sarah and I attended the celebration in Cambridge. Stefano and Maria attended Sarah's funeral.

Maria's taste was everywhere in evidence. In keeping with the name - Good Evening - photographs and frescoes of nighttime scenes in Palermo, Venice, and Florence hung on the walls. After the customers were seated, sniffing the fresh flowers in the center of the table, the waiter brought a platter of bruschetta with garlic bread and green olives, and a small glass of Orvieto - all courtesy of Buona Sera.

As usual, the room was crowded, but they gave me my favorite location, a table at the back wall, opposite the entrance and next to the small service bar, making it easy for me to chat with Maria on her way to and from the kitchen. The table also had the advantage of semi-privacy. It was removed from the center of the room where most of the patrons were seated. As I was to discover, another advantage arose from the flexibility with which they could convert the area to accommodate up to a dozen people.

After Maria and I greeted each other with an embrace and after her tart word about my too-long absence, I introduced her to Sheila and Anna. We settled in and Maria, her jet-black hair tied loosely in back, brown eyes more piercing than ever, came over with a bottle of the Brunello she knew I favored. Sheila looked up at her and said, "So tell me, Maria, is this guy as nice as he seems to be? Is he the real thing?"

As she poured the wine Maria remained silent. I thought she hadn't heard the question - the place was noisy as always. Or maybe she had found the question offensive. She placed the bottle on the center of the table, looked straight at Sheila, and said, "If you have to ask that question, you shouldn't be having dinner with him." She moved on to greet new arrivals, but not before she threw a quick smile at Anna.

Sheila looked at Anna. "What did I tell you? My instinct is foolproof. Burt is not just a pretty face. He's a winner."

Maria took the orders from Anna and Sheila - grilled shrimp for both of them - and, turning to me, said, "The usual, Sid?" I nodded and when she brought us the food, Maria set down broiled veal chops, sautéed spinach, and roast potatoes in front of me.

The evening was a success. Somebody listening would have thought we were old friends enjoying a reunion. It was a balmy night for early April, and the twenty-minute walk home was refreshing. Anna and I walked through the garden with Sheila to her building, and Sheila said, "Well, Burt, is this the beginning of a beautiful friendship?"

A few weeks later, with nothing better to do, I wandered over to the Board room and attended my second meeting. All seven Board members and a handful of residents were in attendance.

When I arrived, they were arguing about the number of pets the residents should be allowed to have. The bald spot on top of Dr. Morton Moody's head was shining in a halo effect, and he was pontificating.

"Pets keep their masters healthy. A tonic easily obtained and easily maintained. The more pets you have, the healthier you are, the younger you feel," he said, citing "university studies" to support his assertion.

"And my first-hand experience with my patients, especially my geriatric patients," Dr. Moody continued, "supports the conclusion to be drawn from the scientific research."

The words marched from his mouth like foot soldiers in close-order drill, encased in precise diction, resonating with incontrovertible truth. "Give a senior a pet and you give him a new lease on life."

"Or her," said Bunny Slack, rubbing one of her long silver earrings between her thumb and forefinger. She was sitting back in her chair, her mop of dyed blonde hair falling all over her heavy makeup.

"Or her *what*?" asked Dr. Moody.

"Give *him* a new lease on life or give *her* a new lease on life."

Looking around at everybody except Dr. Moody, Slack went on, "I hear what you're saying, Morton, but I don't know what you're talking about. I've never had a pet and I feel young as hell. You want animals, you go to the zoo. I say, keep the rule we have. One pet is plenty."

"Look at it this way," Jane Fountain said, "whatever else a dog is, he - or she" - flashing a quick smile in the direction of Bunny Slack - "is your friend. Let me illustrate. Let's say a nice young person moves in with you . . ."

"It should only happen," Bunny mumbled.

Fountain, who looked about forty, seemed to be out of place, partly because she was so young and partly because of the way she was dressed. Most of the women were wearing pants and loose-hanging shirts, and the men had open collars. Fountain wore a tailored suit, a silk blouse buttoned almost to her neck, dark gray stockings, and patent leather pumps. She could have been on her way to a fashionable dinner party.

Fountain continued. "He or she would become your friend, and make you feel better. Same with a pet. What harm could there be if I had a dog and a cat or two dogs or two cats?"

"I'll tell you the harm," Travail said. "You fall on your face slipping and sliding on the dog-doo, you'll want a no-pet rule."

"Not fair," growled Dr. Moody. "We have a pick-up policy and you know it."

"It won't work," said Slack. "Once the galloping herds of animals are roaming the place, it'll be raining turds, fleas, pests, parasites, and we'll be scratching day and night. The barking and growling and meowing will drive us crazy. We'll have rug damage, chewed-up wood. It will be a living hell."

Audrey Woods spoke for the first time. "It is important to be kind to animals."

In the end, Carroll and Rehnberg voted for a two-pet rule, along with Moody and Fountain. Travail and Slack voted to keep the present rule, and Woods abstained - for unstated reasons. We now had a two-pet policy.

After the vote was taken, Travail said, "You'll regret turning this refined place into an animal haven."

He struck me as a man who did not like to have his authority questioned.

Beginning in the middle of April, Sheila, Anna, and I got together once or twice a week. We went to the movies when we could agree on one. Sheila loved card games; Anna was indifferent. We discovered talents and virtues, and uncovered a few blemishes. We talked about books and music and food, among other things. Anna and I had an unspoken agreement to ignore Sheila's level of culinary skill.

During one of our walks, we came upon a distraught mother trying to calm her two small children in the middle of a screaming match with each other.

Sheila looked at Anna and said, "Go do your thing, calm them down."

"Wave my wand."

"It's worth a shot."

Sheila and I hung back as Anna approached the mother and spoke with her for a few minutes. Unsmiling, the mother shook her head from side to side. Anna began to make her way back to us. The mother caught up to her and they spoke again.

This time the mother nodded, and Anna went over to the children, spoke to them quietly, walked with them to the grass nearby, and sat down between them. In seconds the children were in the palm of her hand, listening intently to her soft voice.

Sheila placed her hand on my shoulder, and said, "I've seen her do this before. She has the gift."

If Anna had a gift it was knowing how to listen. She didn't go through the rote motions - eyes fixed on the speaker, nodding or frowning or commiserating or congratulating at the right moment. She would *hear* what the person was saying. And when the speaker had finished, Anna's response was never mechanical or perfunctory. Anna was able to get into the shoes of the person, and, invariably, the person knew it.

And this touch extended to people with varied backgrounds. Anna had befriended Nikki Bullett and could be seen in Nikki's office, listening, nodding, coming back, perhaps, with advice regarding Steven, Nikki's ten-year old son. Anna had no children. She might have been an exceptional mother.

In my two and a half months at the Oasis, I couldn't avoid hearing the favorite topic of conversation among the residents - what the Board was doing wrong, what management was doing wrong. Why in hell were we having a special assessment for the roof replacement? Why hadn't the Board built up our reserves for a rainy day? And the elevators showing their age. Another special assessment?

For the most part the three of us avoided condo-talk. On one occasion I broke the pattern. It was a warm mid-May day, and Anna suggested we have lunch at Buona Sera. She had savored our dinner there a month earlier.

Maria had seated us at one of the three tables on the broad sidewalk just outside the restaurant, and as I dipped the coarse peasant bread into the plate of olive oil, I mentioned the Building Two roof replacement recently completed. I said the new roof had held up well under the heavy rain that had fallen a few days earlier.

I couldn't miss their exchange of glances. Sheila said, "That's a complicated subject, Burt."

"Tell me about it."

"One of these days we'll get into it."

"You've said that before. Why not tell me now?" I asked.

"Why not?" Anna said. "Last year Lars and I felt the bids - all the bids - were far too high, and we wanted the Board to retain an expert to advise us. Travail disagreed. We talked to Efficiency Management, but nothing came of that. The lowest bidder got the contract and did a good job. We still think the price was excessive, but we don't know what to do."

"Are you saying you think there was something improper about the bids?"

Sheila turned toward me. "Something's smelly in the state of Denmark."

"Something's *rotten* in the state of Denmark," I said.

Sheila didn't crack a smile. "Rotten for you, smelly for me."

"Have you talked to a lawyer?" I asked.

"Three," Sheila said, "and they all came up with the same mealy-mouth bullshit. They won't represent individual owners. They'll get into it only if the Board authorizes them to represent the condo."

She adopted a pompous-lawyer tone. *It appears the suppliers may be engaging in criminal practices. But it would be inappropriate to represent individual members in a matter relating to injury allegedly incurred by the entire condominium.* They're telling us we're getting screwed, but they can't do anything?"

Anna kept her silence. She, too, was frustrated, but her reserves of energy on the subject seemed to have been depleted.

Running her hands through her short hair, Sheila said, "The Board has no balls and we don't have a leader we can trust. And the lawyers share the same scriptwriter."

Maria had brought over a carafe of white wine, early on, courtesy of Buona Sera, and toward the end of our meal she joined us for a few minutes. Anna told her how much she liked the restaurant.

"I write travel pieces," Anna said, " and that's been going quite well. I've been thinking about trying my hand at restaurant reviews for suburban papers. If you have no objection, I'd like to begin with Buona Sera."

"So long as you'll say we strive for perfection," Maria smiled.

"I'll do better than that. Suppose I call you, and we'll make an appointment for me to sit down with you and get some background."

Maria beamed, and I saw a friendship taking root.

Toward the end of May, we began to go on two or three day excursions in my green Mustang which I intended to keep forever. They smiled when they saw my vanity tag - "SS" for Sid Silva - and frowned when I told them about the flak I used to take from my business partners who insisted this stood for the SS of Third Reich infamy.

"Why would they say that?" asked Anna.

"I guess they thought I was too bossy."

"Ah, now we find out," Sheila said, glee all over her face. "Burt has a streak of the autocrat in him."

We went to Nashville and saw the Grand Old Opry. We spent two days in the Brandywine Valley in Delaware. We visited Orlando - that one was five days. We would book two adjoining rooms. They laid down the ground rule that I pay for my room, they pay for theirs. But they allowed me to spring for dinner once in a while.

When it was time to turn in at the end of the day, a ritual developed. We'd get to our rooms, and Sheila would kiss me on the right cheek, Anna on the left. Then Anna would say, "Sleep tight, Sid," and Sheila would come up with a parting shot like, "Try not to think about us, Burt, or you'll over-excite yourself."

As we came to know and trust one another, the story of their relationship emerged. When Anna's divorce became final, twenty-eight years earlier, she enrolled in law school, but became disenchanted with the adversarial environment after two years. Anna thought of herself as a healer, not an advocate.

She tried her hand at freelance writing and a variety of editing jobs, but found them unsatisfying. At that point she used some of the money from the divorce settlement as a down payment on an apartment in the Oasis Condominium.

A despondent forty-two-year-old divorcee, lonely and searching for friendship, Anna moved into the Oasis. One day in late April, Anna explored the garden between the two buildings comprising the Oasis. She soaked up the sun and admired the landscaping.

A woman of uncertain years and compact figure sitting on the bench in the garden, invited Anna to join her. The raspy voice belonged to Sheila Marcuse, and within minutes it became clear to Anna that she was in the presence of a singular personality, one who relished social intercourse unencumbered by restraint or inhibition.

Anna, wary of embarking on new relationships, was drawn to the candor that seemed to inform Sheila's every utterance. Nor did Anna's refinement and reserve discourage Sheila's overtures of friendship. Sheila was enchanted with her new friend's guileless transparency.

They chatted for hours that first day, and in the months and years that followed, became close friends. In the fullness of time, Anna found herself talking about her marriage to the philandering physician, her divorce, her erstwhile writing career, and, indeed, her inner feelings.

Sheila matched intimacy with intimacy. She discussed her own marriage to a rock-and-roll drummer, their divorce, her estranged children, and her current relationship with a man named Clarence whose wife was ill. And she discussed, of course, her frustrated desire to be a television personality. Sheila's forthrightness prompted Anna to relate her own disappointments following the divorce.

In the twenty-four years they had known each other, Anna learned that Sheila's deliberate use of raunchy language and faulty grammar camouflaged sensitivity and compassion, and Sheila became aware of the moral strength and resolve that lay behind Anna's sense of propriety.

Sheila's bonhomie was the tonic that restored Anna's self confidence, and Anna's stability was the grounding that held Sheila's erratic circuitry in check. Neither attempted to transform the other, and both benefited from their friendship.

Late one sultry afternoon during a three-day outing to Savannah, Sheila and I were sitting on a stone wall waiting for Anna to return from the restroom. A young woman with bare midriff and a ring hanging from her pierced belly button, was standing nearby, absorbed in her cell phone. She was wearing oversized rectangular sunglasses, cut-off jeans, a tank shirt, and sandals. Above her outside left ankle was a purple tattoo depicting a tongue hanging out from a mouth.

Her voice was loud enough for me to believe she wanted to be overheard. She was saying, "Just you and me. I may never let you go."

She closed her cell phone, and as she reached around to place it into a pocket of her backpack, she gave us a broad grin.

Sheila looked up at her and said, "Sounds real good, sweetheart, just be careful. Make sure he wears something. You know what I mean - protection."

The girl - she couldn't have been more than twenty - switched off the grin, shook her golden mane, and said, "Oh, fuck off," and walked away.

Sheila looked at me. "There's the problem with the young. No respect, no humor."

Then, without missing a beat, she pointed toward the restroom, and said, "You know, Burt, she likes you a lot."

"I like her," I said. "She's a lovely person."

"So?"

"So . . . what?"

"So here's what I think. I think you're scared to get close to her. You think that would be a betrayal of your departed wife. You're afraid to break loose from your grief."

I looked at her and didn't say anything.

As the spring weather became warmer, I came to regard each of them in a different light. I saw Sheila as a valuable friend - for all her shenanigans.

Anna was another story. As she revealed herself throughout the simmering summer, I began to wonder about the sensuality behind that demure demeanor. It was the first time I had entertained such a curiosity in five years. But that's all I did. Wonder.

One of our more memorable jaunts was a three-day stay in the Big Apple where we saw two Broadway shows and heard some big band music in the Village. On the last night, Sheila insisted we go to a cabaret on Eighth Avenue notorious for its racy shows featuring half-clad "dancers." Anna and I protested but Sheila prevailed. After half an hour, they spotted me stifling a yawn. Anna winked at me, and Sheila said, "Don't con us, Burt. Behind that mask of indifference, we know you're horny as all shit."

I was aware of the unorthodox arrangement we had - a man and two women, all in their sixties, behaving like The Three Musketeers.

And I knew the courteous demeanor of the residents disguised their speculation about what they surely perceived to be our lascivious behavior. The gossip machine, always in full gear, must have been curious about this kinky *ménage á trois.* They would have been disappointed to know there was no sexual component to our relationships. Only friendship.

I wasn't above casting a covert glance in Anna's direction when she crossed her legs, or taking in Sheila's décolleté as she leaned forward to pour some wine. I would even tell an off-color story to see what kind of reaction I'd get, just as the two of them were ready with an erotic innuendo on occasion. Sheila never let up on her Burt Lancaster routine, speculating about what a great lover "Burt" must have been in his day.

One morning we were taking a walk through the zoo, and Sheila was in a particularly rambunctious frame of mind. As we watched the orangutans in their cage, she broke us up with her commentary on the mating habits of the species. Later, strolling along an out-of-the-way path we came upon a young couple embracing on a bench.

"So tell me, Burt," Sheila said, "can you still come up with that kind of fervor?"

Before I could deliver some feeble comeback, Anna - a bit out of character I thought - said, "I think Sid Silva can come up with anything he wants to come up with."

Those three months are among my precious memories. We came to respect one another, and after the first month or so, the respect expanded to embrace trust. For the first time in four years I was with people for whom I cared.

Anna and I held our sides when Sheila gave us the ins and outs of her marriage to Rick, the rock-and-roll-band drummer. We had a good time developing a movie, with Nicholas Cage as the rock star and a young Meryl Streep playing Sheila the groupie.

"A young *and lucky* Meryl Streep," Sheila said. "Back in the days when the band was packing them in every night and Rick and I were close, the bass player gave him a tip on the market, and for once he did something right."

Sheila said her ex-husband had invested money in her name in a stock that steadily increased in value. "And the dividends come in like clockwork every three months." Sheila let me know that Clarence, whom I had met at the dinner party, was a "good friend."

Anna told us about her career as a freelance travel writer. And she talked about her early marriage to a young doctor training to be a surgeon. The income from Anna's articles enabled him to complete his residency at a local hospital. Their life together was "blissful," but after two years the marriage began to sour.

"He became cool and distant," Anna said. "I couldn't understand why. Our relationship had been wonderful. I was getting close to my mid-thirties, and we had talked about having children. Maybe when something is *too* good, you'd better be prepared for the fall. I made some inquiries at the hospital where he was an intern."

She learned they called him Dr. Casanova behind his back. Among his countless intimacies, it was speculated, Dr. Casanova had been to bed with roughly half of the twenty nurses on the staff. He was a legend in his own time. One of the nurses who had broken off with him after a few months, opened up to Anna. "He really loves you," she had said. "He never stopped telling me that."

Anna made a face. "It was really gratifying to hear that. But I lucked out. I found a smart, aggressive lawyer, and Dr. Casanova was so filled with guilt that he agreed to a settlement that was super for me."

After the divorce Anna attended law school, but decided she enjoyed writing travel prose more than legal prose. She had met Sheila soon after her arrival at the Oasis.

"And," Anna said with a half-smile, "as long as I remain unmarried, I receive a check every month from the hard-working Dr. Casanova."

I told them that in college I had majored in architecture and minored in literature. And for the first time since Sarah died, I talked about her - how we met when we were both on the staff of the same high school in a Washington suburb. Sarah was teaching writing, and I was teaching great books. I explained how a friend from college, who was the head of a construction business, recognized that my knowledge of architecture would be an asset in his business, and persuaded me to join his company.

"In other words," Anna said with a sympathetic smile, "you abandoned your teaching career and succumbed to the seduction of money."

"That's about right," I conceded, "but I'll tell you something. I never lost my love for books." Even as I said it I knew I was setting myself up for a Sheila wisecrack and she didn't disappoint me.

"Anna, would you reach over there and give this man a medal?"

I told them how close Sarah and I had been and how I had relied on her judgment. And as a measure of the trust that had developed among us, I even told Sheila I had lied when I told her my father had been in the garden supply business.

"You bastard," she said. "I actually believed you. Now I'll tell you something. When you came up to me three months ago at that Board meeting, bullshitting about the rhododendrons? I pretended I didn't know who you were, but somebody had already pointed you out at the market. I instantly thought of Anna."

Anna turned red and I said nothing.

Once, in late July, when Sheila was home with a head cold, and Anna and I were having lunch alone, she told me about Sheila and Clarence. Clarence's wife of twenty-five years, Sally, had begun to show symptoms of Alzheimer's a couple of years ago. It reached the point where on some days Sally didn't recognize Clarence when he came home from work. He had to place her in a private institution in Frederick, Maryland, and when he came to see her two or three times a week, she didn't know him.

Sheila occasionally worked as a substitute teacher, Anna told me, specializing in something called "Contemporary American Culture." Anna laughed. "It covers the field from movies to rock to rap to what she calls fun-fiction, even cooking.

In the course of this work, Sheila and Clarence, who was teaching at the same school, had met and come to like each other. Their friendship ripened to the point where Sheila, from time to time, would accompany Clarence on his visits to his wife.

Six months ago, Anna continued, they went out to Frederick, and sat down with Sally. As Clarence poured tea for the three of them, Sally said to Sheila, "I only wish you could meet Clarence. You'd be so good for him."

"It turned out," Anna said, "that Sheila is, indeed, good for him. He's told me more than once that Sheila has saved his life. They've become very close. When you get to know Sheila, you find out she's a special person. She has a way of drawing people out. She does go on about how wonderful she'd be on TV . . ."

"Tell me about it."

"If Sheila thinks you're a straight shooter she'll go all out for you. But if you're not leveling, watch out. She's the best friend I've ever had."

Chapter 3

One day in the middle of August, Anna was at home working on a piece about our recent excursions for "Where To Go," a local travel magazine. Sheila called and asked me to come over. She had something important to discuss with me. As I walked toward her building, it felt like a tropical rainforest. She opened the door, surveyed my drenched shirt and the droplets on my forehead, and laughed.

"Well, look at you, were you having sex out there in the jungle?"

I had expected the air conditioning to be going strong because she hated the heat, but I hadn't anticipated the arctic tundra. The crowded furniture was huddled together like sheep seeking warmth, and after a while the dull ache began to pester my right knee again.

"Incipient arthritis," Dr. Morgan had said. *Incipient, your ass, Doc.*

Sheila sat me down, served up her trademarked Stale-Danish, and didn't waste a minute. This was my chance, she said, to perform a service for "our community."

"You know what's happening at the Oasis." she said.

"What do you mean?"

"I'm talking about the Board. Travail, really. His father left him a fortune - which he pissed away. But never mind that. He's the worst excuse for a President we could have. Are you following me?"

"I think so."

She got up to get us more coffee and, with her back to me, said, "Travail prides himself that in the four years he's been President, the

30

Board hasn't raised condo fees - even after Nikki Bullett warned him last year the roofs were going to need replacing. The result was the special assessment that's got everybody pissed."

She came back to the table with the coffee, and explained that two Board members, Anna and Lars Rehnberg, had argued for fee increases to build up our reserves to be ready for unforeseen exigencies. They were regularly outvoted, five to two.

Pouring coffee, Sheila said, "Last year we adopted term limits - four years on the Board and you're out. First condo in the country to do it. Travail's four years are up next month so he'll be out, although he wouldn't be re-elected anyway. I want you to run for his seat. We can work it so you'll succeed him as President."

"Out of the question," I said. "No way will I expose myself to that nonsense."

"That's your problem. You don't expose yourself *enough*."

"I like things the way they are in my life. I don't want to become involved with greenspace and pets and financial reserves. And I'm not about to campaign for anything.

Why don't you run and become President? You'd be great."

"I've told you. My true calling is television. *That's* where I'd shine. As President of a condo I'd stink. I need distance between me and my constituents. Like TV. No, you're the man. You'll win in a breeze."

"Look," I said, "I've only lived here a few months . . ."

"Six months."

"All right, six months. I'm not cut out for this kind of thing."

In a mocking imitation of Anna's voice, she said, "I think Sid Silva can do anything he wants to do."

She leaned forward and closed her hand around my forearm with a strength I wouldn't have suspected. Looking hard into my eyes, she said, "We need you. Don't tell me you're afraid of the challenge."

That may have been the moment my resolve began to dissolve.

I said, "Let me think about it."

When those words registered with her, she looked at me with approval. "I knew you were the real thing," she said.

"One word from you and . . ."

"By the way," she said, "am I wrong that you and Anna are finding more and more in common?"

"You're not wrong, but . . ."

"But what?"

"I like things the way they are."

Nor was she wrong about the September election. I defeated my four opponents decisively, thanks to campaigning by Sheila and Anna. They made phone calls, buttonholed people in the elevators and the lobbies, and distributed flyers door-to-door. They told the voters I would bring years of business experience, mature judgment, and unimpeachable integrity to the job.

The Oasis by-laws provided that the seven Board members elect four officers at an "organization meeting" scheduled by the outgoing President a few days after the general election. Sheila and Anna lobbied the Board members on my behalf, and they seemed agreeable to having me as President. Sheila heard through the grapevine that Bunny Slack, a long-time resident, was lobbying her co-Board members to support her for President, telling them I was "new and untried." Sheila heard that the members were now vacillating.

Travail delayed the organization meeting, and it was clear to us that, for whatever reason, he was trying to give Bunny more time to lobby. After ten days, Travail was forced to schedule the organization meeting, and I was elected President. The Oasis had staggered terms for the seven Board members, and, as it happened, the other six carried over. The other incumbent officers were also elected.

After the election, they maneuvered for the President to have a cubbyhole tucked into a corner of the management office.

A month later I walked past the garden, sniffing a hint of winter in the mid-October air. When I got to my cubbyhole at 4:30, I shook off the cold, hung up my twenty-year-old London Fog, took out two shotglasses, poured some Absolut into one of them, and set the bottle next to the empty shotglass.

I took a sip and sighed with small pleasure. Vodka went down much easier than the Scotch I used to drink. I picked up the Journal, and checked out my investments. Uneventful. I pulled out the condo files again. Nothing exciting there, either.

A few days after I had been elected President, I sat down with Nikki Bullett, our on-site General Manager, to get a handle on the services performed by our management company, Efficiency Management of Washington - EM . Nikki was employed by EM, but in practical function, she worked for the condo.

In response to my questions, Nikki said EM managed forty-three commercial properties and seventy-seven residential properties in the greater Washington area. The Manager was Chuck Hardy, and the Assistant Manager was William Stane. EM was a corporate subsidiary of Efficiency Management of America, known as EMA, a publicly traded company with subsidiaries in thirty large cities managing residential and commercial properties in their respective areas.

I asked Nikki to give me all the files for the past year containing invoices for $10,000 and more, and the minutes of Board meetings.

Nikki, who could have doubled for Susan Sarandon on a cloudy day, had a way of looking at you blank-faced, but it didn't take me long to understand she was smart and perceptive. I detected a hint of something more than professional manner, but I couldn't put my finger on it. I'd heard she was divorced.

When I asked her for the files, she raised her eyebrows, and said, "Certainly."

I gave her my Mr.-Nice-Guy Smile. "Do I detect some surprise?"

"Not really, Mr. Silva."

"But something's bothering you?"

She ran her hand through dense dark hair and said, "I guess I'm just a little surprised because Mr. Travail seldom looked at the files. Carlly, I'm glad you're taking an interest in what we do. I'll get them for you."

I plowed through three stacks of manila files containing bills and invoices ranging from dry cleaning of custodian uniforms to brickwork repair to landscaping of our greenspace. Everything looked routine.

I was mindful of the suspicions Anna had voiced some months earlier about the roof replacement bids. I went through the file marked,

"Roof Replacement for Building Two" more carefully, but saw nothing remarkable.

The minutes of the Board meetings didn't contain high drama either. How do we deal with residents in arrears on maintenance fees? Should we allow residents' guests to park their cars in the crowded garage? Such matters as security, redecorating, and the number of pets to be allowed had been argued for at least the past year. The same issues kept popping up, meeting after meeting, as though the Board was unwilling or unable to resolve them.

The minutes of the February meeting stated that management recommended approval of the lowest of the four bids that had been submitted for the Building Two roof replacement. President Travail asked the Board to approve the recommendation.

One thing caught my eye. Board member Anna Carroll said all four bids seemed unreasonably high. Only two small leaks had appeared so far in the Building Two roof, she said, and the Board could take another month or two before going ahead with the replacement. Ms. Carroll moved that the Board delay acceptance of a bid, and retain an independent expert to advise on all aspects of the impending roof replacement. Ms. Carroll's motion was defeated five to two, Lars Rehnberg voting with Ms. Carroll.

These minutes confirmed what Anna and Sheila had told me. The lowest bidder had been awarded the contract, and had done a good job. So I had little enthusiasm for pursuing what seemed to be no more than the product of Anna's and Sheila's imaginations.

Nikki showed up as I finished. "Anything I can help you with, Mr. Silva?"

"I don't think so, Nikki. Everything seems to be in the right place." After a pause, I said, "Tell me, how do you like working here?"

"It's a good job. The people here are mostly friendly, the pay is good, and I especially look forward to working with you."

I smiled. "Why is that?"

"You're a good man, I can tell. Very smart, too."

The files hadn't piqued my curiosity, but now I had a new challenge. What made Nikki Bullett tick?

As I sipped my vodka, Carl Harrison came in with that gimpy walk. As usual, he hung his cane on the corner of my desk, and lowered himself into the only available seat, a pine chair facing my pine desk. His chalk-white hair seemed thinner than it had been at the poker game, and the dimple in his chin - a touch of Kirk Douglas - more prominent. I had my own Burt Lancaster image to live with.

He picked up the empty shotglass I had placed on the desk, poured himself some Absolut, leaned forward, toasted me silently, and took a sip. I detected a whiff of sweet perfume which was not from the neutral vodka. It was now 5:45. Could this aging widower be an afternoon lover?

"Where are we going for dinner?" I asked.

Fixing his rheumy eyes on me, he said, "I hear you made a move on Elsie Turner."

I blinked hard. "What makes you think that?"

"Somebody told me while I was getting dressed a few hours ago."

I was half amused, half embarrassed at Carl's indiscretion. But for all his crudeness Carl was an antidote to the dullness. In any case, I told him, the "somebody" was wrong. Elsie Turner was the flighty woman who lived in my building and had once invited me over for a tuna casserole. She didn't interest me.

But as I sat there, I felt I could pinpoint the root of the problem. A few days before, she and I were on the elevator together. She had been wearing an eggshell skirt that went well with her bright yellow blouse.

"You look very nice today, Elsie," I had said, and she had thanked me with a smile. Maybe I was beginning to act like a politician.

"Who's the somebody who told you this non-story?" I asked Carl. He smiled. "Forget it."

Carl had been to the Buona Sera with me once, and he had shared my view of the restaurant, so we went there again. We ate our way through fettuccini with mushrooms, a small salad, lamb chops, and chianti, not saying much, just enjoying the food.

Maria poured coffee, and Carl once again brought up his pet project - building a community center for Oasis residents. It would be a place where the Oasis community could come together and have guest lecturers, art shows, potluck dinners, musical evenings, bingo games. We could have our monthly poker games there.

He pressed forward. "When Travail was President he was so cheap he wouldn't even put it on the agenda. I figure you're going to build up our reserves. We could add an extension onto the management office. You have the clout to push it through."

I thought about it for a few minutes, and said, "I'll tell you what. You tell me who told you I made a move on Elsie Turner and I'll promise to push for the community center as soon as our reserves begin to shape up - which, if I have my way, will be soon."

Before Carl could answer, his cell phone rang. He said, "Hello," listened, and said, "Hold on."

He smiled and said, "I'll be back in a few minutes," and headed for the sidewalk.

When Maria saw Carl go out the door, carrying his cell phone, she sat down in his seat. "You were here with him before. Looks like a nice guy," she said. "Good friend?"

"Casual," I said. "I pass the time with him once in a while."

She motioned the waitress to bring her some coffee, and said, "You've been here twice with that lovely woman, Anna. How come I don't see her with you any more?"

"We just haven't had the occasion. No special reason."

"No special reason, but she's a special person."

"How do you know how special she is? You've met her twice."

"Five times. She comes by for background for the article she's writing about the restaurant, and we're getting to know each other." She paused. "You and I have been friends for more than thirty years. How many times have I been wrong about people?"

"None I can remember, but what gives you this insight about Anna?"

She placed the coffee cup on the table. "You know how I felt about Sarah, but it's been four years. You need to move on, be close to someone. Not a 'casual friend' using his cell phone on the sidewalk. I would like to see you with someone like Anna."

"It's not that simple," I said. "She's a lovely person, and a good friend, but I'm just not ready for anything more than that."

Carl was maneuvering his way back through the tables, and as Maria got up from his chair, I thought of how very few people could talk to me that way. Maria, maybe Sheila.

Carl sat down and said, "We were on the verge of a deal when I had to leave. The community center for the name who told me you made a move on Elsie Turner."

"Deal."

Carl couldn't wait. "Bunny Slack."

"Bunny Slack, the Board member with all the jewelry?"

"Yep."

"You're not kidding?"

"Not kidding. That was Bunny on the phone just now."

"She's a friend?"

"Close friend."

When you're President of a condo you're the receptacle of a lot of information. Most of it is idle gossip but you never know what might prove to be useful. I filed it away.

When we paid the bill, Carl asked, "What's on for tonight?"

"I have to get up early, get ready to run my first Board meeting tomorrow night."

All the Board members were there. Bunny Slack sat opposite me, her fingers caressing the onyx brooch pinned to her blouse, and Audrey Weeks was still smiling her way through life. Lars Rehnberg looked brawnier than ever. Morton Moody, hale and hearty for his age, looked irritated, as usual, and Jane Fountain, in an ankle-length royal blue print dress, was, as before, conspicuous for her youth and stylish clothes. Anna sat next to me, and greeted me in a low voice with, "You'll knock them dead."

Nikki Bullett sat on my other side, ready to give me whichever files and other information I needed. As it happened, I didn't need her help that night, but it was a comfort to have her there.

Running a meeting was really not a big deal for me. I had presided over so many corporate board meetings that, after a while, I was on automatic pilot. The trick, I had discovered, was to be firm but give in when it didn't cost much. After the conclusion of the agenda items on this night, however, I realized I might have been overly confident.

The agenda was boilerplate and uncontroversial. Only ten residents were there to observe. One of them was Sheila in her running outfit, asking the Board, again, to replant the rhododendrons away from the brick wall. I thought to myself it was probably not worth the effort, but it would be relatively little money. More important, I wasn't about to take issue openly with my unofficial campaign manager. So I agreed with her and the Board approved the change without a whimper. I was riding high.

When we had completed the agenda items, I said I wanted to put the Board on notice that I intended to take the first step toward replenishing our depleted reserves at our next meeting. The reserves were alarmingly low for our anticipated needs, and I would support a motion at the November meeting, that effective the first of the year, our condo fees be increased substantially - possibly as much as seven percent.

I looked around the table. Slack, Weeks, and Moody wore deep frowns. Fountain looked noncommittal, and Anna and Lars Rehnberg were nodding affirmatively.

Bunny Slack pulled herself together. "Hold on. In twenty-six years we've never had a single increase that big. It would be devastating to those of our residents with fixed incomes. We'd better think this through before we go off half-cocked."

Anna said, "I assure you, Bunny, I have empathy for people living on fixed incomes. But we have an aging infrastructure we need to maintain. If we adopt policies designed to meet the needs of the few who, perhaps, should not be living here, we are being unfair to the vast majority of residents."

Anna paused and the room was silent. "We haven't had a fee increase in four years," she added. "The Board has allowed the reserves to fall to an imprudent level. Now we have to pay the price for our foolishness."

Anna was as soft spoken as always, but there was resolve in her voice. Maybe a touch of passion, even anger. I wanted to say "Brava," and give her a hug.

Bunny said, "That was a pretty speech, Anna, but it's baloney. A seven percent increase would be . . . unconscionable."

Turning to me, Bunny said, "I'll tell you right now, Sid, if you continue this reckless course of action you won't get my vote."

"Nor mine," Dr. Pompous Moody said.

"Nor mine," Little-Miss-Muffet Weeks said. "My rule is, don't spend money unless you have to."

"That's my point, Audrey," Anna said. "We have to."

Audrey Weeks seemed to be puzzled. Fountain looked back at each of us in turn, her face impassive.

After the meeting adjourned Anna leaned over to me and in a voice I could barely hear, said, "There's something Sheila and I would like to discuss with you. Could you come to my apartment tomorrow morning? At ten?"

I said, "Of course."

I got home a little past nine and a few minutes later the phone rang. It was Sheila. Her voice raspier than ever, she said, "You ran a good meeting. I'm proud of you."

"Don't con me, Sheila. I lost the support of three out of seven Board members in one fell swoop and the fourth ain't talking. If the vote had been taken tonight it would have been three to three with Fountain up for grabs."

"Fountain will come around," she said. "You set the tone for future meetings. They found out you're gutsy."

"You're calling me to tell me how wonderful I am? What else is on your mind?"

"You'll find out tomorrow morning over coffee and Danish at Anna's place."

I couldn't help but grin. I wondered if these people had an investment in a Danish bakery.

I had only been to Anna's apartment once before. It was imaginative and tasteful. The widely spaced furniture was comfortable, and the area rugs picked up the chocolate hues from the parquet floor. The pictures were nicely framed. I recognized a Winslow Homer reproduction I hadn't noticed the last time.

I looked around and didn't see Sheila. "Where is our friend?" I asked.

Anna said Sheila was unable to be with us. That morning, Clarence, who was teaching all day, asked if she would drive out to his wife, Sally, whose Alzheimer's symptoms had taken a turn for the worse. Sheila had a special way with Sally.

Anna had replaced the dark frame glasses she wore at the Board meetings with lighter, smaller ones. She brought out coffee and pastry in silver dishes, and the Danish was moist and fresh, a treat after Sheila's cardboard leftovers.

"Thank you," I said, "for your support last night."

"Thank *you* for the courage to take an unpopular position. And by the way, Bunny's lofty concern for the welfare of fixed income people is nonsense. She hates to spend money, especially her own."

Anna leaned forward. "Sheila and I want to give you more on roof replacement."

A year earlier, in October, Anna said, the roof on Building Two began to leak, and Nikki Bullett told the Board it had to be replaced the following spring. Nikki solicited bids and passed them on to the Board along with her recommendation that it select the lowest bidder, a company named Security Roofing. At the November meeting, President Travail supported the recommendation. Anna thought *all* the bids looked unreasonably high, and the Board should get an opinion from an independent expert.

The Board disagreed and approved the recommendation, five to two. Anna and Lars Rehnberg, wanting more information, voted against approval.

She paused to take a sip of coffee, and I said, "So it was Travail, Slack, Weeks, Moody and Fountain, for, and Carroll and Rehnberg , against."

"Yes," Anna said.

After the Board meeting, Anna said, she and Lars Rehnberg spoke with Nikki Bullett who told them, again, she had selected the lowest bidder. She had no additional information. Sheila, asserting her rights as an owner, joined Anna and Rehnberg in meeting with Travail to argue that the bids looked too high.

"Sheila has never run for the Board," Anna said. "She'd be a disaster, she says, and she may be right. She'd be arguing with everybody about everything. But Board member or not, when she's riled up, she'll wade in, all guns blazing."

Travail's position was that the Board and management had scrupulously followed accepted procedure. They had solicited bids from the best and biggest roofing contractors in the area, and selected the lowest bidder.

Anna looked up from studying her hands on her lap. "Travail said if we knew how to do it better, show him."

Anna and Sheila told Travail they weren't satisfied, and wanted to go with him to Efficiency Management and have them explain how they thought Security Roofing arrived at the bid price. Travail ridiculed the idea. It would be "silly," and "embarrassing," to go out there. Besides, Travail said, the Board had already approved the bid.

Sheila and Anna threatened to go out there with or without him. He saw they were resolute so he backed down and said he'd go with them. He'd make the appointment.

"The three of us drove to Wheaton. I can still remember the wind shaking the car. Chuck Hardy, the Manager, talked to us."

Anna and Sheila told Hardy they were concerned about the roof replacement cost. They thought the amount of $380,000 was excessive. Hardy told them Security arrived at the price by calculating costs and adding a reasonable profit. They would have no complaints about the quality of the work. "Wait for the first rainfall after completion," he said. "There'll be no leaks."

Hardy took them into the next room to meet Mr. Stane, the accountant. Stane, who seemed uncomfortable, performed what Sheila later called "some razzle-dazzle with the numbers," and they knew they were in over their heads. In the course of the meeting Travail said next to nothing.

"Hardy was courteous and responsive, but we came away dissatisfied."

On the way home Sheila and Anna had tried once more to talk Travail into hiring an outside engineer or a lawyer for some independent advice. He wouldn't hear of it. He thought Hardy and Stane had been, in his words, "forthcoming and helpful."

"You won't find what I just told you in the minutes," Anna said. "I suppose it's too late to do anything about the Building Two roof, but the Building One roof will be up for replacement any time now."

Absorbing Anna's information, I wondered if Travail had been inappropriately defensive of our management company, and if our management company had been inappropriately defensive of Security Roofing.

Anna sipped her coffee. "A friend of mine, an exterior designer just returned from Europe where she was on special assignment for the past year. She's now working in the Richmond area with construction people including a couple of small roofing contractors."

She had called her friend, given her the dimensions of our roof, described the type of replacement, and told her the price we paid. The friend ran it by her people. She got back to Anna the next day and said we overpaid by at least $100,000.

I must have looked surprised. "You remembered, offhand, the dimensions of the roof and the description of the job almost a year after the proposals came in?"

"Fair question. The answer is yes. I've been so upset about this that I suppose I've developed a sense of *mission* about it. I kept detailed notes. I don't know why Travail was so adamant that we accept the bid. I think you should know about it."

I studied the small Tibetan rug her tan loafers were resting on. "I'll get back to you and Sheila. I promise."

I thought about it from the time I left Anna that morning until the following night on my way over to the poker session. Neither Sheila nor Anna was a lawyer, and they had no experience in the business world. But they were smart and savvy, as was Lars Rehnberg, who had also voiced skepticism over the bids.

Did these excessively high bids represent collusion among the bidders? Price fixing or bid rigging? I had been exposed to these practices when I ran Silva Construction.

If the bids were as much as $100,000 out of the ballpark as Anna's friend reported, why hadn't management smelled a rat? Why had Nikki Bullett recommended *any* of the bids and why had Travail been so quick to go with the recommendation? Were the other four Board members who voted with him dupes or knaves?

I flirted with the idea that this was not my responsibility. Whatever happened had not happened on my beat. I hadn't even been living here when the bids came in. But I knew better. I couldn't look the other way. Besides, although the 25-year old Building One roof had not yet shown signs of leaking, it was bound to happen in a matter of months if not weeks. I would have to confront the issue.

The questions rang in my ears, and a sequence of actions evolved in my mind. I would re-read the condo files, more carefully this time. I would have another conversation with Nikki Bullett. Then, I would call my friend, Max, in Chicago. Depending on what Max told me, I might talk to Maurice, and get the legal slant. After all that, I'd sit down with Sheila and Anna and try to sort it out.

When I arrived at the poker game at Ron Sterling's place, four people were there: Ron, bringing out potato chips, Francis Travail, overflowing his chair, Lars Rehnberg, big as life, and Carl Harrison, the Kirk Douglas dimple more prominent than ever. And me.

"Short handed tonight?" I asked. "We're going with five players?"

At that moment, there was a knock at the door, and Carl opened it. In walked Sheila Marcuse, and I said, "I'll be damned. A rhododendron-loving poker player."

Sheila snorted, and proceeded to demonstrate her conversance with the game.

The first time she and I went at each other we were playing draw, and I had been dealt a pat hand - a ten-high straight. Ron, Lars, Francis, and Carl drew three cards, and checked. Sheila drew two cards and bet two dollars. I raised. The others dropped out and Sheila raised me. I called.

She nonchalantly dropped a king-high straight on the table. I said, "You filled a three-card straight. Amazing." She winked at me as she scooped up the chips.

Later, Francis beat out my full house with four of a kind, a rare hand. He wiped his forehead with the back of his hand, looked over at me as he gathered in the chips, and said, "You want to play with the big boys, you got to have the stuff." He looked at the others for approval, but they just glanced away.

Francis was a bloated blow-hard of little skill who was simply lucky that night. Lars posed a more vexing question. An accomplished player, he had bet directly into Travail's putative full house with a lowly straight. The more I saw Lars the more I liked him. But I had to wonder if his spunk sometimes bested his judgment.

This speculation carried a special bite for me. In my long career, my reputation with both colleagues and competitors was that of a circumspect businessman willing to take risks only after carefully evaluating the potential costs and benefits. Lars' go-for-it pluck intrigued me.

The second time I took on Sheila head-to-head, we were playing our modified five-card stud - first card down, next three cards up, last card down. Sheila was showing ace, king, ten of diamonds, and I was showing three, four, five, with a seven in the hole. The others had dropped out. Sheila bet and I called, rashly trying to fill an inside straight. The fifth card was dealt, down, Sheila looked at it, and gave me her blank look.

I peeked, and saw that I had not caught the six. I had nothing. Sheila bet two dollars, and on a just-for-the-hell-of-it hunch, I raised against her three diamonds showing.

"So you filled the straight, Burt," she said.

"You know how to find out," I said.

"Shit," she said, "you would never try to bluff this old pro."

She threw in her cards. I threw in mine and took the money.

After I got home, Sheila called. "How'd you do?" she asked.

"Won forty dollars. How'd you do?"

"Won eighty-five. Tell me something, Burt. Did you have the straight?"

"No more than you had the flush."

"I'm a sonofabitch, I had a pair of kings. By the way, I forgot to tell you something. I've heard through the grapevine that Travail used to play in this game, but he dropped out, said the stakes were too steep for him. Last year he rejoined the game."

Chapter 4

The phone rang the next morning as I poured my second cup of coffee. To my surprise, it was Maria from Buona Sera. The last time she had called was when Sarah died.

Maria asked if I could meet with her at the restaurant at a time when things were quiet. She wanted to discuss a "personal matter." We set up a mid-afternoon meeting for the following week. Could she give me some inkling of what it was all about?

"No," she said. "It needs to be in person."

A few minutes later the phone rang again - suddenly my place was Grand Central Station. This time it was my son, Brad with his weekly call.

*

Brad went to California when he was twenty-four to make his fortune. Now he was in his early forties, and still in California. He was involved in what he called "high tech," the niceties of which eluded me. All I knew was he made a bundle of money, reinvested it into a new venture, and lost most of it. Now, he told me, he was making a living, but nothing to write home about - which he didn't do anyway.

A few months after he had arrived in California nearly twenty years earlier, Brad had called and told us he was going to marry a woman named Paula who, he said, was "very attractive." Her father had lots of

45

money, which Brad claimed didn't interest him. It was my impression that sex played no small role in their relationship.

Sarah and I first met Paula at the "rehearsal dinner" preceding their wedding, paid for by Paula's father, also known as "the King of California real estate." Paula had the look of a thin fox sniffing for prey, her eyes darting here, there and everywhere.

The San Diego paper called the wedding "the event of the year." The guests paraded their Mercedes and Jaguars, compared exclusive vacation sites, and name-dropped their country clubs. Sarah and I stayed to the end, but couldn't wait to get out of there. We went back to our hotel room, toasted Brad with a glass of Perrier, and went to sleep.

When we visited six months later, Brad was subdued. It didn't take us long to figure out what was going on. The "King" wanted Brad to become involved in his real estate business, but Brad was determined to stick with his high tech. The King was disappointed and Princess Paula was livid.

"There's no way," Paula said to Sarah and me, shaking her golden locks, and running her hands down the sides of her angular frame, "that he'll make real money from this off-the-wall computer stuff. My father wants to hand him the keys to the kingdom and all your bulldog of a son wants to do is fiddle with his keyboard while Rome burns."

Apart from Paula's peculiar mix of metaphor, it appeared that Brad had made a mistake in his marriage. There was nothing Sarah and I could do about it except wish Brad luck, and avoid Paula as much as possible.

Later that year their son was born. The name on his birth certificate was Sherman, but Brad called him Skip. We went out again to welcome our grandson into the world.

This time Paula, looking straight at me and pointing to the infant in the crib, said, "That's a mistake and "- shifting her finger to Brad - "he knows I wanted to get rid of it, but the docs said an abortion could screw up an anorectic like me. So I had to go the whole nine months - like going the whole nine yards. You follow?"

They were divorced the following year, and Brad got custody of Skip. We heard the King wanted to fight for custody, but Paula said, "Let him go." The King sent Brad a monthly check for Skip's care. Brad once told us that for the first six years of his life Skip saw his mother once a month. After that, two or three times a year. Brad never remarried.

Sarah and I saw them three or four times a year, and we - mostly Sarah - spoke with Skip on the phone between visits. But as he approached his teens, Skip became aloof, manifesting what is called, I was told, adolescent alienation. During those years, Brad told us, Skip was beginning to exhibit a talent for computers.

When Sarah died, Brad and Skip, in his early teens, flew East for the memorial service. Skip was uncommunicative the entire time.

After Sarah's death Skip and I maintained a mutual distance. My efforts to tear down the war between us had been futile. Earlier in the year Skip had enrolled at a small obscure college in southern California about which he had little to say during our rare and spare phone conversations.

*

"I've got news for you, Dad," said Brad. "Skip's transfer has been approved. Beginning in January he starts at American University in Washington, D.C. They have a great computer department and that's what he wants. His dorm room won't be ready until March or April, so we're looking for a sublet."

I hesitated, mulling it over. In my heart of hearts I didn't want Skip staying with me. But did I have a choice?

"He can stay with me," I said after a moment.

I got to my cubbyhole late that morning, placed the thick brown accordion file on my desk, and pulled out the manila folder marked "Building Two Roof Replacement." I went through it again, this time painstakingly.

The niche I had carved out with my company had been wining and dining the right folks, functions lumped under a catch-all euphemism we called "marketing." My technical knowledge of construction was more academic than operational, and when it got down to the nitty-gritty, I'd call in the engineers. By now, even my imperfect understanding of the construction process had eroded, and I reviewed the Oasis files with some tentativeness.

The folder contained a proposal, dated some two years earlier, from Security Roofing Company, describing the "labor, material, and equipment" necessary to replace the Building Two roof. The description included such things as "counterflashing," "sheathing," "asphalt primer," and "Soprema Sopralene."

The file contained four other roofing proposals submitted within days of the Security bid, from Solid, Lasting, Billings, and District - all similar to that of Security Roofing. Each proposed contract was fixed-price, with a fifteen-year warranty. All the companies were licensed, bonded, and insured.

Under Oasis policy, competitive bids were required for all work over $10,000. The bid price was weighed against quality, and a selection was made. The cost proposals had been as follows: Solid Roofing, $767,250; Lasting Roofing, $675,100; Billings Roofing, $567,350; District Roofing, $482,950; and Security Roofing, $390,750. The Board had approved, five to two, management's recommendation that Security be awarded the job.

I recalled that some six years earlier, my company had installed a new roof on a residential property we owned and operated in Philadelphia. That building had been larger than either of the Oasis buildings. The bids had ranged from $285,000 to $665,000, roughly $100,000 lower than the range of bids in front of me. Even allowing for six-year inflation and different markets, the bid-range difference seemed significant.

I sat down opposite Nikki Bullett who was at her desk. "I want to ask you a few things, Nikki, and it will all be off the record."

She looked at me. It occurred to me that if Sheila thought she had a patented deadpan in a poker game, somebody better tell her Nikki was infringing on the patent.

"When the question of the roof replacement came up, did Travail discuss the subject with you? Ask you questions?"

"No."

"Did he give you any instructions?"

"Only to follow the usual competitive bidding procedure."

"Which is?"

We send out the specs with RFPs - Requests for Proposals."

"Did he give you any suggestions about who should receive RFPs?"

"He said go with the best and the biggest."

"How did you identify the best and the biggest ?"

"I called the trade association, and they said these were the five biggest. I ran it by my boss, Mr. Hardy. He said, fine. Then I called around to other properties and found out who had used these five in recent years. Most said they had been satisfied. The only complaints were against District Roofing - four customers."

"Complaints about what?"

Nikki came around from behind her desk and sat down in a chair next to me. She opened the folder, and pulled out a file called "Customer References and Complaints." She opened the file. "Two said completion went beyond estimated date, and two said there were leaks after completion, and District took too long to fix them."

"When the bids came in, did you discuss them with Hardy?"

"Yes. He said it's a no-brainer. Security is the lowest bidder, and the second lowest bidder, District, has four complaints against it. Go with Security."

"Did you take it up with Travail?"

"He asked me who I was going to recommend. I said the lowest bidder, Security. He said it made sense to him."

"Did anybody else ask to look at the bids?"

"Only two Board members - Lars Rehnberg and Anna Carroll."

"When you reviewed the bids, did it seem to you they were on the high side?"

"In all the time I've been working in this business, I've only had one roof replacement, so I was reluctant to make a judgment on the bids. They did seem high, but I knew in a general way that roof work is costly."

"Did you mention to Travail that the bids seemed high?

"Yes. He said if you want quality you pay for it. Mr. Hardy said the same thing."

"Thank you very much, Nikki. You've been very helpful."

Before I got up from my chair, she turned toward me and smiled - for the first time. "That was easy, Mr. Silva."

"What do you mean?"

"When you said this will be off the record, I thought you were going to speak to me about something personal."

"What would you do if I did that?"

"What *should* I do, Mr. Silva?"

"For openers, call me Sid."

Was she telling the truth? Was Nikki, wittingly or not, part of a conspiracy to insure that Security was selected? And was it routine for her to flirt with the Board president? She aroused my curiosity if nothing else.

Later that day I got through to Max Becker in Chicago. A week later, attaché case in hand, I arrived at Maurice's office for my 9:30 appointment.

Over the years, my company had built and managed hotels in California and Atlanta. We had developed malls outside Boston and Chicago, and built office buildings in Charlotte and residential buildings in Baltimore and Philadelphia. In all of these activities, Maurice Ruffin, consulting with local lawyers, had been our guiding hand in Washington where we were based. But we bid on few jobs in the Washington area because I wanted to keep a distance between headquarters and operations.

Maurice knew his way around corporate and administrative law. He was the managing partner of a fifteen-person "boutique," as the lawyers liked to call it. Judging from the surroundings, they were doing well. Ever pragmatic, Maurice understood that a lawyer's job is less to advise the client he can't do something, and more to tell him *how* he can do it - legally. He had served us well and he and I had become friends, often discussing sports over Scotch into the night.

"Sidney," he said, "I'm glad to see you. You *told* me you were going to hang it up. How long has it been? Nine, ten months? Tell me what's happening."

I filled him in with a sketchy account, and we chatted over coffee and the jelly doughnuts to which Maurice was addicted. His body scoffed at calories and he was trim.

I set my coffee down and said, "You're wondering why I'm here."

"I thought it was because talking to me would be rejuvenating."

"That's part of it. I'll give you the other part. I was elected President of the condo Board where I live and . . . "

He swallowed whole the piece of doughnut in his mouth, threw down some hot coffee, and started laughing. Pulling himself together, he said, "Forgive me, but the very idea is so absurd. Sid Silva, the biggest do-it-my-way hard-ass in the business screwing around with high school politics . . . Okay, the shock has worn off. Please go on."

He kept on chuckling to himself until I said, "Before I continue, let's have an understanding on your fee for this conference. There won't be any."

The chuckling stopped and he became almost morose. He leaned back, sinking into the rich brown leather of his super-executive chair.

"Why is that, Sidney?" he asked softly.

"One, because I don't have the Board's approval to talk to you, so you can't bill the condo, and, two, you're an old friend who billed my business in excess of a million dollars a year for fifteen years. You did good work, but you still owe me."

"All right. I'll tell you what I'll do. You tell me your story and I'll give you my response. Then we'll talk about the fee."

"Fair enough," I said. I gave him the background and told him my concerns. I pulled the Roof Replacement file out of my attaché case and asked him to read through it. When he finished, he placed the documents back in the file, closed it, and looked at me

"I called Max Becker in Chicago," I said. "Remember Max? Fierce competitor, but he liked me. I described the job, and gave him specs, dimensions. He said that given the market in this area, which he knows, all the proposals were $100,000 too high."

"Did he say why?"

"I asked him that. He said, figure it out, or better yet, ask your lawyer."

I told Maurice what Anna's decorator friend had said, and this time Maurice was quiet for more than a few seconds. He drummed his fingers on the desk. "Sounds like they're deciding who gets which job and at how much. Remember that time on the coast, the boys wanted you to join their 'club?' I managed to talk you out of it and saved your ass. Three of them ended up serving time plus big fines."

I laughed. "There was no way I was getting into bed with those guys. I ran it by you to stroke you, let you think you were brilliant. And was that a mistake. When I got your bill that month, they had to call the rescue squad to revive me."

Maurice said it was possible that Efficiency Management was the choreographer. They'd get a piece of every job, and if they were doing this with roof replacement, they could be doing it with brick, tile, elevator repair, electric and plumbing work.

"Let's assume it's bid rigging," I said. "What do we do now?"

"You retain me to conduct an investigation. My people will identify the residential and commercial buildings that have used these companies during the past few years. If we get what I think we'll get, we take a package to the Justice Department."

Maurice said that the government would issue subpoenas. If the documents showed collusion, Justice would file complaints. Maurice would then put together the victims and file a class action suit for triple damages - "treble" damages as he put it.

"By the time it's over," he said, "your condo will give you a trip around the world, first class, your choice of companion."

I placed my lukewarm coffee on the desk. "You're moving too fast. My Board doesn't even know I'm here. Carlly, I'm not sure I want my condo tied up in endless lawsuits talking to lawyers - no offense - with depositions and judges and appeals."

I told him I wanted to fish around. Depending on what I came up with, maybe I'd talk to Efficiency, and if they were not responsive, I'd go to Security Roofing. I'd ask them to explain how they arrived at their price.

Maurice put his hands behind his head, leaned back in his chair, and lifted his eyes to the ceiling. "Mistake, Sidney." He dropped his eyes to mine. "Efficiency will be ready for you. They'll cooperate, you're a client. So will Security Roofing, you're a customer. They'll show concern, but they're not going to tell you anything you don't know."

If there was in fact a conspiracy, Maurice said, my visit to Efficiency would give Security notice that I intended to talk to them. By the time

I got to Security they would be well prepared to demonstrate that everything was on the up-and-up.

"What are you going to show them? The other three proposals? They'll shrug and say it's vigorous competition."

"At this stage," I said, "no visible lawyers. I just wanted to see if you confirmed my gut feeling. You did."

Maurice ignored what I had just said. "Then what do you do? Tell them you talked to an expert who said all the proposals were a hundred thou too high? They'll say they'd like to talk to this expert. I do indeed remember Max. He'd never forgive you if you involved him. At least let me go with you if you talk to Security."

"Not yet."

"Let me ask you something. When are you going to discuss this with your Board?"

"In due time. Right now it's premature and I want to . . ."

"Be a hero. Show your Board you single-handedly tracked down the bad guys. It ain't gonna work."

He fiddled with the papers on his desk. "What happened to the Sidney I once knew? Gutsy, yes, but careful, weighing the odds. Now I'm seeing go-get-'em and damn-the-torpedoes."

"In those days it was just business, not personal. Now it's personal."

"At least do this much. See what you can dig up. Then come back and we'll talk."

 I got up, shook hands with him, and headed for the door. He said, "Okay, today's a freebee, but when you come back, and you will be back, no more freebee."

After I left I took a long walk. I had been pretty sure Maurice would say it looked like collusion, but I needed to hear it from him. And I had been certain he would try to talk me out of dealing directly with Efficiency Management.

That's why I left out the last thing Max had told me. It would have strengthened Maurice's resistance to my going to them. It had come at the end of the conversation, almost as an afterthought. "The Manager of Efficiency Management in the Washington area is Chuck Hardy," Max said. "If you have any dealings with him, be careful."

"What do you mean?" I asked.

"Just be careful."

My Mustang responded well to a sixty degree temperature on a crisp dry early November day, and it hummed contentedly when Anna and Sheila were in the car. The ride was smooth as we cruised into the Maryland countryside. Sheila had suggested we get away from the condo for our "confab."

I briefed them on my review of the file, my interrogation of Nikki, my talk with Max, and my session with Maurice. We stopped for soft drinks at a roadside stand. Nobody else was around and we sat down at a picnic table set in the middle of scruffy grass. As three crows watched us from a fence, I outlined the three options I saw.

Under the first option, I would schedule an executive session of the Board to inform them fully. I would then recommend that the Board retain Maurice, and we would step aside and let him take over. Board resistance would crumble when I told them the lawyer's fee would be twenty percent to a third of the amount recovered. The downside could be a Board member who would inform Hardy, giving him and his co-conspirators time to prepare for the legal assault and destroy incriminating documents in their files.

The second option was to do some investigating on our own and see if we could come up with enough to warrant a confrontation with Hardy - an "unassailable set of facts," in Maurice's words. The problem here, I said, was that the three of us had no professional experience with investigative techniques. We wouldn't even know what we were looking for. As amateur gumshoes we'd flounder until we came up with nothing.

The third option was to walk away and forget the whole thing.

Sheila broke her silence. "Walking away is unacceptable, and the first option gives me a pain in the ass. When I was involved with lawyers during my divorce it was like sinking into quicksand while they're sucking every last buck out of you."

"Maurice is not like that," I said. "He's aggressive, but I've never known him to be untruthful or unethical."

Sheila placed her hands flat down on the seat of the backless bench and leaned forward. "Maybe so, but I think lawyers should be a last resort. I vote for Option Two."

"What do you think, Anna?" I asked

"I think we should conduct a limited inquiry, and see where we go from there."

I was irritated. "What *kind* of 'limited inquiry?'" I asked. "I don't think we know what we're talking about."

Sheila looked at Anna. "Shall you tell him or I?"

"I will." Anna said. "Sid, we have a secret weapon."

"What's that?"

"You mean, '*who's* that.' It's Lars Rehnberg."

In the course of the afternoon confab more questions had come to my mind that I wanted to put to Nikki Bullett. It was late and I wanted to catch her before she left for the day so I put on some speed as we headed back.

A few minutes before we would have crossed into the District, I saw flashing lights in my rear view mirror. I switched on my direction signal, pulled over onto the shoulder, and shut off the ignition. I watched through the mirror as a Maryland State Police car pulled up behind me, lights still flashing.

A black policewoman with a no-nonsense look got out of her car, and came up to the passenger side of my Mustang, away from the traffic. She was wearing a nameplate that said, "Duncan." She had to be nearly six feet tall.

Sheila, next to me, pulled down her window, and the three of us smiled at Officer Duncan so sweetly you'd think she was about to tell us we'd won the Maryland lottery.

"May I see your license and registration, please?" she asked.

I reached across Sheila, got them out of the glove compartment, and handed them to Officer Duncan. She took them back to her car and after a few minutes she came back and gave them to Sheila who held onto them.

Officer Duncan looked over at me, and said, "When's the last time you consumed an alcoholic beverage, sir?"

"Last night at eight o'clock. One shot of vodka."

"You were doing fifty-five in a thirty-mile zone, sir, and I have to cite you. Are you driving on business time or leisure time, sir?"

"Business time," I said.

"I could write this up as reckless endangerment which could mean suspension, but I'll call it exceeding the speed limit. Will you promise you'll observe speed limits from now on?"

"Absolutely, officer. Thank you."

She glanced around the car, taking in Sheila and Anna, and from the beatific expressions on our faces, she must have thought we actually had won the lottery. Sheila placed the license and registration back in the glove compartment, and I got back on Connecticut Avenue, observing every traffic sign in sight.

Despite the delay, I caught Nikki Bullett just before she left, and asked if she could spare me an extra fifteen minutes. She said she'd be happy to do that.

"Do you know much about the roofing business, Nikki?" I asked.

"In my previous jobs, we had only one roof replacement. But I have a rough idea of what happens."

"Can you give me the highlights?"

"Contractors use the 'hot mopped down' process or the 'glue-down' process. Everything on the roof is petroleum based and the essential material is asphalt which is melted to adhere to all sections of the roof. They apply 'sheets' to the roof - 'mop-down,' 'torch-down,' and 'top.'" She paused. "Is something wrong?"

"I'm just trying to understand how it works. By the way, do these contractors have a trade association?"

"Yes, WARA. The Washington Area Roofing Association."

"That's the outfit you called to find out their biggest members?"

"Yes."

"Who did you speak with?"

"Well, I knew that Jane Fountain works there so I had them put me through to her. She's an Oasis Board member."

"I know."

In mid-afternoon, Buona Sera bore no resemblance to the busy gathering place that I had come to know - bustling with energy, animated with conversation, and redolent of fresh basil. Maria and I were the only people in sight, and silence reigned.

I took a sip of espresso. "Where is Stefano?" I asked.

Maria smiled. "He's taking a break. He'll be back in an hour."

"He's all right?"

"He's great. I'm fortunate to have a husband like him."

"That's wonderful. So tell me, *mia cara*, what is this personal matter that can't be discussed over the phone?"

"It's about my nephew, Mickey. Maybe you forget, but you met my sister, Theresa, at Laura's graduation ten years ago. Tall, hair lighter than mine?"

"How could I forget? She's one of the few women I've ever met who's better looking than you."

She took my hand "I can still remember Sarah rolling her eyes every time you tried to bait me. I love you, Sid, I truly do."

"I love you, too. So what's with Mickey?"

"Well, you've heard this before. Abusive father - they were divorced ten years ago - and a good mother, Theresa, who loses control over her rebellious son."

At an early age, Mickey exhibited a tendency toward violent behavior. His father beat him, which exacerbated the violence. After the divorce, Theresa attended counseling sessions with Mickey, and the therapist recommended that Mickey channel his energies into athletic activity.

He played basketball in high school, and upon graduation enrolled at George Washington University, continuing to live at home. During his second year, he received accolades from the local press for his play as guard on the varsity basketball team.

"He's about six-one, powerfully built, strong, all muscle," Maria said. "And he's bright. He's good with numbers and he loves to read about the business world - he studies the financial pages all the time. He was getting good grades in college, and had his mind set on a career in accounting or possibly economics."

But toward the end of his second year at GW, Mickey began to work out at a gym on the other side of town. Before long, he was hanging around with some men who frequented the gym, and Mickey had become uncommunicative with his mother. Theresa sneaked into the gym one afternoon and observed Mickey in the company of these men. According to Theresa, "One look at this gang and you knew it was trouble."

At the end of his second year, Mickey dropped out of college to the surprise of his family and the shock of his teammates. His explanation was that he had become "bored" with college, and he began to spend less and less time at home.

A few weeks before, the police had come to the house to question him about a 3 a.m. robbery at a high-end women's clothing boutique. Outside and inside locks had been picked and the combination lock to a vault broken. Listening from the kitchen, Theresa heard Mickey deny knowing anything.

Then the police questioned Theresa. When they asked her what time Mickey had returned home on the night in question, she said 11 p.m. But she remembered clearly that it had been more like 5 a.m. After the police left, she confronted him and he said it was "nothing you need to get bent out of shape about."

"Stefano and I talked to him," Maria said, "and he told us to mind our own business. His father moved out of town and has nothing to do with them. Would you talk to him, Sid? I know you both have an interest in basketball. That could be your angle. I think he'd respect you. It probably won't help, but we're desperate."

I had no interest in the special problems of the young, and no desire to play Uncle Sid to this troubled kid. But the request was coming from Maria.

"Give me his phone number. I'll give it a shot."

Chapter 5

A few nights later, Sheila called me at six and said it was imperative that I come over immediately.

"What is it?" I asked.

"Just get your ass over here. Now!"

As I knocked at her door five minutes later, I could hear the sound of "Eleanor Rigby." Sheila opened the door, threw her arms around me, and gave me a mammoth kiss on the lips. Clarence came up to me and shook my hand. "Congratulations," he said.

I walked in and saw balloons hanging and floating all over the place, making the living room look more cluttered than ever. Anna threw *her* arms around me, kissing me on the cheek.

"What's going on here?" I asked.

Anna spoke first. "You've got a BIG birthday coming up and we decided to celebrate tonight so we'd know we'd snare you while you were unsuspecting."

"When I'm seventy," Sheila said, "I hope I look as sexy as you."

"He's not seventy yet," Anna said, "three more days."

"Which makes him a Scorpio," said Sheila. "If he loves you he'll go all the way for you. Stick with you in good times and bad. And the most important room in his home is the bedroom."

I was so caught off-guard that for once I was speechless. We sat down and they had white wine, and ice cold Absolut for me.

Sheila, irrepressible, wouldn't let up. "What do we call him," she asked, "when he crosses the big threshold? How about The Viagra Kid? Will he graduate from senior to elderly or elderly to senior?"

Anna said, "Elderly senior citizen."

"Elderly senior citizen," said Sheila, "who can't rise to the occasion any more."

"That reminds me of a routine Mae West used to do," I said.

Sheila came right back. "Yeah, where she says, 'Is that a gun in your pocket or are you just happy to see me?' Burt would have to say, 'It's a gun, but it has a silencer'."

I squinted my eyes. "Oh, what the hell is the name of that movie?"

"See what I mean?" Sheila said to Anna. "He's having a senior moment."

After a while they came up with broiled veal chops, sautéed spinach, and roast potatoes, and served a Brunello di Montalcino from Tuscany. Anna did the cooking.

"How did you know my birthday was coming up?" I asked at the end of the meal.

"Remember three days ago," Sheila said, "we got stopped? While Officer Duncan was favoring you with her words of wisdom, you were, naturally, giving her your full attention. I looked at your license and got the date."

"Tricky," I said. "How did you know this is my favorite meal?"

This time Anna spoke. "Well, you remember that time at Buona Sera when Maria asked you if you wanted the usual? I also talked Nikki Bullett into giving me the name and phone number of your son, Brad, from the next-of-kin folder in the office. I called him in San Diego to confirm it and he did."

"You've been busy beavers," I said, attacking my veal chop.

After we opened a second bottle of the Brunello and finished dinner, they pushed a sofa and a couple of chairs off to the side, and no sooner had they cleared a small space then Sheila and Clarence were dancing.

Anna pulled me up and said, "We're going to dance."

I smiled. "That's not my thing. A dancer I'm not."

"I won't buy that," she said. "We went to all this trouble because we like you. The least you can do is reciprocate with a dance."

I sat silent.

"You know what?" Sheila threw in her lot from the dancing space. "You're afraid to dance with us. *That's* what it is."

There it was again. The challenge.

Anna was a good dancer, lithe and graceful. Later we switched partners, and Sheila, whose dancing was on my inept level, had me laughing so much, I lost track of my old Arthur Murray moves. At one point she took the lead and I followed compliantly. She leaned in and said, "This hasn't happened for a while. Am I wrong, Burt?"

"*What* hasn't happened for a while?"

"This excitement."

"*What* excitement?"

"We're reacquainting you with the pleasures of the flesh, and we don't want you to explode in uncontrollable frenzy. So just take some deep breaths and you'll be all right."

After a few minutes, the arthritis in my right hip decided to pay me a visit. But no way would I tell Sheila about that. Funny thing, though. When I resumed a turn on the dance floor with Anna, the pain was gone. Meanwhile, Sheila and Clarence cleared the table - they refused to let me lift a finger.

Sinatra was singing - *Fairy tales can come true, it can happen to you, if you're young at heart* - and Anna had snuggled into me like we'd been there a hundred times. Before I knew what was happening, I said I was happy to be with her.

She brought her mouth up to my ear, and whispered, "I think you know how I feel," and we were dancing like one person. Sinatra was finishing. *And if you should survive to a hundred and five, look at all you'll derive out of being alive. And here is the best part, you have a head start, if you are among the very - young at heart.*

At about eleven, Clarence said, "We're lucky men. Two beautiful women all ours tonight. We're lucky men, wouldn't you agree?"

"Wholeheartedly."

The following week Anna called and invited me for dinner. She brought out a glass with ice and a bottle of Absolut from the freezer.

As she set it down next to me, I studied the muted stripe and the crease of her medium-gray pants, and her gray-black shirt buttoned up to her neck, almost hiding the silver necklace. Her deep auburn hair was loosely tied in a bun, giving her a self-assured and faintly regal appearance.

We ate the grilled tuna under the glow of lighted candles. Count Basie was softly rollicking, and the Napa Valley Chardonnay was refreshing. This time she allowed me to help clear the table, and we were in the kitchen, putting the dishes in the dishwasher. I set down the plate I was holding and kissed her gently.

"You make me feel better than I've felt in a long time," I said, holding her hair back from her face, and looking into her eyes.

"The next time you come here," she said, "I hope you'll stay a while so you might want to bring your toothbrush. It'll be soon, but not tonight. Can you deal with that?"

"I can deal with anything you want me to deal with," I said.

A few days later I called Anna and asked her to dinner.

"Next time," she said. "This time I'd like you back here. 7:30, okay?"

"Okay."

I immediately went out and bought myself a new toothbrush.

Anna and I lived two floors apart in Building One. I ignored the elevator and at 7:29 climbed the two flights and rang her doorbell, slightly out of breath. She opened the door and I looked at a transformed woman.

The prim countenance and the sharp, almost stern, features had disappeared. In place of the loosely-tied bun of a few nights ago was a ripple of silky hair flowing almost to her shoulders. This time the auburn of her hair seemed to be graced with a touch of chestnut-red. Her long neck and prominent cheek bones now enhanced her softness. She wore no jewelry.

I poured Absolut onto the ice while she sipped white wine. Duke was playing "I Let a Song Go Out of my Heart," and Hodges' alto sax was, as always, breathtaking.

Occasionally glancing at each other across the small teak table, we peeled and ate our grilled shrimp slowly. We talked about architecture and her writing and the big band music we both loved and we even covered some art. The Winslow Homer was still there.

At one point she said, "You must miss your wife."

I said I did but the pain had subsided and I thought I was adjusting reasonably well.

"How about Dr. Casanova?" I asked. "Do you miss him?"

She sipped her wine, put it down, and said, softly, "I miss him like you would miss a hard kick in the stomach. The biggest bad break I ever had was marrying him. The biggest good break was finding out about him in time to get on with my life."

I helped her clear the table and sat down in the living room. She came over and sat down next to me and mentioned some of the men she'd seen since her divorce.

"They were all right. Well-mannered, well-educated, treated me well. Just no sparkle. How about you? Have you been close to any women since Sarah died?"

"No," I said. "Up to now, none."

We sat for a while listening to Ellington playing "In My Solitude."

Pulling my new toothbrush out of my pocket, I said, "I feel more relaxed than I have in quite a while."

She glanced at the toothbrush, and got up, a thin smile on her pale face. But it was enveloped in nervousness and hesitancy. "I think I've gotten a little ahead of myself."

"What do you mean?"

She paused. "I've led you on, and I know I'm sounding like a high school girl. I'm afraid to take the plunge. I'm sorry, Sid. To me, something like this is . . . I don't know any other word to use . . . a commitment. I understand you probably don't see it that way."

"Look," I said, wearing my kindest smile, "if you take the plunge, I promise to rescue you."

She looked straight at me, no smile. I tried again. "Neither one of us is a spring chicken, Anna, and it seems to me that after a certain age one is entitled to extract whatever entertainment value is left."

The words were hardly out of my mouth when I knew I had just given a new meaning to the word "blunder."

63

She leaned forward. "Just because you're over sixty, your emotional needs don't change. For me, making love has to be more than 'entertainment value.' Those men I told you about? I made love to one of them once, and afterwards, he laughed and said it was the nicest diversion he'd had in a long time. I broke it off."

This time the silence was longer and we avoided eye contact.

I took a few steps, came back, and sat on the other end of the sofa. "Let me try to sort this out, at least for myself. For five years I've avoided any kind of intimacy with anybody. You've stirred up feelings I thought were long dead. Talking to you, looking at you, makes me feel whole again. You've brought a renewed purpose to my life."

Her face was impassive, but I continued. "The more I see you the more I want to see you. What I just said about entertainment value was dumb. I have trouble taming my wise-guy impulse. Can I declare a commitment? I don't know. But when I'm away from you I'm consumed by the desire to be with you. I care for you. I care *about* you."

It suddenly hit me that I meant every word I had just spoken.

She stared at me for a long time. At last she said, "I never thought I'd hear you talk that way." She got to her feet and looked down at me. "I would like to dance."

We held each other closely, and after a few minutes we were gliding closer and closer to the corridor leading to the bedroom. When we reached that corridor, I took her hand and we walked into the bedroom. She gently pulled the bed covers back, finishing with a flourish. She looked at me and whispered, "Voila."

We sat on the edge of the bed, and she said, "Let's try to remember it doesn't matter what we do so long as we both want to do it."

I unbuttoned her blouse and unclipped her bra. When we were undressed she lay back on the sheets, her eyes never leaving mine as I lay beside her. Our breathing was already strained. We held each other, gently at first, more insistently later. In no special order of importance, we encountered hesitant gestures, mistiming, and concerned glances. I sure as hell didn't make love the way I had forty years earlier.

But then, I've never been one who calibrates fulfillment on an efficiency-of-performance scale, and it was clear to me that neither was she. Afterwards, lying there next to her, I couldn't remember the last time I had felt so contented.

The next morning we slept late. As we were having a light breakfast in the kitchen, Anna set down her coffee and gazed across the table at me. "I never thought I would feel this good again. Even if it turns out to be a passing interlude, I'm glad it happened."

"As far as I'm concerned," I said softly, "this is not a passing interlude. I can't promise you - us - years of bliss. But I'll tell you this: I don't want it to end."

I broke off a piece of toast. "By the way, why do you say you never thought you would feel this good again?"

She sat quietly. "I went through a bad time a few years ago. I was lethargic, down all the time. I couldn't stop feeling sorry for myself. Sheila helped me pull myself together."

"How did she do that?"

She looked sharply at me. "Do you really want to know how . . . I'm sorry. Of course you want to know. It happened in the space of a few hours."

Anna related the events of those few hours, and I listened.

One midsummer day Anna asked Sheila what was wrong with her. "I haven't written in years," Anna said. "I can't meet a man I respect, or worse, who respects me. Am I a loser?"

"Stop it," Sheila said. "It ain't that complicated. You married a guy, you found out he's a schmuck, and you ditched him. Never happened before, right? You're healthy, you're good- looking, you've got a nice trim bod and you're sharp as hell. If I were a man I'd be all over you. So drop the self-pity shit and get with the program."

"What's the program?" Anna had asked.

"Start writing again, find a good hairdresser, get some clothes that don't look like Salvation Army discards, and if you see a guy you like don't be afraid to wiggle your ass."

Anna considered this. "I don't see many men I like."

"Tell me about it. For every good man out there, there are twenty losers. Twenty? Fifty. When I discovered Clarence, it was like finding an orchid in a thousand weeds. You keep on going 'til you strike pay dirt. You don't strike pay dirt, you keep on going."

Taking her friend's advice, Anna resumed writing articles about restaurants, movies and plays, the same kind of writing that supported her then-husband through medical school. She found a new hair stylist who talked her into a flowing look for her auburn hair, and she bought new, stylish clothes. It had been a long time since she felt good about herself.

"When I first laid eyes on you at that Board meeting," I said, "I knew right then and there I wanted to get to know you."

Anna smiled. "Actually, I had heard about you before that Board meeting."

"Oh?"

She laughed. "I'm telling you things I never thought I would tell anybody." After a pause, she related how she first heard about "the new man in town."

"I was on my way over to Sheila's apartment I can still remember carrying my bag of Danish in the face of the freezing wind that day. The thirty-second walk felt like an hour. And I was out of sorts. I was tired of talking about 'the conspiracy,' but I knew there was no avoiding that subject. You know how tenacious Sheila can be."

Another reason for Anna's consternation, she said, was Sheila's notion of body comfort. When the weather outside was frigid, Sheila set the thermostat at eighty-five degrees. In the heat of summer, Sheila kept it at sixty-four. To prepare for the over-heated apartment, Anna was wearing light cotton pants and a thin blouse under her wool parka and boots. In the summer Anna wore heavy clothes when visiting Sheila.

"Come on in," Sheila said, opening the door. "It's a bitch out there, ain't it?"

While Sheila was hanging up the parka, Anna went to the kitchen. She pushed Sheila's stale pastry to the far end of the oversized table behind the toaster oven, reached into her bag, and placed her own freshly baked Danish on a plate. She sat down, smelled the coffee, and looked around.

On her many visits to Sheila's apartment, Anna said, she was taken by the contrast between the kitchen and the rest of the apartment. In the kitchen, order reigned - clean dishes stacked in their cabinet, dirty dishes in the dishwasher, forks, spoons, and butter knives separated in the cutlery tray, cutting knives at attention in their magnetic holder, utensils aligned, and napkins and paper towels in their respective dispensers.

The rest of the apartment was another story, Anna said. "You've been there. What do you think?"

"Sheer chaos," I said, and we began to laugh. Caught up in this indictment of Sheila's sense of taste, I couldn't stop. "The living room is an unruly mass of gridlocked chairs, coffee tables, and sofas all competing for space. The paperbacks spill out of the bookcases. Picture frames are out of line, and the two rhododendrons at the balcony door look like they were last watered during the Civil War."

Anna told me about the time Sheila had asked her to fetch a cookbook from the bedroom while she prepared one of her "super-suppers." Making her way through the minefield littered with torn blouses, T-shirts, bras, and pantyhose, Anna glanced at the unmade bed and worn drapes hanging askew, and was reminded of a street strewn with trash that had not been picked up in weeks.

When Anna felt their friendship could withstand criticism, she asked, "How come your kitchen is so orderly and the rest of the apartment so . . . casual?"

"Eating is the second most important thing we do, honey, so everything has to be in place. I don't have to tell you what the most important is."

"No, you don't. But in that case, why is the bedroom so messy?"

"In the sack with a guy, I like messy. Each to her own taste."

Sheila set her coffee on the table, sat down opposite Anna, and reached for the stale pastry behind the toaster oven as though she hadn't noticed its position had shifted.

"Let's recap," Sheila said. "All three lawyers gave us the same bullshit - won't take on individual owners. They'll represent the condo with board approval. We ain't going to get board approval. I say talk to more lawyers. I can't stand them, but we need them."

"We've been through this," Anna said. "In seven months we'll elect a new president of the board. That will be our opportunity to turn the board around."

Sheila's hands went to her hair again. "All right, listen up, there's a new man in town. I'm walking over to the Safeway yesterday with Elsie Turner, and she tells me about this new resident. Widower, been here two weeks. You won't believe this, she says, he's a dead ringer for Burt Lancaster. We get inside the store and Elsie says, 'what do you know? There he is at the check-out counter.'"

"What's his name?"

"Sid Silva."

"How old?"

"Late sixties. When you meet him I want you to turn on that smile you love to hide. Show some interest, come on to him. Get out of your shell, let yourself go."

"I should throw myself at him? You haven't even met him."

"Have I ever been wrong?"

"That's a nice story," I said, "but you didn't throw yourself at me."

"Not so you'd notice. Now, all of *that* made all of *this* possible. But . . . I want to give you full disclosure as the lawyers like to say. I still have a few hang-ups."

"Unlike me," I said, "a model of mature rational behavior. Speaking of Sheila, should we tell her we've become pals?"

"Yes. You think?"

"Why not?"

"She'll be almost as excited as I am."

After that evening, when Anna and I got together, sometimes we slept together, sometimes we didn't. I cherished every moment, and I knew that if the love boat ever ran aground, I was going to have some bad moments.

After Anna had told me a week earlier that the "secret weapon" was Lars, Sheila had given me some background. Some years ago, before she had met Clarence, Sheila had "a spring fling" with Lars, a widower. It wore off, but they'd been friends ever since. He had operated his own detective agency in Washington for more than forty years, and was in the process of retiring when Sheila met him. His clients, she said, had been impressive.

Sheila had elucidated. "Big time - Congressmen, corporations, wealthy families. Even the CIA, he once hinted. Investigating Hardy would be a piece of cake for him. *If* he's willing to work with us. Lars is from Minnesota. He's honest and dependable."

Anna had said, "I know him through the Board and through Sheila. He's a straight-shooter. How well do you know him, Sid?"

"Just from the Board meetings and the poker games," I had said. "He seems to be a nice guy, level-headed. I just don't understand how he's going to prove that Efficiency Management conspires with its suppliers."

Sheila had come back with, "Lars used to tell me, there's a saying in the business. 'Let's see where it takes us.'" Then she said, "Maybe you ought to have lunch, get to know him a little before we all talk."

Maria had it right about her nephew, Mickey. He was a strapping young man with the body of a young Lars Rehnberg.

When I called, I said I was an old friend of his uncle, Stefano, and his aunt, Maria. I told him that Maria had remarked that he was a terrific basketball player. Since basketball was a longtime interest of mine I thought it might be nice to compare notes on the subject. Also, I said, I understood he was talented in accounting and business, and I had an idea I'd like to kick around with him.

He had declined, politely, to meet me for lunch, saying he was too busy. I suggested we have a late afternoon beer at a Georgetown lounge I knew, and after some hesitation he agreed to meet me there. The place was empty and the morning-bar smell of antiseptic still lingered in the air. After a handshake, we ordered two beers. The bartender asked Mickey for an ID, and, sure enough, he had turned twenty-one the month before.

We took the beers to a table in the corner, and I opened up with, "I understand you play pretty good small guard and you're not afraid to shoot from the perimeter."

He laughed. "Maria should have been my agent."

"She showed me the press you got while you were at GW. Very impressive."

We talked at length about the game, getting around to the Knicks in the sixties and seventies, and the Lakers in the seventies and eighties and the Bulls in the nineties. When I told him Michael Jordan was the greatest athlete ever, Mickey shrugged. But when I said that Jordan's key strength - more than his uncanny eye, his timing, his physical power - was his ability to concentrate, to focus, I had his attention.

After awhile we got around to what he was doing. He told me he regularly read the leading financial journals as well as annual reports and other corporate information. He mentioned that he worked out at the gym several times a week.

I asked him why he dropped out of college. "To put it bluntly," he said, "I already knew a lot of the stuff they were teaching me, and the rest of it was boring."

In the space of a half hour or so I found him to be an engaging, articulate young fellow. At no time did either of us refer to the gym crowd Maria said he had been seeing or the police visit to his house.

I told him about my business background, and said I still had some clout with my old company. If he were interested I might be able to get him placed in the accounting department of Silva Construction & Maintenance - as they still called it. That kind of job would give him "hands on" experience in the area of his interest - corporate finance.

He thanked me, said he would think about it, and let me know. We sipped beer quietly. After a few minutes, he looked at me and said, "Tell me something, Mr. Silva . . ."

"Sid - please."

"Okay. Tell me, Sid, why are you here talking to me?"

I paused for a few seconds, and framed my reply in measured cadence. "Because one of the most decent people I've ever known is your aunt, Maria, and she loves you, and she asked me to talk to you because she thinks you may have lost your way, and I happen to know something about that phenomenon. She thinks maybe I could help you, and I'm willing to try to do that if you're willing to work with me."

He finished off the last of his beer. "What does that mean? Work with you."

"Trust me. Give me the benefit of your doubts. Loosen up with me. Which brings me to my next point. How would you like to go to New York with me and see the Knicks play the Wizards at the Garden? I have a contact for tickets."

"You're not putting me on?"

"Do I look like that kind of a guy?"

When I asked Lars Rehnberg to be my guest for lunch, he said, somewhat formally, that he would be pleased. I took him to Buona Sera because it was my experience that it's easier to talk freely in a noisy restaurant than in a quiet one. I introduced Maria to him, and the way she hung around our table, I thought she'd swoon before lunch was over.

I was right about the noise because the strong, silent Swede opened up, and we had a good time comparing the Bulls in their heyday to the Celtics in theirs to the Knicks in theirs. For a while there, I thought I was talking to Mickey again.

We both expressed our admiration for Anna and Sheila. "They're wonderful," I said, "and very different. Anna reserved, Sheila gregarious. And yet they click together."

"I know," Lars said, "but then, opposites attract. Even their dreams are different. Anna would love to publish a travel book, and Sheila never stops hoping she'll get a slot on television. She ever mention that to you?"

"Once a week." We laughed.

At one point I was walking toward the restroom and passed Maria. I said, "Good looking guy I'm with, don't you think?"

She took my arm, and whispered in my ear, "A little jealous are you, Sid?"

I moved on, muttering, "More than a little."

"You should be."

Toward the end of our calamari salads, I said, "I asked you to lunch, Lars, because I wanted to get to know you better outside of the poker games, and it's been a pleasure talking to you. There's something else I want to run by you. Could you come to my place tomorrow morning at ten? Sheila and Anna will be there."

"I'll be happy to do that."

Later that day I walked over to the market to pick up orange juice. On my way home I ran into Elsie Turner on the sidewalk. Her thinning red hair standing up straight in the breeze, and her wide-bottomed culottes flapping in the same breeze, the queen of the Casserole Brigade was overjoyed to see me.

"Where have you been?" she asked, shuffling in toward me. "Why haven't I seen you around?"

There couldn't have been more than six inches between us. I stepped backward. "Which question do you want me to answer first?"

She laughed loudly and said, "I love your sense of humor, Sid. We have to see more of each other, and I'm going to remedy that problem right now. I want you to come over tonight for my tuna casserole which I make with extra cream sauce. No excuses."

My mental reflexes weren't what they once were, and I walked into my own trap. "That's very nice of you, Elsie, but I'm tied up tonight."

"I'm free for the next five nights. Pick your choice, or better yet, all five nights."

"*Your* sense of humor's right up there, too. This is the first time we've talked for longer than fifteen seconds."

"That's my point, dummy. Look what we're both missing."

"I mean, let's take it one step at a time."

"Not at *our* ripe age, buster," she said, coming up close again.

The thought crossed my mind that I might be imagining this conversation. I slung the plastic bag with the orange juice over my shoulder and said, "Let me get back to you."

"All right," she said, this time moving into the two-inch range. Peering at me through the Ben Carllin glasses sitting low on her nose, she said, "But the offer expires in thirty days - so I'll be waiting." She laughed again and went on her way.

I detested tuna casserole - with plenty of cream sauce, with a dollop of cream sauce, or with no cream sauce.

Chapter 6

If someone had told me back in May, when I was getting to know Sheila and Anna, that six months later the three of us would be ensconced in my apartment, briefing a big blonde bruiser about corruption in the condo, I would have been surprised. If someone had told me we'd be planning some kind of *investigation*, I would have laughed outright.

We reported our suspicions to Lars that the Oasis might be the victim of illicit activity, and we passed on everything Nikki and Max and Maurice had told me. We gave him our feeling, in descending order of enthusiasm from Sheila to Anna to me, that we should conduct a preliminary investigation and then see where to go from there.

Lars listened carefully, his head tilted at a slight angle. He focused on whoever was speaking to apprehend every detail, every nuance. He reminded me of the sticky tape my father used to hang from the ceiling to catch flies. Everything touching it stayed there.

When we were finished, we fixed on Lars who was bent forward on his chair, looking down at the floor, hands on his knees. "Let me be sure I understand," Lars said, looking at me. "This lawyer-friend of yours, Maurice, recommends that we turn the whole thing over to him. If we go for a confrontation with our management company or with Security Roofing, he says line up some hard facts before we do that. Do I have that right?"

I said, "Yes," and glanced quickly at Sheila and then at Anna. They were with me. The operative word in what Lars just said was "we." He was on the team.

He seemed to be reflecting. "Somehow I'm not surprised."

Lars recapitulated - how the bids looked high, how Travail "soft-soaped" Anna and him about the care they'd taken in the selection process, how Travail said it would be a waste of money to retain an independent expert. And how the Board backed Travail.

Rehnberg took a small bite of Sheila's Danish, and sipped some coffee. He chewed slowly and swallowed. "The most obvious conspiracy, if there is one, is between Security and its competitors. Fix the price of roofing jobs."

He reached for the fresh pastry Anna had brought over, and his hand hovered over it like an eagle pausing in mid-flight. "But," he continued, "we should consider other possibilities. Each set of suppliers could have *their* own agreements to fix prices. Have we analyzed our costs in other areas over the past few years?"

They all looked at me. "No," I said.

Rehnberg said, "And maybe our own management company is involved."

"What do you mean?" Anna asked.

Rehnberg picked up the pastry, and placed it on his plate with a delicacy I wouldn't have associated with him. "If all of them or most of them - and we're talking a big 'if' here - are fixing prices, then each set of suppliers is like a spoke in a wheel, and the wheel needs a hub. How many properties does Efficiency Management handle?"

Again, they looked at me. "I understand about one-hundred-twenty - counting both residential and commercial," I said.

"Every property," said Rehnberg, "has certain ongoing needs. Plumbing, electrical jobs, brickwork, painting, roof replacement, elevator breakdowns. And these needs are not discretionary. If a water line breaks down, you need a plumber - fast."

Sheila fidgeted in her chair. "So?"

"So in order to make the thing work efficiently, they would need somebody to direct the operation. At what level does the price get set? Whose turn is it for the next job? What's a more logical place to run the show than the management company?"

"What's in it for the management company?" Anna asked.

Rehnberg nodded. "A piece of everything under the table."

"Assuming this is happening," I said, "the management company would need reliable information at the source of each property."

Lars and I stared at each other and Anna and Sheila stared at both of us. Anna broke the ice. "You're referring to Nikki Bullett, I assume," she said.

"Yes," I said. "And - or - somebody on the Board."

"Travail until recently?" Anna asked.

"Maybe," I said. "But who now?"

I looked at Rehnberg. He shrugged. "It's possible they have people in some or all of the various properties on their payroll. In the case of a condo, a member of the Board would serve their purpose. It doesn't cost much to bribe somebody in a situation like this."

Anna broke in. "If these companies agree among themselves who gets each job and for how much, why would they need an inside person?"

"Make sure everything stays on track, steer it back to the game plan if it's going off course," I said, glancing at Lars who nodded. "Somebody to keep an eye on things and keep you informed."

After a silence, Lars said, "I take it you want to know what I think we should do."

The three of us nodded.

"We should move slowly. Suspicions can be unfounded, and it's easy to get carried away. I can do some fishing, see what I come up with."

"Fishing for what?" I asked.

"Let me think about it," Lars said. "I'll develop a plan and go over it with you in about a week. For the time being, I think the four of us should operate informally and confidentially. Sid can always go to the Board later."

I think a spark of excitement triggered our quick agreement.

I made sure the November Board meeting had only one item on the agenda: fee increase for the next calendar year. I wanted to give everybody, Board members and residents, plenty of opportunity to express their opinions.

Money always claimed their interest, and the meeting was well attended. But another tension was present this time. To some residents a substantial fee increase would amount to a public repudiation of the previous Board for their negligence. Others would be happy to forgo that satisfaction for the sake of no increase.

Lars moved that we increase fees by six percent, effective January 1st. Anna spoke in support of the motion, and Bunny, Audrey, and Morton argued that a two percent increase was sufficient. I called for comments from the residents before the Board voted.

They were divided. Sheila spoke with passion to the effect that the time had come for us to "pay the piper," and half a dozen residents, including Carl Harrison, echoed her remarks. Some burly guy I hadn't seen before said that if the Board voted the six percent increase, he would assume "the Board wanted to drive the residents into the poorhouse." This statement received a smattering of applause.

Francis Travail, of all people, supported an increase. "When I was on the Board," he said, "in trying to keep the fees low, we failed to anticipate some of the expenses coming up. I think we now have no choice but to rebuild our reserves. But the Board should limit the increase to three percent."

Not if I could help it.

The burly guy was frantically waving his hands in my direction. I recognized him again and he said, "It would only be fair to have the Board vote by secret ballot."

"Why is that?" I asked.

"So as not to embarrass anybody."

"There's nothing to be embarrassed about," I said. "Board members vote their conscience. If their vote is unpopular, what will happen? Impeachment? We will vote openly." I wasn't about to let Jane Fountain or anybody else off the hook.

At the conclusion of the resident comments, I said, "All the Board members have expressed opinions except you, Jane. Would you like to do that before we vote?"

"Yes," she said. "I don't like the increase one bit but it's necessary."

That did it. The motion carried four to three.

The poker game was at Sheila's this time - she'd become a "regular" - and Carl and I walked over to her building. Out of the corner of my eye I saw him fidgeting the way he did when he was gearing up to provoke me.

"I hear you're going full steam with Elsie," he said.

"Is there no end to this juvenile gossip?" I asked, throwing up my hands. "I suppose you got this from your dependable source, Bunny, who got it from Elsie in person."

"There's no need to be prickly about it. If you've got eyes for this woman why deny it? Although your friend, Anna, might be less than ecstatic."

I stopped short and faced him. "Let me speak plainly. The woman stopped me on the street. She asked me to come for dinner. I said I'd get back to her. She lives in our building. I run into her. Nothing more. There is no romance here, budding, full-blown or anything in between. Can you get all of that straight? And leave Anna out this."

"Hey, you want to form a relationship with somebody, that's your business. I just don't understand why you're so defensive about it."

To free up space for the poker game, Sheila had jammed the already overcrowded furniture into a corner, and it looked like she was having a fire sale. She had set up a table on the same floor area where I had danced with her and with Anna a few weeks earlier.

The same players as last time were there. This time I had a special incentive - go head to head with that wiseass Carl, put him in his place. And *murder* Francis. My chance came twenty minutes into the game in a hard fought hand of seven-card stud. Sheila, Ron, and Lars had dropped out. Francis, Carl and I were left.

After seven cards had been dealt two questions confronted me. Did Francis have a flush? Did Carl have a full house? This was a situation where I was guided by "tells," those unconscious quirks - a nervous tic, a particular gesture, a clearing of the throat - that sometimes give the opponents a clue.

My take on Francis was the perpetual veneer of sweat on his face. When the perspiration became profuse, he thought he had a winner. Placing his chips into the pot in a neat stack indicated tentativeness. Tossing his chips in carelessly suggested confidence. Carl's tell was not subtle. He couldn't stop grinning when he thought his hand was a winner.

After I had raised them both, Francis wiped his forehead again with the back of his hand, and threw in his cards, and Carl, grinning, also folded. So much for tells. I collected the chips, and threw in my hand without showing it to anybody.

Francis, visibly angry, said, "What's going on here? You didn't show your hand."

"I didn't have to," I said. "Everybody folded."

"This is getting to be a cut-throat game. I like a friendly game."

We all looked at him, but nobody cared to follow up.

On the way back to our building after the game, Carl said, "I've got to hand it to you - lucky in love, lucky in cards."

"Carl," I said, "tell me something. Did you have a full house?"

"Hell no. I only had the two pair you saw, kings over jacks. What'd you have?"

"Two pair, queens over deuces. Your kings over jacks would have won." I didn't believe him, and I was sure he didn't believe me. Both of us were lying.

After we were seated in Anna's apartment, Lars prefaced his report on Hardy with a rundown of the sources he had unearthed including neighbors, friends, relatives, co-workers, classmates, police reports, college records, and Hardy's mother, still living in Queens. Lars pulled out a pocket notebook to which he referred as he spoke.

Anna asked if she could take her own notes, and Lars said, "By all means." He told us the following as recounted in Anna's notes which became part of the condo papers.

> Harold Hardy, one of 11 children, dropped out of high school and worked on construction crews. Harold married Agnes and they had two children, Charles, called "Chuck," born in 1938, and Guy, born in 1941. In the winter of 1950, when Chuck was 12 and Guy was nine, Harold got off the work crew one Friday afternoon, and stopped by the neighborhood pub with his co-workers. Harold was in no hurry to get home because it was meatless Friday, and Agnes would have fried carp which he detested. He ended up drinking in the pub until 9:30.

Harold arrived home at 9:45, and found Chuck, Guy and Agnes listening to the radio in the small living room. He said to the boys, "Shut that damn thing off and get your ass in bed, NOW." Agnes said, "Don't talk to them that way, they're your sons." Chuck and Guy had seen their father whack their mother in slapdash fashion, but the intensity and duration of the beating that night surpassed anything before. Chuck and Guy got in front of their mother to shield her. Harold hit Chuck in the jaw, knocking him to the floor, and then kicked Guy in the left hip, resulting in a permanent limp. Harold promptly fell asleep on the sofa. Agnes called the police, but when they arrived, she changed her mind about cooperating, and she and Chuck declined to furnish statements. The police said they were powerless to stop or challenge this "domestic violence."

Four years and many beatings later, Harold got home at midnight, his belly filled with beer. When Agnes said, "You never spend time with your family," Harold knocked her off the sofa, picked her up by her hair, and proceeded to hit her in the face with his fist. Her screams woke Chuck who rushed down stairs, and brought a chair down on his father's head. Agnes told Chuck, who was now 16, "Get out of here and find a job. You have to get away from him." She gave him $2000 she had stashed away over the years, and he left that night Guy had slept through all of it.

This time Agnes and Chuck did furnish statements, and Harold was arrested and arraigned. He pled guilty, and the judge enjoined him from "touching Agnes in any manner except with her consent." A few weeks later Harold left. Agnes later heard he was living with a woman a few miles away. They never heard from him again.

Chuck moved into a room, finished high school, and with a partial scholarship, more help from his mother, and part-time work on construction sites, enrolled in St. John's University. In college, Chuck was known as a loner. At the beginning of his second year, however, he began to keep company with a classmate named Maureen Hanrohan.

Maureen told Lars what happened. One night after a movie they took a booth in a hamburger joint near the campus. Sean Tobin, a classmate, dropped by the booth and chatted with Maureen. Chuck became sullen. When he dropped Maureen at her sorority building, she said, "I know you're mad. Sean is a friend, nothing more. You shouldn't be jealous."

"I don't like the way you looked at him."

A week later, Sean Tobin was found at midnight in a semi-conscious state behind the same hamburger joint. He told the police he had been hit from behind and was unable to identify his assailant. The investigation produced no leads. Maureen never went out with Chuck again.

Sean told Maureen he hadn't told the police that his assailant had said, "This is for Chuck." When Maureen reported this to the college authorities, they considered earlier reports of his "hostile behavior toward classmates and faculty members." They told Chuck he was no longer wanted at St. John's. He left.

Beginning in 1958 he worked on construction sites in Brooklyn and Queens, and did well. He was a hard worker, bright, and became a foreman with one of the companies. During this period he spoke with his mother and brother every week, and sent them a "hefty" check every month.

In 1964 Chuck enlisted in the Army Reserves to pick up extra money, and in 1965 he was called to active duty. Assigned to a Corps of Engineers unit, he was sent to Vietnam where he was awarded the Bronze Star for saving the lives of four comrades at risk to himself. In the course of this effort, he incurred a severe head injury, and was awarded the Purple Heart.

Throughout his three years on active duty, Chuck had his paycheck mailed directly to his mother. Hardy was honorably discharged from the Army in 1968, and returned to the construction industry, moving up into the management ranks. He continued to send money regularly to his mother.

In 1975 he took a job as General Manager with Efficiency Management of Washington (EM) in the

Washington D.C. area. EM was well known in the industry. In 1975 the President, Jack Roth, and his family held the majority of the stock.

Chuck soon discovered that EM was living off its past reputation. He observed indifference among the owners, sloppy control, missed deadlines, and laziness among the supervisors Intolerant of waste and inefficiency, Chuck spoke to Jack Roth within a few months after his arrival, detailing the problems he saw. Roth, then 79, waved him off. The more Chuck persisted, the more Roth resisted Chuck's demands for radical change. They had loud nasty arguments, overheard by employees.

In mid-1976 Efficiency underwent a series of events that changed the nature of the company. In May two employees reported for work at eight a.m. and found Jack Roth on the floor of his office, severely beaten. Roth was known to be in his office by seven a.m. The police report included employee statements that Hardy and Roth had been arguing for weeks and that Hardy had "a bad temper" and had "exploded" at Roth the day before the beating. The police were unable to tie these alleged actions of Hardy to the beatings, and no charges were filed.

Roth, now 80, immediately announced he would shortly retire. Neither Roth's son, Nathan, nor his daughter, Eva, nor any other member of the family had the desire or competence to operate the business.

When Chuck visited Roth in the hospital, according to Eva who was present, Hardy said the only way to protect the financial welfare of Roth's family was for Roth and his hand-picked board to appoint Chuck president, and sell Chuck 55 percent of the stock for the amount of $550,000. At the same time, EM would lend Chuck the amount of $550,000 to be repaid over 20 years. When Roth, feeble in the hospital bed, said he would rather sell EM to an independent company, Chuck said, "EM ain't worth a damn and you know it. With me running it, you'll do well in your declining years." Chuck stared at him, his face blank. Roth agreed.

County records showed that in September 1976, Charles Hardy, at the age of 38, acquired 55 percent of the stock of EM in consideration of $550,000. This amount, which some observers believed was significantly less than "fair and reasonable," was matched by a loan from the company to Hardy, to be repaid over 20 years. Hardy became President in October, and immediately brought in William Stane, whom Hardy was said to have known in New York, as Chief Financial Officer. At the same time a man named Gus Hadley joined the company. He appears to accompany Hardy everywhere, and is said to be Hardy's "bodyguard."

In 1984 Efficiency Management of America, Inc. - EMA - acquired Efficiency Management of Washington and operates it as a subsidiary. EMA is a publicly traded company listed on the American Exchange, and doing business in most of the 50 states. Hardy is a Vice-President of EMA, and Manager of EM. The CEO of EMA is said to be "pleased" with the performance of the subsidiary under Hardy's leadership. In 1994 Hardy was designated "Manager of the Year," and his annual compensation was substantially increased. Hardy has come into possession of a significant amount of EMA common stock. Stane stayed on as local comptroller.

Hardy is six feet, two inches tall, balding, paunchy, and "works out" regularly at a gym.

"That's it so far," Lars said. "The next phase, if you give me a green light, will be more about his personal life. After that, we'll go over the plan I'm developing."

Sheila spoke. "So what have we got here? A tough, smart, hard-working success story with a temper who saves his comrades in battle and beats up on them when they're not in battle. He takes care of his mother. And don't forget the two head wounds. Still a little woozy? We need more."

Anna said, "When we met him, I thought he was just an aggressive businessman who played by the rules. Now I know better. He's violent. You have my vote."

"Your sources are good, Lars," I said "Hardy won't know we're looking at him?"

Lars shook his head. "Extreme discretion. Couple of other things. Any ideas on who, if anybody, is Hardy's inside person?"

"I'm sure there's someone," Sheila said, "but I can't prove it."

"Who?" Anna asked. "Travail is no longer on the Board."

"Building One was constructed at the same time as Building Two," Sheila said. "It's up for a new roof very soon. You can bet your sweet ass we'll get phony bids again. They'll need a friend on the Board. It can't be Travail and it ain't Sid or Anna or Lars. So we're talking about Bunny Slack or Audrey Weeks or Morton Moody or Jane Fountain."

"Or Nikki Bullett," I said.

They looked at me and nodded.

Lars asked, "Who knows these people?"

"I run into them," Sheila said. "Bunny's always saying we should have lunch. I can't tell where Weeks is coming from. Moody's a fuddy-duddy, but I can talk to him. Fountain's okay, a little stuck on herself."

Anna said, "I've talked to Fountain. She works downtown for the trade association, and does some lobbying. And, as Sid told us, she's the one Nikki Bullett spoke with to get information about roofing companies."

Lars suggested that we make one-on-one assignments.

Sheila nodded. "We'll each set something up. Lunch, dinner, anything. See what we come up with."

I shook my head. "Whoever the spies are, they'll be on their guard."

"So what?" Sheila said. "Worst case, we learn nothing. What's the downside?"

"All right," I said, "but we proceed cautiously, walk on egg shells."

"You can do better than that, Burt," Sheila said. Lately, Sheila had taken to letting me know when she thought my cliches were insufficiently fresh for her taste.

"What are the best fits?" Lars asked.

"Sheila for Slack and Moody," I said, "and Anna can take Fountain. I'll do my best with Weeks. Bullett I talk to all the time. I'll try to draw her out."

Sheila's enthusiasm was spilling over. "I've got a feeling about Audrey Weeks, Burt. Take her to a big time restaurant and loosen her up.

83

Show you're interested in her. She's lonely and everybody can use a new friend."

"If I come on too strong, she'll know something's wrong. I'm not a gigolo."

Sheila grinned. "Maybe not, but you know how to do it. Think of your hundreds of Hollywood affairs, Burt."

Anna rolled her eyes.

"While Sid is giving Audrey a new lease on life," Sheila continued, "I'll go to work on Bunny. We'll have lunch and commiserate about the treachery of men. Anna, you'll try your hand with Fountain?"

"I'll try," Anna said.

"Good," Lars said. "Now, I think we should have a name for our group."

Sheila yelled out, "The Avengers."

I said, "The Trustbusters."

Lars, smiling, asked, "How about The Warriors?"

Anna, holding back, said, "I suggest the Task Force."

We adopted "Task Force." There could come a time when we'd want to review a record of what we'd done, and we decided to keep minutes of our meetings. Anna agreed to be the secretary, but for the time being our group was accountable to no one except ourselves, and "minutes" and "secretary" might be inappropriate words. "Notes" and "Note taker" would be better.

Sheila said, "Let's call the notes 'the condo papers.'" We agreed.

I suggested that I keep the condo papers in my apartment underneath my underwear in the bottom drawer of my bedroom dresser. They smiled.

"This may sound adventurous," I said, "but it's serious. And nothing said at a Task Force meeting ever leaves the room."

As we broke up, Anna said, "We're grateful for your help, Lars."

"Are you kidding? I'm back in the saddle again."

A few days later I was hurrying over to my office to meet Carl for what had become our weekly late-afternoon vodka followed by dinner at Buona Sera. Thanksgiving was around the corner and, after a week of unseasonably balmy weather, a chill had abruptly appeared. I had neglected to throw on a sweater and was too lazy to go back for it, so I was moving fast in the cold semi-darkness of the greenspace area.

Tripping on a rock that had found its way onto the pathway, I fell hard, and my left leg scraped along the flagstone. As I sat there, rolling up my pants leg to survey the damage, I sensed a flurry of motion. It was Bunny Slack, running and pulling up in front of me like an express train screeching into the station.

"You've hurt yourself. Let me help you."

"Thanks, Bunny. I'm okay, just a small cut."

She got down on both knees, placed her arms under my bleeding leg, and, lifting the leg, examined my "wound" with the scrutiny of a watchmaker. In the midst of her inspection, her long, heavy gold necklace fell against the cut, and I winced.

"You see?" she said. "This has to be washed and treated immediately. Take my arm and I'll help you up to my apartment."

I told her I was fine, but she was persistent, and within five minutes I found myself half-reclining on an overstuffed sofa she must have inherited from her grandmother. She washed my leg, applied some peroxide, and placed a large Band-Aid on top of the gash.

The bleeding had stopped and the sting had subsided. As I started to get to my feet I said, "Thank you very much. I appreciate it."

"Slow down, big boy," she said. "There's a price for this medical service. You have to have a glass of wine with me."

I was already fifteen minutes late for my vodka date with Carl, and the thought of sipping wine with this frugal Florence Nightingale was uninspiring. But it would have been unkind to walk away, so I sat down on a chair facing the sofa with a smile.

She poured some nondescript white wine. Fingering her necklace with one hand, she raised her glass with the other, and, said, "You know, Sid, just because we disagree about some condo things doesn't mean we can't be friends."

"To friendship," I said.

I sneaked a look at my watch. Another ten minutes, I figured, before I could make a graceful retreat.

She leaned back on the sofa and crossed her short legs, again caressing her necklace. "I know you're close to Sheila Marcuse and Anna Carroll. And I know you're fond of Elsie Turner - and Carl Harrison, too. I think that's wonderful. They're all fortunate to have you as a friend. I hope you'll add me to your circle of friends."

Sheila, Anna and I had never sought to conceal our friendship, and after Carl's jibes about Elsie I knew *that* story had done the rounds. But Don Juan was not the persona I wanted to project. Or did this overture of hers represent something else? Was she Hardy's person on the Board, aware that as President I was the best source of reliable information?

"I'd be pleased to call you a friend, Bunny. We'll talk some more, but I'm late for an engagement, so thank you again for everything."

I arrived at the office twenty minutes late and Carl was annoyed. I'd planned to tell him I had been tied up on the telephone in my apartment, but I knew at the first opportunity Bunny would relay the entire episode to him, complete with bells and whistles. So I told him what had happened, leaving out the "circle of friends" nonsense.

"Ho, ho, ho," he said. "Silva, the Great Lover. You've surpassed my wildest dreams. They all want you, my friend, but you can't have Bunny. She's *my* special buddy. Come to think of it, why don't we do a double date? Me with Bunny, you with Elsie."

The first order of business at the next Task Force meeting was Lars' report on his investigation of Hardy's personal life. Following is Anna's transcript in the condo papers:

> In 1980 Hardy, 42, married Brandy Buffington, 44, in Maryland. In that year she made three formal complaints to the police, alleging that Hardy had beaten her. No charges were filed. That marriage was annulled in 1981. There were no children. Ms. Buffington is now living in Los Angeles. She never remarried.

> The search uncovered no record of any further personal involvements, including marriage, until 1987. In that year Hardy, 49, married Elsie Harris, 54, in Maryland. In an uncontested proceeding they were divorced in May,1996. Her whereabouts are unknown.

In 1997 Hardy,59,married Melody Minton,66,in Maryland. Melody's divorced daughter eventually moved in with Melody and Hardy. The three of them reside in Potomac, Maryland in a ten-room house for which they paid $1.4 million. Some of the neighbors say they regularly see Hardy playing ball in their yard with his stepdaughter. According to these neighbors, "Mr. Hardy seems normal."

There is no record of Hardy ever having been arrested. The FBI has no file on him.

When Lars finished his report he said, "What do you think?"

The words were hardly out of his mouth when Sheila said, "We're talking WEIRD. Start with the age thing. A woman takes up with a younger guy, no big deal. If Burt were twenty years younger than me I'd give Anna a race for her money."

She looked at Anna. "Joke."

Anna feigned a pained look. "Sheila, it is not weird, as you put it, for a man to marry an older woman. Maybe it was once. No longer."

Sheila kept going. "But this is different. The first wife is two years older than him and he beats up on her so bad she never remarries. The second wife is five years older and she's missing in action. The third wife is seven years older - the spread is widening."

"I never told you this," Anna said. "I was two years older than my husband. Do you consider that weird?

For once Sheila was quiet.

The next stage of the Task Force meeting was to hear reports from those assigned to check out the four Board members. Anna said that Jane Fountain would not be available for another month. I said I had been derelict in not calling Audrey Weeks. I would do so. Sheila said Moody was out of town, returning January. The following condo paper is Sheila's report of her lunch with Bunny Slack as transcribed by Anna.

On November 20, Sheila and Bunny had lunch at La Pomme on Connecticut Avenue. Bunny launched into an examination of the pros and cons of the unattached men at the Oasis. Sheila was impressed with the scope and depth of her knowledge. So-and-so is a nice guy, but all he talks about is his hip surgery. So-and-so has big bucks but if he takes you to a movie he thinks he's a big spender. So-and-so goes right home when the evening is over and doesn't call until he's "horny again" a month later.

Bunny said she "understands" that Sheila, Anna and Sid Silva are "good friends." Sheila acknowledged that.

Throughout the evening Sheila tried to steer the conversation toward the infrastructure of the Oasis but Bunny was steadfast in her refusal to talk about anything except men - and jewelry. She often referred to her collection of necklaces, bracelets, and the like.

As they walked home Sheila threw what she called a Hail Mary pass. "They did a good job on the Building Two roof replacement, don't you think?" she asked. "We paid through the ass," Bunny said. "It damn well better be a good job."

Did Bunny object to the price? "Hell, yes. I told Travail we're paying too much and he said, If you know how we can get equal quality at a cheaper cost, show me. I couldn't, so I just went along with the rest of them."

Anna said, "She was playing it straight with Sheila or she deserves an Oscar."

"If she's their gal," Lars said, "she knows Sheila was one of the trouble makers who went to Efficiency Management. She'd claim to have been outraged at the high bids."

Lars then outlined the balance of his investigative plan. As I listened to the details of his clandestine operation, I wondered if the others shared my apprehension.

When he finished, I spoke first. "Let me get this straight, Lars. You're proposing that we bug Hardy's office phone. You call it 'electronic surveillance.' I call it illegal wiretapping. I doubt that a lawyer could use the tape in court, or even take it to the government. Not to mention we could go to jail. Maybe we should rethink this one."

"Rethink, reshmink," Sheila said. "We have to *do* something. The Task Force was formed for a reason. The lawyers wouldn't help us, and we have nothing to show the government. Lars knows what he's doing. He's done it - what, Lars, a hundred times?"

Lars looked at me as he answered Sheila. "Something like that. Let me check out the place. I'll be cautious. You're right, Sid, tapping into Hardy's phone *is* illegal, and nothing we get that way can be used as evidence. But it could give us leads."

"See what we come up with," Sheila said. "It will either be junk, like Hardy harassing one of his ex-wives, or it will be useful. After all, Hardy probably talks constantly to his - what's the word, Sid? Co-conspirators? What do you think, Anna?"

Anna was concerned, of course, about illegal actions, but she felt that Sheila had a point. There was nowhere to turn except the Task Force.

"Lars," Anna said, "if Sid is right, what *could* we do with the telephone tapes?"

Lars stood up, stretched his arms, and looked down like a man trying to remember where he parked his car. Imposing looking. I guessed about six-three, mostly muscle.

"Think of the tapes as a road map," he said. "If we go to Hardy we'll know what we're talking about. Naturally, we're not going to tell Hardy we tapped his phone. But the tapes should give us leads to make our pitch to him more convincing."

He added that if we struck out talking to Hardy, we could take a transcript of the tapes to Sid's lawyer- friend, Maurice, and ask him to read them on a hypothetical basis. The transcripts would give Maurice leads.

While he waited for new equipment to arrive, Lars would scout out Hardy's building and take pictures. After that was completed, he'd propose a course of action, and we could form a collective judgment as to whether the risk was worth the possible benefit.

"Meanwhile," Lars concluded, "I think Sid should follow up with Weeks, Sheila with Moody, and Anna with Fountain. Maybe we'll learn something to make the surveillance unnecessary. Remember, though, whoever it is has likely been told about your trip last December to Efficiency Management. They'll be on their guard."

Sheila, Anna, and I must have sensed, at some level, that our enterprise was bound to be flawed. But Lars' experience and professionalism gave us a sense of confidence. We encouraged him to set the agenda, and he obliged us all too readily. I could have told the three of them, of course, that I would no longer be associated with these activities, and detached myself. But, like them, my adrenaline was flowing.

Chapter 7

Two days later I swallowed hard and called Audrey Weeks. She wasn't home and I left a message. It was early evening and time for the second of the three Absoluts I allowed myself every day. I put on my Peggy Lee CD and relaxed in my twenty-year old recliner. *You had plenty money nineteen - twenty two, you let other people make a - fool of you . . .*

The phone rang, and I held off picking up the receiver until Peggy admonished, *Why don't you do right? Like some other men do.*

"Mr. Silva This is Audrey Weeks. I'm returning your call."

"Thanks, Audrey. I called you for a couple of reasons. The first was to ask you to call me Sid."

After a pause she said, "All right."

"The second reason was to ask if you would have dinner with me. Get your off-the-record impressions of the Board, which direction we should be headed."

After a second pause, she said, "That would be fine . . . if you think it's proper."

"Why would it not be proper?"

"Well, we're both members of the Board, and our being out together and all, it might look funny. But I'll be glad to do it if you think it's permissible "

What were we going to do? Make out on the sidewalk?

"I think it's okay. Are you free tomorrow?"

"Yes."

I took her to Buona Sera, assuming the VIP treatment would impress her. Wrong. I could see from the start that Audrey was uncomfortable in the informal-close-together tables. Worse yet, Maria gave me an indifferent look and assigned us another waitress.

Audrey was wearing a fixed smile and a tailored powder blue suit, and I was wearing my navy blazer. We were a study in blue. She ordered Perrier, and I had my third and final Absolut of the day.

I tuned into avuncular mode. "So tell me, how do you like being on the Board?"

"What do you mean?"

"I mean, do you enjoy it? Is it fulfilling? Do you find it interesting?"

"We do it as good citizens. I'm not on the Board for fun."

"What *do* you do for fun?" I asked with a polite smile.

"Well, I like to sew. And, let's see . . . oh, yes, you know those cards you get in the mail with the picture of a child? 'Have you seen me?' Well, I save them in albums, one for the girls, one for the boys."

"You do?"

"Yes, you never know when you might see one of those poor things."

I toyed with breaking my rule and having a fourth Absolut. She ordered minestrone and a salad. When the waitress asked what she would like for her main course, she said, "This will do, thank you."

"Would you like a glass of wine?" the waitress asked.

"No, thank you, but I would like some more Perrier."

I threw caution to the winds and ordered the Absolut, a New York strip, rare, with all the trimmings.

"I gather you're not a big eater," I said, mustering a broad smile.

"I'm five-three and a hundred-ten pounds," she said. "You must be about six feet and, oh, I'd say one hundred-seventy-five to a hundred-eighty pounds. So a big meal for me would be starvation for you."

Her fixed smile broadened into a grin.

"You're not too far off," I said

After that explosion of conversation we discussed the weather in tedious detail as we waited for the food.

By the time Audrey had eaten half her soup and half her salad, which was all she wanted, I had cleaned my plate.

"How do you like living at the Oasis?" I asked.

"It's a secure place, and most of the people are well behaved. How about you?"

"I like it a lot. Good location, nice people."

"Yes, but I think we spend too much money. We're not cautious enough. I know you felt you had to replant those rhododendrons but things like that drain our reserves."

I took a sip of water. "I certainly agree we should be careful how we spend our money but the rhododendrons may not be the best example of imprudence. The cost of replanting them came to a hundred-twenty-five dollars."

"Well, a better example was the redecorating we did four years ago that came to over fifty thousand dollars. It could have waited another few years."

This was probably as close to an opening as I was going to get. "You may be right about that. I wasn't on the Board then. But some things are necessary. We really didn't have a choice on the Building Two roof replacement, did we?"

She looked directly at me, smile still in place. "No, we didn't, but those prices surely were high."

"Really. Did you raise the issue at a Board meeting? Or mention it to Travail?"

"I called Mr. Travail and he was rather abrupt with me."

"How so?"

"He said stick to my sewing and leave pricing matters to him."

"What did you say to that stick-to-your-knitting routine?"

"I don't knit, I sew. I said nothing. You may have noticed I'm not the most aggressive person in the world."

"Why did you vote to accept the bid?"

Her facial expression was, I thought, the personification of innocence. "Mr. Travail felt so strongly about it, I didn't have the heart to vote against him."

She declined dessert and coffee and I paid the bill. When we got back to the Oasis, I walked her to her apartment.

She opened the door with her key, turned around to face me, and asked, "Would you like to come in for a Perrier?"

Her smile was still in place as I told her I was tired, kissed her on the cheek, and went home.

The Task Force met a week later, and I told them about my dinner with Audrey Weeks, omitting the nightcap invitation. When I finished, the room was silent.

Anna finished taking her notes, and, looking at Lars, asked "Another great actress?" He shrugged.

Next it was Anna's turn. Ever organized, she had already drafted her report on Fountain. She put the original in the condo papers file, and handed out copies to us.

> I called Jane Fountain and asked her to lunch or dinner. We agreed on the day after Christmas. She said things are hectic at work, and she welcomed this time to relax.
>
> She is Public Relations Director at the National Association of Property Managers, and is in charge of the NAPM newsletter distributed to 455 members and 2450 associate members who provide services and materials purchased by the members. She also engages in lobbying, and frequently attends trade receptions, luncheons, dinners.
>
> I said, casually, "Seems they did a good job on your roof last spring." (She lives in Building Two.) She said, "As far as I know that's right." She laughed. "We haven't had any leaks. That's my test." Then she said, "I know you voted against the recommendation, Anna, and you may have been right. I just didn't see what else we could do."
>
> I said I assume the roofing companies that bid for the Oasis job are associate members of NAPM. She said, "Absolutely. Anybody who's anybody in this business is a member of NAPM. As a matter of fact, Nikki Bullett called me for some info to help her on the roof replacement."

I asked if she gets to see the members. She said, "Oh, yes. I've met many of them at one time or another. In fact, William Stane from Efficiency Management, the Oasis management company, was in just last week. He took me to lunch."

Nobody had much to say after reading Anna's report. Finally, Sheila spoke up. "Hardy can't be *this* obvious. Plant a spy on the Board from his own trade association."

Nobody disagreed.

Sheila told us that Moody and his wife were out of town for the holidays. That assignment would have to wait a few weeks.

Lars gave us his plan to place Hardy's phone under electronic surveillance. Step one, photographing the outside area around Hardy's office with a zoom lens, had been completed. He showed us the pictures, assuring us he had been careful.

The second step would be installing the "bug." He had arranged for a van with commercial markings to be parked during working hours a few blocks from Hardy's office. Inside the van Hardy's phone calls would be monitored and taped.

Who would be doing the taping inside the van? Lars said it would be "Ben," someone who had worked for Lars for twenty years.

Who would pay for all this? I offered to split the costs with Lars. He wouldn't hear of it. "I pay. Haven't had this much fun in years. There'll be enough juice in that phone for Ben to work the tape for a month. After that we'll pull the bug."

I said I would pay for the cost of the van and Ben's time. Lars said he would split it with me. Sheila said the four of us should split everything, and we all nodded. The next words popped out of my mouth like empty bubbles. "I'll go with Lars to install the bug." Why did I say that? To show off in front of Anna? Because I was caught up in the fervor?

Lars, looking dubious, said it would be better for him to go alone. Before I could say that on second thought Lars had a point, Sheila importuned on my behalf. "Give Burt a break," she said, "he needs the excitement." Lars relented, reluctantly.

The next day, Carl Harrison was in my cubbyhole for the vodka preceding our weekly dinner. He sat down, picked up his Absolut, and said, "I know I'm good but I never thought I was that good."

"What are you talking about, Carl?"

"We mentioned Bunny Slack the other day?"

"So?"

"So I'm over there and we're relaxing afterwards . . . I forget what they call that."

"Post coital."

"How did you know that?" he asked.

"I read it in a book."

"Post coital. She says, Carly - that's her pet name for me - you're the best. I say, better than Travail? He was her special friend before me, but you knew that."

"No, I didn't."

"Considering you're the President, you don't know much about what's happening around here. Anyway, she says, Travail's a loser. His daddy left him big, big bucks and he threw it away on stupid investments. She doesn't understand how he can live here."

It was ten o'clock Sunday night, the best time to break and enter a commercial property, Lars said. And it was just after Christmas, a quiet time of the year in a non-retail section. We were on our way to Wheaton, Maryland, some fifteen miles outside of Washington. I was fidgety. We were about to violate I didn't know how many laws. But Lars' concentration had a calming effect.

"We'll go in through the front door," Lars was saying. "I got a shot of the lock and it won't be a problem. I have a flashlight - no other lights. We're going to install a simple bug, only in Hardy's phone. I'd like to do the secretary's phone to find out the incoming calls, but I want to keep it short and sweet, get out of there in five minutes."

Lars and I had studied the rough sketch of the layout that Anna and Sheila had made from their recollection of their visit. Once again, we went over it, including the outer office where the secretary sat, Hardy's inner office, and Mr. Stane's "inner-inner" office.

Lars said, "Now, please do exactly as I say - no more, no less."

"Right."

I felt a little flushed, and glanced over at Lars. Stolid, imperturbable.

He parked his four-door black Lexus a block away from Hardy's office, and didn't lock it. We were in a warehouse district, and no other cars or people were in sight. The cul-de-sac was motionless and quiet. Lars put on a pair of thin rubber gloves, picked up a small, fabric bag, and we walked at a moderate pace to the small Efficiency Management building. Lars got the door open in about twenty seconds.

Inside, he taped a porous cloth around the bulb of his flashlight and switched it on. We made our way into the inner office. As he went to work on the phone sitting on the desk, I watched him unscrew the mouthpiece The gleam of the dimmed flashlight reflecting a yellow cast to his hair. A Nordic God of the electronic underworld, he was deft, precise, with not a wasted motion.

I remembered Sheila and Anna telling us how they went into Mr. Stane's tiny office tucked behind Hardy's desk, where Stane did the "razzle-dazzle" with the numbers. I decided to take a quick look at it.

As I approached the door I heard Lars mutter, "All done," and out of the corner of my eye saw him pick up his fabric bag. The events of the next thirty seconds occurred rapidly, and later, when I tried to recapture the scene, everything was in fast forward.

I opened the door. The next thing I knew, I registered a blur of motion hurtling toward me, and what felt like a vice with prongs, had clamped onto the calf of my left leg. I was outraged that the dog had not selected my right instead of my left leg which was not entirely healed from my slip a few weeks ago. I became aware that the dog's purpose was to keep me in place. And I remember the enormous quiet.

I absorbed the sting of pain, and, through the semi-darkness, watched the stocky, motionless, black body of the dog whose teeth were fastened onto my leg. He-or she- never once barked or growled or made any other sound.

But I did. Trying to keep my voice down, I said, "Lars, help me."

Lars sprung through the open door, sized up everything in a mini-second, and said, "Don't move."

Soundlessly, he went back into the outer office and was back in a few seconds. In his right hand was a syringe which he plunged into Fido's back. The teeth loosened on my leg and Fido keeled over and lay still.

Lars sat me down in the outer office, and went back and closed the door to Stane's office. He locked the outside door, leaving it as we found it, and half carried me to the car. He drove about ten blocks and parked under a street light.

"Let me see it," he said, and, wincing, I pulled up my pants and raised my leg.

"Damn," he said.

"What?"

"He tore through your pants. He may have some threads still stuck in his teeth. But we can't go back so let's hope he swallowed all of it."

Lars said there was little blood and he didn't think it was serious, but he headed for the emergency room at Holy Cross Hospital where somebody would treat the wound and give me tetanus and rabies shots. It was easy for him to say it didn't look serious. All I knew was it began to hurt like hell.

I guess Lars was a little vexed with me. "You promised," he said, "to do exactly what I said. Did I tell you to open that door?"

"No. I screwed up."

I was grateful that he did not say, "I told you not to come."

Despite his optimism about my leg, Lars pushed the Lexus, and we were at the hospital in ten minutes. The emergency room doctor cleaned and bandaged the wound, and gave me the shots. She had the temerity to tell me the surface was barely broken and it was only a superficial flesh wound. Stay off your feet for a few days, she said. She asked us to describe what happened, and we said we were walking on the street and the dog came from out of nowhere, held onto me for a few seconds, and dashed off.

"Third case like that this month," she said.

On the way back to the Oasis, Lars said, "I was taught to carry that syringe on a job, but this is the first time I've had to use it. He'll be out for an hour. After that, he'll be fine and nobody will know what happened. He's a rottweiler. Despite what you've heard, that's a gentle dog. This one was trained to keep intruders in place, not to hurt them."

"Two things I don't understand," I said. "Why don't they keep the dog in the outer office or in Hardy's office. Why in Stane's inner office? And if they want to keep a watch dog there, why not have one that barks, to scare intruders away?"

"Whatever they're concerned about must be in Stane's office. As to intruders, they don't want to scare them away. They want to come in the next morning and find the intruder sitting there with that vice around him."

We got back after one in the morning, and there were two messages from Anna on my machine. Where were we? How did it go? It's 12:30, why aren't we back yet?

I called her and told her what happened. She said she'd be right over and I told her I was okay, the pain was lessening. I said I'd see her tomorrow.

Five minutes later Anna was at my door in her bathrobe. She looked at my leg and asked, "What did they say to do for that at the hospital?"

"Stay off my feet for a day or two."

"Not a problem," she said, pulling off her robe.

Ben, whom I never did get to meet, delivered the tapes to Lars at the end of each day, and the Task Force met at my place each night to listen to them. Sheila and Anna were able to identify Hardy's voice from their visit with him a year ago. The calls during the first week, Monday through Friday, dealt mostly with routine business between Hardy, uniformly solicitous, and his customers about roofs, prices, and schedules. None of the conversations that first week was with roofing companies.

There were two calls on Thursday, however, that had us sitting up straight. The tape captured everything said from the time Hardy picked up his receiver in response to his secretary's buzz. The first of these two calls was clocked in at 9:30 a.m.

Hardy: "Yeah?"

Secretary: "It's Ms. Buffington."

Hardy: "I'll take it. [Click] Brandy, what are you doing up so early? It's 6:30 in LA. Are you OK?"

Buffington: "I'm fine, Chuck. But the check didn't come on the first like it usually does."

Hardy: "Oh, shit, I forgot to tell you. I had a little cash flow problem. It's okay now. The check'll go out today."

Buffington: "I'll be looking for it. What about the EMA stock? Should I sell it? Buy more? Or what?"

Hardy: "Hold it. Bye."

(Disconnect.)

Sheila was the first to speak "What was that all about?"

"Strange," I said. "He gets out of his first marriage with an annulment and then sends her money and stock. Could there be a generous streak behind all that ugliness?"

"Or a guilty streak," said Anna.

"You two are living in a dream world," Sheila said. "She's got something on him, and he's paying her to keep her mouth shut. The money stops, she shoves it to him."

The second call came at 4:55 p.m.

Hardy: "Yeah?"

Secretary: "Pete Slarsky."

Hardy" "I'll take it."

(Clicking sound)

Hardy: "Pete, my man.

Pete: "Are you alone?"

Hardy: "No one's in here, but I want to be careful. That gum-chewing bitch listens in sometimes. I'll call you right back on the private phone."

(Disconnect)

100

Lars and I looked at each other. There was another, hidden phone somewhere in Hardy's office. We had missed it.

The first week of tape-listening had ended, and it was my turn in the poker rotation. Anna, who didn't play, said she'd help me set it up. The full set of players were present this time: Lars, Sheila, Paul, Francis, Ron, Carl, and me - plus Anna, watching.

In the course of a game of seven-card stud, Lars flipped the fourth open card to everyone. No pair was showing, and nobody had the makings of a straight or a flush. Francis held a king, the highest card in sight. My four up-cards were a three, six, nine, and jack. I had another jack in the hole, and with one more card to go, the most I could hope for was two pair or three jacks.

My seventh card was a useless deuce, and I ended up with a pair of jacks. High on the board with his king, Francis bet. Paul folded, and Sheila called. Not proud of my jacks, I called because a bet from Francis meant nothing, and because any pair was capable of taking the pot against the sorry lot of cards spread out on the table.

Lars raised which also didn't necessarily mean anything. Over the course of our games I had seen Lars go on the offensive, holding scanty ammunition. Ron dropped out, and Carl, Sheila, Francis and I called. Lars turned over a pair of kings he had in the hole. Sheila, Carl and I threw in our cards, but Francis came up with another king, putting him in an apparent tie with Lars. But Lars' next highest card was a ten while Francis' was an eight.

Lars scooped up his chips, and Francis said, "I don't like the way you play."

"What do I do that you don't like?" asked Lars.

"With that skimpy pair of kings, you should have called," said Francis.

"I was hoping to scare you all out. In any case, I won, didn't I?"

"But it wasn't nice, the way you did it. You squeezed more money out of us when you didn't have to."

"With all respect, Francis," I said, "he followed the rules, and he's playing the game the way it's supposed to be played. And what are you complaining about anyway? As you once said, You want to play with the big boys, you have to have the stuff."

Francis sat there scowling, and didn't say a word.

As the others were leaving, Lars said he'd stick around and have another beer, and Sheila said she'd join him. Anna and I cleaned up, got ourselves a beer, and sat down.

"Well," Lars said, "we missed the boat on the secret phone. I have to go back."

"When do we go?" I asked.

"No offense, Sid, but this time just me."

Sheila couldn't wait. "Burt doesn't get to bond with his canine buddy again?"

"Which reminds me, Lars," I said, "suppose that phone is in Stane's office?

"I'll have my syringe ready."

Lars went back to Wheaton the next night, Sunday, and accomplished his mission without mishap. He found the other phone in an unlocked drawer in Stane's desk, and had no need to deal with Fido who was nowhere in sight.

I would never understand how we could have been so uncomprehending, so obtuse as to attach no significance to the unexplained absence of the dog.

The Monday through Thursday tapes were once more routine, and Hardy never used the secret phone. Friday was Christmas day and no calls were on the tape. Sheila missed the Tuesday night Task Force session because she had Morton Moody, the Board member, and his wife, Agnes, to dinner at her apartment. She told them it was to celebrate their return from Florida.

She gave us her report, a model of brevity, on Wednesday, before our tape session:

> Sheila had Morton and Agnes Moody to dinner on Tuesday, February 6. She spent the evening trying to get them to talk about anything other than their respective golf games. When Sheila found an opening to bring up the roof replacement, all Moody would say was 'We got a good deal -lowest price, best quality.'

> Sheila said Moody is no more a Hardy spy than Burt is in his sexual prime. She served corned beef and cabbage and they LOVED it.

Anna and I exchanged smiles.

I had been engrossed in my Elmore Leonard book most of the morning. It was 11:30 and I decided to go for a walk so I could feel virtuous the rest of the day. I threw on a heavy jacket and rang for the elevator. The door opened and my heart sank to see Elsie Turner standing inside.

She ushered me in with a grand gesture. "What do you know? My lucky day."

"Nice to see you, Elsie."

"It can't be *that* nice," she said. "You never did get back to . . ."

At that moment the elevator abruptly ground to a standstill in mid-floor, and the door remained closed. We looked at each other, concern on my face, a grin on hers.

A few elevator stoppages in my building had occurred over the past several weeks, and I knew that Nikki Bullett was looking into it. On each occasion, the repair personnel arrived after about an hour, eased the elevator down to the lobby floor, got the door open, and made the necessary adjustments in the mechanism. But it was becoming apparent that some form of major repair was imminent. This was the first time I was a victim.

I picked up the emergency phone, reported that we were stuck, and asked them to expedite our rescue. They assured me we'd be extricated within an hour.

Elsie moved toward me. "What do they say in moments of crisis?"

"I give up."

She moved in closer and I stepped back until I was up against the wall. "Always make the most of a bad situation," she said.

I began to laugh. "Elsie, you are a special piece of work."

"You don't know how special." She circled my neck with her arms. "Let's make a deal," she said. "Whatever happens in the next hour will never cross either of our lips."

"'Either' means one or the other. Between us, we have four lips."

"Let's find out."

She kissed me softly, and I gently pushed her away.

"Elsie, this is crazy."

"Why?"

"Because it's inappropriate. Besides, I've never done it standing up."

"You've got to be kidding. Have you led such a sheltered life?"

"Elsie, I like you, I really do. But we just don't know each other that well."

She sighed. "Your deadline for tuna casserole expired six weeks ago. But I'm going to give you a special exception. Be at my place at 7:30 and all will be forgiven."

My mind on the elevator, I accepted her invitation. That kind of hasty decision may have been a function of the aging process, but in my self defense, I was condo President, and it behooved me to be courteous to my constituents. We were freed from the elevator in half an hour. Later, I told Anna about my adventure with Elsie and the invitation to dinner.

Anna laughed, and said, "I'll be waiting for a full report."

Elsie's apartment was on the same floor as Anna's, and I made my way past Anna's door like a kid slinking off to play hooky. I knew the stealth was silly.

I was in for a surprise - several of them, in fact. My first surprise was that Elsie looked fetching. She wore a beige tailored outfit over a burgundy blouse. Her apartment was exquisitely furnished, and her CD was playing the 1927 Louis Armstrong "West End Blues." An even bigger surprise came when she handed me an Absolut vodka on the rocks with a twist. I figured that one out. Oasis grapevine.

The $64,000 surprise came when she said she was tired of tuna casserole, and served lamb chops. This night was turning out to be less painful than I had anticipated.

The food was good, and the conversation was pleasant. After I helped her clean up, we sat down on opposite ends of the sofa, listening to more Louis. Pretty soon we began talking.

It was just after ten, and I said, "Thank you for a delightful evening. It has been lovely, but I'd better be going."

She said, "Before you go, Mr. President - I voted for you, by the way - you should be aware that I could tell you a few things I think you'd like to know about."

"Oh?"

"Things that have been happening around here."

"What do you mean, 'around here?'"

"The Oasis."

"What things?"

"I can give you background that you can't get anywhere else."

"So tell me."

"This is information only to be shared with friends."

"Aren't we friends?"

"The last time we met you said we hadn't talked to each other for more than fifteen seconds. We could spend a little more time together, then - maybe - become friends. Who knows? Only you may not be up to that. It seems to me you're always hiding behind an impenetrable screen to shield you from I-don't-know-what."

The challenge again.

I remembered that late Indian summer day in October, 1952. I'd been back from Korea about a year, teaching great books to high school seniors. Being a Korean veteran hadn't hurt my application. Teaching was what I had always wanted to do. I had been seeing a colleague named Sarah, and we were making noises about getting married.

The class had ended and I was alone, grading papers. The mixed aromas of new textbooks and old chalk hung over the room. There was a light tap on the door and I looked up to see my old college buddy, Danny Jenkins. We'd kept in touch intermittently. After an embrace and some reminiscences, he had said, "Proposition. Join my construction firm. With your talent for architecture and my business savvy we'll get rich."

I told him I was flattered, but money was less important to me than the satisfaction I was getting from teaching.

"Tell you what," he said. "You come with me and if you're not happy after six months, I promise to get you reinstated in the school system."

He told me his contacts with the local government and the school board would ensure that he could do this.

I declined his offer a second time.

He persisted. "You know what I think? You're afraid to take the plunge. You tell yourself you're comfortable and secure in this academic cocoon and you're scared to get out there where the ice is thin and the fish are waiting for the bait. You're risk-averse."

That last is probably what got to me. I *was* risk-averse and cautious, but I disliked being seen that way. I took him up on his offer, and after six months he asked me what I wanted to do. I said, "Stay here."

*

Now I was confronted by this attractive-well-dressed-good-cook-full-of-surprises-Louis Armstrong-fan telling me she would give me important condo information if we became friends. And, surprise of all surprises, I was beginning to like her.

Even if we became "friends," whatever that meant to her, she would probably string me along, trickling out the information. I suspected her "information" was useless gossip. Anna mattered to me more than any information this woman might share with me.

Still, Elsie had me interested. My challenge was to *coax* the information out of her.

"You own your apartment which means you have a substantial investment in this place. If there's something I should know as President, it's in your self-interest to tell me."

"Friendship is more important than money," she said without smiling.

"We *are* friends, aren't we?"

"Getting there, maybe. I'll give you the subject, then it's up to you."

"You're on," I said.

"It's about the roof replacement. Your move."

I exhaled slowly. One passionless kiss would surely not be disloyal to Anna. I brought my lips to hers, and to my astonishment the smell of lavender came floating out of her half-open mouth, the same sweet scent that had once adorned Sarah's very presence.

In my four months as President, I had adopted the practice of dropping in on Nikki two or three times a week, and she'd fill me in on Oasis happenings. It was mid-morning, and before I walked over to her office I put on my poncho. It had been raining over the four-day New Year's weekend. Not a hard rain, but steady, never letting up.

As I stood in front of her desk, shaking the moisture from my poncho, she said, "Well, it's happened. Leaks into two top floor units in Building One over the weekend. They're small and can be patched, but the roof needs replacing."

"When should it be done?" I asked.

"Early spring, like April. Now's the time to send out the RFPs."

"Same companies?"

"Maybe one more."

"Get them ready but don't mail them. Let me see them before they go out."

'Okay, Sid."

I picked up the small photograph of a young boy that was always on her desk. "Suppose you come into my office and tell me about that good-looking lad over a bagel and coffee. How does that sound?"

"Like an offer I can't refuse."

We went into my cubby hole, and, slicing the bagel, I asked, "What's his name?"

"Steven."

"Solidly built guy from the picture. Looks like he has the makings of an athlete."

She laughed. "He's only ten and already placed second in his wrestling class."

"You must be proud of him."

She looked at me for a few seconds. "I *am* proud of him. He's a good boy."

When Sarah's scent of lavender floated out of Elsie's mouth, my impulse had been to pull away. But she beat me to it. She had pushed me off and sat upright.

"That was about to get interesting," she had said, "but we're not ready. In the meantime, you showed me you're sincere. So I'm going to whet your appetite."

She had paused and I said, "I'm all ears."

"All right, one thing for now. Our management company? Efficiency? I was married to the head guy, Chuck Hardy, for nine years. Next move is yours. Good night."

Now, a week later, the Task Force met to hear Lars' report on Nikki Bullett. This was Anna's transcript.

> Nikki Bullett (nee Mardson) was born in Cleveland, Ohio in 1955. She attended the University of Ohio for two years and then left school to work in the property management field in the Cleveland area. In 1984 she moved to Washington D.C. and was employed by the Dixon Company which is engaged in, among other things, property management. In 1992 she was hired by Efficiency Management Company, and assigned as Property Manager to the Oasis Condominium on Connecticut Avenue. She currently holds that position.
>
> In 1988 Ms. Mardson gave birth to a son, Steven. The father is unknown.In 1993 Ms. Mardson married Oliver Bullett. The marriage ended in 1995 with an uncontested divorce. Subject has retained her married name. In 1998 Oliver Bullett filed a petition for custody of Steven Bullett whom he alleges to be his son.

"So why did she move to Washington? And who is Steven's real father?" Sheila asked. "And what's with this Oliver Bullett?"

"Everybody has a story," Anna said. "It doesn't have to be sinister."

I thought hard about where to take Elsie, finally deciding on Buona Sera. I didn't tell Anna about it. I still don't know why. When I telephoned Maria to make reservations for two, her manner began with warm anticipation and ended with icy correctness.

"I look forward to seeing you, Sid. You'll be here with Anna?"

"No, I'll be with another woman who is important to me from a business viewpoint. So please give us some VIP treatment, will you?"

"I assure you, Mr. Silva, you'll be treated with our usual courtesy and respect."

The restaurant was crowded and noisy as usual, but as I had suspected, Elsie liked it. When Maria came over I introduced them and Maria said, "I'm pleased to meet you, Ms. Turner. Any friend of Mr. Silva is welcome here."

"That's some testimonial," Elsie said after Maria left the table.

I had my usual and Elsie ordered liver and onions which she said were superb. We went through a couple of glasses of Brunello, and the conversation flowed smoothly. It was no stretch to see that one could get to like this woman.

On the way home, I asked Elsie to tell me about Hardy.

She married him, she said, some ten years earlier, on the rebound from a brief love affair. She had been fifty-four. When they were in the presence of others, Elsie said, Hardy behaved like a teddy bear. When he was alone with Elsie, the teddy bear revealed a temper. One night they argued over some petty matter, and he slapped her. After that it got worse. He never injured her seriously, but slapping her face became a habit.

"An occasional Scotch," she said, "no other drugs. I understand it's now 'frequent' Scotch. I'd look at him and I'd see a man who slapped me. Why didn't I leave him sooner? I guess I thought it would stop. Then I became afraid to leave him. I'm not sure you'll understand, but I came to believe I deserved everything that was happening to me."

After nine years of marriage, they had some disagreement and he hit her on the jaw with his fist. That elevation of the violence, she said, turned out to be providential. It gave her the impetus she needed to leave him.

We got to her apartment at the Oasis and she invited me in for coffee. She was wound up, shaking a little, having dredged up the bad memories.

After a few minutes she said, "After the divorce I went back to my maiden name, Turner. He knows where I am, but he's never bothered me. In fact . . ."

"What?"

"You're discreet?"

"If nothing else."

"The word in the office was that he made a lot of money. Something called executive stock options. A few years ago he began sending me a check every month. The divorce decree gave each of us our personal possessions and that was it. I called and asked why the monthly checks. He said it was something he wanted to do. Strange, isn't it?"

"And he wants nothing in return?"

"Nothing. Last year he sent me a certificate for a thousand shares of common stock in his company, Efficiency Management of America - EMA. Told me to hang onto it. As of this morning it was trading at $51."

Something wasn't ringing true. "What is this guy? A saint in monster's clothing or a monster in saint's clothing?"

"He can be charming, ingratiating, but the man I knew was mean. At the end of our first year he put me to work in his office. What he did to me was kid stuff next to his business dealings. Look, Sid, I'm really tired, but call me and we'll talk some more."

I said I would. I wondered if Anna would understand. I needed to find out more about Hardy.

The Task Force played the tapes five nights a week throughout December and up to the middle of January. We listened to innocuous personal calls between Hardy and his wife, and between the secretary and her girl friends. Two calls were placed by Stane, exhorting a woman named Florence to reconsider her decision not to see him anymore. She told him he was "polite," but would always be a "cold fish."

All of Hardy's business calls were placed to or received from properties he managed. No roofing company, elevator repair company, or any other supplier, provider. or contractor placed or received a call. Every call we listened to reflected routine business transactions or personal chit-chat. Not one call suggested illicit or unethical activity.

Lars felt that going back and removing the bugs wasn't worth the risk, and we quickly concurred. We had reached a dead end.

PART TWO

To me, fair friend, you can never be old,
For as you were when first your eye I ey'd,
Such seems your beauty still.

William Shakespeare
[1564 – 1616]

Sonnet 104, 1.1

Chapter 8

My grandson, Skip, arrived in the middle of January with his backpack, portable CD player, cell phone, and bottled water. We embraced perfunctorily and exchanged a few pleasantries. When I asked what kind of food he'd like me to stock, he said, "Whatever." After the first fifteen minutes the conversation petered out.

He took over the second bedroom, and by the end of the second day he had adorned the walls with an array of posters. I looked them over, and recognizing nobody I asked him who they were. He sighed, as though irked at my ignorance.

"Over here," he said, pointing his forefinger, "is Radiohead. Next to them is the Dave Matthews Band."

He crossed to the opposite wall and faced the four posters arranged side by side, each one lower than the next. All four were photographs of unkempt-looking men. "This guy," he said, pointing, "is Method Man. The next guy is Ghostspace Killah, and the next one is Rza. The guy on the right is Ol' Dirty Bastard. They're all with Wu-tang Clan."

"I see," I said.

During the next few days tortured sounds passing for music permeated my apartment. When I asked Skip if he could make it softer, he nodded, and from that time on he listened through his earphones. For the balance of his stay with me the silence that followed the incessant din of those first two days was a restful melody to my ears.

On his second day, I told Skip I had leased a car for him to use to drive to his classes until the dorm was ready. He said, "Thanks." That was it. One night toward the end of his first week, a vaguely familiar smell floated out of his room. I knocked at his door and said I was sorry, but no drugs in the apartment.

He said, "Come on, man, I see you throwing down that vodka every night before we eat. That will hurt you more than grass."

Regardless of other considerations, I said, alcohol was not illegal. He shrugged and said, "I'll be out of your face real soon." He closed the door softly as I stood there.

I was aware that teenagers go through stages, and one has to ride them out. But Skip's attitude was coarse sandpaper rubbing against my emotional skin. Was there no way to get through to my grandson, to penetrate that surly indifference?

A few nights after the cannabis incident, we were seated at the kitchen table, chewing on some pizza I had ordered in. At one point the tomato sauce had caked onto both our chins, and as we wiped away with our paper napkins his eyes lit on me for a fraction of a second. Was that a hint of a smile? A faint flicker of possible détente? I was emboldened.

Still working on my chin, I said, "Skip, I've got a little problem here at the condo I'd like to run by you. Get your reaction. Your ears only, I'll trust you."

I told him about our suspicions.

"Why don't you go to a lawyer?" he asked immediately.

"I did talk to a lawyer, but I wanted to see what we could come up with ourselves."

He wiped the last of the cheese off his chin and said, "You're bored and you want to stir up excitement in your life."

I hovered between resentment of his presumptuousness and respect for his insight.

"Maybe a little. But before we become involved with the lawyers I want some confirmation that we're onto something."

"Why not get into his phones?"

The kid was quick. "We tried that," I said, refilling our glasses with diet Coke, and wondering if he understood the legal implications of what I'd just told him.

"And?"

"Nothing useful. Routine business and small talk."

I took a sip of the Coke. "You understand, Skip, this was not entirely . . . uh . . . legit. Tapping into somebody's phone can get you in . . ."

"I know all about that. How long did you do it?"

"About three weeks."

"They're not using the phone to do their stuff, they're using e-mail."

"You mean on computers."

He sighed. "Yes, Grandpa, computers."

"So we're screwed," I said, hoping my choice of idiom might bring us closer.

"We're not 'screwed,' Grandpa." The sarcasm was inescapable. So much for vernacular as a binding device. "All we need is a good computer."

"What good would a computer do?"

"We get into his e-mail, see what the bad guys are saying."

"You're telling me you could do this if you had a computer?"

"No sweat. Dad said he'll buy me one for the dorm, but I don't think he'll spring for the quality I want."

"Wouldn't we be violating the law?"

"I don't know."

"You're saying it may be illegal, but we might not get caught. I don't like it."

"Grandpa, whatever I say, you lecture me."

I took a swig of Diet Coke. No question, I was critical with him, but my *purpose* was to help him. His *perception* was a grumpy grandfather who nagged and nagged.

"Suppose I bought you a new computer. We'd set it up here and then you'd take it with you when you move into the dorm."

He placed his Coke can onto the table. "You'd do that for me?"

"For me."

I reported to the Task Force Skip's belief that we could get into Hardy's e-mail. I said I was dubious that he could do it, and, more important, it might be illegal.

Sheila said, "Go for it." Lars leaned toward giving it a try, and Anna was hesitant. I said I thought we should limit the exercise to Skip and me. If we got into trouble, the three of them would be shielded from liability. Out of the question, they said. All or none.

I told Skip that Anna, a good friend of mine who lived in our building, wanted to meet him, and had invited us to dinner. Skip begged off, saying, "You'll have a better time without me. I'll send out for pizza, like that. I'll be fine."

"I think you'll like her, and she cooks up a great meal. Do this for me, Skip."

"All right, but I'm gonna leave early."

Anna said, "Nice to meet you, Skip," and he threw her a half-smile. She took our drink orders - bottle of Bud for Skip, no glass, and my usual vodka. As we sipped our drinks, Anna slipped a CD into the player. The sound surrounded the room.

Article man, particle man,
Doing the things a particle can,
What's he like? It's not important,
Particle man.

Skip's mouth hung open, his polite smile became a broad grin, and he began to move to the beat and hum along with the melody, such as it was. On the next verse, or stanza, or whatever they called it, Anna sang along with the CD.

Is he a dot or is he a speck?
When he's underwater does he get wet?
Or does the water get him instead?
Nobody knows, Particle man

When the track was completed, I asked, "Who is that band?" I tried to keep disdain out of my voice.

Before Anna could answer, Skip said, "They Might Be Giants." He turned to Anna, and said, "How do you know about these guys?"

"I've been listening to Flansburgh and Linnell for more than ten years. Remember 'Boat of Car?'"

"You have to be putting me on. You know 'Boat of Car?'"

115

"Sure I do. How about 'Your Racist Friend,' or 'Youth Culture Killed my Dog'?"

"Far out."

Anna sat down next to him on the sofa. "Listen, my friend, I was there at Darinka in the East Village the night everybody in the audience - a hundred of us - had an acoustic guitar, and played "Mr. Tambourine Man" along with the band. You know how they got their name?"

"No."

"From a 1971 movie starring George C. Scott."

"Who's he?"

"Big star in his day."

Skip peered at her. "I'll bet you don't know Fugazi."

"Of course I do. They're originally from Washington. You know what 'Fugazi' stands for?"

"No."

"Phrase from the Vietnam era. FUCKED UP, GOT AMBUSHED, ZIPPED IN."

For the first time, I listened to Skip laugh out loud. "How about Lucinda Williams?"

"Happy Woman Blues."

"Jesus."

Anna slipped into the kitchen, and Skip, barely noticing my presence, said, "Oh, man, that is one cool woman."

Anna, came back, gave me a smile, and asked us, "How do you like your steak?"

"Rare."

"Rare."

"Perfect," she said.

As Anna went back to the kitchen, Skip winked at me. He actually *winked*.

After our coffee and apple pie, I went to the bathroom at the end of the corridor. As I was returning, still out of sight, I heard Anna say, "You must know, Skip, that your grandfather is a very special person."

I heard him say, "Yeah, he's okay."

Skip and I had scheduled our search for a new computer for the next day. He said, "How about we take Anna with us?"

"I can ask her."

"Shit, Grandpa, she'll do anything you say."

"You've been smoking that stuff again."

Anna, Skip and I went to five stores, looking at computers for the better part of the morning. It was 12:30, and I suggested lunch at an Italian place in the mall. Anna asked Skip what kind of food he wanted, and he said Mexican, especially burritos.

Anna said, "I declare that this is Skip's day. Mexican it shall be."

Skip looked at her with something close to adulation.

After lunch, at a store in the same mall, we found Skip's "super" computer. "What's super," I said, "is the price. Let's look some more."

"Hey, Sid," Anna said. "What day is this?"

We both looked at her blankly, and then Skip broke out into a grin, and said, "Skip's day."

I bought the computer.

That afternoon Anna and I took a walk. "I didn't know you like that so-called music," I said.

"I've loved that so-called music for years."

"Aren't you a little old for that stuff?"

"Up yours."

"You and Skip seem to have something going."

Anna turned to me and smiled. "Jealous?"

"You bet your ass."

We walked along quietly, and I said, "He really likes you. You must know that."

"I like him, too. He's going through a tough period."

"He's been going through a tough period since he was two weeks old. His mother is a spoiled airhead obsessed with money. To say she's neglected him is an understatement. Maybe, without realizing it, he sees you as the mother he never knew. No, more like a sister. And Brad . . . I don't know. He tries, but something's missing. As for me, I can't make a connection. Maybe all of life is a tough period."

"Sweetheart, spare me the philosophy."

I laughed. "Done. What's your secret with him? Is it just the music?"

We walked on for several more minutes, and she took my hand and led me to a bench. We sat for a while, and she said, "Remember I told you about my marriage? The promiscuous husband? I left something out. When I found out what Dr. Casanova was doing to me, I was two months pregnant. I'd been planning to tell him on his birthday, a week off. Two days later I had an abortion. I've never regretted doing that. I couldn't bear bringing his child into the world. I've never told this to anybody, not even Sheila."

She paused. "I guess I've always felt a connection to kids."

I put my arm around her and we sat quietly.

Lars, Anna, Sheila, and I were gathered in my apartment. Skip asked the four of us to take seats, and standing in front of the small group, he gave us a run-down on what he proposed to do. He described the various methods to gain access to Hardy's computer.

The computer, Skip explained, would be password protected, so we would need to identify the password. One way to do this would be simply to guess. We knew a little about Hardy and his business, so we could try out words or acronyms that Hardy might favor, such as "management," "properties," or Hardy's wife's name, "Melody."

I had briefed the task force on what Elsie Turner had told me, and I wondered out loud if he might be using "Elsie," as his password.

Sheila scoffed, "From what you told us, all he wants to do is forget about her." She threw her hands up in the air. "Talk about a needle in the haystack."

Skip tried all the names to no avail. "You're right," he said. "Guessing is usually hopeless. There's a better way."

He explained that most people have a tendency to write down their password and place it in a handy place. If somebody could snoop through Hardy's office he might be able to find the password. As though on cue, all of us looked at Lars. Even Skip.

I had selected New York instead of Washington to see a basketball game so Mickey and I would have more time to get to know each other. It hit me that having Skip along might make for a smoother trip I knew that neither of them had ever been to the City, and who knows, I thought, maybe getting to know Mickey would be good for Skip.

When my scalper-friend finally answered his cell phone, I asked if he had three tickets to the Knicks-Wizards game at the Garden. He said "No problem." As it turned out, Skip was delighted.

The three-and-a-half hour train ride was uneventful. Absorbed in Carl Hiaasen's latest Florida romp, I glanced across the aisle now and then at Skip and Mickey playing around with Mickey's lap-top.

They were a study in contrast. Skip, eighteen, scrawny like his mother, with a haggard look, spoke in spurts of "Cool," "Man," "Chill out," "Sucks," and "Bummer." Mickey, twenty-two, dense black hair crowning his six feet of brawn, evidenced a composure behind which, I suspected, was a coiled spring ready to strike.

As they launched into a war game on the computer, I watched them covertly. Their play was competitive, but, clearly, Mickey was taking the lead, showing Skip new techniques, new approaches. It was also clear that Skip respected him At one point I saw them exchanging e-mail addresses.

At 6 p.m. we checked in at the Hotel Pennsylvania, opposite Madison Square Garden, where I had reserved a room for them and a room for me. The game was scheduled for 7:30 and I suggested a bite at a nearby restaurant, but they were eager to get into the Garden and, as Skip put it, "Grab something between the quarters."

The Garden, as always, was a spectacle of klieg lights zooming in and out of the seats and onto the playing floor, and blaring rock music amplified to a decibel level designed to challenge aural tolerance. Mammoth replay TV screens hung by invisible wire, and ubiquitous placards advertised everything from banks to hospitals. The throngs of Knicks fans were raucous and fiercely partisan.

When we cheered as the rookie Washington guard made his fourth three-pointer, the crowd around us chanted, "Beginner's luck," and "Back to the sticks, hicks."

At the end of the first quarter, the Knicks were leading by five, and we went upstairs to the concession stands, where we each had two giant hot dogs, everything on, French fries and beer. At the end of the second quarter the game was tied, and to celebrate our team's comeback, we had one more hot dog each. When the third quarter ended, the Knicks led by twelve, and the final score was Knicks, 101, Wizards, 97.

The Brooklyn-accent-loudmouth sitting behind us bellowed his verdict. "You guys'll never beat the Knicks. NEVER."

"Next year," I said, turning half-around. "We're rebuilding right now."

"I'll see you here in ten years. You'll still be rebuilding."

Skip and Mickey were grinning ear-to-ear.

"Let's take a look at Times Square," I said, "ten minutes away, walk off the hot dogs. First, let me give you both a tip. I used to come here on business. When you're walking around in New York, especially at night, you take pains not to look like a tourist. You proceed with a determined gait as though you know where you're going, you avoid eye contact, and you never gaze up at the skyscrapers or stop to look at anything else."

They responded to this advice with condescending bows in my direction.

Times Square mesmerized them, as I had suspected it would. They gaped at the electronic signs, peered into the theatre marquees, and stared at the wannabe starlets strolling and trolling the streets. In short, they disregarded my words of caution, but, I had to say, I so enjoyed their enthusiasm that I never once pulled them up short. Besides, other tourists were doing the same thing.

It was now close to 11 and we set out back to the hotel. We walked down Broadway for a few blocks, and at 38th street we crossed over to the east side of Seventh Avenue. Just after we passed 37th street we came upon a bronze statue of "The Needleworker" in front of a large building. I told them the statue was a tribute to the garment workers who had worked in this area since the turn of the century.

The three of us were stooped down, reading the inscription at the bottom of the statue when out of the corner of my eye I saw a darkly-clad wisp of a figure emerge from the shadows of the building. It was a short man with a scraggly nest of beard, and he approached us. His arm described a rapid arc, and upon completion, the hand at the end of the arm held a pistol pointed at Skip's left temple.

"Stand up and keep quiet," the man said, "or I'll blow his head off."

We slowly rose, remained motionless, and said nothing. The man continued to point the pistol at Skip.

"You, old man," he said, "get out your wallet nice and easy, no fast moves, and hand it to me. Nothing funny or he's toast."

In slow motion I reached into the inner breast pocket of my jacket, fished out my brown morocco wallet containing four credit cards and $200 in twenties and tens, and handed it to him. To my surprise my hand was steady. His gun hand, too, was unwavering as he seized the wallet with his other hand and chanced a quick glance at the cash.

In a blur of motion Mickey fixed a lock on his wrist, twisting it downward. The gun skittered along the sidewalk ending up in the gutter. Now with two hands on the man's wrist, Mickey picked up his right knee, and brought the wrist down hard on the knee. The man leaned over and uttered a groan so plaintive, so desolate, that for a moment I almost felt sorry for him. Almost.

Mickey's right arm went up high and came down with a chop on the back of the man's neck like a silent jackhammer. He fell to the sidewalk, twitching.

Mickey took three steps to the gutter, and prodded the gun with his shoe until it fell into a drain hole. "Let's go," he said, retrieving the wallet from the man's hand, and handing it to me.

"Shouldn't we get the police?" I asked.

"No. We have to get out of here - fast. Trust me on this one."

I saw three couples walking north on the west side of Seventh Avenue. They were laughing together and evidently had not observed the incident. No one else was in sight.

We walked the four blocks to our hotel briskly without conversation, and once we were inside the lobby, I could not stop trembling. "Let's go to the bar," I said.

They ordered beer and the bartender, to my astonishment, didn't ask either of them for an ID. That was fine with me. I had a double Absolut.

After a while, I said, "You saved our asses back there, Mickey."

"Yeah . . . well . . . if you ever need me again, just yell."

"I'll remember that." I slept badly that night.

The next day on the train going home, while Skip was taking a nap, Mickey and I talked about the attempted holdup. I told him I admired his equanimity under fire, and he said he had been similarly impressed with my performance.

"When you pulled out your wallet real slow, your hand wasn't shaking," he said.

"I know, but my knees were trembling and my arthritis was howling up a storm. To tell the truth, I'm still pretty shook up."

After analyzing the strengths and weaknesses of the Knicks and the Wizards, I not so subtly brought the conversation around to Mickey's situation. I raised the subject of a job at my company again, and, initially, he was unenthusiastic. I told him I had spoken to the chief accountant who was a good friend. As it happened, they had an open slot in their department, and my friend said he would be happy to interview Mickey.

I said he had nothing to lose if he went over there and talked to them. They could discuss a full-time job or, if Mickey decided to return to college, a part-time job. After some hesitation, Mickey decided he would take me up on the suggestion. "Thank you," he said, "you're a good man."

Chapter 9

With every opportunity that came his way, Carl Harrison kept after me to place the subject of a community center on the agenda for a Board meeting. I had told him the time wasn't ripe. I would get to it after the Board disposed of more pressing business. But Carl was not to be deterred. We were walking over to Lars' apartment for a poker game, and he didn't waste a moment.

"You have to hard-sell them," he said. "Make them understand it will improve the quality of our lives. Bingo, parties, pot luck suppers, catered dinners, lectures, bridge games, our poker games, even dances. We can bring in a CD player and . . . "

I threw up my hands. "You've told me all this before. I understand. Don't you believe me?"

"I get the feeling you're playing along with me, but I don't hear commitment."

"Okay, I'm committed. It will come up on the agenda when its time is due. What else is new?"

"Well, my granddaughter is coming to stay with me for a few weeks. I'll show her the Capitol, Washington Monument, Jefferson Memorial. You know, usual tourist stuff."

"That's great, Carl. Is she in school or what?"

"She's in her second year of college in Kansas, and very smart for twenty-four. Her name is Karen, and let me tell you, she's one hell of a looker. A good head for business, too, and lots of drive."

"Most second-year students are nineteen or twenty, aren't they?"

Carl said that Karen dropped out of college for a few years. She wanted "hands-on" experience, and found a job with Tallmark in Kansas City. They rotated her through marketing, accounting, and corporate finance.

"She came up with some hocus pocus interpretation of the accounting laws," he said, "and the company was able to avoid reporting executive stock options as expenses in the financial reports. They boosted her salary. When she told them she was going back to college, they begged her to stay, but she figured she'd better get her degree."

Carl told me that Karen's parents lived in Los Angeles, where her father managed a high-risk investment firm with a stable of wealthy clients. He had little time or interest in his wife, Carl's daughter, and even his own daughter, Karen. He was driven by money.

"When she came home from her senior year in high school with four A minuses and a B plus, her father told her, that's nice. After you make your first million, come see me. The only hero in her life is her father, and he treats her like a piece of shit."

"My grandson, Skip, is from L.A., too."

"I know. I was sitting with him on the bench the other day. Nice guy. Not too talkative, though."

"Yeah, well, he has to learn how to relate to adults. We'll introduce him to Karen. Maybe they'll be good for each other."

"Good idea."

When I called Elsie Turner and asked her to dinner again, she said, "That Italian place you took me to, can we go back there?"

I set up a time when I'd pick her up. Once more, I didn't mention this to Anna.

Maria greeted us cordially and promptly turned us over to a waitress. We ordered wine, held off on the food, and talked. The edginess Elsie had exhibited when I last left her was still perceptible, and we weren't seated five minutes before she resumed discussion of her former husband. She said she could now look back and analyze her situation with a clarity she had never been able to invoke at the time.

They had a maid who cleaned, cooked, and washed clothes. Hardy was generous with his money, and encouraged Elsie to buy new clothes and have lunch with her friends at pricey restaurants. But if she said something he didn't like, he would snap at her. Later, the snaps turned into slaps.

"Those slaps probably satisfied his sexual desire as much as the bouncing around in bed he forced me to do."

After the first year of marriage, Elsie worked her way through a few flirtations, as she put it. Suspicious, Hardy asked her to work in his office as an "administrator," where he could "keep an eye" on her.

"I hope you understand, Sid, I detested him, but I was petrified. I mean, scared to death of him every day."

Once, when she told him she was thinking of leaving, he said, "I don't think that would be smart."

Elsie sighed. "The worst part was that I began to feel shame. I know that's hard for you to relate to. I was *ashamed* of myself."

The tremors in her body had returned. I said quietly, "Maybe you don't want to talk about this right now."

"I *want* to talk about it."

As she disclosed more nightmarish details of her existence with Hardy, I steered her gently in the direction of her work in his office. She was reluctant to talk about this.

"I know that as President you have an interest in our management," she said. "Will you promise that no matter what happens, nothing I tell you will get back to that man."

"I promise."

Hardy assigned her the job of maintaining an ongoing file of certain documents. These included notes and memos of telephone conversations and conferences between Efficiency Management and its suppliers.

"He told me to keep the file in chronological order," said Elsie, "but he cautioned me not to read anything, or I'd 'regret' it."

That caveat caused her curiosity to overcome her fear. She proceeded, surreptitiously, to read the documents. At first, she attached no significance to the "agreements" and "revised agreements." Nor did she have any interest in the parties involved - electricians, plumbers, roofing suppliers, maintenance and repair companies.

After a few months she read a memo from Hardy to "All Members of the Club." Elsie's recollection was: **"REMEMBER: KEEP NOTHING IN WRITING. DESTROY A PIECE OF PAPER AFTER YOU HAVE READ IT, INCLUDING THIS ONE."**

This was the moment when Elsie suspected that Efficiency Management was likely involved in questionable activities, and was the sole repository of these documents.

She remembered a week or so later coming upon a memo to "All Club Members" from a plumbing company. As best she could recall, the memo said, " Make sure you have your phones checked regularly for taps. If the law enforcement boys found out about our 'Club' we'd all be in deep shit. Ha, ha."

Elsie's knowledge of business matters was limited, and she couldn't understand why they should be in "deep shit." But after studying the documents more carefully, she figured out that their purpose was to keep the price high. The stealth attending the transactions led her to believe that their activity might have been unlawful.

"Did you think about making copies of these documents, maybe show them to a lawyer?" I asked.

"He watched every move I made. I only read the stuff when he was out of the office. Whenever I used the Xerox machine, his spies watched me like a hawk."

"You made no copies of anything."

"That's what I'm saying."

I asked if any of the documents were copies of e-mail. She said no documents she handled were e-mail. The company was just beginning to install computers at the time she left, and Hardy was in the process of learning how to use them.

During her three years at Efficiency Management, Elsie maintained a file of hundreds of documents, and her suspicions of illegality grew with each new reading. But she lived in constant fear of Hardy and she did nothing.

When she finally summoned up the resolve to leave - after the fist to her jaw - she scooped up the money she'd been hoarding, moved into a cheap motel, and hired a lawyer. She saw Hardy only once, some eighteen months after she left, in front of the judge who granted the final divorce decree.

We left the Buona Sera at 10:30, and she wanted to walk back to the Oasis despite the blustery January wind. Inside her apartment, she poured herself a glass of water, and sat down, pale and trembling. She hadn't offered me anything to drink, and I stayed on my feet.

"I've never told any of that business stuff to anybody before," she said. "Not even to my lawyer."

She placed the water glass on a table and, shaking even more, looked up at me. "I'm going to ask you something you'll think is weird. Will you lie down with me and hold me? Just hold me?"

The more I was with Elsie the more I had come to like and, indeed, respect her. This distressed woman sitting in front of me was not without substance and character. She was light-years removed from the senior coquette trying to cajole me into sharing her tuna casserole. But lying down with her and holding her were not on my agenda.

We stared at each other and after a time she silently mouthed the word, "Please." I couldn't say no.

Fully clothed, we lay down on top of her bed covers, and I put my arms around her, our bodies pressed close, and she cried quietly. When my fingers lightly touched the back of her neck, a moan issued from deep inside her, and I initiated a gentle, circular motion on her neck and upper back. As her tremors and tears gradually subsided, she whispered, "Don't stop doing that."

I continuing the soft massage. After about five minutes, I said, "There is something very personal I have to tell you, Elsie. If I do this much longer my hand will fall off."

I had expected a guffaw or at least a good-natured grunt. When I heard no response, I pulled away slowly to get a look at her face. She was sound asleep, snoring softly. I went into the kitchen, made myself some coffee, left the kitchen light on, took the coffee into the living room, and sat down in the semi-darkness.

After a few minutes I felt restless, and wandered around the room, straightening the pictures on the wall and reading the return addresses of the unopened mail that had been tossed onto the small desk tucked away in a corner - all routine. On impulse I opened the top drawer of the desk and saw a stack of files. The first was marked "Battered Women," and ignoring that one, I skimmed through the others. They were uninteresting.

The deep bottom drawer was empty except for a thin letter-sized manila envelope with the word "Confidential" hand-printed on its face. The flap was closed with conventional metal prongs, but was not sealed. I opened it and removed the contents consisting of two Xeroxed documents.

The first document was dated five years earlier.

AGREEMENT

The undersigned agree to the following terms:

1. Chuck Hardy will use only the suppliers whose names appear below for work on the more than 100 properties Chuck manages;

2. Bids on all jobs in excess of $10,000 will be rotated among these suppliers as determined by Chuck;

3. All bids will be submitted on the basis of a percent above the going rate as determined by Chuck;

4. Chuck will have the final say on resolving all disputes. Chuck will receive ten percent of the fee on every job as compensation for his efforts in organizing and maintaining this agreement;

5. As a show of good faith all parties to this Agreement shall purchase a minimum of one thousand shares of the common stock of Efficiency Management of America, Inc. (EMA) within 30 days from the date of this agreement. Over the past three months the value of this stock has ranged from $35 to $40. The company is in sound financial condition and both its short range and long range prospects are positive.

6. The purpose of this Agreement is to increase efficiency in our service to our customers.

Signed,

The document was signed by the presidents, CEO's, or managers of thirty-five firms, together with company addresses. The signatures were grouped by relevant category: HVAC (heating, ventilation, air conditioning); roofing maintenance & repair; tuckpointing; painting; landscaping; tree removal; elevator maintenance & replacement; plumbing, electrical; sewer cleaning; road surfacing & repair; concrete repair; and swimming pool maintenance.

Beneath the other signatures appeared that of Charles Hardy, Efficiency Management.

The second document in the manila envelope was a certificate stating that Elsie Turner owned 500 shares of the common stock of Efficiency Management of America, Inc. (EMA). When I had checked stocks of interest to me in the Journal that morning, EMA had been listed as closing at $51. The value of Elsie's stock exceeded $25,000.

I bent the prongs back around the flap, replaced the empty envelope in the desk drawer, folded the two thin documents lengthwise, and placed them in the inside pocket of my overcoat hanging in the hall closet. As soon as possible I would have copies made and replace the documents in the envelope.

I poured more coffee and thought about what I had found. *You made no copies of anything*, I had asked. *That's what I'm saying.* Elsie had lied. I didn't delude myself that the lies somehow justified my "borrowing" the documents. But one thing was certain. I could no longer trust her. Nor, for that matter, could she trust me.

Why had she lied to me? Why was she holding onto the Agreement between Hardy and his thirty-five co-conspirators? What in the world was she doing with five-hundred shares of stock in a company whose regional manager she detested?

First, the loopy loon. Next, the all-suffering victim. Now, the enigma.

After an hour, Elsie came into the living room and sat down next to me.

"How are you feeling?" I asked.

"I'm better. I want to thank you for what you did in there. You're a good man."

"You're a good woman. Do you mind if I ask a few more questions?"

"Be my guest."

"Couple of things I don't understand. When you moved in here three years ago, you changed your name. You wanted to steer clear of that guy. You must have checked out the name of the management company. Didn't that deter you from moving here?"

"Even before I left him, I heard he'd taken up with somebody. He's never bothered me since the divorce. He knows I live here, but he couldn't care less where I live."

"Did you consider going to the police about his abusive treatment?"

"Come on, Sid. Even I knew what would happen if I did that. They'd investigate and decide it was a 'domestic disturbance' and leave. Then I'd have to face him. Besides, what was I going to tell them? That he slapped me two or three times a week?"

"Did you consider going to a shelter?"

"That's not my style."

"Did you seek help from your friends?"

"I had no friends."

She paused. "I regard you as a friend so I'll give you a piece of advice. Be careful with that man. I saw him abuse his employees when he didn't think anybody was watching. Some of them quit, but others stayed because they needed the money. He puts on a good front - polished, polite, deferential. But when he's angry, he loses control."

It was after midnight when I got back to my apartment. Anna had left a message at ten - just when we were leaving the restaurant. I returned her call the next morning.

"Hi," I said. "How are you?"

"Fine. Didn't you get my message? You didn't call last night."

"I got back too late."

"Oh?"

"We haven't talked in a few days. What's new?"

"Nothing. How are things going with your grandson?"

"Very well. He's really a whiz on the computer. I plan to have him speak to the Task Force at our meeting tomorrow."

"Good . . . well, I'll see you there."

"What's your hurry? How about lunch today?"

"No, thanks."

"Is something wrong?"

"Where were you last night? Just curious."

I told her about my dinner with Elsie and recounted what Elsie had told me about her marriage to Hardy and her exposure to his business.

"Sounds like you had an interesting evening," Anna said.

"Well, I learned a lot."

"Look, Sid, I'm not good with indirection. I don't go to sleep before midnight so I assume you got home well after that."

"That's right. We got back after twelve."

"Then what happened?"

"What does that mean? Nothing happened. I went home."

"Why do I have the feeling you're not leveling with me?"

Whatever unarticulated understanding I thought we had, how could I find a way to tell her that Elsie and I had lain down on her bed together, our bodies up against each other, and that nothing in that experience fell within the broadest definition of erotic - or romantic - behavior?

How could I possibly make her understand that for all the hollow sound of the words, I had performed nothing more than an errand of mercy? I considered myself proficient in expressing my thoughts and feelings, but this was beyond my capabilities.

Or was it? I could have assumed the mutual trust we had developed would enable her to digest the unvarnished truth, however unpalatable. Why didn't I trust her as I wanted her to trust me? Why didn't I tell her exactly what happened?

Instead, I prevaricated. I said, "She was very upset after telling me her story and she needed to talk it out so we went back to her apartment and had coffee and I let her go on until she was calmed down. I got home too late to call you. Why don't we have lunch and talk about it there?"

"If there's one thing I can't tolerate, it's being conned. I'll see you at the meeting." She shut the phone. Earlier in the conversation I thought

I had dodged a land mine. Now I knew better. I knew that my equivocation had triggered a small doubt in her mind. I knew that a chink in the armor of our affection had made its incipient appearance.

I was getting into my pajamas after the eleven o'clock news that night when Skip came in, wearing what could have almost been called a grin. I followed him into the kitchen as he gulped down milk directly from the carton.

I poured some into a glass for myself and asked, "What's new?"

"Your friend, Carl, introduced me to his granddaughter this afternoon. Her name is Karen. We went to a movie tonight."

"What did you think?"

"She's pretty cool."

The Task Force met at my place to hear Lars' report of his third nightly visit to Efficiency Management, this time to find the e-mail password. I explained that Skip might help us, and they nodded their acceptance of him as a sworn-to-secrecy ex officio member.

Before Lars began, I told them what Elsie had disclosed to me about Hardy's business dealings. The consensus was that this merely confirmed our suspicions. I made no mention of the "borrowed" documents. Anna said nothing.

Lars told us he made a cursory survey of the office. Again, no dog was present. Wearing surgical gloves, he scrutinized desk surfaces and drawers, file cabinets, closets, and bathrooms. He looked under rugs and blotters and on top of shelves. He examined trash receptacles for paper that might be Scotch-taped to the sides. He scanned the telephone directory, private address books, and business manuals for handwritten notes.

Frustrated, he decided to explore the three light fixtures hanging from the ceiling in Hardy's office. He got up on a chair, reached over the first fixture, and dipped his hand into and around the shell. As he gazed straight up, blindly sweeping his hand along the curve, he caught sight of a barely visible spherical device attached to the bottom of the fixture which he recognized, to his horror, as a hidden camera.

He peered at the other two fixtures and discerned similar devices. He replaced the chair and departed the premises. Instead of achieving his mission objective, locating the password, he discovered he had been under surveillance.

Sheila spoke first. "They ditched Fido and replaced him with a camera. You're in the movies, Lars. I hope you were wearing that red Angora sweater I like."

"Maybe," said Anna, "the camera was in place even before he got rid of the dog. Maybe both Lars and Sid were under surveillance the first time. And Lars, again, when he went back to plant the bug in the private phone."

Anna said that would explain why we came up with nothing from the phone taps. Hardy could have viewed the video tape, she said, and saw two trespassers placing a bug in the main phone. Later, he saw Lars on the tape placing the bug in the private phone. He made sure that all phone conversations from his office were sanitized, and he simply left the bugs in the phones.

Sheila said. "Smart dude."

"What did he think," I asked, "when he saw Lars on the third visit looking for something? Did he guess it was a computer password?"

We looked at one another in silence.

We discussed the use to which Hardy might put the video tapes. There was unanimity that he wouldn't take them to the police, demanding that they identify and apprehend this trespasser.

"My picture is on file in the District, Maryland and Virginia from the old days," Lars said. "But you're right, there's no way he'll go near the police. He'll try to identify me through his private sources."

"Then what?" asked Anna.

Lars shrugged and silence prevailed.

"Well," Sheila said, "we're screwed on the e-mail."

Skip came to life. "Not necessarily. Grandpa, didn't you say that Efficiency Management is a subsidiary of a national corporation?"

"Yes, Efficiency Management of America. They call it EMA. It's headquartered in New York, publicly traded, offices in thirty cities."

"Then we'll hack into their mainframe and snoop around through their e-mail archives. We'll get into their current e-mail, and maybe some of their deleted e-mail."

Skip took hold of the meeting. Sitting at his state-of-the-art computer, he guided us through hacking, raiding, and other computer esoterica, and analyzed recent innovations. His method was simple yet sophisticated, succinct yet comprehensive.

He highlighted the pitfalls and "ripple effects," and identified concealed nuances. When he strayed from the theme - how to get hold of Hardy's e-mail- it was not for long. He listened to our questions and answered them responsively. He said he would "fool around" with the computer for a few days and come up with "a tentative plan." Skip held our attention - the visiting teen-age professor delivering erudition to his flock of awed senior citizens.

The Task Force members thanked Skip for his presentation, and after they left, I reinforced their remarks. I told Skip he had done a good job in laying everything out to us, and I was proud of him.

"No problem, Grandpa." He headed toward his room, stopped, and turned around. "Uh . . . I don't want to get you mad, but is it okay if I smoke a joint in my room? I'll keep the window open and be on the lookout for the fuzz."

"Just don't tell me about it.

On the train back from New York, Mickey had said, "You're a good man." Too many people had been telling me that lately. Maybe I *was* a good man, but not a responsible one. My grandson was about to violate multiple laws at my behest. Lars had engaged in unlawful trespassing and wire tapping. I could comfort myself that he was an adult with plenty of experience. But who had encouraged him?

And Anna, the only woman after Sarah whose affection I cherished, was now disenchanted with me. When I called to make a date for dinner, she declined. After I pressed her a bit, she said she thought we should "take a vacation from each other."

When I asked her why, she said, "Maybe I'm being unfair, but I'm not comfortable in our relationship. I'll continue working with you on the Task Force, but that's all. I can't spell it out. It's the way I feel."

"With all respect, Anna, you owe me more than that. Why aren't you comfortable with me? Why don't you want to be alone with me?"

"I don't trust you anymore."

"What does that mean?"

"I think we should leave it at that."

Didn't trust me? Did she know I hadn't leveled with her about Elsie? Was it too late to walk her through the details of what happened that night? The threads of my reinvented life were beginning to unravel.

Chapter 10

Skip was ready for another Task Force session. The meetings were now held at my apartment where the super-computer would reside until Skip took it with him to the dorm in about a month. Sheila asked, "Some goodies tonight, Skip?"

"Actually, yes. First, I bought a virus and sent it to Hardy . . ."

"WHAT?" said Sheila. "You sent a virus to Hardy? We're trying to KILL him?"

"We want to look at his e-mail, right? This is the quickest way to do it."

Skip explained. He bought a virus from a "black hat hacker" - I would reimburse him, Skip said. He installed the virus in Efficiency's computer by sending them an e-mail purporting to be an advertisement for industrial vacuum cleaners. The virus, attached to the fake e-mail, triggered a program that monitored Efficiency's typed keys, enabling Skip to identify Hardy's password and capture everything typed on his computer.

"Is that what is called a Trojan Horse?" asked Lars.

"No. A big company would catch on to a Trojan Horse right away. What I'm using is easier to deploy and harder to spot."

Skip was now capable of reproducing all of Efficiency Management's computer files onto his own computer. He had received the files for a twenty-four-hour period, including e-mail to and from Hardy. Skip printed them out and distributed copies to us. One set of what we

136

obtained went into the Condo File. Most of them dealt with routine business matters, but some were of special interest.

TO: Chuck, Ron, Ed, Jerry, Sam

FROM: Chuck

Chuck's turn for the interior painting job for Leisure Retirement. The RFPs will go out in two weeks. The bidding will be as follows: Ron, $64,750; Ed, $61, 200; Jerry, $60,500; Sam, $57,100; Chuck, $55,850.

The replies came back to Chuck as follows:

"Great!" "Okay," "Fine," I'm on board," and "Will Do."

TO: Chuck

FROM: Charlie

Problem. The jerk from the Douglas Project likes the brickwork job we did last year, and wants us to do Douglas. (We were 7% higher than Ed like we was supposed to be.) I tell him we're full up right now. Then why did you bid? We thought at the time we could do it. He's pissed and says we honor the bid or he'll spread the word we're unreliable. I had to go along.

The reply had come twenty minutes later.

To: Charlie

From: Chuck

That is BULLSHIT. You could have told him no way, you're up to your ass in work. Unless you broke the Agreement and came in lower than everybody else. I've told all of you a hundred times don't be greedy. Stick to the Agreement and we'll all make money. Break the Agreement and we go back to jungle warfare. You want cutthroat again?

The reply to the reply had been sent five minutes later.

To: Chuck

From: Charlie

I did NOT break the Agreement. So don't tell me that. Anyway, I didn't sign the contract. I'll call him and tell him it's impossible for me to do the work. He can spread whatever stories he wants. By the way, have you thought about what's bothering us? 10 % is too high. We think 5% is fair.

"It's what I suspected," said Lars. "Hub and spokes. Hardy is the buyer. Directs the operation, works out the pricing schedule with the sellers, keeps them in line. But there seems to be discontent in the ranks. It sounds like Hardy takes ten percent of the profits and the troops don't like it."

Once again, everybody expressed appreciation of Skip's computer proficiency.

Anna asked, "Is it possible they could trace the virus to this computer?"

We looked at Skip in silence.

"Not a problem," he said. "By the time they get around to it - *if* they get around to it - me and the computer will be out of here. There's no way they'll find me in the dorm in the middle of hundreds of computers, most of them hacking all over the place."

I got up and took a step toward Skip, fixing him in my gaze. "Skip, I want you to cancel the virus, erase the whole thing, pull out, or whatever the hell the terminology is."

He shook his head. "We don't even have anything about the Oasis yet. Hey, we're just starting to strike pay dirt."

"We *struck* pay dirt. We have what we need. It's time to cut our losses. I want you to do it *right now*. No arguments, no negotiations, no discussion. KILL IT."

He must have read something in my look or heard something in my voice because he said, "Okay, Grandpa."

When the meeting broke up the people went into the bedroom to retrieve their coats. "Please stay a minute," I said to Anna. "I need to talk to you."

"I don't think so."

I waited a few minutes for Anna to get home and called her.

"Anna, I'm coming up. I want ten minutes with you. Then I promise to leave."

I hung up the phone and walked up the stairs to her apartment. She opened her door, purposefully looking at her watch, and neither of us said anything. I sat at the end of the sofa and delivered my pitch. She remained standing near the door, expressionless.

Everything I had told her about Elsie, I said, was true. But I had left out part of it. I told her about the two dinners. I related all the events of that last night with Elsie, from beginning to end in exacting detail.

"That's everything that happened. Nothing more, nothing less. I shouldn't have been coy with you on the phone. I had nothing to hide and I behaved as though I did."

I paused and added, "I suppose some people contrive suspicious circumstances out of innocent ones so they can hoard an ongoing supply of guilt."

Anna had once told me I was one of the most guilt-free persons she'd known, and I thought this reference might soften her resistance. It didn't.

I said she was right to be offended and angry. I got up from the chair, my hands outstretched. I asked for the opportunity to make amends. If she still believed she couldn't trust me, then she should say so and I would walk away and not bother her anymore.

I sat back down. "You've restored my sense of purpose. Maybe that's a strange thing for an old guy to say, but that's how I feel."

She walked over to the other end of the couch and sat down, and a long silence descended on the room. She glanced at me once or twice and I glanced at her once or twice, ships passing in the night.

"I think you're sincere," she said, "but cut out the groveling. Get rid of that contrite expression, it doesn't look good on you."

Anna leaned forward, regarding me like an entomologist studying an insect under her microscope. Did she see a cockroach? Or a deformed butterfly?

"The reason you didn't tell me you were lying on the bed with Elsie and stroked her neck was because you couldn't imagine I'd believe nothing else happened. *That's* what has me ticked off. You didn't trust me so how can I trust you?"

She said she had run into Elsie earlier that day and thought Elsie looked out of sorts. If I had told her the entire story that next morning she would have believed me.

Another silence. I didn't dare look at her.

"You play fast and loose with the facts, Sid. Maybe it's your business background. You once said you didn't know if you could declare a commitment to me. Commitment isn't the issue. What I need is total, unreserved honesty. Everything up front, nothing held back. I don't know if you're capable of that."

We looked at each other and said nothing.

"Are you capable of that?"

"With you, yes."

"Maybe we should take it one step at a time. Are you willing to try a trial period?"

"Yes."

She got up off the sofa and walked toward the door. I followed her, hope stirring.

"One more thing, Sid."

"Yes?'

"Before we resume any intimacy, let's find out if we can repair our friendship."

I had made copies of Elsie's documents, and deposited them with the other condo papers in my bottom drawer. When Elsie asked me to come over, I put a set of them in my pocket to return to *her* bottom drawer when she stepped out of the room.

As we sipped herbal tea, I was prepared for a fresh flood of information further indicting Hardy. But she fooled me.

"I want us to be straight with each other," she said. "I know sometimes I come on like a space cadet with half her marbles gone. But you know that's not my whole story. I want us to be friends and no more. Can you handle that?"

"Of course."

"Good. That's behind us. Now, I'm going to hit you up for something. I've been helping out twice a week at a battered women's shelter. Something I want to do. They need money badly. Would you be willing to make a contribution?"

I pulled out my checkbook and asked, "How much would be appropriate?"

"Whatever you think. Maybe a hundred dollars?"

"Made out to whom?"

"Network of Battered Women."

I wrote out a check for five hundred dollars and handed it to her. She got up, walked around to me, gave me a kiss on the cheek, and said, "Thank you for that."

Elsie reminded me of my promise that Hardy would never hear of her involvement. She warned me again to be careful in whatever dealings I had with him.

"He can be smooth. Big-hearted like your kind uncle. But whether it's money or power or whatever, you cross him, he'll go after you."

She never did leave the room that day. My opportunity to replace her papers never arose because I was never in her apartment again. But I didn't know that then.

I called Anna and told her about my meeting with Elsie. "We drank herbal tea, and I contributed to the Network of Battered Women. Elsie warned me again about Hardy's temper, and then I left."

"Sid," Anna said, "I'm not your probation officer."

"You said everything up front, nothing held back."

She laughed. "Touché."

Nikki Bullett called to remind me that I had asked to see the Requests for Proposals for the Building One roof replacement before they were mailed.

There were five RFPs to be mailed, each consisting of five pages of detailed specifications. These RFPs would surely generate a flurry of e-mail activity among the boys, and I had second thoughts about insisting that Skip kill the virus. But after what Elsie had told me, the thought of Hardy tracing the virus to Skip's computer was sufficient for me to know I had done the right thing I told Nikki to send out the RFPs.

Mickey called to tell me he talked to the people at my old company. They liked him and he liked them, and he now had a part-time job in the accounting department. He was going back to college the next semester.

"I appreciate what you've done for me, Sid. I owe you big time."

"My pleasure. I understand you and Skip are e-mail correspondents."

"Yeah. He taught me how to play computer games through the e-mail. He's a nice kid. Just trying to find himself. "

"Who isn't?"

A week after Nikki had mailed the RFPs, Skip asked me if the Task Force could meet. I asked him why, but he only smiled, and said we would all find out at the meeting. When we filed into the computer's temporary home - my den - Skip was already in his seat, a cat-that-swallowed-the-canary look on his face.

"Before you blow your stack, Grandpa, let me explain. I was all ready to cancel the virus like you said and then I figured, one more shot. This time we came up with gold."

Seething, I remained silent. Skip handed out copies of the e-mail communications he had retrieved. Most of them, he said, were called IMs - instant messages. The first was an IM exchange between Nikki Bullett and Chuck Hardy.

> Bullett: I mailed out five RFPs this a.m. I sent you copies through the mail.
>
> Hardy: I'll look for them. Silva signed off?
>
> Bullett: Yes, he's conscientious. Wants to see everything.
>
> Hardy: Yeah, he's a good man.

Sheila wondered if Nikki Bullett "was in league with the bastard." Lars and I were in half-agreement, and even Skip was nodding vigorously.

It was Anna who restored perspective. "Let's not forget she's Hardy's employee. He's her boss and pays her salary. All she did was send him copies of the RFPs. That sounds legitimate to me. I don't think we should convict her on the basis of this evidence."

The second IM exchange was between Hardy and Travail.

Hardy: How's my favorite ex-president?

Travail: Fine. How are you, Chuck?

Hardy: This guy, Silva. What's your take on him?

Travail: Knows his way around Smart, tough.

Hardy: It might be a good idea for you to feel him out, get across to him what a good job was done on the first building. Make him understand that quality doesn't come cheap. You follow me?

Travail: Yup.

Hardy: Take him to lunch at the Broth-L and send me the bill.

Travail: I'll do it.

Hardy: And, hey, we're due for another boys' weekend. What do you think? Atlantic City or Vegas?

Travail: That's a hard one. The girls are better in Vegas but the tables are friendlier in Atlantic City.

Hardy: Come to think about it, maybe we'll try San Juan this time.Get a big suite. A little change in color if you follow me.

Travail: I could deal with that.

Hardy: I'll be in touch soon. And by the way, keep me posted on this other stuff.

Travail: Sure thing.

Sheila couldn't contain herself. "Look what we learned about Burt. He's smart and he's tough. I never would have known it. And he's going to get a freebie at that cowboy whorehouse, the Broth-L. We'll want a blow-by-blow, Burt. Ha, ha. What say I bring a TV camera crew and interview you after the lunch?"

Skip could hardly restrain his glee.

"Well, well," Lars said. "Bullett's not the only one on his payroll. She only gets a straight salary. Francis gets women and gambling even though he's no longer president."

I asked Lars if he could do a background check on Travail. He said he would expedite it.

The final round of e-mail was between Hardy and the roof replacement group.

> To: Roofing Bidders on Oasis, Building One
>
> From: Hardy
>
> You've all received the Oasis RFPs by now. The bids will go like this. Majestic - $855,150, Superior - $760,500, Solid - $645,350, Security - $590,450, District - $487,500.
>
> District will get the job. As always, destroy this NOW.

Maurice had once told me that although most white collar criminals are careful to avoid anything in writing, documents sometimes turn up. Maurice had speculated whether this sloppiness was the result of ingenuousness or arrogance. Maybe a combination.

The roofing replies, all signifying compliance with Hardy's instructions, came back the same day. Our discussion on this one was brief. It was time to talk to Maurice.

I showed them the Agreement and EMA stock certificate I had taken from Elsie's drawer. Except for Anna, they all threw questions at me. How did I get the documents? Did Elsie give them to me? How did I get her to do this?

I said I stumbled upon them on Elsie's desk while she was taking a nap. I copied them and would replace what I had taken. I told them I would put these documents and the e-mail and the bugged phone tapes in my bottom drawer with the other condo papers, and give all the material to Maurice.

The room was quiet, and I sensed their embarrassment. If Elsie had been taking a nap while I was in her apartment, that strongly suggested an intimacy between Elsie and me. They were uncomfortable with the tension this surely created between Anna and me. How right they were. I said nothing more.

I was reluctant to rebuke Skip in the presence of the others. Holding my anger in check, I conceded he had come up with valuable documents. I didn't know how we would be able to use them, but one way or another they would be useful. Nevertheless, I said, I had asked him to stop the process and he didn't.

"I'm trying to get through to you. This guy can be trouble. Kill the goddamn virus right now, in front of all of us."

He went through some arcane process on the computer keyboard, and after about five minutes, he said, "Done."

Then he grinned and said, "Relax, he's not going to go after a kid like me.

As I expected, Francis Travail called me. He'd been up to his neck in personal matters, and congratulated me on winning the election.

"I'd like to take you to lunch," he said.

I said, "Thank you."

"How's tomorrow?"

"Fine."

The Broth-L, on L Street, reproduced, or purported to reproduce, the décor of an Old West house of ill repute. The walls were a deep scarlet textured material covered with black and white photographs of brothel scenes from the 1880's. The hostess, a buxom matronly type, seemed to be coming off a long night. Sitting on a bar stool behind the reception desk, she wore the nameplate, "Madam." The deep slit in her ankle-length skirt was prominent, and she was wearing a kind of bodice over a sheer blouse.

She found the reservation, snapped her fingers for somebody to lead us to a table, and said, "I sure hope yew cowhands'll find what y'all lookin' for."

Travail, staring at her bodice, said in contrived Texas accent, "Ah think we've found it, *madam.*"

Our waitress, sporting a dyed-blonde bouffant under a ten-gallon cowboy hat, was wearing a mini cowboy-style fringed skirt with boots up to her knees. She greeted us with a twangy, "Howdy, pardners, my name's Pat. What can I rustle up for you today?"

Travail grinned and asked me, "How about a drink first?"

I said, "Double Absolut on the rocks."

Travail ordered a Bud and said, "Fun place, isn't it?"

I could have come up with plenty of words to describe the place - boring, tedious, tasteless were some of them - but "fun" was not among them. "Sure is," I said.

He asked me how it was going as President.

"Fine."

There was a moment of quiet and then he said, "I was glad to see the Board voted to replant the rhododendrons away from the brick wall."

I laughed. "Right."

He toyed with his glass of Bud. After a little bit he said, "I'm sure you've found out that as President you have to make your peace with the residents. And speaking of peace, that Sheila Marcuse is a piece of work, isn't she?"

I never got to express my admiration for his clever way with words because Pat strolled over, placed her pointy-toed boot on the top rung of my chair, her skirt riding high on her thigh, and looked over at Travail from under her wide-brimmed hat. "How about another Bud, stud?" she asked.

Travail smiled and nodded yes. She looked down at me, grinned, and said, "I'd ask you the same, pardner, but I don't know what rhymes with vodka."

I returned her grin. "You could say, how about another salute for the Absolut?"

She smiled - it was almost genuine - and said, "Hey, what a team we'd make."

The menus were in the form of eight wooden slabs connected to one another with a twined lariat. The slabs were shaped like the profile of a nude woman with exaggerated busts and buttocks. The hungry customer turned the pages by reaching for the outsized nipple on the breast.

We both ordered the house specialty designated in the menu as the "broth of the brothels" - stock-of-beef-stew. After another pause, Travail said, "You know, I was on that Board for four years. I know something about where the bodies are buried. If there's anything I can help you with, don't hesitate to ask."

"Thanks. I appreciate that."

"I want to warn you about the Treasurer," he said. "Lars means well but he has a tendency to make a mountain out of a molehill."

"Like what?" I asked.

"Well, he'll spot some minor discrepancy in an invoice and act like it's the Brinks robbery. You have to stay on top of him. Anna, too. She gets a little carried away. People like that can twist things out of shape."

I took a sip of the Absolut and said, "They take their job seriously."

The same film of perspiration I had observed at that first Board meeting I'd attended began to form on his face. "Well, I'm glad to hear that, but you should understand there are some nut cases around the place. Take the Building Two roof replacement. We picked the lowest bidder with the highest quality and from the way they reacted, you'd think we gave the store away."

He took out a handkerchief and wiped his face. "Let me give you the benefit of my experience. You're always going to have people getting riled up when they don't know what they're talking about. We did everything right - RFPs, competitive bids, the whole enchilada. We have a first class roof with a 15-year warranty for the lowest price bid."

I had reached the end of my rope, and wanted to say: *"Hardy and his cronies put it to the Oasis, and I intend to make them pay. And that includes you, you puffed-up piece of shit. I mean to see this through, and you can tell that to anybody you want to."*

Instead, I bit my tongue. "Well, as I think about it, Francis, you make a good point. I've got plenty to do as President. As you say, we got a quality job at the lowest price. So why look for trouble that doesn't exist?"

Travail wiped the sweat from his forehead for about the third time. I could see the relief on his face. "Good man," he said.

"Still, those bids were pretty high. And as you know, Building One is about ready for a new roof. It'll be interesting to see what *those* bids look like."

He looked at me blankly.

147

When the bill came, Travail said, "My treat," handed Pat his credit card with one hand and ran his hand across her backside with the other.

Her eyes roaming the room, she flashed a toothy smile, and said, "Don't be fresh now, pardner," and walked away.

Travail looked at me and said, "I just *love* this place."

The beef stew was fair.

Chapter 11

I asked Nikki if the bids had come in. She said none had been received, but we should have them all within the next week. As she spoke my eyes were drawn again to the photograph of Steven, her ten-year old son, sitting on the desk. I remembered she had told me Steven had placed high in his wrestling class. "How's the wrestling champ?" I asked.

As I took a chair in place in front of her desk, a glum look came onto her face. I placed my hand on her arm and said, "Nikki, what's the matter? What is it?"

"It's nothing, Sid. I'm sorry."

"Please tell me what's the matter. You never know, maybe I can help you."

She dried her eyes, placed her hands in her lap, and looked at me for a few seconds. "I haven't even told this to Anna Carroll, and she's my best friend here. I need to talk about it. I can trust you, Sid?"

I looked at her and said nothing.

"Of course I can trust you. But my story may be more than you want to know."

"Try me."

"All right. Ten years ago I was living with a man, Oliver Bullett. He made me feel good and I was crazy about him. One day I found a note. He would always remember me. He was gone."

She opened a fresh box of Kleenex, and let it sit there. She got up, poured coffee, sat down, and stared at me, longer this time. "Maybe I'd better give you the whole thing."

*

Nikki Mardson grew up in Cleveland, Ohio. Her father was a traveling salesman, and her mother was an alcoholic who dabbled in real estate. When Nikki entered high school she became aware that she was a talented student who liked boys. She earned a scholarship to the University of Ohio where she excelled, finishing fourth in her class at the end of her first year.

In her second year she met a third-year student. She fell in love, and "we launched into it without fanfare." Nikki thought she was one of the lucky ones, meeting the man with whom she'd spend the rest of her life, and not yet twenty-one. When she told him she was pregnant, he wished her luck and went out of her life. In her naiveté Nikki had believed her lover had reciprocated the need she had for him.

Her parents never found out about her pregnancy or the abortion she managed to obtain. The post-abortion period was painful. She suffered depression and remorse, dropping out of college, and telling her parents she was tired of "the academic environment." She hung around the house doing nothing.

Up to this point, Nikki had fixed her eyes on the opposite wall. Now she shifted her gaze to me. "If this gets boring, you'll tell me, won't you," she said

"Yes, I will."

After six months she shook off her lethargy and, at her mother's suggestion, went to work for a property management firm in Cleveland. Partly as a result of the tips on the real estate business her mother had passed along between drinking bouts, she readily accommodated herself to the management milieu. In this period she had a few romantic episodes each of which ended after a few dates.

A Washington D.C. property management firm lured her from Cleveland. She moved up the ranks quickly, and by the mid-'80s she was carrying out higher level assignments. Despite her success at work,

Nikki, now in her mid-thirties, felt a gap in her personal life. She met Oliver Bullett at a computer training workshop and after a brief dating period he moved into her apartment.

For the first year their life together was "near bliss." During the second year their relationship deteriorated. Nikki wanted marriage, children and stability. Oliver was not ready to give up "the good life" - nightlife, travel - he enjoyed with Nikki's money. Nor was he able or willing to hold onto a job.

The day came when she found the departure note on the kitchen table. A month later Nikki discovered she was pregnant despite her precautions. She could not bring herself to endure another abortion, and besides, she wanted this baby. She named the baby Steven, nursed him for a month, hired a nanny and went back to work.

A few years later she was introduced to Chuck Hardy at a trade association meeting - she met Jane Fountain at the same meeting - and he enticed her with a substantial salary increase into coming with Efficiency Management. A short time later she was assigned to the Oasis as Property Manager.

She heard nothing from Oliver Bullett until Steven was five, when Bullett returned. He had missed her, and wanted to move in with her and their child. Nikki resisted his overtures, telling herself he had revealed his "true feathers" in that kitchen table note. He persisted, avowing that he'd changed, that he loved Nikki and Steven, and that he was prepared "to settle down." Lonely and eager for affection, Nikki weakened, but said she would live with him again only if they were married.

He agreed, and they were married in a civil ceremony. For the first year they got along, but Bullett couldn't find a job that suited him and Nikki continued to work. During the second year they quarreled. The marriage fell apart, and they agreed a divorce was best for all. Nikki held onto her married name for the benefit of Steven.

Again, Oliver Bullett dropped out of Nikki's life. He would call two or three times a year to talk to Steven, and sometimes he remembered to send his son a birthday present. On infrequent occasions Nikki received a check for child support drawn on a Texas bank, but the sporadic checks were for less than half the amount specified in the settlement decree. She never bothered to complain to the court.

Two years after Bullett's second departure, Nikki met the owner of a prosperous neighborhood hardware store. Clean-cut, hard-working, and self-effacing, Joe Fowler was a middle-aged bachelor who was the mirror opposite of Oliver Bullett. After six-months, Fowler moved in with Nikki and Steven, who was now ten.

Fowler and Steven took to each other. For Nikki, Fowler was a dream come true. He treated her with a sensitivity Nikki had not previously experienced, and they began to discuss marriage.

One night, a few months after Fowler had moved in, Nikki was putting away the dinner dishes while Fowler was instructing Steven on the subtleties of chess. The door bell rang and there on Nikki's doorstep was Oliver Bullett with a trim young woman whom he introduced as his new wife, Kate.

Over the ensuing weeks Nikki learned that Kate was a childless widow who had come into a substantial amount of money after her husband died in an automobile accident. Kate was unable to have children of her own, and Bullett wasted no time in letting Nikki know that he and his new wife wanted ten-year-old Steven to live with them in Texas, and were prepared, if necessary, to petition a court for custody.

For this flake of an ex-husband to show up out of the blue and demand custody of a child he barely knew was to Nikki a travesty of fairness. Bullett argued that he and his affluent wife would give Steven a secure privileged life in Dallas with advantages that Nikki, however well-intentioned, could never offer. Nikki, who rarely lost her temper, told them to get out of her house.

Bullett did, indeed, file a custody petition. His attached affidavit alleged, among other things, that the mother of the subject child was a person of questionable moral standards, living out of wedlock with a man she hardly knew in the same household as Steven. The affidavit recited that Bullett was "repulsed" at the thought of his son witnessing the "daily depravity" taking place.

Nikki retained a lawyer whose name she found in the Yellow Pages. He was routinely late for appointments and unprepared for depositions. Even to Nikki's untutored eye, his paperwork was sloppy and error-ridden. But Nikki had no previous exposure to lawyers, and she assumed this modus operandi was par for the course. Besides, his fees were modest and affordable.

Eager to cooperate, Joe Fowler accompanied Nikki at several of her conferences with her lawyer. He was willing to furnish an affidavit, appear before the judge, testify before a jury, and do anything else the lawyer thought would be helpful. The lawyer instructed Fowler to remain out of sight.

Following a three-month flurry of motions and affidavits, the judge ordered an informal conference in his chambers with the parties and their attorneys. The discussion was tense, and at one point Nikki whispered to her lawyer, "Why don't you say what we talked about before - Steven stays with me and his father visits him once a month?" Her lawyer ignored her and Nikki asked the question aloud.

The judge did not respond. He announced that on the basis of what he had heard he was inclined to award custody to the petitioner. Urging the parties to discuss a compromise embodying rotating visits, he set a date for a hearing.

As Nikki and her attorney were leaving the building she remembered she had left her glasses in the conference room Smiling her way past the judge's secretary, she opened the door without knocking. The judge and Oliver Bullett's attorney were sitting on the sofa, talking, drinks in hand. Nobody else was in the room. After recovering her glasses, Nikki left quickly and told her lawyer what she had observed and questioned its propriety. He said, "You're imagining things."

Nikki's lawyer urged her to settle. If they went to trial, he said, there was a possibility that the judge would ask young Steven to take the stand and he would be asked whether he would rather live with his mother or his father. The child would bear long-time scars from such an experience.

Nikki paused, looked at the far wall again, and then came back to me. "I will never forget his words," she said.

"Even if your kid says he'd rather live with you," Nikki's lawyer said, "I don't think that will sway the judge. You heard him. He's ninety percent of the way toward your ex-husband. If you lose at the hearing

I predict the judge will give you visitation rights every weekend. If you settle you'll get the same thing. Why should you incur the stress and expense of a big battle? It makes sense to settle."

Nikki wondered if her lawyer had cold feet about litigating. "I don't want 'visitation rights,' I want my child living with me. Besides, I can't fly to Dallas once a week. I thought the mother gets the child," she said. "Why don't we fight them?"

"Because you are in fact living with a man out of wedlock in the presence of your ten-year old son. I assure you, that doesn't bother me, but I can see the judge is disturbed by this. I don't see him turning around. Settle."

"Couldn't we have a jury?"

"Wouldn't matter. Settle."

"Well," Nikki said, "did I give you an earful?" Her eyes were moist.

"You did. Will you do this for me? Write down the name of the judge, your lawyer's name, and the name of your former husband's lawyer."

"I will, but why?"

"I'll try to help you, no promises, no guarantees. You've had some bad breaks, but you have a few things going for you. You're strong and you're smart and your values are in the right place. I have a lot of respect for you. Not only that, I like you."

"I like you, too, Sid. And you're a good listener."

The next day I showed up again at Nikki's office. "Would you mind if I asked you a few questions?" I asked.

"Like what?"

"How well do you know Chuck Hardy?"

"He interviewed me for the job, and then I've seen him at a couple of professional functions. Almost all my dealings with him are by phone and e-mail."

"I've never met him. What is your impression of him?"

"Off the record?"

"Absolutely."

"Totally dedicated to his business. He's been fair with me. Good salary, raise every year, bonus at Christmas. He has a temper, though.

I overheard him berating a sales agent at one of the functions. I won't tell you the language I heard."

"Is that it?"

"Well, if you want rumors . . ."

"I love rumors."

"His secretary calls me once in a while when he's out. She tells me stories. He wants everything his way. She says he explodes if he thinks somebody is not following his orders or hurting his business. Why do you ask?"

"Just curious."

She looked at me again with that blankness that always got to me. "Why are you trying to help me keep my son?"

"Because I'm a wonderful person."

I went back to my apartment, and listened to Maurice's message returning my call. He had been out of town the day before. This time I reached him immediately. I told him the subject I wanted to discuss had nothing to do with Oasis business, and gave him the background on Nikki Bullett, outlining the events she had related.

"It sounds to me like she has a half-ass lawyer," I said. "Do you know a good domestic relations lawyer?"

"I sure do. Good friend of mine. John Miller, one of the best in the country. His specialty happens to be custody battles. His batting average is about .850."

"Will you do this for me? Lean on him to represent Nikki. Given what you just said I'm sure his plate is full. As soon as you tell me he'll do it I'll have her call him. And ask him to send all bills directly to me. This is important to me."

"I'll try, but I ain't promising nothing. Now tell me - why are you doing this? Do you have something going with this young lady?"

"Maurice, you're beautiful."

I hadn't seen Audrey Weeks since the last Board meeting. When I saw her sitting alone in a neighborhood café I went over to her. Everything was in place - limp handshake, tepid smile, inert eyes.

I asked if I could join her for lunch. She hesitated, slowly placing her glass of water alongside her salad.

"I guess it's all right," she said.

I sat down opposite her, pondering the litany of small misfortunes that had shaped the life of this forlorn creature. I ordered a sandwich and we sat in silence for a minute.

I smiled and asked, "How are the missing children doing?

"It's so good of you to remember, Sid. I now have over four-hundred photographs. I keep looking, but so far without success."

She sipped her water, put it down, and looked out the window at the sidewalk. "Poor things," she muttered.

The waitress came with my order and again conversation was suspended as I munched on the sandwich and she picked at her half-eaten salad.

I put the sandwich down and said, "You know, the RFPs for the Building One roof are about to go out."

Before Audrey could respond, the voice of Bunny Slack rang out. "Well, now, what do we have here? A romance in the making?"

Bunny pulled up a chair from the next table and squeezed in between us, her face flushed with excitement. "So what are the two of you cooking up?"

"Sid just told me the RFPs for the roof replacement are about to be sent."

"The bids come in, we pick the lowest one, end of story."

"I guess that's right," Audrey said. "Why would we select a higher bid?"

Anna, Sheila and I would talk to Maurice. Lars said the less he had to do with lawyers, the better.

We wanted Maurice to confirm that he believed illegal behavior had occurred, and that the Oasis had the basis for a lawsuit. Finally, we wanted to know how much money it would cost the Oasis, and how much the Oasis could reasonably expect to recover.

And we had questions concerning our own liability. We had bugged the phone, and stolen the e-mail. Computer law was in its infancy, and

I suspected Maurice might not be able to address the e-mail issue with his customary confidence.

When we arrived, Maurice had already brought out the doughnuts and coffee, and as we progressed, I was glad to see he was suspending his wise-guy routine. He read through the e-mail we had appropriated and the Agreement signed by Hardy and the thirty-five suppliers and providers. He looked at us without expression.

Sheila asked, "What do you think, counselor?"

"These documents point to antitrust violations. If I'm right, your condo and others may have been substantially injured."

"Hold on, counselor," Sheila said. "Say it in everyday English. What did these guys do that hurt our condo, and how do we prove it?"

"The antitrust laws say that competitors cannot agree about the price they're going to charge. That's called horizontal price-fixing. We may have here a situation where they agree about who's going to come in with the lowest bid, and get the job. They rotate which one submits the lowest bid. That way, they keep the price artificially high. That's called bid-rigging. It's unlawful for them to agree among themselves, as well as with the person feeding them the business, in this case Hardy."

"So who are the bad guys here?"

"Potentially, all of the thirty-five who signed the agreement, including Hardy."

"So what happens to these bad guys?"

"The Justice Department investigates, and if they come up with reliable evidence, they file a criminal suit. If they can prove their case to a jury or a judge, the bad guys face heavy fines or jail terms or both."

"What did you mean about reliable evidence?"

"You must convince the judge that the documents are trustworthy and have not been illegally obtained."

Anna spoke up. "We have a potential problem on that last point, don't we?"

"Yes, we do. Hypothetically, if this e-mail is real, I doubt we could use it - one, it would be argued that it was stolen and is not admissible, and, two, it could result in a lawsuit against all of you for stealing it."

"So what's your recommendation?" Sheila asked.

"That Sid seek approval from his Board to retain counsel. If I were to be retained, I would conduct an investigation."

Before he could continue, Sheila asked, "What does that mean?"

Maurice smiled. "That means we interview other properties that may have been similarly injured. Then we take everything to the Justice Department. After the Department filed complaints, we would file our own lawsuit seeking triple damages."

Anna said, "How long do you estimate it would take for the Oasis to be compensated?"

Maurice laid out the timetable. His investigation would take a couple of months. The Justice Department preliminary inquiry would likely be three to six months. This would be followed with subpoenas and depositions - another six months to a year. Negotiating a settlement could extend from three to six months. If a settlement were not reached, Justice would litigate in federal District Court. Meanwhile, our civil suit would have been prepared and filed.

Anna smiled. "And then there would be appeals, isn't that right?"

"Possibly."

"You're talking five years," Sheila said.

"I would say more like two to three years."

Sheila threw her hands out. "We're senior citizens. Two years is an eternity. Some of us won't even buy green bananas." After a pause, she said, "What kind of money would the Oasis be looking at?"

"Six figures, maybe seven."

Maurice looked at me. "What do you intend to do?"

"I know you think it's a mistake for me to talk to Hardy, but he is, after all, under contract to the Oasis. He's accountable to us, and I don't think it would be inappropriate for me as President to ask him some questions about the bidding process."

"What would be the purpose?"

"Do a read on him, get a feeling whether he might be reasonable about settling."

With a quick glance in the direction of Sheila and Anna, Maurice thumbed through the date book lying on his desk. "I know you're an highly intelligent man, Sid, but ten months ago I recommend you stay away from him. My advice is unchanged."

As we left I asked Maurice to send me a bill. He laughed and said, "Meeting these lovely people has been recompense enough."

We argued all the way home, not whether we should talk to Hardy, but *who* should talk to him. Sheila and Anna believed their previous exposure to him would give them a crucial edge. The insight they had gained could make a difference in our ability to penetrate whatever meretricious story he might offer.

I said their previous exposure to this sociopathic time bomb would be a drawback, not an advantage. Furthermore, the meeting would go better limited to one-on-one, Hardy and me.

"Your macho streak is showing," Sheila said.

I just looked at her.

They argued that the hidden cameras may have been operating at the time of Lars' and my first clandestine visit to Hardy's office. Therefore, they said, it made sense for the two of them to go back to Hardy without me. They dropped that line after seeing the look of incredulity on my face.

But they were adamant and so was I.

"Look," I said, "I'm this far away from laying everything out to the Board and recommending we retain Maurice. I appreciate your zeal, but it's either me alone with Hardy or no meeting at all, and I go to the Board."

I underestimated them. They understood my obsessive need to confront Hardy with or without them, and they called my bluff. The three of us will go, they said, or we can forget about the meeting and I could go to the damn Board.

"Suppose I just go and don't tell you," I said.

Anna looked like I had hit her with a wet towel.

"Then I'll know I was wrong when I called you a straight-shooter," Sheila said.

Why did I say we should think about it for a few days, and then make an appointment with Hardy for the next day? And not say a word to them.

The easy answer would be that it was the challenge, the opportunity to best an adversary. But if a "challenge" was so central to my psychic well-being, I might well have addressed the challenge of restoring Anna's trust. Was it possible that deep-down I *wanted* Anna to give up on me? That I nurtured a notion that to love Anna was to betray Sarah?

Negotiating the forty-minute drive quickly, and arriving five minutes early, I took in the area. In the daylight this time, I could see the industrial neighborhood more clearly than I had during my night with Lars and Fido. Only warehouses and plain-front offices were in sight. Hardy's office was located at the end of a shallow cul-de-sac.

The small reception area was as quiet during the day as it had been in the dead of night. A sullen-looking man with a plaid jacket and grey pants, mid-to-late forties I guessed, was sitting next to Hardy's office, his chair tipped back against the wall and his eyes half closed. His thick black hair tied in a ponytail and his five-day growth were apparently the mark of macho chic.

The teen-age gum-chewing secretary went through the door behind her and came back after a few seconds. "You can go in now." A tall, solidly-built man, maybe late fifties, got up from his chair and walked around the beat-up pine desk. He looked me over as he clasped my hand. His hands, large and hard, were almost twice the size of mine.

"I've been looking forward to meeting you, Mr. Silva. I've heard good things."

"You have a pretty good reputation, yourself. Please call me Sid."

"Sure, Sid. Friends call me Chuck. And this guy is our accountant, Bill Stane."

Thin and dour-looking, Stane was perhaps ten years younger than Hardy. His hands were small and soft. Shaking hands with him was like gripping a soggy noodle.

"Bill will be in his office back there if we need his expertise on the numbers." Stane nodded to me, and went into the adjoining office, closing the door behind him.

Hardy looked more like a lab than a grizzly bear, as he had been described to me. He was bald with a soft smile and hard eyes. I detected a small gut behind the high-rise, well-pressed gray trousers. His shirt was blue striped, open at the collar, and he wore black tasseled loafers.

The gum-chewer brought in coffee and cookies on a tray, and we sat around the desk. Hardy extended the cookies, and I shook my head. "Watching my weight."

"Tell me about it, " he laughed, taking a cookie and dipping it in his coffee.

"So how do you like being president? Lots of responsibility and complaints about everything, mostly trivial. Am I right?"

"You've got it. Everything from not enough guest parking in the garage to pets."

"I saw that last one about pets in the minutes Nikki sends me. Broke me up."

"Speaking of Nikki, she's efficient and responsive. We're fortunate to have her. You must feel the same way."

"Absolutely. She's a gem. Lucked out with her."

Hardy opened his drawer and brought out a box of Coronas. Looking at me, he raised his eyebrows, and I shook my head again. He selected a cigar from the box, placed it between his thick lips, lit it with a long kitchen match, puffed, and exhaled slowly.

"I'm sure you know we manage a lot of properties, Sid, but the Oasis is the jewel in our crown." He smiled. "Silva, Silva. Aren't you in the construction business?"

"Used to be. I'm retired."

"I remember. Silva Construction. You put up commercial buildings, and you managed some. I'll bet building them was more fun."

One thing that hadn't yet happened to me in my so-called senior years was memory erosion. What Hardy had just said was almost word for word what I had told Travail at the first Board meeting I had attended eleven months earlier.

"Right," I said.

"Sounds like you did what I do. Keep the shareholders happy, the employees in line, and the union off your back. Watch the competition, and make the customers happy. Lots of balls in the air. One of these days we should compare notes."

Hardy placed his cigar onto the ashtray. "Well, my friend, what can I do for you?"

"You'll recall the Building Two roof replacement. Now Building One is ready. I was looking through the files the other day and I had the feeling that Building Two's bids were on the high side. I thought maybe you could give me a better understanding of how the bids were arrived at, and see if we can't get a better deal this time."

As I put my questions to him - some feigned, some genuine - his manner reflected a desire to be helpful. Hadn't I previously acquired business experience with RFPs and bids? I had, I said, but I wanted to hear it in the context of this business.

"Besides, Chuck, old guys like me get rusty."

Hardy laughed. "I'll bet."

He walked me through the bidding process, telling me nothing I didn't know, but I wanted to see how he handled it. The RFP - Request for Proposal - is just what it sounds like, Hardy said. It is a request with specifications sent by the buyer of labor and material to competing sellers asking that each seller submit a "proposal" describing in detail the manner in which he would perform the job, accompanied by his best price.

The buyer, he continued, compares the proposals and makes a selection. Price is not the sole factor. The buyer also considers reputation. Sometimes quality trumps price.

I would remember his reference to quality over price.

"That helps me understand the process," I said, "but why was the cost of our roof replacement last year so high?"

He said they followed usual procedure. Nikki drafted the RFPs and Hardy reviewed them. When the bids came in Nikki made a recommendation based on the price-quality factor, and Hardy and Travail signed off.

"*And* the condo got top quality. No leaks since the job was finished. Right?"

"Right, that's what we expected. But I ran the numbers by somebody I know and he thought they seemed high." I scratched my head as though confused. "Maybe I'm off base, but I wonder if these vendors got together on the price."

His expression didn't change. "Always possible, Sid, but not likely. It's unlawful for the vendors to communicate with one another about their proposals. I know these people - we work with them a lot. If they were fooling around, their lawyers would find out and be on them like a ton of bricks. You know that."

"Yeah . . . I hear what you're saying." I remembered Travail telling me Lars was making a mountain out of a molehill. "Maybe I'm making a mountain out of a molehill."

"I don't mean to be glib. If these guys are screwing around, it hurts me as much as you. Tell you what. When the new set of bids for Building One comes in, we'll go over them together."

"Sounds good."

He picked up his cigar, flicked the ash toward the ashtray sitting near the edge of the desk, and took a drag. He exhaled, and some of the cigar smoke drifted my way. I relaxed, and experienced that exquisite pleasure I had so missed. It had been twenty years, but addicted I would always be. I took his smile to be a tacit sign of simpatico.

"What do you like to do, Sid? For kicks?"

I paused. "I read, I listen to music, I go to the movies . . . and I play poker. We have a regular game at the condo."

"Love that game," he said. "Played night and day in Nam."

"I played night and day in Korea." I could almost get to like this guy.

"Shit," he said, "we've got a lot in common. Got a place for me at the poker table?"

"Say the word."

"What stakes?"

"Quarter-half."

He changed the subject. Clearly a dollar - two-dollar man. Or more.

"Ever do blackjack?"

"Yeah, but not recently," I said.

"I understand you're a widower, Sid. My condolences."

"Thanks."

"Nikki tells me your grandson is staying with you. How's he doing?"

"He's all right, usual teenage problems."

"A grandson is important in your life." He took a last, deep puff on the cigar. "How about lunch one of these days?"

"Sure - okay."

"I'll call you."

I concentrated on the drive back. If there was something illegal going on, it would be a hard nut to crack. Should I abandon the entire escapade? Destroy the condo papers, disband the Task Force, ask them to forget everything, and stay away from the lawyers?

Walking away stuck in my throat because I took seriously my responsibility to the Oasis. I decided to get the Board's approval to retain Maurice. I would turn everything over to him, and accept his decision.

Sooner or later I'd have to tell the Task Force about my meeting with Hardy. Anna and Sheila would be furious that I tricked them out of attending. So I delayed calling a Task Force meeting. I decided to dribble the ball for a while.

After a movie Skip and I dropped into Buona Sera for a late evening bite. Sitting at a small table near the kitchen in the sparsely populated restaurant were Anna and Maria conferring over coffee. Anna had told me she and Maria were on the phone together at least once a week. They had become good friends. Still, I was surprised to see them.

We walked over to their table and Anna's face lit up when she saw Skip trailing behind me. "What's happening, my main man?" she asked.

Skip shrugged. "Little of this, little of that."

She said "Excuse us" to Maria and me, and sat down with Skip three tables away. Anna continued to see something special in Skip, and Skip sensed this, perking up in her presence. I knew that even if Anna and I were getting along, she would be sparing in telling me what she and Skip had to say to each other.

I chatted with Maria, and when Anna and Skip returned, Maria invited us to join them, but I said we didn't want to intrude, and we took a table at the other end of the room. I sneaked a glance. They had resumed their discussion, Anna no doubt telling Maria about her problems with me, and Maria defending me. Or maybe they were comparing notes on the best sauce to have with rigatoni.

Chapter 12

The Task Force met the next day without Skip who no longer attended the meetings. I told them I had met with Hardy.

Sheila spoke first. "You said we'd think about it and you'd talk to us. You lied."

"I felt it was important to go alone."

After I summarized the meeting, Lars asked, "How did he strike you?"

"He seemed to be a nice guy. He was courteous, he listened to my questions, and was responsive. He and his boys may be playing illegal games, but I have to say, I enjoyed talking to him. We talked about poker. He even asked about Skip."

For the first time, Anna looked directly at me. "What did he ask about Skip?"

"Just how was he doing. He said a grandson is important in my life."

"How did he know about Skip?" Anna asked.

"Nikki mentioned Skip was staying with me. It's not a big deal."

Anna was not satisfied. "You were talking business. Strange he brought up Skip."

Lars felt it was time to seek Board approval to retain an attorney, and disband the Task Force. The others agreed, Sheila reluctantly. If Hardy had no spy on the Board he would not know we had retained an attorney unless and until he received a Justice Department subpoena - six months to a year. If there was a spy, Hardy would know immediately.

A few minutes after they left I called Anna, and as I had anticipated, she had gone from cool to frigid. I said it was an unexpected surprise to see her at Buona Sera. I asked if she would have dinner with me.

"No, thank you," she said.

"Look, I know you're disappointed that I went to see Hardy by myself, but I thought it was important that I confront him alone."

"You don't get it. We were going to do this together. I didn't know it was going to be a one-man show. You didn't tell me. *Before* you went, not afterward."

"Because you would have protested. I didn't want to argue with you and Sheila."

"You have your priorities, I have mine."

"Fine."

"Okay.

I had figured I wouldn't hear from Hardy for a couple of weeks, but he called a few days later. "How you doing, my friend?"

"Hanging in, Chuck."

"You free for lunch tomorrow?"

"Sure."

"Know the Broth-L?"

He damn well knew I "knew" the Broth-L. "Yeah, Travail took me there."

"One o'clock."

Everything looked the same. At her post near the entrance was the voluptuous hostess with the nameplate, "Madam," wearing the same ankle-length deep-slit skirt. Different waitress this time. In place of "Pat" with the bleached-blonde bouffant under the ten-gallon hat, was "Suzy-Q," a short pixy-type, black bangs covering most of her forehead. The cowboy-style fringed skirt, and boots to the knees were the same.

Suzy-Q opened up with, "Nice to see you again, Mr. Hardy." Turning to me, she reverted to formula. "Howdy, pardner, my name's Suzy-Q. What can I rustle up for you all today?"

Chuck's overtures to the waitress were polished next to Travail's crudities. When Suzy-Q brought the drinks - Absolut for me, Lone Star for Hardy - Chuck said, "Let me give you a piece of advice, sweetheart."

No doubt expecting the worst, she said, "Yes?"

"Don't ever change your hair style."

She moved on with a wide grin.

Later, over thin steaks, we talked about business, and I found myself reminiscing. "It was a roller coaster. Sometimes the phone would ring twice in a whole day, and I thought we were on the skids. Then, out of the blue, a couple of big-time new customers would walk in, and we'd be up to our necks in work for months, sometimes years."

He ran his fingers down his cheek. "Bet you planned ahead for those bad times."

"You're right. We were always throwing profits back into the business - modernizing, keeping up with the new stuff."

"That's not what I meant. It's okay to re-invest in the business, but my rule is take the money while it's there, and not worry about the fine points. Worry about yourself. You know what I'm talking about - I think we're cut from the same cloth."

"I hear you, but we did that. We took care of ourselves."

"Good. We should get together more. Now and then I set up a junket for friends - Vegas, the islands, a little get-away. Booze, blackjack, poker, whatever. I'm planning one in San Juan over Memorial Day. Travail will be there. Give it a shot?"

"Sounds good, Chuck. If I can go, I'll get in touch with you."

"Let me make reservations for you."

"Thanks. I'll handle my own arrangements if I come."

"The more I see you the more I like you. I wish you were part of my team. That's not business-bullshit, I mean it."

"I hear you. Forty years ago we would have made a good team."

On impulse, I added, "What's the most important thing in your life?"

"You're kidding."

"No."

"Make sure I treat people the same way they treat me. That make sense?"

"Yup."

When Suzy-Q gave Hardy the check, he pulled out a crisp fifty-dollar bill, made sure I saw it, folded it once, neatly, and handed it to her. Resting her hand on his shoulder, and looking straight at me, she said, "Am I lucky to have a friend like this, or what?"

After Suzy-Q went on her way, I said, "You made her day, Chuck."

"One of these days she's going to make *my* day. My rule is, one hand feeds the other. You follow?"

"Yup."

Nikki called to say all the bids had arrived. I stuck the copy of Hardy's six-week-old e-mail to the Building One bidders in my pocket, picked up the bids, and went into my cubicle. The bids were signed with first and last names and company.

Their bids adhered to Hardy's e-mail schedule to the last dollar. District Roofing came in with the lowest bid, $487,500, as Hardy had instructed. Security Roofing, which had been the lowest - and winning - bidder two years earlier for the Building Two roof, was now the second lowest bidder. Hardy made sure each player got his turn at bat.

The background files on the bidders indicated that all five companies were in good financial shape and were reputable. I examined the customer comments that Nikki had obtained from some fifteen properties that had used these companies for roof replacement over the past two years following our Building Two roof replacement.

Almost all of the customers complained about the cost, but most of them were satisfied with the quality. Five customers, however, were unhappy with District Roofing for reasons relating to performance as well as cost. Work was completed weeks after the original estimate, and District's explanation was "unsatisfactory" and "unresponsive." New roof leaked for a month, and District was laggard in correcting the deficiencies.

The comments about the second lowest bidder, Security Roofing, were uniformly complimentary regarding performance. In conformance with Hardy's e-mail instruction, Security's bid of $590,450 was $102,950 higher than District's bid of $487,500.

Hardy's predetermined winner was supposed to be District Roofing. Something was telling me the condo would be better served by the second lowest bidder, Security. The hundred-thousand-dollar gap was formidable, but Security had a good track record with the Oasis, and the five complaints against District - double the number two years earlier - were red flags. Hardy's frustration would be an extra bonus.

"What is stopping us from going with the second lowest bidder?" I asked Nikki.

"Nothing," she said, deadpan in place.

"Is it ever done?"

"Sometimes, not often."

"Would you recommend against doing that?"

"It's strictly your call."

"Do I need the Board's approval?"

"Ordinarily, management selects the bid and the President signs off, but if you want Security for $100,000 more, you'd better have the Board behind you."

"Do you think we should run it by Hardy first?"

"Your call."

"Okay. Let's see if I can make the Board see the light."

"They won't like the extra money. You'll have to spell it out to them."

I was developing a guarded feeling that Nikki was clean. At the same time, I knew that selling the Board on Security was going to be tough.

Maurice woke me up at seven a.m. John Miller had agreed to represent Nikki Bullett. Miller's plate *was* overflowing, but Maurice applied the pressure. He told Miller he would regard it as a personal favor if Miller would squeeze Nikki into his schedule.

"This cost me big time, you owe me," Maurice said as I cradled the phone between my chin and elbow, trying to spoon coffee into my Krups. "Want to know why?"

"Do I have a choice?" I asked.

"We're both seven handicappers and he wants me to give him four strokes when we play next week. That's a heavy price to pay. I trust you understand."

"I don't know what you're talking about."

I was sitting at Nikki's desk when she arrived that morning at 8:50. I said she had a new lawyer and if there was any way to hold onto her son he would figure it out.

"His name is John Miller and I'm told he's good. Call him this morning and tell his secretary you're calling on the recommendation of Maurice Ruffin. It may be a couple of days before he returns the call. Tell him you're a friend of mine. When you meet with him, give him everything about your personal life. Spare no detail."

She sat motionless, staring at me, and for a moment I thought I was looking at incomprehension. But I realized it was stupefaction.

"Remember," I said, "this guy is a good lawyer, but he's not a magician, so let's not count our chickens yet."

"I understand that, but at least I'll always know I did everything I could."

She threw out her hands, palms up. "My God, I just realized, his bill will be huge. I hope he'll let me work out a payment schedule."

"Don't worry about that."

"What do you mean?"

"The bills will come to me."

"That's very nice of you. I'll arrange to reimburse you on a monthly schedule. It might be a while before I can pay you back, though."

"No, no. Just forget about the money."

Again, she gave me that deadpan stare that would have melted me on the spot if I'd been ten years younger. Maybe fifteen.

Board meetings were required by law to be open to any resident or owner who wished to attend. There were two exceptions. If the purpose of a meeting was to discuss legal questions involving possible litigation or performance of staff personnel, the president scheduled an "executive session" to be attended only by the board members. No other residents or owners would be present, not even Nikki Bullett. "Executive sessions" were confidential.

I placed the issue of bidder selection of the Condo One roof on the agenda for the next open meeting. At the conclusion of that meeting, I would announce there would immediately follow an executive session, and after we had cleared the room, we would take up the question of retaining Maurice. I hoped that hitting them cold with the retention-of-attorney issue might be to my benefit.

The monthly Board meeting took place a few nights later. In addition to the seven Board members, four residents and Nikki were in attendance.

Arriving at the meeting ahead of time, I watched each of the other six members walk in. The first was Dr. Morton Moody. Unsteady of gait, his head shaking, he wore a skeptical expression, as though he had made up his mind to oppose whatever I proposed.

Dressed in a beige linen suit, Jane Fountain came in just behind Moody. Her air of insouciance suggested that no bad news I might impart was likely to disturb her poise.

Audrey Weeks and Bunny Slack followed Fountain a moment later, Audrey with a touch of lipstick on her upper front tooth. She wore the same vacant smile with which she had favored me some months earlier when I had kissed her cheek outside her door.

Emerging from beneath Bunny's pancake and eye shadow was the image of a strong-minded woman who looked ten years younger than she was, and was still capable of dispensing pleasure to deserving people. She twirled both her loosely-fitted watchband and the adjacent dia-mond-studded bracelet throughout the meeting.

Anna and Lars, who knew my plan, were the last to arrive. They had poker faces.

I recited the background and the current bids. I gave my reasons for recommending that we award the contract to Security Roofing.

Bunny led the charge. "This beats all. You are asking us to spend $100,000 just because this District Roofing company has complaints against it. Everybody gets complaints. What's the big deal? I never heard of not going with the low bidder."

Dr. Moody jumped in. "You're losing it, Mr. President, you're off the wall. You're wasting condo money. Of course we have to go with the low bidder."

Audrey, to my surprise, provided a touch of - unintentional - wry humor. "Unless you have a hundred-thousand dollars you're willing to contribute to the condo."

Bunny looked at me. "You can't be serious."

"Of course he's serious," Anna said. "A new roof is a long-time thing, and it behooves us to stick with the company that performed well two years ago."

Lars said, "Anna makes sense to me."

It was Jane's turn. "I understand where you're coming from, Sid. Quality of the work is no less important than cost. If the difference were less significant I might feel it's worth the extra money. But a hundred-thousand dollars is a bit too rich for my blood."

The vote was four-to-three for District. I had lost.

Following my announcement that an executive session would follow, we cleared the room. I discussed the Building Two roof replacement, including the cost. Outlining the current status of the Building One roof replacement, I reminded them that even their selection of the lowest bidder, District, earlier that evening, would still cost $487,500.

I said I had given the two-year-old Building Two bids to each of two friends experienced in related industries. They had told me the bids were excessive.

I then reported an off-the-record discussion with an attorney I knew and trusted. This "behavior," he had said, had the "earmarks" of conspiratorial conduct. If the Board retained him he would conduct a preliminary investigation and report the results of his inquiries along with his recommendations. I said it would be prudent to retain him.

"Hold on," Dr. Moody grumbled. "You're going too fast. All you're telling us is some friends of yours, flying by the seat of their pants, said the bids are 'excessive.' You've got to do better than that, Mr. President. What's the name of this shyster?"

"Maurice Ruffin," I said, "and he's no shyster. He's a first-rate lawyer."

"So he's a first-rate lawyer," Bunny said. "Big deal. What you're saying . . . it's like I tell you I had a mild headache two years ago and you want me to have surgery."

"That's good, Bunny," Dr. Moody said. "I'll remember that one."

"What I'm proposing," I said, "costs us nothing. He conducts his investigation and comes back to us with his recommendations. No fee.

Then we decide what, if anything, we want him to do. We can kill it at that point if we want to."

Bunny sat up straight. "I've never ever heard of a lawyer who will work without getting paid. Maybe he won't call it a fee, but he'll find a way."

"Bunny," I said, "any arrangement we make will be what is called a contingency. His fee, if it gets that far, will come out of our eventual recovery. In any case, let me assure you, Maurice has irreproachable integrity. He is highly ethical."

Bunny rolled her eyes. "Ethical, schmethical. If you're a lawyer you're a liar." She slipped her bracelet higher on her arm. "Required course, first year law school. Lying one-oh-one."

"All Sid is proposing," Anna said, "is that we call in a disinterested professional to advise us. It's not to the lawyer's advantage to mislead us. If he recommends we proceed, knowing we have no case or a weak case, he will do a lot of work and end up with zero compensation. He's not stupid."

"How do you know that?" asked Dr. Moody.

"FOR GOD'S SAKE, stop a minute. This *conversation* is stupid." In all the many times I'd been with Lars, I had never heard him speak in an abrasive tone.

He continued, his voice softer, but his irritation intact. "Sid is proposing a no-lose scenario. We get a legal opinion at no cost. We can thank the lawyer for his efforts, tell him to drop everything, and pay him no money. Or we can instruct him to continue."

"I don't like it," said Bunny. "You get involved with lawyers and before it's over their hooks are sunk into you, and you pay."

Dr. Moody, still shaking his head, said, "I'm with Bunny. Not necessary. We had a tummy ache two years ago and you want to call in a high-paid gastroenterologist."

"My analogy was better," Bunny said.

"Jane, Audrey," I said. "You've been quiet. Do you have opinions?"

Audrey spoke first. "My intuition tells me not to look for trouble. Do you know of a single leak in Building Two since the roof was replaced? Leave well enough alone."

Fountain shifted in her seat. "It's not the quality of the work we're concerned about, Audrey. It's the cost." Turning to me, she asked, "What would you estimate our eventual recovery might be, Sid?"

"If the only victims of the conspiracy turn out to be the Oasis and other local properties, my guess would be low six figures," I said. "If the conspiracy can be proven to be wider - covering a three or four-state region - could be more."

Bunny emitted a noise akin to a snort. "Your pal, Maurice, what would his cut be?"

"Somewhere between a quarter and a third of the final amount coming to us."

Jane said, "So if our final recovery were, say, $150,000, we would come out of it with at least $100,000."

"Correct."

"No tax?"

"No tax."

Bunny made the snorting noise again. "Who pays his ongoing costs?"

"We do," I said.

Jane placed her elbows on the table, hands on her cheeks, and leaned forward toward me. "These ongoing costs, Sid. What kind of money are we talking about?"

Ongoing costs, I explained, would cover out-of-pocket expenses like telephone, Xerox, outside investigators, expert witnesses such as accountants and economists, and depositions. Month-to-month costs would vary, of course.

Jane persisted. "Can you translate that into dollars?"

"The first few months would be minimal, under a thousand dollars a month I would say. More later. It could get up to two thousand a month."

"For how long?"

"I'd say two or three years."

Jane sat up straight. "So the condo could be laying out ten to twenty thousand dollars a year for, say, three years. In the aggregate, we could be looking at expenses of more than fifty thousand dollars before we recovered anything. *If* we recovered anything."

"Possible, Jane," I said.

Dr. Moody frowned. "You're trying to talk us into a huge, irresponsible gamble."

"For once the Doctor put it right," Bunny said. "We could easily end up losing over fifty thou based on pure speculation. Not for me."

Audrey spoke up. "I have to say, gambling is not what our condo is about."

Jane looked at me, and said, "I'm sorry, Sid. I know you're trying to act in the best interests of the condo, but it sounds too chancy. Based on my experience, proving a conspiracy is not easy. I'd still be willing to try it except for that monthly outlay."

I waited a moment before continuing. "Is there anything else anybody wants to say?" After a silence I said, "Then I would like to hear a motion."

Lars moved we retain Maurice for the limited purpose I had described. Lars, Anna, and I supported the motion, and Bunny, Morton, Audrey, and Jane opposed. The motion was defeated, four to three. Hardy would undoubtedly receive a detailed account of the meeting. He would be a happy camper.

I had lost both votes, but Audrey's little throw-away - *gambling is not what our condo is about* - had planted the seeds of an idea in my mind. Maybe the time had come for me to play with the high rollers.

Sheila had asked Lars, Anna and me to drop over for coffee after the meeting. Not a resurrection of the Task Force, she had said, just a get-together. The "confidentiality" of executive sessions was ignored at the Oasis, and we spoke freely.

"For a while there, I thought Jane was with us," Anna said. Was there an undertone of sympathy for me from Anna? I doubted it.

"I did, too," I said. "Could I have a small vodka, Sheila?"

On her way to the liquor cabinet, Sheila said, "Bunny Slack is the spy. I don't buy that call-it-like-I-see-it bullshit. She's smart, and believe me, she ain't afraid the lawyers will rip us off. She's got some other reason for keeping them out of it."

"Something I never got around to telling you," I said. "Carl Harrison, who is close to Bunny Slack, told me she used to sleep with Francis Travail."

"So there you are," Sheila said. "First, Travail gets off the Board and off Bunny, and then Bunny inherits Travail's spy duties and gets on top of Carl."

"Does Hardy pay her the same way?" Lars said. "Studs and casinos?"

Sheila laughed. "Straight cash."

Anna said, "Audrey Weeks is too innocent to be true. That talk about leave well enough alone. What does that mean? She can't be serious."

Lars asked, "What about Moody? Something more there than we see?"

Sheila laughed again, louder. "Casting Moody as James Bond. That's like casting Audrey Weeks as Marilyn Monroe."

Anna turned toward me. "How is Skip doing?" she asked.

"He's been seeing Carl Harrison' granddaughter, Karen. His dorm is almost ready, and I'm thinking about a farewell party. I would ask the three of you to come, of course, and Mickey, Maria's nephew. They've become good friends. What do you think?'

"Wonderful idea," Anna said. "I'll make something special."

Sheila gave me one of her mischievous looks. "You know, Sid, despite the problems you're having with your Board, it pays for you to make nice. They've seen Skip around the place, talked to him on the elevator. It wouldn't hurt to invite all of them."

I dropped into Nikki's office at 10 a.m. the next morning. "Tell me something. Did you call Hardy this morning to tell him the Board voted to go with the lowest bidder?"

"No, he called me five minutes after I got here at 9, and let me tell you, he was in one good mood. Asked if I had a good time at the meeting last night. Strange question."

"What else did he say?"

"I'm doing a great job. Could have knocked me over."

"Do me a favor? Don't send the contract to District until I give you the word."

"Done. And keep all this to myself?"

"Thank you.

When I suggested a going-away party, Skip said, "Okay with me." I called Mickey, Fountain, Weeks, Moody, and Slack. They would be "honored" and "delighted" to come.

Then I thought of Elsie. I'd been feeling a little sorry for her and I invited her. She said she "would be pleased" to be part of the celebration. Finally, I called Carl and invited him and his granddaughter, Karen.

"Hey," he said, "We accept. Karen was just telling me this morning at breakfast how 'cool' Skip is. You think they might have something going?"

"Why not?"

The tone of the party was congenial. My concern that the age disparity might create awkwardness, turned out to be misplaced. Anna made a roast beef, Sheila a potato salad oozing with mayo and oversalted coleslaw, and Lars brought wine.

The presents for Skip ran the gamut from dictionaries to three new hip-hop CDs from Mickey. Anna and Skip spoke about his curriculum as Dr. Moody and Bunny Slack listened. Skip said, "My main thing is the computer."

Dr. Moody said, "That's the wave of the future, young fellow."

Bunny, rolling her eyes, said, "Thank you, Morton, for that valuable information."

Turning to Skip, Bunny said, "I'll bet you're a whiz on the web."

"Yeah, pretty good."

Jane Fountain worked the room, dispensing cheer, her all-black pants suit hanging loose. Early on, she got me alone. She wanted me to understand her vote against retaining a lawyer. She had to be guided by her experience, and this was where she came out.

A fleeting fantasy seized me - Anna dressed in that same black outfit Jane was wearing, waiting to meet me in the bar of an intimate hotel perched in the hills overlooking a village in the heart of Tuscany. For years I had yearned to visit that part of the world.

My idyll evaporated with the sounds of Lars regaling Mickey with tales of the accounting problems he used to have in his private investigating business, Mickey nodding appreciatively. The veteran telling combat stories to the young warrior.

Carl arrived with his granddaughter, Karen. When he introduced us, her eyes locked onto mine for perhaps a second too long, and I saw myself as she must have seen me. A grumpy-looking old man, pouches folded over sunken cheeks, staving off boredom and cynicism. And I saw a fresh rose in early blossom with a touch of cunning in her eye.

Mickey and Skip played a computer game, the rest of us talking idly about the condo. Anna, smiling, tapped her glass for quiet, and made some brief remarks. She said Skip was gifted, and older people could learn from young people. Skip glowed.

Toward the end of the evening I noticed Skip and Mickey slipping into Skip's bedroom and closing the door. Ten minutes later, Anna asked me, "I wonder what happened to Sheila and Carl's granddaughter. I haven't seen them in a while."

I stuck my head inside Skip's room, and saw a haze of smoke curling around the open window. Sheila and Karen were stretched out next to each other on the bed, heads propped up by pillows, Mickey sitting on one side of the bed, feet firmly on the floor, and Skip on the other side in the same position. Karen was passing a thin cigarette to Mickey.

"Pot break," Sheila said, laughing.

Later, after everyone had left, I walked Mickey to his car. "You think Karen and Skip are becoming friends?" I asked.

"Maybe, but she bothers me. I can't put my finger on it. I just don't trust her."

A few days later I drove Skip to his dorm. We walked around, Skip pointing out campus landmarks. We returned to his building, avoiding eye contact.

"Listen, Sid, I appreciate everything you've done. I'll stay in touch."

Some eight years ago when he was ten, I had said I'd like him to call me Sid because that's what my friends called me. After that request he had steadfastly refused to call me anything except grandpa. Until now. Did this signify a ray of hope?

Chapter 13

I slept late and lounged around with coffee. Checking out EMA in the Journal, I did a double take. A week ago the stock was trading at $52. It was now down to $24. The story reported negative earnings, and hinted at financial irregularities. Lots of disappointed people out there, I thought.

I dropped in on Nikki Bullett to see if I could coax more information out of her. She reached for a yellow pad brimming with handwritten notes, and her face brightened with a sparkle I'd never seen before. "I was about to call when you came in. I got a couple of phone calls in the last hour that will interest you."

"I'm all ears."

Referring to the pad, Nikki said, "First and foremost, Mr. John Miller called. My ex-husband withdrew his petition for custody of Steven. It's all over. Steven belongs to me - and Joe Fowler. We're going to be married in two months. Small wedding. You and Anna will be invited. Can you believe all this?"

"Hold on. You're going too fast. Why did he withdraw the petition?"

"My first lawyer I told you about? The paper shuffler? He never even *thought* about a background check."

Nikki said John Miller had hired an investigator in Texas who learned that Nikki's former husband, Oliver Bullett, and Kate, his "wife," had in fact never been married. The same argument Oliver was using against Nikki - Nikki and Joe Fowler living together - applied to Oliver and his non-wife.

Glancing at the yellow pad, Nikki took a breath and continued. The investigator also discovered that after Kate's husband had died in an automobile accident, the Dallas District Attorney's Office conducted an investigation into the circumstances of the accident. They concluded that Kate and Oliver Bullett had conspired to arrange the death of Kate's husband and make it look like an accident.

Kate and Oliver were indicted by a grand jury for conspiracy to commit murder. The District Attorney's principal witness, the driver of the car that killed Kate's husband, disappeared a week before trial. The D.A. proceeded to trial anyway, but his case was fatally flawed without his main witness, and the jury acquitted both defendants.

John Miller sat down with Alice Larson, the attorney for Oliver and Kate. If they went to trial, Miller said, the jury would be told about the non-marriage between Kate and Oliver Bullett, the indictments and the mysterious witness disappearance.

According to Nikki's notes, Alice Larson said, "I know about the non-marriage. That's a non-issue They're getting married tomorrow. As for your other argument, there's no way the judge will admit evidence of a Texas case ending with acquittals, a case totally irrelevant to a custody matter in the District years later."

Miller handed Ms. Larson a decision that had come down from the District of Columbia Court of Appeals three months earlier. At this point, Nikki read word-for-word from her notes. The decision held that "evidence of a previous trial in a 'foreign' jurisdiction is admissible in a custody case to establish a rebuttable presumption of bad moral character even if that trial had ended in acquittal."

Ms. Larson offered a settlement much like Nikki's first lawyer had sought. Miller told her there would be no settlement of any kind. Either she withdraws the petition or they go to trial. A week later the petition was withdrawn.

Nikki was beside herself. "It was withdrawn with prejudice. That means they can never file such a petition again. You're the kindest man I ever met and John Miller is the best lawyer in history."

"That's great, Nikki. I'm delighted."

"I still want to repay you for the legal fees. Maybe over time, like five years. Would that be okay?"

"We covered that before. It's out of the question. Forget about it."

She touched my arm. "I will never forget what you've done for me," she said. "I can't thank you enough. I'll do anything for you."

She was a teen-age girl enticing an older man to try his hand. "Anything?"

Raising her eyebrows, she said, "You call it."

"Tell me more about Hardy."

"And here I thought it was about to get interesting. All right. I'm told he's made a ton of money. Stock options, whatever. Also, somebody told me something, but I can't remember right now. By the way, this is off the record?"

"Everything between you and me stays between you and me."

She grinned. "Good. Now, the second phone call. One of the electrical suppliers Efficiency uses a lot, guy named Ed Runco. I went out with him after Oliver took off and before I met Joe. Didn't work out, but he still has eyes for me."

She blinked her eyes in a mock-coquettish fashion that had me laughing. "I lead him on," she said with a blush, "so he'll keep me in the loop. He tells me stuff he shouldn't and it stays with me, but I think you'll want to know about this one."

Nikki said that Runco had called that morning, "all bent out of shape." The stock value of EMA had been plummeting, Runco told Nikki, and Hardy had never advised anyone to sell. "We've all lost big money," Runco said, "and not a word from Hardy. He had to know this was going to happen. We've had it with this bastard. All of us."

"What is that all about?" Nikki asked me.

"It's a long story, but thanks, that's helpful. Anything else new with Hardy?"

"Same old, same old . . . no, wait, I just remembered. He's going to San Juan with Mr. Travail over Memorial Day. His secretary told me she reserved plane tickets and hotel reservations for them in a suite at the Ritz-Carlton. And he had her go to his bank and draw out cash plus open up a line of credit with the hotel."

This confirmed what Hardy had told me as to when and which city. Now I knew which hotel, but I was still curious about the money. "Did she tell you how much?"

"A fifty-thousand dollar line of credit and fifty thousand dollars in cash . . . if Hardy ever found out I talked to you about him . . . "

"Don't even think about it. It won't happen."

A wave of restlessness had come over me. I was angry at Hardy for ripping off our condo, perturbed at Anna for her holier-than-thou sanctimony, annoyed with Sheila for her off-the-wall frivolity, disappointed in Lars for the reckless way he had used his expertise, and vexed with Skip for his adolescent stupor. I was irked at Jane Fountain for the control freak she was, and exasperated at Moody, Slack, and Weeks for their unwillingness to act in the best interests of the Oasis.

Mostly, though, I was disgusted with myself for allowing hubris to propel me into this misadventure, and late that afternoon when Carl Harrison came limping into my office for our weekly drink and dinner, my customary simpatico was absent. I was in no mood to swap banter with him and listen to accounts of his sexual exploits.

He settled back in his chair, sipped his Absolut, and began to snipe away as usual. After pestering me about the community center and berating me for the good cards that consistently came my way in the poker games, he decided to home in on the personal.

"I hear you and Anna had a falling out - if that's the right way to put it."

I held my vodka short of my lips. "Anna and I are good friends. Period."

"If you say so. But I hear she's pissed at you."

I placed my glass on the table and looked at him for a few seconds. "What goes on between Anna and me is not your business."

I reached for the glass on the table, but my hands were trembling and I placed them in my lap. "It's time we had a Carl exchange. We have dinner once a week, we play poker, we chew the fat, but we don't share intimacies. So fuck off."

For the first time since I'd known him, his face reddened. He drained the rest of his vodka, placed his glass on the table, and I saw that *his* hands were trembling. He looked at me, "I've never heard you talk this way. You really are pissed."

"With good reason."

His eyes never leaving the bottle, he asked, "May I have another?"

"Be my guest."

He poured some vodka into his shot glass, his hands still unsteady. Leaving the glass untouched, he muttered, "I guess you see me as some kind of low-life."

"Close."

"That's a bad rap considering how I go to bat for you."

I was silent.

"Don't you want to know about that?"

"I really don't give a shit, Carl."

"I never heard you use language like that," he said.

"You already said that."

"I'll tell you anyway. Bunny's been bitching about your pushing to get a lawyer. She says you're throwing condo money around so your lawyer friend will get rich."

"She's not supposed to be talking to anybody about an executive session."

"A rule made to be broken. You want to hear more?"

"Yeah."

"She says you tried to get the Board to retain the lawyer because you've got some kind of cozy arrangement to split his take."

"Sonofabitch."

"You're sounding more like me than I do."

"I'm out of sorts and you're not helping."

"I guess Anna's not helping either."

I looked at him hard, and for the first time since high school I thought about starting a fist fight.

He raised both hands high in the air as though I were pointing a gun at him. "I'm sorry. You want more?"

I nodded.

"She says you tried to screw the condo out of a hundred thou because you've got some deal with the second lowest roof bidder, too."

Nikki had said she did not tell Hardy about the Board's vote, and I believed her. But Hardy knew, and it was my strong guess that Bunny told him. But why did Bunny pass it on to Carl Harrison of all people?

There was only one answer. Hardy wanted me to know he had a pipeline. When Bunny told him I had tried to award the job to Security and retain Maurice, he let her know he wouldn't mind my finding out he knew what had happened. Bunny knew that Carl, a rumor-spreading *agent provocateur*, and I met once a week.

"I want you to know," Carl continued, "I defended you. Getting a lawyer made sense to me, and giving the job to the more reliable company was the right thing to do."

"Thank you."

Was Carl no more than an unwitting messenger? Or was he in bed with Bunny in more ways than one?

"Listen," he said, "I wasn't going to tell you this because you're being so shitty, but I want you to know what sticking up for you cost me. I came on so strong about what a terrific President you are that she got pissed at *me*."

With mock-impersonation in his voice, he said, "*I'm going to have to think about our relationship.*"

"Why are you telling all this to me?"

"Because I'm your friend."

I reviewed the sequence of events in my mind.
- All the bids are in.
- The Board defeats awarding the contract to Security and retaining Maurice.
- Hardy, up-beat, calls Nikki. Somebody, not Nikki, had told Hardy the Board had selected District Roofing, and voted not to retain Maurice.
- The conspirators are angry with Hardy for not telling them to sell their EMI stock.
- Nikki gives me information about Hardy's San Juan junket.
- Hardy lets Bunny know he wouldn't mind my finding out what he knew.

A week later, nursing the tail end of a cold, I was sipping my late afternoon Absolut to the sound of Peggy Lee singing "Fever." A minute into the song my door bell rang. I opened the door and Anna was standing there.

"May I come in?"

I asked if she would like wine or coffee, and to my astonishment she asked for an Absolut on the rocks with a twist, the way I took it. She'd been having sleepless nights, she said, and the vodka might calm her.

"How have you been?" she asked.

"Edgy."

Looking at me, she took a sip of the Absolut, and said, "I've been thinking about us. Have you?"

"Have I what?"

"Been thinking about us."

"Day and night," I admitted.

She placed both hands around the glass of vodka and stared at it. "It's time to stop punishing myself and you as well."

I leaned forward to insure that not a word, not a syllable, would elude me. Yet, I couldn't contain myself. "Let me say, Anna, I . . ."

"Please - let me finish."

"Sorry."

She put her vodka glass to her lips, held it there, set it back onto the place mat sitting on the glass coffee table, and leaned back. "You are one mixed bag, Mr. Silva."

Again, I couldn't hold back. "Who isn't?"

"Ninety percent of the time it doesn't matter to me. You, I care about. Sheila says you're a dissembling bastard, but she sees a lot of good in you. You behave shabbily and hurt me. Then I find out you help people when there is nothing in it for you."

She placed her hands on her seat adjacent to her thighs. "Who is this person who means so much to me? Have I been sleeping with Dr. Jekyll or Mr. Hyde?" She plucked a Kleenex from the table, but her eyes were dry and she held onto it and began to laugh, softly. I tried, with little success, to join in with her.

After a time Anna told me what had happened. Maria, for all her assimilation, had hung onto some of her old-school ways. She had kept her silence about the assistance I'd given Mickey. This was an internal family matter - in Maria's eyes I was part of her family - and it was a cultural imperative that messy family matters not be discussed outside the family.

Maria had listened to Anna's rendering of our difficulties. Despite Maria's affection for Anna and me, she felt it would be inappropriate to act as a referee. Some weeks later, as Anna's disposition had shifted from agitation to dejection, Maria decided that tradition be damned, she would relate the story of my helpful hand to Mickey.

The second stage of Anna's resurrection - *my* resurrection - occurred when Nikki, elated over her new-found lawyer, shared with her friend, Anna, the story of how I used my "connections" to do this "good deed" for her, and, indeed, at my cost, not hers.

Anna asked, "May I have another Absolut?"

We talked into the evening. She ticked off the things I had done to offend her. It had become difficult for her to take me at my word. When Dr. Casanova had deeply hurt her, she lost the ability to trust, to stretch a point now and then. She had placed herself inside a "rigid unreal straitjacket."

"Nobody is a nicely-wrapped package of integrity and judgment. When you said we're entitled to extract whatever entertainment value is left, I thought that was coarse, but now, I'm not so sure. What are we supposed to do, wait for moral perfection?"

With a smile of semi-apology, Anna reflected. "There may be some higher being, who takes the measure of a person in terms of the kindness he's shown, and weighs that against the harm he's done, and comes out with a final tally. My responsibility is to be tolerant of people's shortcomings, including my own, and do what makes me feel good."

Elated, I felt a perverse urge toward jocularity. *Can we dispense with the philosophical disquisition and get down to business?* But I kept my mouth closed and managed to resist snatching defeat from the jaws of victory.

She looked at her watch. "It's 8:30. Is it too late to call Maria and see if she can squeeze us in? Assuming you want to resume our friendship."

On our way to the restaurant, I told her about Hardy's exuberance in his phone call to Nikki. Clearly, he had been informed about the two Board votes. I said I'd give two-to-one he got it from Bunny. Anna agreed.

"Are you still worried that Skip may be in jeopardy?" I asked.

"Yes. When did you last talk to him?"

"Two, three days ago."

Anna turned to me. "It's time you talked to him in person. I'd like to be there."

Maria greeted us without so much as a raised eyebrow. "No menus tonight," she said. "You eat what I bring you."

After ravioli, Maria brought us her "signature" dish, grilled veal chops. Toward the end of a wonderful evening, Maria stopped me on my way to the restroom.

"How did you do it?" she asked.

"Pure charm."

Everything was on the house. Arguing with Maria was futile.

A few days later, Anna and I set out for our prearranged meeting with Skip. Before we left, I had stopped off to speak with Nikki.

"Has Hardy said anything more about the roof job?" I asked.

"Not a word. He's pretty much left me alone the past few days."

We pulled up in front of the off-campus coffee shop and sat in the car, observing Skip inside, gesturing, laughing, and participating actively in what looked like an animated "rap session" with his classmates. This was a student comfortable in his environment.

When we entered the café, he came over and led us to a booth at the far end. He was genuinely delighted to see Anna, but at the same time he was fidgety, no doubt wondering why we had asked to see him.

Skip and I sat opposite Anna. After the coffee arrived, Anna said it was nice that Skip had made friends and was enjoying college. But he should think about transferring.

"Young people make mistakes," Anna said, "and so do seniors. We used bad judgment on this foolishness, and we're paying a price. We understand your reluctance to leave, Skip, but it would be better if you were away until this blows over."

Skip put up his hands. "Wait a minute. 'Til *what* blows over?"

Anna covered the familiar ground. Hardy had surely identified the virus in his computer and traced it to Skip. Hardy surely knew we had tried to retain counsel, and award a contract to a firm that was not supposed to win the bid. It was essential that Skip understand we were dealing with a man with a history of destructive behavior who was now outraged and knew Skip was involved.

"You've said you trust me, Skip," she said. "Maybe we're being over-cautious, but we think you should go back to the west coast."

Skip placed his clasped hands on the table, and looked around the room, then back to his hands. "You're both hysterical. I'm not going anywhere."

"I know your father has been on the phone with you about this," I said. "He found a good college in San Diego with a first-rate computer department. You'll have an apartment overlooking the Pacific Ocean. Everything you could possibly want."

"I'm staying right here."

His roaming eyes lit on Karen, Carl Harrison' granddaughter, who was entering the café. He got up, grinned at us, and said, "Have a nice day." He blew a soft kiss in our direction, and went to meet Karen.

One of Lars' former employees was now the head of the campus security police at AU. Lars talked to him, and the man promised to instruct his people to keep an eye on Skip. Lars wondered if we should hire professionals to conduct additional close watch of Skip. Anna said yes. I said I didn't think it was necessary. My call, of course.

Sitting on the bench between the buildings, I was absorbing the horticultural signs of spring. Wearing a deep scowl, Morton Moody ambled over to my bench and asked, "May I sit down with you?"

Extending my hand toward the scene in front of us, I said, "My pleasure."

He sank down cautiously as though he were testing the strength of the bench. "This may be your treasure, but for the rest of us it's a burden."

I enunciated slowly. "I said, my *pleasure*, not my *treasure*."

"Same thing," he said. "Your treasure or your pleasure, still my burden."

"I meant it would be my pleasure for you to sit . . . never mind. What's new in your world, Dr. Moody?"

"Thanks to you, we almost had the privilege of paying an extra hundred-thousand dollars for the new roof." He tried to cross his feet, didn't quite make it, and asked, "Tell me, where did you get the nerve to push so hard for this Security company?"

"It made sense for the reasons I presented at the meeting. The decision to push for something is at the discretion of the presidents."

"That's what I thought. The residents make that decision through the Board."

"No, I said the *presidents* make that decision, not the *residents*."

"Presidents, residents. You tried to spend a huge chunk of our money for nothing."

I raised my voice slightly. "I did what I thought was best for the Oasis."

"You forget you were elected President, not Dictator."

"What are you suggesting? That I be impeached?"

"I'm suggesting you have been running this Board as if it's your personal fiefdom."

I turned half way around on the bench to face him. "Since I've been President, every important decision has been submitted to the Board for a vote."

"Translated, you do what you want to do and expect the Board to rubber stamp it."

"Like what?"

"You push through an obscene fee increase, try to hire your buddy lawyer to pursue a frivolous allegation, try to have us pay a disgraceful premium to hire the *second* lowest bidder. You line up your flunkies. I don't know what you have on Rehnberg and Carroll, but they do whatever you say. But for Fountain you would have prevailed."

"I'll tell you what. I'll write out a check for $100,000 right now and deposit it in the Oasis account. Will that make you change your vote?"

"Don't patronize me, buster. You think I'm an old fool entering the first stages of senility. Well, let me give you the news. I still know when I'm being taken for a ride."

"I'm sure you do, but in this case you're imagining conspiracies that don't exist."

"I thought that's your department."

I got up, took a few steps, then came back, standing in front of him. "What is biting your ass, Dr. Moody? I have the feeling I'm missing something."

"Don't use that vulgar language with me. Save it for your poker games. Since you ask, I'll tell you what you're missing. The Board is supposed to be democratically elected, acting in the best interest of the owners, not in the members' personal interests."

"What are you referring to?"

"I'm referring to cozy deals with lawyer friends, sweetheart deals with contract providers. My nose tells me we're not done with that chicanery. You're riding high, Mr. President, but remember what they say. The higher they go, the harder they fall."

"You're out of order. I resent your implications."

"If the shoe fits wear it."

I sat back, looked around, and kept my mouth shut for a minute. Then I spoke carefully. "Will you do me a favor, Dr. Moody?"

"What?"

"Come to my place and have a cup of coffee with me."

"Why should I do that?"

"I want to get to know you better, and sitting down together over coffee might be conducive to that end."

His glance was just short of incredulity, but he said, "If you insist."

Laboriously, he made a move to get up. I extended my hand to help him and he brushed it away, sharply.

We sat in my living room, sipping the freshly brewed good stuff I had been saving for what I hadn't known. Now I knew. The conversation was sparse - "Nice place." "Thanks." - and I knew if there was going to be some kind of détente, ambiguous as it might be, I would have to initiate it. I put on a CD of the Brahms Second Piano Concerto, hoping it might have a calming influence on him.

We listened to those first three whole tones followed by the triplet followed by two more whole tones. I started to say something, but he shushed me. He stared straight ahead, and after a few minutes, said,

"That could be the Philadelphia with Ormandy conducting and Serkin playing. Recording from the middle fifties."

"*Very good.* How could you tell?"

"Ormandy took Brahms faster than most conductors. Brahms is special to me."

"To me, too."

"You don't strike me as a man who would like the likes of Brahms."

"I don't strike me, either, as a man who would like the likes of Brahms."

That evoked a flicker of a smile. "You wanted to get to know me better. What do you want to know?"

"Well, I already know we both like Brahms. What about your family?"

"There's just my wife, Agnes, and me. We spend time in Sarasota where we play golf and own a condo apartment. The condo is called Golden Harvest."

"Are you on the Board of Golden Harvest?"

"Hell, no, wouldn't be if they paid me. You think we've got problems with the Oasis? We've got the real thing down there - collusion, bribery, you name it."

"We're not without a touch of that here."

Looking at the ceiling, he said, "There he goes again." He lowered his eyes and sipped the last of his coffee. "What about your family?"

I gave him a rundown, and as an afterthought, I talked about Skip and my difficulty in communicating with him.

"At least you have a grandson," he said.

"What do you mean?"

He motioned for more coffee, and after I refilled our mugs, he looked directly at me for the first time. In a steady voice he said, "We had one child, a daughter, Grace. She drove a date to her senior prom and dropped him off afterwards. She was on her way home when a truck slammed into her. Killed on the spot. That was forty years ago."

I remained silent and, finally, said, "I'm sorry."

"We've learned to live with it. You can learn to live with almost anything. I'm even learning to live with old age."

"What kind of medicine do you practice?"

"Used to practice. Internal medicine. One day ten years ago I pre-scribed the wrong drug because I misheard the patient. Nothing ter-rible happened, but I knew it was time to hang it up. Even with these so-called state-of-the-art gadgets in my ears, my hearing won't win any prizes. And I know I can be cantankerous. Goes with the territory."

"I'm getting up there myself, and I know about grumpy."

"You can call me names, but I'm not frumpy. My appearance is fastidious."

"*Grumpy*, Dr. Moody, grumpy, not *frumpy*."

We laughed, and he said, "Call me Morton. Just consult more openly with the Board, will you?"

"Count on it," I said.

Chapter 14

The next month was tranquil. The campus security people called Lars once a week, and reported nothing suspicious. Skip revealed no sign that he was aware of their scrutiny. When Skip told me he had signed up for courses straight through the summer, Lars asked his friend to continue the surveillance at least during the summer. Anna and I reached the point where we could joke about my erstwhile duplicity. I was determined to be straightforward, tame the impetuous devil in my nature, and walk away from challenges.

The Board meetings were less rancorous. Fountain, the professional, contributed constructive input. Moody was less obnoxious than usual, even joking about his hearing loss. Slack, ever the parsimonious gadfly, missed no opportunity to offend someone, but her attacks now seemed to be softened. Weeks sat quietly in her pool of loneliness, and Lars and Anna were, as always, stalwart in their support of sensible policies.

I flattered myself into believing this kinder, gentler accommodation was the result of my conciliatory approach. Moody's criticism, for all its abrasive tone, may have had an ounce of merit. I conceded to myself that I had been heavy handed in pushing my agenda. I tried a lower-key approach and they seemed to respond in kind.

I called Skip, and he told me he had won an award for computer proficiency. Karen had been commuting from her Midwest college to see Skip. She had been accepted to AU Law School. She would move East in a few weeks.

The poker games had assumed a predictable pattern. There were the players who hung in with unpromising cards; those who "ran a bunny" - bluffed; those who bet "on the come" in the hope that a mediocre hand would develop; and those who handled defeat gracelessly - players "on tilt."

Sheila and I, the go-for-it players, secretly disdained the take-no-risk players, Carl and Travail. They in turn regarded us as reckless high-rollers. The solid middle-of-the-roaders, Lars and Charlie, were circumspect in their disapproval of both extremes.

The continuum of impaired hearing and vision ranged from mild to severe, and generated its own distinctive banter. On one hand Sheila bet and Travail called her. As she laid down her cards, she said, "Flush, my friend."

Travail, straining to read her cards across the table, said, "What do you mean, blush? Why should I blush?"

"I said flush, not blush," Sheila sighed. "Francis, if I kick in fifty percent, will you get a new hearing aid and better glasses?"

After the game Carl and I conducted a postmortem on the greenspace bench. On one hand I had held five, six, seven, eight, and had drawn a nine to the open-ended straight. Holding three tens, Carl had called me. Now, sitting in the moonlight, he asked, "Which one did you catch?" Instead of telling him the truth, the nine, I said, "The seven," indicating I had filled an inside straight - a "gut shot," one of the longest odds in poker.

He looked up at the moon. "You live right. Well, unlucky in love, lucky in cards."

The campus security people continued to report no irregularities. We resurrected the triumvirate activities, Sheila and I playing serious cribbage, Anna joining in reluctantly. In late April we drove to Montreal for a long weekend, this time with Sheila's friend, Clarence.

Upon our return from Canada, I learned that nothing had changed. No word from Hardy. A sense of normalcy prevailed.

There was a telephone message from Skip. "Hi, grandpa, thought I'd say hello. While you were away, we . . . uh . . . got some info about Hardy Oh, . . . it's nothing. Forget about it. Hope you had a good time. Bye."

What the hell was this all about? *We got some info about Hardy.* Who was "we"? Karen and Skip? Info about Hardy? And why the return to "grandpa" from "Sid"?

I called and caught him in. "How you doing, young man?"

"Great. Did you all have a nice time in Canada?"

"Yes, we did. Skip, what was your message about? What did you and Karen do? What was the information about Hardy? And how did you get it?"

"Everything's going fine."

"Are you alone right now, Skip?"

"No."

I related the conversation to Anna. It seemed to us that someone - probably Karen - had come into the room, and Skip did not want her to hear whatever it was he was trying to say. Anna felt we should see Skip sooner rather than later. I called him several times, finally reaching him, and after setting up a meeting, I asked, again, about his earlier message. He was unresponsive, saying only, "See you then, grandpa."

"By the way, Skip, just you, Anna and me as usual. Okay?"

"Yeah."

When we arrived at the same coffee shop the next day, Skip was waiting for us, and, to our surprise, Karen was with him. I didn't comment. Carl's appraisal of his granddaughter as a "looker," however subjective, had merit. But she had taken on a spare appearance. At Skip's farewell party, I saw a fresh rose. Now, the rose was faded.

Skip led off the discussion, telling us he had briefed Karen on everything he knew about our exploits. This irritated me, but I kept my mouth shut, and I avoided questioning him about his cryptic telephone message. Once again, Anna told Skip it would not be a bad idea for him to transfer to a college on the west coast.

His eyes glued to Karen, Skip said, "Karen just got here. She's planning to go to law school here. Why should we transfer?"

Looking at me with untroubled eyes, Karen asked, "Why *do* you want Skip to transfer? Why are you worried?"

"Not worried, Karen," Anna said, "just concerned."

Ignoring Anna, her eyes still fixed on me, Karen said, "Is it about Hardy?"

"Yes," I said.

"Has Hardy ever said anything to you about Skip?"

I was becoming the chief spokesman for Anna's belief that Skip had to leave. Although the intensity of my concern may have been a notch below hers, I had learned to trust her judgment.

"He made a reference to Skip."

Smiling, Karen said, "What was the reference, if I may ask?"

I said, "He asked about him."

Still smiling, Karen, said, "I understand, but what exactly were his words?"

The rose was on her way to become a thorny lawyer.

"'Nikki tells me your grandson is staying with you. How's he doing?' I said, 'fine,' and he said, 'A grandson is important in your life.'"

They looked like two people discovering they had been hoodwinked.

Skip said, "He asked how I'm doing, and he said I'm important in your life, and we should be concerned about this?"

Karen jumped in. "Skip *is* important in your life."

"Of course he's important."

"Maybe," Karen said, "somebody mentioned Skip to him without your knowing - like the property manager, Nikki, or the so-called spy on the Board - and he was just being nice to you. You are, after all, his client. "

"Nikki did mention Skip to Hardy," I said. Skip hadn't just "briefed" Karen, he had regurgitated every detail of every event.

"If he found out you tried to hire a lawyer, and tried to pick a bidder he didn't want, and he's angry, how would it help him to hurt Skip? If that's what you're getting at."

Her wide open blue eyes were pools of innocent curiosity, but I detected mockery behind her ingenuousness. "That's a good point, Karen. You must understand, we're dealing with a man who'll strike out at somebody if he feels his plans have been thwarted."

"Then why did you thwart him in the first place? Assuming your priority is to protect Skip, why did you try to get the Board to do these things?"

My respect for her intelligence was now competing with my distaste for her sarcasm. Why was this twenty-four-year-old girl friend of my eighteen-year old grandson giving me a hard time? And why was my grandson so reticent?

Anna touched me, signaling me to hold back.

"Sid could go to the Board," she said, "and tell them he's thought about it, and he's glad they turned him down on the lawyer, and he's glad they voted for the lowest bidder. But he'd be violating his obligations to the condo."

Anna paused. "Unless . . . is there something Sid and I don't know?"

I knew, and I believed Skip knew, that Anna was obliquely referring to Skip's mysterious phone message - and Karen be damned.

We looked at one another blankly, except for Skip whose eyes were resolutely focused on the lunch counter at the far end of the café.

"Skip," I said, "look at me. What was in your computer that I don't know about?"

Before Skip could answer, Karen cleared her throat. "So the only way out you see is for Skip - and me - to transfer somewhere far away."

"Yes," said Anna.

Karen looked at Skip. "Skip?" she asked.

"No way."

She looked at Skip with those same untroubled eyes. "Who would want to hurt this guy? He's a sweetheart." Skip glowed.

"Skip," I said, "I'd like to talk to you alone. Could we take a walk?"

Karen looked at Skip, and pointed to her wrist watch.

"Later for that, grandpa. I have a class, and I've got to go." They got up, waved a quick goodbye, and were gone.

I had assumed that sex was the glue that bound Skip to her. Did something more account for her Svengali-like hold over him? And what did she see in *him*? A pet?

I called Mickey, Maria's nephew. What I intended to do did not require that Mickey be with me, but some sixth sense said, have him there. Besides, he might supply a modicum of fun to the enterprise.

"Can you meet me tomorrow night at Buona Sera? Seven o'clock?"

"No problem."

I called Anna, and said I was going to have dinner with Mickey at Buona Sera. "Do you mind?" I asked.

"Of course not. Are you planning to do something rash?"

My laugh was false. "Well, to tell you the truth, I was planning to order lamb chops instead of veal. That's pretty rash for me."

"Why do I have trouble believing you?"

I got to the restaurant at 6:30, before the rush period, and Maria sat me down at the semi-secluded table for two on which I always had first claim. I watched her greet guests and lead them to their tables, chatting in that warm professional manner of hers. I had always been impressed with her ability to compartmentalize.

At one point, she came over and said, "Why are you having dinner with Mickey?"

"I like him, and a couple of hours with him gets my mind off my troubles."

She looked at me skeptically. "You're hatching something."

Mickey arrived, his brawny, six-one frame all muscle, even more prepossessing than I had remembered. Clean living agreed with him. Maria got up from the table, embraced him, and said, "Be careful with this man, sweetheart."

Mickey laughed. "Yeah, I'll be careful."

Maria glanced at the line of customers forming near the front door, turned on her proprietress-smile, and went about her business.

Mickey told me he loved school and the job at Silva Construction was great. He'd even been talking to my successor about a full-time job in the accounting department after he graduated. We ordered our meal, and Mickey shared some gossip about high-level people who had arrived at Silva Construction after my departure. I laughed and relaxed.

As we had our dessert and coffee, I told Mickey everything that had happened from the time I was elected to the Board until the present. I took him through each event, step by step, sparing nothing, including detailed reports on the crucial Board meetings.

"Hardy," I said, "has put together a conspiracy that is hurting the condo, and at the moment we're helpless to do anything about it."

"I hear you. What can I do to help you?"

I avoided a direct answer and we talked for another thirty minutes, drinking our way through too much coffee. Every so often Maria would come idling by, her antenna at full strength. Without so much as a wink, we automatically launched into basketball talk when she came within ten feet of us.

Again, he said, "What do you want me to do?"

I hesitated telling Mickey my plan. Maybe I was afraid he would laugh out loud. I said I needed him to be with me when I came face to face with Hardy.

"You met with him in his office and had lunch with him. Why see him again?"

"I'm not sure." I was sure, but I wasn't ready to share it yet.

"I'll do anything you want," Mickey said, "but I don't get it."

"I'll tell him what I know about his activities."

"What will you do when he says, I don't know what you're talking about?"

"He'll know that I know."

Mickey looked puzzled, but was quiet.

"We'll talk some more," I said, glancing quickly in the direction of Maria. "In the meantime, please keep all of this . . ."

"Are you kidding? Not a word."

I got Skip on the phone. Would he like to spend a weekend with me in San Juan? Mickey was going, too. Get away from the grind? "No thanks," he said. He was "tied up with classes." Evasive as usual.

Hardy was next, and when I accepted his invitation to San Juan, he was hardly evasive. "That's great, Sid. It's on me, of course."

I said I'd pay my own way and added, "See you at the Ritz-Carlton."

Damn, damn. Hardy had not mentioned the hotel when he said his junket would be in San Juan. It was Nikki who had told me it would be at the Ritz-Carlton, and I had assured her of confidentiality. *Everything between you and me stays between you and me.*

And now I had betrayed her. My mind had been preoccupied with a dozen things, and the words had come dribbling out of my mouth like spittle from a senile man.

After a brief pause, Hardy reiterated, "I'm glad you're coming. See you there."

Had I been saved by the bell? Or had he caught it, and was biding his time?

The next day Mickey and I strolled around the greenspace in the mellow May air, and I guided him to the bench between the buildings. That hallowed bench where Anna and I had conducted our first, untroubled, conversation a year earlier.

We sat down and I said, "How'd you like to go to San Juan?"

"Wow . . . okay, I'll bite. What's it all about?"

"Hardy will be there with Travail. He invited me."

"So *this* is what you're talking about. What do we do there?"

"I'll play some blackjack with them, and then I'll get them over to the poker table. I've been on a streak in our condo games, and I believe in streaks."

"How much do you expect to win?"

"Maybe six figures. I'll steer him to the no-limit table. I'll win."

Mickey looked at me as though I had suggested we tell Maria the food at Buona Sera was tasteless.

"Suppose you *lose* six figures?"

"Brad gets that much less when I die."

"It's crazy, but as I told you, I'll do anything you want."

"I invited Skip, but he's tied up. By the way, you like to play blackjack, right?"

"I know the basics, but I'm not a whiz. Don't take offense, Sid, but you sure have a pair of balls."

Huffing and puffing, Francis Travail caught up with me the next day in the cheese aisle of the supermarket. He looked like a superannuated steam engine, clinging to memories of the old days when he chugged ahead and nothing could stop him

"Tell me what's going on in your young life," I said.

"Hanging in. Be out of town for a few days. A quick get-away." He mustered a wink that must have cost him precious energy. "Little of this, little of that. Get my drift?"

"I think so. You're up for some fun."

"Isn't that what it's all about?"

Had Hardy told Travail I'd be in San Juan? Was Travail playing games with me?

While Anna was preparing her chili, I thought about the best way to break the news about my trip to Puerto Rico with Mickey. I had begun to lay a foundation by telling her how relaxed I was with Mickey and how he had earned a vacation. At that point I experienced a rare moment of epiphany. Instead of giving her a dissembling "cover story," why not simply tell her the truth? I rushed out the words.

"Hardy invited me to San Juan. I plan on winning a lot of money and giving it to the Oasis to induce the Board to retain Maurice and hire Security Roofing. Mickey will be with me."

"What in the world are you talking about?"

"Hardy asked me to join one of his so-called junkets in San Juan. I'm going to take him up on it, and try to roll over him at the poker table. You were at the Board meeting. The votes boiled down to a question of money. Right?"

"That's true, but you're talking about fifty to a hundred thousand dollars. I can't believe you're serious."

"Believe it."

"Have you ever played poker in a casino?"

"Now and again."

Anna glanced at me as we sat down. I put the radio on, softly, and we ate.

"You were saying Mickey will be with you?" Anna said.

"Yes. He went through a tough period, and he seems to have straightened himself out. I thought he'd like a break."

"Maybe deep down he's a surrogate for what you had hoped Skip would be like."

"Could be. As a matter of fact, I invited Skip, and he said he was too busy. Anyway, Mickey also loves to play blackjack, and so do I."

"So you're going there to test your skills at the tables. Drink some wine, get some sun on the beach, look at the sexy women."

"That's about it, plus win some money."

"Suppose you *lose* some money.'"

"I'll be disappointed."

"When do you plan to do this?"

"Memorial Day weekend."

"You do understand I think this is crazy."

"Yes."

"Are you giving me the whole story?

"Yes. This time yes." Damned if I do, damned if I don't.

I had planned that Mickey and I would talk about timing and strategy on the plane to San Juan. But the flight was bumpy, and we held off on the discussion.

We picked up the car I had reserved at the airport in case we had a chance to explore the island. There was little traffic, and we checked into the Ritz-Carlton at noon. As I was signing in, out of the corner of my eye I saw Mickey checking out the minimally clad women standing around the tiled lobby. A few were checking out Mickey, too.

It was as I had imagined. Everybody seemed to be infused with geniality. The locals were eager to please the tourists, and the tourists were good natured. The weather was glorious, the beaches stunning, the restaurants first rate, and our suite and amenities were designed to confer good cheer upon the most captious misanthrope.

It was one in the afternoon, and Mickey suggested we discuss our plans at the pool while the sun was high.

"Good idea," I said. "Our friends checked in yesterday, and they won't be hanging around a swimming pool. They'll be at the blackjack tables or in suite 703 with hookers."

"How do you know their room number?"

"Inquiry at the desk - told them I'm planning a special surprise for some old friends. That and a twenty-dollar bill."

We took adjacent reclining chairs on the pool deck. There must have been close to fifty people in the area, most of them intermittently applying cream and oil to already tan bodies. Nobody, not even the topless women, was sunburned.

The pool was large, with bridges, trestles, long-curving slides, and underwater passages. Within my range of vision was a "water bar" where drinkers could sip their margaritas and rum punches sitting on stools set in the water.

The women in the pool area, from eighteen to fifty, showed their interest in Mickey with side-long peeks, over-the-shoulder glances, and outright stares. Mickey, a neglected sprout finding sunlight and water, basked in the glow of their attention. A few women smiled at me, no doubt figuring I might be an entrée to this Adonis, probably my grandson.

Lying on her stomach next to Mickey was a woman whose black hair fell half-way down her bare back. She lifted her head to take a measure of Mickey. A few minutes later, she sat up topless, straight as an arrow, and I looked at the tattoo of a cupid's heart on her shoulder. Running through the heart from bottom left to top right was an arrow. Next to the bottom of the arrow were the initials "BG." Next to the top of the arrow were the words, "Mr. Lucky."

The woman turned to face Mickey, gave him an angelic smile, handed him a small tube, and said, "Would you be good enough to rub some of this on my back?"

"My pleasure," said Mickey, and played it as though this request was routine. The woman, maybe forty, resumed her stomach-down position, and Mickey massaged the lotion onto her back. When he was finished, she turned her face up to him, said, "Thanks, honey bun, my name is Beth Goody. I owe you," and turned back onto her stomach.

Mickey turned toward me. "I could get to like this place."

"If I can tear you away from your fans I'll give you my plan. I'll point out Hardy and Travail, and you'll drift around the blackjack area, watching them. I'll find a slot machine where they won't see me. When I think the time is right, I'll join them at their table. They'll be expecting me . . . OH, SHIT, here they come, hookers and all."

Sporting a terrycloth robe and sandals, aviator sunglasses framing his hooded eyes, Chuck Hardy came striding into the opposite end of the pool area like a Roman emperor surveying his vassals. Waddling behind him was Travail, decked out the same way, and in Travail's wake were two blonde voluptuaries in bikinis even scantier than the one Beth Goody was wearing. They were making a bee-line for the water bar.

"Time for us to move," I said.

We gathered up our towels, my P.D. James book, Mickey's "Modern Accounting Procedures," and were out of there in seconds, but not before Mickey leaned down to Beth and said, "See you around, honey bun."

In our suite, we sipped Evian. "They had sex," I said. "Then the girls wanted to go to the pool where they could advertise their wares. They'll get rid of the girls quickly, and head for the casino. That would put them at the tables around three."

Mickey shook his head. "I don't think so. I say the girls got them to the pool first so they can work up their appetites and negotiate for more money. They'll be back in their suite with the girls in about an hour. Tables around four."

Pretty sophisticated for a kid, I thought. I went with his scenario.

Sarah and I used to play blackjack occasionally in Atlantic City. We lost a little more than we won, but we loved the action.

Mickey and I worked out a strategy. I explained that it was not unusual for two or three people to stand behind the blackjack players, watching and silently second-guessing the play. Mickey could blend in and wander inconspicuously among the tables, keeping a covert eye on Hardy and Travail. I would feed quarters to a slot machine where I could watch the blackjack area.

"Tell me what you know about the game," I asked.

"Highest number up to twenty-one wins. The players are dealt two 'up' cards. The dealer gets the first card 'down,' second card 'up.' An ace plus a ten-value card is blackjack, and beats everything except another blackjack. That's a 'push,' a tie."

"Also," I said, " the players are competing against the dealer. Different from poker where the players compete against one another."

It was late afternoon - almost four - when we entered the gargantuan "gaming room." The place shrieked with energy, neon lights everywhere. But no windows, no clocks. Sections for roulette, poker, craps, baccarat, and blackjack were roped off separately. The din of the slots was pervasive, interspersed with pleas of "BE THERE" from the crap tables. I could faintly hear Sinatra singing. *I Tried So, Not To Give In.*

Hordes of people, from twenty-somethings to eighty-somethings, roamed the place, most of them in jeans and sneakers. Everybody was busy, and nobody appeared to be out of place in the garish ambience.

We were smack in the middle of one of the safest, most secure places in the world. I knew that security personnel mixed with the crowd, watching for any sign of errant behavior, and that ceiling cameras peered down on all of us like unseen stars in the sky searching for the anomalous cheat, the pickpocket, the drunk.

I surveyed the large blackjack area until I spotted Hardy and Travail. I pointed them out to Mickey, and said that in a short while they would be absorbed in the game. After I bought a pouch filled with fifty dollars worth of quarters, I selected my slot machine and dispatched Mickey on his assignment.

"Keep your eye on me," I said. "If I should need to talk to you, I'll touch my nose twice - like this. They shuffle the six decks every twenty minutes or so. We'll wait for the next shuffle - takes five minutes - and meet in the men's room."

I believed that blackjack, like poker, was eighty percent luck and twenty percent skill. With slot machines, skill played no role, and after thirty minutes of non-cerebral exercise, I was coasting, about even, when a voice I knew cut through the cacophony of the slots like the sound of a fingernail scratching on a blackboard.

"I'll be damned," Chuck Hardy said. "Sid Silva in person. Finds me even though I never mentioned the Ritz-Carlton."

"A high roller like you stays at the best - and this is the best."

"How are you doing on the machines?"

"Dead even."

"You want to make money, blackjack is the way to go."

Pointing, he said, "I'm going to the john. You get rid of your kiddy quarters, then come with me. You'll see your friend, Travail."

I had forgotten about the men's room near my slot machine. I checked out the thick wad of hundreds in my wallet before Hardy came back. We walked over to the blackjack section.

Exuding good fellowship, he put his arm around my shoulder. "Glad it worked out for you to be here." As we used to say, Hardy was playing it fat, dumb and happy. But his mind had to be racing.

"Been okay, Sid?"

"Fine. Business good?"

"Couldn't be better."

Hardy was at one of twelve blackjack tables, each containing seven stools in a semicircle facing the dealer. Every table was connected to the adjoining table by a purple velvet rope, preventing the customers from trespassing into the area behind the dealer. In that forbidden area, impeccably behaved men in dark suits and women in tailored slacks monitored the dealers, discreetly observed the customers, and, from time to time, conferred softly with one another.

A sign on the table said, "Minimum Bet $100, Maximum Bet, $5000." Six stools were occupied. The "third base" stool, to the dealer's immediate right, was empty, and Hardy motioned me to sit there. It was 4:45.

Gamblers tend to indulge superstitions, such as choice of attire (wear the striped blue shirt) and gastronomic rules (eat a hard-boiled egg one hour before playing). I was no stranger to these rites, placing a ten-dollar bill in the side pocket of my pants on the theory that Alexander Hamilton would impart some of his fiscal brilliance. I observed another stratagem. If I felt uncomfortable with a person sitting next to me, I bet the minimum. If I took a liking to that person, I'd up the bet. But I tried to put that nonsense out of my mind.

As of now, I am part of the action.

The perky dealer, in her mid-forties with short red hair, is wearing a name tag, "Dolly." While she shuffles the six decks, diligently observing each step of the house-prescribed procedure, I survey the other six players.

Travail is sitting in the "first base" seat, to the left of the dealer, directly opposite me. He is wearing jeans, like Hardy, and his linen plaid shirt is a duplicate of Hardy's. I had noticed that same shirt in the window of the lobby boutique, with a price tag of $235. Travail sees me, does a double take, gives me a thin smile, and looks inquiringly at Hardy. So Hardy hadn't told him I would be there.

"Look who I found, Francis, we lucked out," Hardy says, sitting down in the center of the semicircle. "He's going to teach us the ropes."

"Don't hold your breath," I say with a smile. I wonder how much money Hardy had slipped Travail before they sat down to play.

Next to me is an Asian woman of grace, exquisite cheek bones, and indeterminate age. Sketches of pagodas adorn her ankle-length dress. When I arrived, she had smiled and extended her hand, helping me mount the high stool. Privately, I call her "Exotica." Reaching into my pocket to tap Hamilton three times, I think I'll like Exotica.

To Exotica's right is a girl in jeans, stringy dirty-blonde hair, and an inch of pudgy midriff framing the bottom of her tight-fitting sweater. On the street, I would peg her at eighteen. Within everyone's hearing, she turns toward Exotica, and says, "I still don't get this game. Daddy gave me a thou for my twenty-first birthday? He said *that's it*, so, you know, I'd better win. You look like you know what you're doing. You'll help me, no?"

"I'll be happy to make suggestions," Exotica says, "but please understand there are no guarantees."

"Oh, compared to me you're a pro. You know what I mean?"

I dub this one, "Airhead."

To Hardy's right is an elderly woman in a faded print dress. The sour-dour expression on her heavily lined face must have been stamped onto her from birth. Her repertoire does not seem to include smiling. "Grumpy."

The seventh player, lanky, taciturn and in his forties, sits between Grumpy and Travail. The lapels of his blue blazer are impeccably rolled, not pressed, and he must think his red-flowered tie is a magnet to women. I've seen him before. Where? Long black hair tied in back, five-day growth. I've got it! Of course. When I went to see Hardy this guy was sitting outside Hardy's office, leaning against the wall. "No-shave."

Dolly finishes shuffling the six decks, and is placing them in the "shoe." I push twenty one-hundred-dollar bills toward her, and, with a smile and a "good luck," she places twenty blue chips in front of me.

Hardy is an aggressive player. He behaves well despite the free Scotch the "drinks girl" brings him.

After five or six routine hands, Hardy bets a thousand dollars and is faced with the bane of blackjack players, a sixteen. When do you "hit" - take another card - a sixteen? The dealer must hit with sixteen or less and "stay" - take no more cards - on seventeen or more. The player may hit or stay. "Smart money" says the player should hit a sixteen against the dealer's seven through ace, and stay with a sixteen against the dealer's two through six.

A ten and a six are face up in front of Hardy, and Dolly's up-card is a six. Defying the experts, Hardy hits his sixteen, receives a two, and stays with eighteen. Dolly flips her down card, an eight, giving her fourteen. She turns a six, giving her twenty. Dolly wins.

Grumpy's grumbles to herself when she loses, which is most of the time. After Hardy loses with his eighteen, Grumpy half-turns toward him, and mumbles, loudly enough for everyone to hear, "Never hit a sixteen against a six."

Hardy pauses, and points a warm smile at Grumpy. "You're absolutely right, ma'am. I wasn't thinking. If I'd listen to you, I'd be all right. You know your stuff."

Grumpy squeezes out a hint of a grin "The way my cards are falling tonight, it doesn't matter. But thanks, you're okay."

Hardy, the charmer without peer.

Exotica and I begin to swap comments about the play of the cards. When I'm dealt natural blackjack twice in a row - ace and face card - she says, "You live right." On the very next deal, Exotica hits a twelve with a nine, and I counter, "Look who's talking." We're enjoying the repartee, and with a winning streak going, I'm making heavy bets.

Mickey and I maintain periodic eye contact. I see him walk over to the nearby lounge, order a small bottle of mineral water, return to a close-by table, and catch my eye. He is ready whenever I need him.

During the first couple of hours, there's no stopping me. I'm dealt blackjack one hand out of six, paying one and a half times the bet. And I'm now betting two to three thousand dollars per hand. I'm hitting sixteens with fours and fives, and splitting aces, catching nothing but face cards for twenty-one. I'm ahead by about $11,000.

Hardy, on the other hand, has lost about $7,000 by my rough estimate. He is getting terrible cards and is playing them recklessly - a doomed combination.

Travail tries to emulate Hardy in the play of his cards, and outdoes Hardy on booze consumption. His cards are no better than Hardy's, and as Travail's losses mount, his mood darkens to match that of Hardy. Perspiration lines Travail's forehead, and the Scotch is beginning to take its toll.

At one point, Airhead has a pair of queens in front of her. She asks Exotica, "I split these, right?"

Exotica quietly says, "You always stay with twenty. Never, never split two face cards, pair or no-pair."

Dolly, a six showing, turns over her down card. It is a ten giving her sixteen, and, as required, she hits the sixteen. It is a five for twenty-one.

As Dolly pulls in the chips, Airhead glares at her and says, in an abrasive whimper, "Not fair. Where did that five come from? Inside your bra?"

No-shave drools out a smile from across the table, "Now calm down, li'l darlin', Dolly's just doing her job."

Airhead switches her stare from Dolly to No-shave, and her eyes reveal a spark of interest. No-shave says, "Come with me to the lounge over there. I'll buy you a drink and we can talk about it."

Eyebrows raised, Hardy shoots a dire look in the direction of No-shave who then says, "Let's make that later, l'il darlin', I've got a small streak going right now."

Later, when Dolly is replaced by Judy, a no-nonsense type, Exotica is on a small winning streak, and bets $250, her biggest bet of the night. She is dealt the deadly sixteen against Judy's nine. Exotica leans toward me and says, "What do you think?"

"Do it."

Exotica taps the table lightly with her forefinger, indicating, "Hit me," and Judy deals her a five for twenty-one. Judy flips her hole card, a seven, and is required to hit the resulting sixteen. It's a four, giving her twenty. Exotica wins. She turns toward me and, in a tone of mock-wonder, says, "You're a genius."

"It takes one to know one," I say, and we laugh.

Hardy looks at me, and says, "You've got it all going, Sid. Good cards and a beautiful new friend from the enchanting East." He pauses and decides to remind me of his pipeline. "But Anna's not going to like this romantic development in your life."

A few minutes later, Exotica gives me a pat on the back and a quick smile, and moves on. It is 6:45.

Airhead takes Exotica's seat and says, "You'll help me, won't you?"

"If I can, but don't count on it."

Exotica's departure and Airhead's proximity spell the end of my streak. I bet the minimum, but it doesn't matter. By 7:45 I've lost my winnings and I'm even. By 8:30 I'm out $5,000. I tap Hamilton repeatedly to no avail. I'm trying to ignore Airhead, but she won't stop pestering me for advice. The superstition is being validated.

In the same period, Hardy's worm has turned. Everything - the cards, his play - is going his way. He is placing maximum - $5,000 - bets, and winning four out of five times. By eleven, I figure his winnings have to be in six figures.

Around 8:45 Travail, perspiring freely, places five blue chips in the rectangle in front of him. This represents $500, more than he has bet all evening. He is transgressing an inviolable principle of the tables. Increase the size of your bets when you're on a winning streak, bet the minimum when you're losing. Cut your losses.

Travail is dealt an ace and a six, a "soft" seventeen. He has the option of counting the ace as a value of one, giving him a total of seven, or as an eleven giving him a total of seventeen. Dolly, who has returned, says, "Seven or seventeen."

Dolly has a six showing. When Travail said, "I'll stay with these," everyone at the table - even Airhead - is still. The greenest neophyte knows you *always* hit a soft seventeen against a four, five, or six. Dolly flips over her down card, revealing a ten. Her ten and her six give her sixteen. She is required to take a hit. She does, and deals herself a three for a total of nineteen. If Travail had hit, *he* would have been dealt the three which would have given him twenty.

As Dolly scoops up Travail's chips, Hardy finally loses his cool. He leans toward Travail. "Everybody knows you hit a soft seventeen, Francis. You getting old or what?"

His voice raised a notch, Travail says, "Mind your own business, Chuck. You play your cards, I'll play mine."

Hardy half rises from his stool.

At this point the pit boss with a slight resemblance to Robert De-Niro leaves his section, and walks around the table to the players. He whispers something in Travail's ear. Moving along, he whispers something in Hardy's ear.

Glancing at Travail, Hardy says, "Time to cash in our chips, Francis."

Two more rules at the blackjack table. You never antagonize the dealer and you never argue when the pit boss suggests that you need a break.

It is almost 9.

Chapter 15

I caught Mickey's eye, and beckoned him to join us. Hardy, Travail, and I got up from our stools, and so did No-shave. Pointing toward him with his thumb, Hardy said, "This is Gus. He's my bodyguard."

Gus - No-shave - nodded slightly, but did not extend his hand. I said, "Why do you need a bodyguard, Chuck? Looks to me like you can take good care of yourself."

"You never know."

The four of us made our way to the cashier cage to redeem our chips. Gus walked with a decided limp, slowing our pace, and Mickey quickly caught up with us.

"This is my friend, Tony." I said.

Hardy stopped, and looked "Tony" over, from his sneakers to his jet black hair. He shoved out his hand to Mickey, and looking at me, asked, "Your bodyguard?"

"Do I need one, Chuck?"

"How should I know?"

His eyes went back to Mickey. "This is a dude not to mess with. What's your last name, Tony?"

Without missing a beat, Mickey said, "Delano."

"Where are you from, Tony Delano?"

"The Washington area," Mickey said.

Hardy shifted his glance to me, and I said nothing.

We walked over to the cashier's box, and I watched Hardy push the container overflowing with blue chips toward the chubby, bald cashier wearing a white shirt and clear-framed glasses. It took him about five minutes to count the chips, from time to time scratching numbers on a small white pad.

When the cashier finished, he looked at Hardy and said, "$151,250."

Hardy had won three times as much money as the cash he had brought with him. He said, "Sounds good to me."

The cashier smiled. "Are you planning to play some more?"

"Hell, yes," Hardy said.

"Suppose I give you ten thousand in cash, the rest in the form of a voucher you can cash in with the hotel cashier or use it to play with?"

"That'll do it. Hundred-dollar bills, please."

After Hardy filled out the tax form, the cashier made out the voucher check, placed 100 hundred-dollar bills into a black leatherette zippered pouch marked, "Guest of Ritz-Carlton," and handed the check and the pouch to Hardy. Travail cashed in chips amounting to a hundred-ten dollars, representing, I was certain, a big loss. I had lost close to $20,000, but for some unfathomable reason I was not dispirited - not yet.

Flushed with his winnings, Hardy said, "Who's up for a little Texas Hold 'Em?"

This was the question I was on the verge of asking, and I was pleased that he got there first. "Hey," I said, "you read my mind. I'd like to take a half hour break, go to the room, freshen up. We'll meet you at the poker tables."

When we got inside our room, it was 9:30. I told Mickey a hunch had crossed my mind. I'd like him to play poker with the rest of us. I would, of course, stake him.

"I know the game, but I've never played in a casino," he said.

"I'm going to give you a crash course on Texas Hold 'Em."

As we munched on candy and bottled water from the mini bar, I explained the system. Remember, I said, the players compete against one another, not against the house. The house takes a cut from each pot.

The player to the dealer's left places a wager called the "small blind." The players to his left posts another bet called the "big blind." These bets establish the ante. The first player after the big blind has the opportunity to match the big blind, raise, or fold, and the process continues around the table.

The house dealer distributes two cards, face down, to each player. Then the dealer lays five "community cards," face down, in front of him or her. After each players peeks at his two cards, betting begins, and each players can call, raise, or fold.

"Are you following so far?" I asked.

"Pretty much."

The dealer turns up three of the five community cards lying on the table. This is called the "flop," and each player can check, call, bet, raise, or fold in turn, considering the value to his hand of some or all of the cards in the flop.

Now the dealer turns over the fourth community card - the "turn" - and once again, the players can check, call, bet, raise or fold. Finally, the fifth card, or "river," is turned up, and the last round of betting takes place. Any or all of the players can use any three of the five community cards - the "flop," the "turn," and the "river" - along with their two down cards in formulating the best five out of the seven cards, and determining how to bet - or not bet.

"I'll give it my all," Mickey said.

"Can't ask for more."

Once more, I'm part of the action.

It is now 10 o'clock. Six men and two women are sitting - some straight up, some sprawled out - around a poker table. Two of the men and one of the women are wearing baseball caps, and all of them are trying, unsuccessfully, to look relaxed. Hardy, Travail, No-shave, Mickey, and I are standing around watching, because all ten tables, some accommodating eight players, some six, are full.

After a few minutes, a pleasant looking guy in a suit and tie comes over, and says, "All of you waiting for a table?"

"Yes," we say.

"We're opening a new table, six players. It will be no-limit stakes."

"Beautiful," Hardy says.

We sit down, and again I take the seat on the extreme left. The chair next to me is empty, and the others occupy the remaining four chairs.

The handwriting is on the wall beginning with the very first hand. The flop is a seven, king, and six, the turn is a four, and the river is a six. My down cards are a five and a six. I have three sixes, and in the last round I bet $10,000. Hardy raises $20,000 and I call. He turns his down card - two kings, giving him three kings. Hardy's winning streak at blackjack is carrying over to Texas Hold 'Em.

Over the next hour I'm constantly patting Alexander Hamilton in my pocket, but Hamilton is having none of it. Hardy is on a remarkable roll. The other three seem to be breaking even. Hardy's money is coming from me, and I've twice dipped into my line of credit with the hotel. I'm now playing ultra-conservatively, folding on promising down cards and calling instead of raising, even when my hand is auspicious.

Hardy keeps winning and I keep losing. And he is anything but magnanimous in victory. "Beginning to understand the game?" he asks after edging out my queen-high straight with a low flush.

By 11:30 I've stopped calculating how much money I've lost. I'm playing with that gambler's hope that it will change, that nothing stays the same. At midnight I'm staring down into my depleted pile of chips, reviewing in my mind the dumb things I've done in my life. Coming to San Juan has to be at the top of the list. *Now* I'm dispirited.

"Hello again."

The sound of Exotica's voice penetrates like a sudden burst of sunshine on a wintry day. I help her into the seat next to me, and she smiles, no doubt remembering the reversed process on the blackjack stools a few hours ago.

"Where have you been?" I ask.

"Here and there."

Hardy can't resist. "Ah, Miss Mysterious, you're back. Anna won't like it, but maybe you'll bring your new friend some Chinese luck." I'm hoping that Hardy is as clairvoyant as he is insensitive.

Exotica plays warily, betting with good cards, but raising infrequently. Travail, No-shave, and Mickey continue to be up a little, down a little. My cards are improving, and I'm playing more aggressively. As Hardy's winning streak begins to wilt, my despair begins to fade.

Hardy ignores the cut-your-losses rule and is betting large amounts of money. He scowls when he loses, and the breezy wisecracks attending his earlier behavior have become petulant jabs. On one hand Mickey wins a bigger-than-usual pile of chips, and Hardy looks at the table in front of him. "Mr. Delano thinks he's something special. He'll find out he's nothing before we're through."

Even Gus, the bodyguard, is not spared from Hardy's bad-tempered potshots. After Hardy's ace-high straight loses to Gus' flush, Hardy glares at him. "Just don't forget your place here." As the downward slide of his cards accelerates, the Scotch takes its toll. The affable charmer without peer has metamorphosed into the petulant loser without grace.

At one point Hardy rises from his chair, looks at his three neatly stacked piles of chips, says to the house dealer, "I'm going to the restroom," and walks away. The dealer places a "marker" on the table in front of Hardy's chair to save his place. When Hardy returns a few minutes later, he tosses the marker at the dealer, looks at the three stacks, and asks, "What happened to my fourth stack?"

"There were three stacks when you left, sir," the dealer says. Hardy looks questioningly at Gus who says, "He's right, Chuck. Three stacks."

"What did you all do? Divide up the fourth stack?" Nobody at the table meets his gaze. Could this be a manifestation of clinical paranoia? Am I witnessing the disintegration of his psyche?

A few hands later, Hardy makes a mammoth bet, and on the strength of my down cards - a pair of jacks - I raise. The others drop out, and Hardy and I swap giant raises. The flop doesn't help me, but the turn is a jack - more bets and raises - and the river is, astonishingly, the fourth jack. The odds are now astronomical that I have the "nut" - the controlling hand.

Hardy makes his biggest bet of the night, and I raise. Hardy raises, I raise, Hardy raises, and I raise again. Hardy says, "I don't want to take *all* your money," and he calls me. Hardy has a full house and I have four jacks. I've now recaptured my losses, and I'm ahead. Hardy's scowl is now etched in place.

We play for another hour, Exotica and I trading whispers. "I'd throw it in." "I'd go all out with a pair in the hole." I have won a lot of money.

Hardy's losing streak is avalanching, and he has long ago shifted from winner to whiner. He sees us whispering, but can't hear what we're saying. Looking at the dealer and pointing to us, he says, "Do we have to put up with this steady stream of bullshit?"

"There is no house rule, sir, prohibiting conversation between the players - so long as they keep it low."

Hardy has figured out that Exotica is a charm for me. "Why don't you go back to the blackjack tables?" he says to her. "You look tired. You'll do better over there."

"I think not," she says. No smile.

At 1:30 Travail folds after the flop, and Mickey wins the pot with a pair of fives. Travail says, "I've had enough." "Me too," says No-shave, ignoring Hardy, and after a nod from me, Mickey says, "Me too."

"It's fine with me if you want to keep playing, Silva," Hardy says.

"No, thanks."

As we collect our chips and get ready to leave, I turn to Exotica and ask, softly, "Tell me, what is your name?"

"Sandra, but my friends call me Exotica. They think that's sexy. When you have a chance, tell your obnoxious buddy that I was born in New York, and my roots are Vietnamese, not Chinese. And by the way . . . I hope all goes well with Anna."

We walked toward the cashier, and Hardy said, "Come to my room for a drink." The gruffly spoken words were more of a command than an invitation.

Last in line, I watched the others cash in their chips, and I estimated that Mickey, Travail and No-shave came close to breaking even. The big loser was Hardy who watched closely as I signed the tax form and as the cashier carefully counted my chips and gave me a certified check for just over $200,000. Most of it was from Hardy.

There was no conversation in the elevator or along the seventh floor corridor. When we got outside Hardy's room, Gus - No-shave - promptly sat down in the chair propped against the corridor wall outside Hardy's door.

Once inside the large suite, Hardy carried his black pouch into one of the two adjoining bedrooms, closing the door behind him. In a few minutes he came back, went directly to the mini-bar, and poured four miniature bottles of Johnny Walker Black into glasses with a splash of water. I knew Mickey would have preferred a beer, but he took the glass of Scotch without a murmur.

Hardy handed out the drinks, and we all sat down near Travail. I was about to make my toast - "To each of us according to what he deserves" - but Hardy beat me to the punch.

"Tell me," he said, "You took me up on San Juan, okay. But one thing I still don't get. How did you know we'd be at the Ritz-Carlton?"

I set my drink on the small table between Travail and me. "This place is the best, and you stay at the best."

Hardy, showing signs of frenzy as the staggering amount of his losses began to sink in, turned away from me and looked sharply at Travail. "Something bothering me, Francis. On that last hand you folded after the flop. What were your down cards?"

"Pair of deuces."

"You folded with a pair in the hole? The river was a deuce, you would have had three deuces. Are you fucking stupid?"

"Get off my back, Chuck. I don't have to take this from you."

Turning back to me, Hardy whacked his forehead with the palm of his hand. "It just came to me. That nerd secretary of mine is always bullshitting with Nikki Bullett. The *nerd* told Bullett we were coming to this hotel. And Bullett and you are in bed together - in more ways than one. Those two bitches are dead meat."

"What does 'dead meat' mean?" I asked.

He drew his hand across his throat.

Travail was ashen. He opened his mouth to speak.

Hardy glared at him. "Shut the fuck up."

Travail, now unsteady and perspiring profusely, got to his feet, and looked at Hardy. "You're not going to hurt them, are you?"

Hardy was breathing hard. In a hoarse voice, he said, "For the last time, shut up."

"I can't believe this. Violence was never part of our arrangement."

Showing control I found remarkable, Hardy carefully placed his Scotch on the linen coaster sitting in the middle of the table and got to his feet. From the time we entered the suite, the entire exchange of words had been conducted softly, and even now as Hardy turned toward Travail, a fog of silence enveloped the room. He walked casually over to Travail, and I expected a stream of obscenities to come pouring out of Hardy's mouth. Instead, he wrapped his hands around Travail's throat.

I glanced at Mickey who reached Hardy in a single stride, and applied a chop to the back of his neck. Hardy came down, motionless, on top of Travail's inert body. Mickey pushed Hardy off Travail and I felt both their neck pulses.

"I think they're okay," I said. "It's probably the booze more than anything. The old guy will have a sore throat and the back of Hardy's neck will ache for a few days."

"They'll come out of it in a few minutes," Mickey said. "Let's get out of here."

We passed Gus sitting outside the room, his eyes closed. I said, softly, "Good night, Gus." No response. He was in the arms of Morpheus.

We walked quickly down the empty corridor, turned a corner, and came to a house phone near the elevator. I picked up the phone, and got the desk. "We heard some noise coming out of 703. You might want to get somebody up there."

"Who is calling, please?"

I hung up the phone, and looked at my watch. It was 2:15.

We considered taking the stairs to avoid being noticed, but I didn't feel up to climbing three flights. The elevator arrived, and standing in the rear, weaving a bit, was Beth Goody, the black-haired belle from the swimming pool.

"What do you know?" she said, a titillated tremor in her voice. "Honey bun, my masseur." She switched her glance to me. "And his mentor. The masseur and the mentor. May I buy you both a drink?"

Before Mickey could speak, I said, "We'd be honored."

Mickey blushed, but kept his poise, and the three of us went down to the lounge off the lobby. We sat at the bar, Beth between Mickey and me. It was apparent she had already consumed a fair amount of alcohol.

We ordered three Scotches - I didn't dare switch to vodka, not with the plan I had in mind - and I said, "What did you play tonight, Beth?"

"Craps, and that's the last time."

After a second round of Scotch, which I diluted with as much water as possible, Beth said, "How long we been here in the lounge?"

It was 2:30, and we had been in the lounge about fifteen minutes. I reached around her and touched Mickey's arm, signaling him to be quiet. "Since 1:30, around an hour."

"Well," she said, "the time went fast. I'm going to the john. After that, I trust one of you guys will escort me to my room." She laughed. "Maybe both of you."

Mickey helped her off the stool, and we watched her walk to the ladies' room. I said, "I'm going to bed. Here is my credit card. Pay the bar bill with it, and sign my name. Then spend as much time as possible with her."

"Is that an assignment, Mr. Silva?"

"Think of it as a challenge. I'll explain later."

Mickey nodded, and asked no questions. The corridors and lobby were empty, the desk clerk probably taking a cigarette break in back. I got to the room at quarter to three and was sound asleep in ten minutes.

I woke up at 4:30 to go to the john. Mickey was not there I had my best night's sleep in a long time, and I woke up at 11:30, refreshed. I tiptoed into the next room and saw that Mickey was sleeping peacefully. I didn't know when he had returned to our suite.

As I headed for the coffee machine in the kitchenette, the phone rang.

"We should talk," Hardy said. "I wanted to talk last night, but I lost control with Travail. I assume it was your buddy, Mr. Delano, who stopped me. I thank him for that."

"So talk."

"No, head-to-head. I'll meet you at the swimming pool."

"I've seen the swimming pool. Besides, I can't think of anything you could say that would interest me."

"Try me. It will be worth your time. Anywhere you say."

"All right, the old city. There's a hotel there - El Convento. It used to be a convent. Perfect for you, Chuck Two o'clock. How's Travail?"

"He took the noon flight. Don't bring the stud with you. This will be one-on-one. Got that?"

"Yeah."

I woke Mickey, and after he had showered and drunk some coffee, I told him about Hardy's phone call. I said I had no doubt that despite Hardy's one-on-one admonition, our new friend, Gus, would be somewhere in the area.

"I want you there out of Hardy's sight, but you are not to tangle with Gus. Will you promise me you won't have any physical contact with that guy?"

"Yeah."

"Say it."

"I promise."

I had read about El Convento, a restored 350-year-old Carmelite convent set in the center of Old San Juan. Celebrated for its restrained old world charm, the hotel was the antithesis of the posh Ritz-Carlton. El Convento seemed to take pride in the absence of a casino and the diminutive size of its pool.

I dropped Mickey in the parking lot, instructing him to keep his eyes open and fit into the background, unobtrusively. If he spotted Gus, Mickey was to watch him, and if he saw a sign of anything disturbing, he was to summon hotel security.

At two on a Sunday afternoon the lobby had the solitude of a mausoleum. The only people in sight were an elderly couple having tea in a far corner. I heard no rattle of dishes, no music, no subdued exchanges between waiters. It was silent except for the faint sound of German drifting over from the tea-drinkers.

Hardy arrived five minutes after I did. He claimed his cab driver had doubled the normal fare. "I need a drink to get the taste of that spic driver out of my mouth."

After the waiter took our order - black coffee for me, Scotch for Hardy - he said, "You're one hell of a poker player. I have to admit you did a job on me. I haven't lost that much in years." Throughout our entire conversation he rubbed the back of his neck every few minutes.

"Eighty percent is the cards."

"Maybe so. When the Chinese chick came back the cards turned your way."

"She's Vietnamese, born in New York."

"Slanty-eyed is slanty-eyed, but this one had something going. Why didn't you make a move on her?"

"How do you know I didn't?"

He laughed. "Now you're talking." He drank some of his Scotch. "You come down here with the kid. You hook up with me, you take a big chance at the tables and come away with - a hundred-fifty? Two-hundred? What's this all about?"

"I thought it would be fun and I was right."

"All right, let's get serious. First thing, are you wearing a wire?"

I just looked at him.

"No, of course not. You're a smart guy. I'm going to tell you a few things, and you'll see I'm not as bad as you think. Then I'll make you an offer you can't refuse."

He took another swallow of his Scotch and water. "But before we get into that, we need to settle up on the money you stole last night. You give it back to me, and I give you my word, there'll be no questions asked. Then we can get down to business."

"What the hell are you talking about?" I said.

Another swig and a pause. "Don't make me do it, Sid. I'm starting to like you. I really don't *want* to report you and the kid to hotel security."

For once I had anticipated him. Waiting for the elevator I had reflected that as the enormity of Hardy's losses sunk in, his rage would surface.

A few scenarios had occurred to me. He had seen the cashier hand me a check for more than $200,000. But he would assume I had come to San Juan with a big wad of cash, and stashed it in the vault in my room. He would tell hotel security that when he and Travail fell asleep after drinking too much, Mickey and I broke into his vault and stole the money he had placed there. The way he saw it, the security people would find the cash in my vault.

The time spent with Beth Goody later that evening provided an unexpected alibi for a crime Mickey and I had not committed. Hardy figured I might give him a chunk of the cash I had taken with me from Washington to avoid hassle. Even if I convinced security this was legitimately my money - the casino knew how much I had won at poker, and they knew they had given me a check - my embarrassment would make his fabricated story worthwhile to him.

The irony was that before I left home, I had fleetingly thought about, and rejected, breaking into his vault at some point with Mickey's help. Stealing was not my style.

"I'm sorry, Chuck. Somebody stole some money from you?"

A longer pause and another swig. "Give me back the pouch with the money or I'll have you holed up in a cell for twenty years with AIDS-infected spics."

I shook my head. "You're starting to annoy me. I had nothing whatsoever to do with any theft. I've never stolen anything in my life."

"You want me to believe you didn't see me go into the bedroom with the pouch? Do I really look that dumb?"

"When we got inside, I stood next to Travail and looked at the ocean. I didn't know if you went to the bedroom or the bathroom or whatever. None of my business."

He stared at me. "Just before I came here I checked the vault. The pouch was not there. After you stole it, you put the cash in the vault in your room, right?"

"Never use those vaults."

"You know nothing about my money being stolen."

"Nothing."

"After Travail and I were out of it, what did you do?"

"Had a couple of drinks and I went to bed."

"And this so-called Tony?"

"Went carousing, I guess. Not my business."

"When are you going back?" Hardy asked.

"Wednesday." That wasn't quite true. My plan was to follow the venerable adage - take the money and run. Our tickets were for Wednesday, but Mickey and I would drive to the airport early the next day, Monday, and get on standby.

"Hotel security will be talking to you."

He drank some Scotch and locked his eyes onto mine. "Sometimes I know where you're coming from. Try to retain a lawyer, try to go with the *second* lowest bidder, Security. Those are things I expect from you. But to place taps on my phones, get into my e-mail, steal my money, get your grandson to blackmail me, that's not like you. Doesn't fit your profile."

"I steal your money? I'm blackmailing you? You're in some fantasy world."

"Elsie gave you the papers to fuck me up- she'll get what's coming to her. Then you gave them to your grandson and his girlfriend to do the job."

I raised my voice. "I do not know what you're talking about. That's the truth. You're totally off base."

"You're good, I'll give you that. All right, try this on for size. I withdraw my complaint about your theft. My lawyers are ready to go to law enforcement to bring criminal charges for breaking into my office, tapping into my phone and my e-mail, and for extortion and blackmail. I'll call them off. You give me your word you won't go back to your Board to retain a lawyer and to switch to Security."

I tried to string him along. "Interesting. Tell me about your arrangement, and we'll see."

"What arrangement?"

"The arrangement to rotate the bids among your providers."

Ordering another Scotch, he acknowledged the existence of a "loose" group. "We bring some order into an inefficient system so everybody can benefit. We service our customers better. Not working as smoothly as I'd like, but it's still good for everybody."

I asked him what role Travail had played. "No role, just a good friend despite what you saw last night."

He had almost finished his second Scotch and was staring at the glass. "Look, sometimes my temper gets the best of me, but I mean well." He ordered his third Scotch.

I said, "Tell me about your first wife, Brandy Buffington, out there in California."

He raised his eyebrows. "You've done your leg work. She hits me up for money."

"You checked the phones in your office and found bugs in them. What alerted you to do that?"

"The dog. I found bloody threads in her teeth. That meant she had been holding on to somebody. That got me thinking and we found the bugs. We placed the cameras in the light fixtures, but you know all that. Now, my proposal."

Hardy said his lawyers had "strong evidence proving" that Lars and I had engaged in trespassing and planting bugs in phones, felonies punishable by fine and jail. Other evidence would show that Skip, acting on my instruction, had illegally "intercepted" e-mail from Hardy's computer. After turning over this evidence to law enforcement, Hardy's lawyers would file a civil suit seeking damages against Lars, Skip, me, and the Oasis.

"We're talking millions on that stuff alone." Hardy said. "On this new stuff the sky's the limit plus jail time for all of you."

"What 'new stuff' are you talking about?"

"Please, Sid, you steal my money, now you want to bullshit me. I'm talking about your brazen attempt to extort money from me, using your grandson as your flunky."

"You're talking riddles. I don't know about any 'new stuff.' Anyway, the case against you for price fixing and bid rigging is air-tight. Efficiency Management of America will have to pay out *tens* of millions. By the time you get out of jail, they will have thrown you to the wolves. You'll be toast."

Hardy changed his tack, insisting that the so-called bid rigging was ineffectual. He said his lawyers called the scheme "nugatory." Although my lawyers might be able to piece together a "bare-bones case," the damages would be minimal, "a token amount."

"It doesn't amount to shit," he said. "Whatever understanding we had, they break it as much as they follow it. You might prove a half-ass *attempt* to rig bids that failed."

"Maybe so," I said, "but you'll still go to jail."

Hardy snorted loudly. The couple drinking tea turned around in their chairs, and I smiled at them, reassuringly.

"No way." Hardy said his lawyers would show that he and his co-conspirators were the gang that couldn't shoot straight. His lead lawyer called them "the Toonerville Trolley Tinkerers - wannabe crooks who couldn't get their act together."

Hardy gave me examples of deals gone bad, co-conspirators acting "only in their selfish interest" who openly flaunted Hardy's authority, and "double-dealing" members who subverted the goals of the conspiracy.

"Doesn't matter," I said. "EMA will throw you out on your ass."

"If the shit hits the fan, yes, EMA will be pissed. If they ditch me, my stock options and my golden parachute will take care of me. It won't come to that. By the time we're done, the jury will feel sorry for us. Your best bet is to listen to what I have to say."

"What do you have to say?"

"I know that awarding Security the contract and retaining your lawyer-friend went down the drain with your Board. But I also know you've got a stubborn streak, and you'll try to find a way to turn them around. I say we back off, settle for a stand-off. I'll call off my lawyers and you give me your word you'll do the same."

I looked at him. "You might collect a few thousand for the break-ins, but your bid-rigging and inside trading would come out at that trial. Our lawsuit will cost EMA millions. But I'll tell you what I'm prepared to do. You pay the Oasis $500,000, and we walk away. EMA will never know a thing."

Hardy motioned for another Scotch. I had lost count. Smiling, he said, "You take risks, you're a con artist. I can relate to that. You've got a pair of balls."

First Mickey said that, then Hardy. It must be true. "You screwed us out of a lot of money, Chuck. How can I walk away?"

"Let's stop the dancing. Me, I'm trying to hold on to a good thing and keep in check my 'anger management problem,' as Elsie used to call it. You, you lost your sharp edge after your wife died. Why don't we play the cards we're dealt?"

"My cards say we need compensation."

"Last offer. I don't report your theft to security. Take twenty-five out of the pouch, and give me the rest back. I don't sue you for breaking and entering, the wire-taps, blackmail. You leave the Board actions stand, and stay away from lawyers."

"No deal, Chuck. I need five-hundred thou for the Oasis."

"Trust me on one thing. You don't want to become my enemy."

Without taking his eyes away from mine, he waved his hand in a "come here" motion. I looked in the direction of the wave. Gus and Mickey were standing outside the lounge, watching us. They appeared to be having a quiet conversation. Gus walked toward our table, Mickey following.

"Gus," Hardy said, "this man doesn't get the picture. He wants to be my enemy. Sit down and explain how we deal with enemies."

Gus looked in the direction of the elderly couple in the corner, and Hardy said, "Don't worry about them. Just do your thing."

Pulling up a chair to my left, Gus seized the four fingers of my left hand, and began to squeeze. Mickey came up behind Gus, applied his thumbs to the hollows behind his ears, and Gus immediately let go of my fingers. All this transpired in about five seconds and was accompanied by silence.

Mickey nodded toward the exit, and I said, "We're out of here, Chuck."

"Don't fuck with me, Silva," he said. "You'll regret it."

On the way to the hotel, I said, "What were you and Gus talking about?"

"He was telling me that Hardy was mad as hell because Gus fell asleep outside the door last night and didn't see us leave. He wants to make amends with his boss."

"You broke your promise not to have physical contact with him."

"Yes, I did."

"Thanks. I think he was about to crush my fingers."

I intended to drive to the airport early Monday morning and avoid dealing with the security people. But after we got back to the room late Sunday afternoon, there was a knock on the door, and a middle-aged man, a tall young man, and a shapely woman stood there. I invited them inside. The older man said it had been alleged we had stolen money from a guest's suite, and, in apologetic tone, he said they were required to investigate.

Their questions were put respectfully, but pointedly. On the preceding evening, where were we from 6 p.m. until 6 a.m.?

I gave them a detailed account of the nature and timing of my slot machine activity beginning at 4 followed by my session at the blackjack table from about 4:45 to about 8:45. Mickey said he was observing the blackjack tables in that time frame.

I added that we went to our room to freshen up and take a rest, and beginning at about 10, we played poker. We quit poker at about 1:30, ran into Beth Goody, a hotel guest, and had drinks with her in the lounge until about 2:30. At that time Mickey escorted her to her room and I returned to my room and went to sleep.

The young man asked Mickey if he went inside Ms. Goody's room with her.

"Yes."

How long did he remain with Ms. Goody in her room?

"Two, three hours."

The young man asked, "What did you do during that time?" His colleagues looked at him blankly, and he said, Spanish accent intact, "I withdraw the question." They asked Mickey for Beth Goody's room number and he gave it to them.

The security woman said that an unidentified person had called the desk at 2:17 to report some noise in Room 703. Was that person either of us? No, we were at the bar with Ms. Goody at that time.

Had we been in Mr. Hardy's suite on the preceding evening. We had not. Did we know Mr. Hardy and Mr. Travail? Yes, we did, but running into them in San Juan was a coincidence. Did we have any objection if they spoke with Ms.Goody? Absolutely none.

With our consent, they conducted perfunctory body and room searches. They glanced at the vault which was wide open, empty.

Before they left, the older man said, "We know your winnings at poker last night were large. Could you tell us where that money is?"

I took the certified check from my wallet and showed it to them.

They thanked us for our cooperation, and we never again heard from the hotel.

Mickey and I drove to the airport early the next morning. Standby got us onto the next flight, but we had to sit apart.

On the way home, Mickey said, "Tell me what happened at El Convento."

"He wants to settle everything - no lawyers, no lawsuits. He won't bring charges in connection with breaking and entering or wire tapping."

I didn't mention Skip's blackmail. I needed to find out about that for myself.

"And you would do what?"

"Leave the Board decisions where they are. No lawyer, no Security."

"Anything else?"

"I wanted $500,000 for the condo."

"And?"

"He said no, I said no deal. The rest you saw. Now let me get to a more interesting subject, honey bun. Did you have a pleasant time with the black-haired bombshell?"

"Very pleasant. We talked for a while. I gave her my number, and she said she'd be in touch."

"That was it? After that professional massage job you gave her at the pool?"

"That was it."

"I checked at 4:30 and you weren't there."

"We talked a long time. As you've taught me, virtue is its own reward."

"I'm proud of you. You're discreet. And discretion is the better part of . . .?"

"Fun."

Chapter 16

The first thing I did when we got home was set up a Board meeting for the following week. The second thing I did was call Skip. I needed to see him immediately. He said that was "impossible," and this time I abruptly ended the conversation.

I gave Anna an account of the trip, omitting nothing, and told her about my phone call with Skip. She called him and left an urgent message. Skip returned her call a half hour later. Anna was able to set up a meeting later that day.

We met at the same off-campus coffee shop, and, again, Karen was with him. I led off. "I've been told that the two of you are engaged in some kind of blackmail scheme. I need to know what this is all about. No evasions, no doubletalk, no bullshit."

"Who told you that?"

"NEVER MIND who told me. I'm not getting through to you. You're in big trouble, and if you don't level with me I can't help you. ARE YOU BLACKMAILING HARDY? YES OR NO."

"Blackmail," Karen said, rolling her eyes. "You've already told us the man is weird. Sounds like he's paranoid. Why do you believe him?"

"Karen, this is not a game. The man is dangerous. You've got to level with us."

Ignoring what I had just said, she continued, "Maybe he's just putting pressure on you to lay off him."

Could she have a point? After all, he made up the story about my theft of his money. Maybe he was making this one up, too. It was hard for me to believe that Skip, or for that matter, Karen, was so stupid as to become involved in blackmail.

But I persisted. "He's pressuring me, all right, but you're giving him the ammunition. How can I get you to come to your senses? First, tell us what you've done, and then we'll get you out of town. It is IMPERATIVE that you do this."

Anna said, "Sid is right. Please tell us what you have been doing."

Skip began to say something, but Karen took over. "We go to class, listen to music, and enjoy each other's company. Is that all right?"

"You are in trouble," Anna said.

"Skip," I said, "I'm pleading with you. Tell us what's going on."

"Chill out, grandpa. Nothing's going on."

After we got in the car, I said, "They're lying, of course."

"And they can't even do that right," Anna said.

I reached Maurice in his office at 7 a.m. and told him what I contemplated. He was "astonished" at my "audacity," and questioned my judgment, but found no legal impediment to my plan. I deposited $50,000 in my account and $150,000 into an escrow account. Depending on what happened the escrow money would go to the Oasis.

Despite the frenetic few days in San Juan and my disquiet over Skip, the next few days were calm. I mused on the greenspace bench, watching the forsythia's fading yellow flowers anticipate spring's departure, and the early dogwood blossoms herald the imminent arrival of summer. I took walks, read Graham Greene, and was even reduced to daytime TV - five-minute spans were all I could tolerate.

I called Skip regularly to no avail. He was steadfast in denying any illicit activity. On the last call he said he was excited because he had qualified for a limited-attendance advanced computer science course.

A few days before the Board meeting a light bulb came on. Jane Fountain would be the key to the outcome of that meeting. I called and asked if I could take her to lunch.

Buona Sera was crowded, the way I liked it. I arrived first and Maria gave me my table in the far corner near the kitchen. I ordered Pellegrino and white wine. The waiter returned and showed me the label on the bottle of wine. As I nodded I saw Jane at the door, and watched her make her entrance.

She surveyed the room and waved to me, her tall frame erect, and her turquoise blouse in harmony with the maroon frescoes on the wall. Her presence was commanding, and she made her way forward with the pro's talent for instilling trust in strangers with a smile. If I passed her on the street, I'd wish she were a friend.

We shook hands, and without hesitation she poured the bottle of mineral water sitting on the table while the waiter was uncorking the wine. Pulling off her glasses, she looked at me across the table.

"I want to thank you again, Sid, for inviting me to Skip's going-away party. He's going to be a star at college. You must be proud of him."

"I am. He's had some rough spots, but I hope he's coming out of his teen-age fog."

"I'm sure he is."

Smoothing down her long auburn hair with both hands, she glanced around, her eyes coming back to me. "This place is a real find."

We sipped wine, ordered lunch, and talked about the condo and its inexhaustible supply of eccentric residents. She didn't miss a cue, and her act was close to flawless.

Everybody had an act, I thought, by which we want the world to identify us, and by which we conceal our foibles. As Jane and I engaged in perfunctory chit-chat, I thought about the acts of the people who, for good or for bad, were now part of my life.

Anna's act was calm-rational. Sheila's was blunt-vulgar. Lars' was dead-on sober. Sid Silva, who pretended he was thirty when was creeping past seventy, played the role of Gruff Old Impulsive Guy with Heart of Gold.

My thoughts wandered to the other Board members. Moody, who was already eighty when he had been thirty, ceaselessly polished his curmudgeonly cynicism. Bunny had worked up an I'm-tough-but-I'll-go-to-bed- with-you-if-you-have-enough-money-or-influence routine. The core of Audrey's act was meek confusion. Which of these Board members' acts concealed disloyalty and disdain for ethical behavior?

Skip turned out a pretty good act - smart-alienated-misunderstood-antisocial teenager. Carl Harrison was adept in playing the role of the lascivious old guy whose paramount mission was getting laid and talking about it. And Karen, whom I barely knew, exhibited clear-eyed intelligence and young ambition. But what was she really all about? And what was Skip doing in her life?

And what about Hardy? His act said, look at me, I came up the hard way and evolved into an amiable-but-tough successful businessman. But sooner or later the ugly side of his performance emerged.

The most professional performance was Jane Fountain's late-Twentieth-Century savoir faire. Her choice of clothes, facial expressions, body language, and articulateness were seamlessly integrated. If on occasion she seemed to hesitate or falter, such a misstep had likely been programmed along with everything else. Did the mask ever come off?

Half way through our salads, she mentioned the up-coming Board meeting. "What is that all about?" she asked with a smile.

I decided to be vague. "Just some lingering business I'd like to resolve," I said.

"Ah, Mr. Mysterious."

I remembered Hardy's 'Miss Mysterious,' and Exotica flittered through my mind.

Toward the end of our conversation, Jane said, "Once again, Sid, I want to say I felt I had to vote against your proposals. As you know, I support you most of the time. But I could not in conscience support the significant outlay of money with uncertain benefit."

I believed she was sincere.

"Now," she said, "I'd like to raise a personal matter. I hope I won't offend you."

"You are incapable of offending me."

"Thank you. You've observed, I'm sure, that I'm a direct person. Subtlety is not my strong suit. I don't do obliqueness. And I especially feel I can be direct with you."

She sipped her wine, apparently uncomfortable. Or maybe not. Maybe this, too, was programmed.

"I understand that you and Anna are no longer seeing each other." She raised her hand. "I know this is none of my business, so tell me to drop it and I'll drop it."

"Please go ahead."

Another sip of her wine, and I detected a faint flush on her face. That could not have been programmed, not even from this consummate pro.

"If there comes a time when you are a free agent, so to speak, I would be interested in seeing you socially."

I found her attractive, and the devil inside the Old Sid was urging me to play along with her overture. See what happens. But the New Sid prevailed. "I'll try to match your candor. It's true that Anna and I were not seeing each other, but we're back together. Your interest is flattering, and I'm honored to think of you as a friend."

We sat quietly. I smiled and said, "While we're both in this Carl state of mind let me ask you this. There is a giant-size disparity in our ages. Why would you want to go out with an old codger like me?"

"Age has nothing to do with how I feel about somebody. I'm forty-five, and you have twice the vitality and substance of the tired, hollow divorced men my age I go out with. You're engaging and interesting, and, if I may say so, appealing."

"So are you. I'll say it again - I'm lucky to have you as a friend."

I walked home slowly. Intelligence and tact informed Jane's appeal as much as physical attributes. When she is on the Hill, I thought, dazzling the politicians with charm, she must be something special to watch. But was she more than an ambitious lobbyist? Could I be wrong? Was this a theatrical flirtation, part of a masterful routine?

My musing wandered from Fountain to Nikki Bullett. Was there more to Nikki than I was seeing? She could have said, "I think we should run this past Chuck Hardy first." Had she called Hardy and told him what I was planning to do? *He's been fair with me.* I would be loathe to condemn her for declining to jeopardize her good job. Was this responsible mother, struggling to hold onto her child, covering up for her boss?

Or was Nikki aware of and repelled by Hardy's illegal conduct? *Strictly your call.* Was she engaging in a silent conspiracy with me to thwart Hardy?

All the Board members showed up at the meeting. The usual half dozen residents were in attendance. I said it was important, in my view, that we revisit a couple of issues. At this open meeting I was raising, for the second time, the selection of the roofing contractor for Building One. At our last meeting, I said, we discussed this at length, and the Board voted to award the contract to District Roofing.

I had argued that we should go with Security Roofing, but five of the members had expressed concern about the additional cost of roughly $100,000. Tonight, I was prepared to contribute $100,000 to the Oasis treasury in an effort to induce a majority of the Board to vote to hire Security.

"You'll recall our discussion," I said, "in which we expressed the pros and cons for more than an hour. I hope we can keep tonight's discussion on the shorter side."

After Lars moved that the Board reverse its position, and award the contract to Security, the questions poured forth. "What is going on here?" asked Moody. "Why are you giving the condo a hundred grand just so this Security outfit can put on the new roof? Do you own a piece of Security? What's in it for you?"

"I have no interest of any kind in Security," I said, "and I don't know anybody who works there. My sole reason for asking you to award them the contract is because it is in the best interest of the Oasis."

Peering at me, Audrey said, "I thought this was settled last time. Why are we arguing the same question again?"

"Because there is a new ingredient in the recipe - my contribution, which means the Oasis will pay no more for the tried and trusted Security than it would for District."

Fingering a necklace of small pearls I hadn't noticed before, Bunny followed up on Audrey's point. "You have a lot of nerve making us come here to talk about something we already disposed of. I don't think you have the authority to take up the same issue we've already decided."

"Later, Bunny, I'll show you the part of the bylaws giving me the authority."

Moody looked at each Board member in turn. "I've been around longer than anybody here, and I'm trying to tell you something. In the history of condos nobody has ever done anything like this - handing their condo a hundred thousand dollars. For what? So we can get the better roofing company? Tell me another one."

His gaze came to me. "I'm sorry, Sid. I know you to be a good person, but what in hell is happening to you? Why are you doing this?"

"So I can be a trail blazer." No smiles.

Jane had been biding her time. "Why *are* you doing this, Sid?"

"Because I want to."

All of them were staring at me. I bit the bullet. "I won a lot of money at poker - outside the Oasis. To me, this is like found money. It may sound crazy but I attach more importance to the welfare of this condo than keeping the money. I don't need it."

Jane turned to Nikki sitting next to me as always, and who had not yet opened her mouth. "Nikki, what was your recommendation?"

"District."

"Why?"

" Because it was the low bidder."

"In your experience, is it appropriate to select the second lowest bidder?"

"If the Board believes Security will do a better job than District and is willing to pay the extra money, then it is perfectly appropriate."

Moody asked, "Where did you win this money?"

"I'm sorry, Dr. Moody, that's my business."

Bunny again. "I heard through the grapevine he won it in San Juan at a casino. I don't think our condo should accept gambling money."

Audrey again. "I agree. It's just plain wrong to use ill-gotten gains for the condo."

Jane again. "It is absurd to question the source of the money unless it was obtained illegally which it was not. I believe Sid. In any case, how he obtained the money is not our business. *Our* business is remedying our problems. I will support the motion."

The room was silent for a few seconds, and I called for a vote on Lars' motion. The Board selected Security by a four-to-three vote, Jane voting with the majority.

Before adjourning the meeting I notified the members there would be an executive session as soon as the room was cleared.

I led off. "I want to revisit the question of retaining a lawyer. The Board rejected this because the case was too speculative, and we would have to pay costs, possibly as high as $50,000. Okay, I am willing to contribute $50,000 to the condo with the understanding that if we prevail, the Oasis will pay me back. The Oasis is in a win-win situation."

The remainder of the closed session paralleled the open session. Similar questions, similar answers. "We've already voted on retaining a lawyer - we said no. Why are we revisiting that issue?" *The Board was unwilling to undertake ongoing costs in the face of an uncertain result. I will cover those costs out of my pocket. The condo can't lose.*

"What's in it for you?" Same answer as before. *The Oasis has come to play an important role in my life. It gives me satisfaction to contribute to its welfare.*

"What is your special arrangement with this Maurice guy?" *I have no special arrangement with him. He's a friend, but this is a business transaction, and everything is up front and visible.*

"Your company used him. Were there kickbacks?" *Never, and that's offensive.*

Jane expressed admiration for my largesse, and voted for Lars' motion which carried, four-to-three. Security would put on the new roof, and Maurice would represent the Oasis. This time Hardy was going to be one hell of an unhappy camper.

I dropped into Nikki's office at ten the next morning. "Tell me something. Did you call Hardy to tell him the Board voted to go with the second lowest bidder?"

"No, he called *me* five minutes after I got here this morning at nine. He was in a foul state. He already knew the Board selected Security Roofing, and he questioned me. Why hadn't I told him? I said I didn't think it was all that important. Why hadn't I talked the Board out of it? I said that's not my job."

"What else did he say?"

"Only that you're making a mistake, but it's your decision."

Has the contract to Security been sent yet?"

"It will go out this afternoon with the other mail."

"Don't wait for this afternoon. Get it out right away."

She said, "No problem," and on impulse I winked at her. She smiled, paused, and returned the wink.

The results of the Board's "confidential" decision to retain counsel washed through the residents like a tidal wave. *Best news I've heard in a long time. We're going to be in the money. Say goodbye to fee increases.* A few dissents were heard. *Why are we paying a lawyer for something that could well be a loser?* But for the most part, elation reigned.

Sheila called. "There's excitement in the air. I know this TV camera guy. Let me come over tomorrow with him. He'll tape my interview with you. *What made you suspicious? How did you select the lawyer? What do you estimate your recovery will be?* You know, like that. We'll peddle the tape to a local channel."

"Sheila, calm down. No interview."

"You don't understand. I'm serious. This has genuine news value."

"There will be no interview. *Nada, niente, rien.*"

Security completed installation of the Building One roof six weeks to the day after they began the job. Our independent inspector said it passed muster.

One day in July, I said, "An Italian professor is giving a lecture tomorrow at the Smithsonian on the glories of Tuscany. Want to go?"

Anna perked up. "I've never been to Italy. There's no place I'd rather hear about."

The lecture was informative, covering art, literature, music, architecture, wine, and food. The professor finished at 10:30, and we dropped into Buona Sera for a late bite. The place was nearly empty, and Maria sat down at our table with a glass of wine

"We're thinking about ten days in Tuscany," I said. "What do you recommend?"

Anna stared at me, her face a study of ill-concealed shock.

I smiled, and Maria said, "Well, I come from Sicily, so I'm preju-diced. I studied art in Florence before coming here. Tuscany is not Sic-ily, but you could do worse. I'll lay out an itinerary. You'll fly to Milan, rent a car, take a two-day drive, ending up in Florence. You'll take day trips out of Florence and come home rejuvenated."

Walking home, Anna said, "You see? You did it again. You unilat-erally took charge without a word to me. How do you know I want to go to Italy?"

"You said there's no place you'd rather hear about than Italy."

"So you make no distinction between a two-hour lecture and a ten-day trip."

"I thought you'd be delighted to be my guest in Italy."

"I *am* delighted. It's your habit of not talking things over before-hand. But that's your style, you're not going to change. Neither am I, so let's get on with it. Besides, I can write a travel piece about the trip."

When I ran into Elsie at the local market I was taken aback. The color was back in her face and her eyes were clear. She told me she felt much better than she did the last time she saw me. Talking to me had made a difference. She would always be grateful.

"I hear you and Anna are together again. That's good, she's a special woman."

"I know. By the way, Anna and I are off to Italy next week."

"Wonderful. I know you'll have a great time. How long will you be away?"

"Ten days."

I called Skip repeatedly, each time hearing, "Leave your message at the beep." He didn't return the calls, and when I managed to reach him directly after a half a dozen tries, I said, "I need to know exactly what you and Karen have been doing with Hardy. Can't you get it through your head that there is nothing more important in your life right now than telling me the truth? TELL ME."

Irritation in his voice, he said, "There's nothing to tell you. I have to go now." He clicked off the phone.

Over the next several days I left messages, but he never called back. If truth be told, I, too, was irritated, and somewhere in the back of my mind was the notion that "I'll be damned if I let that brainless grandson of mine spoil my trip to Italy."

The flight to Milan was uneventful. We slept, read, and watched a Tom Cruise movie. In between, we talked as though we had been close friends for fifty years.

At one point I pointed out a middle-aged couple sitting across the aisle two rows in front of us. "You can tell they're not married," I whispered.

"I give up. How do you know?"

"Look how closely she listens to every word he says, how her eyes can't leave his face, how devoted she is to him."

"I'm like that with you."

"Very funny. From you I get massive indifference."

She punched my arm with more zip than usual.

The landing was smooth. We picked up an Alpha Romeo at Malpensa Airport, circled around Milan, and found our way to the autostrada going south. After an hour, we reached our first destination, Piacenza, in late morning. We drove to the Locanda del Lupo, an Eighteenth Century inn Maria had recommended.

We slept like rocks for a few hours, and when we awoke we drove to Parma. Guide book in hand, we walked around the Duomo, and gazed at the Corregio frescoes. The highlight of the day was the bustling market. Our eyes were glued to the extravaganza of fresh produce, fish, and meat. After being assured it would hold up fine for ten days, Anna bought a chunk of Parmigiana-Reggiano to take back to Sheila.

The next day we drove into Bologna, walked around the long arcaded streets, and continued on to our hotel in Florence. I glanced around our room, spotted the terrace, and said, "Come out here with me for a minute."

Anna and I gazed across the Arno River at the Ponte Vecchio and the celebrated Uffizi Gallery. "This is beyond description," she said. "This cries out for an article."

Taking advantage of the dry and sunny weather, we must have seen more in that one day than any tourist in history. Each Michelangelo was more breathtaking than the previous one. Each Donatello more majestic. Standing in front of the Della Robbia bas-reliefs of children laughing, dancing and singing, we held hands and smiled.

Anna browsed through a bookstore, and bought a picture book - Italian text of course - of well-known Italian TV news personalities. "Sheila is going to love this book," Anna said.

We got back to our room, took a long nap, and it was close to nine when we awoke and went down for drinks. At Anna's urging - "When in Rome . . ." - I ordered campari and soda instead of vodka.

"We've been gone two days," Anna said, "and it's all like living a dream."

"You're right, but you're the difference between a wonderful trip and a dream . . . You know, I can't help thinking, I may have overreacted to Hardy."

"All bluff?"

I signaled for two more campari. "Could be. There's a good chance his lawyers will settle the conspiracy case, and he'll get off with a stiff fine, no jail. He has to know that if he does something extreme, I bring in the police, and if that means exposing our own dumb actions, so be it. He may be crude, but he's not stupid."

"Let's put the bastard out of our minds.

"Anna, you used a cuss word. I'm shocked, shocked."

"It won't be the last time, buddy."

Again, on Maria's recommendation we had dinner at Camillo, near our hotel. As Maria had suggested, we began our meal with ribolita - vegetable soup with beans, cabbage, carrots and chunks of bread.

Picking up my napkin, I said, "This soup is something to write home about."

"Which is exactly what I'm going to do when we get back to the room. I'll write to Sheila and Skip about this trattoria."

By the time we got back to our room it was 11:30, but for some reason - probably the long nap - we weren't tired. Watching the passing parade from our balcony, we shared a glass of Orvieto, and after a while we began to yawn. We switched off the TV, got undressed, and slipped into bed.

"I'll write the postcards tomorrow," Anna said.

As though on cue the phone rang.

Anna looked up at me. "Who in the world can that be?"

"Probably a wrong number." I grappled around, picked up the phone, and in a half-whisper, said, "*Pronto.*"

"Is this Sid?"

I recognized the voice "Mickey, I know it's early where you are, but it's almost midnight here. What's going on?"

"I'm sorry to bother you, Sid, but I thought you ought to know something. It's about Skip."

Mickey explained that Skip and he exchanged e-mail almost every day. Three days ago, Skip's e-mail stopped coming. Mickey kept on e-mailing him with nothing coming back. Mickey called Skip on his cell phone. No answer, just the message. Then Mickey drove over to Skip's dorm, went to his room, and left a note on his desk.

As Mickey left the room "a man in a suit" asked Mickey if he was looking for Skip. The man asked Mickey to come with him. They walked over to another building and went into a room marked, 'Security.' Two more "dudes in suits" were there and they asked Mickey how he knew Skip and other questions.

"I guess they believed me. They told me Skip has been missing for three days. They called his father in California and he had no idea where Skip could be. I asked Maria what we should do, and she said to call you right away. She had your itinerary."

I said we would be there as soon as possible. We drove that night back to Milan, stayed at a motel near Malpensa, and managed to get on a flight early the next day. We dozed fitfully, and we talked. Maybe, Anna said, Skip and Karen decided to elope. Maybe, I suggested in desperation, he decided to take a cross country bus and pay his father a surprise visit, and the bus hadn't arrived yet.

"Maybe," said Anna, "he's just having a prolonged pot party."

But we knew better. Something was wrong.

I had called Mickey from Malpensa Airport, and he was there to meet us at Dulles with more disturbing news. He had gone back to the campus to try to pick up additional information. The security people, who were getting to know and like Mickey, told him that Karen, too, had been missing for what was now four days.

On the drive from Dulles to the Oasis, I called Maurice on Mickey's cell phone and set up an appointment for 7:30 the next morning. I reached Maria on the cell phone. She had called all the local hospitals and there was no record of the admission of Skip Silva or Karen Harrison.

From my apartment, I talked to Brad in California. He was, understandingly, agitated. Skip had never done anything like this before. For Skip to "pull off a disappearing act," he said, "was unthinkable." Brad would catch a mid-morning flight and be at the Oasis by late afternoon the next day. I arranged for Lars and Anna, and at Anna's suggestion, Sheila, to be with me at Maurice's office early the next morning.

I called Carl Harrison and told him his granddaughter was missing along with Skip. He was distressed, of course, and I said I would keep him informed, and would be in touch with him after talking to Maurice.

A torrential rain fell out of the sky as we left the Oasis on the following morning, and Lars, a skillful driver, was forced to pull over and wait for a respite. We arrived at Maurice's office ten minutes late, and he had coffee for everybody. His secretary wasn't due for an hour.

I summarized our situation.

"Who was the last person to see him?" Maurice asked.

"As far as we know," I said, "the security people on the campus."

"It's now been five days since they're missing?"

"Yes."

"We have to bring in the District police right away. I know Lt. Blake in Missing Persons. I'll set up a time for you to talk to him today. I think you and Mr. Harrison should go, nobody else."

Lt. Blake could see us at eleven that morning. I called Carl from Maurice's office to alert him. We got back to the Oasis at 9:30, and I decided to check my message machine before meeting Carl. As I approached my apartment I heard stirring inside.

I unlocked the door, opened it, and saw Skip and Karen sitting on the sofa. A mass of welts and bruises covered Skip's face. His upper lip protruded, and he was holding his left arm at an awkward angle. When he opened his mouth to speak no sound emerged. Karen's eyes were swollen and framed in black. A red line ran from the lobe of her right ear to her jaw line.

"My God in heaven," I cried out. "What happened?"

The words crawled out of Skip's mouth like worms emerging from a hole. "It's a long story, Sid."

Medical attention had to come before I listened to Skip's "long story." Carl Harrison and I drove them to a nearby hospital. In the waiting room Carl asked me what had happened, and I told him everything I knew - which was not much.

After an hour, the resident came out and told us she had sedated both of them. We could see them, but she cautioned us to hold off talking to them.

"There are lesions, deep but not critical," she said, "and our prelim indicates no concussions. It will be a week or so before they are back to normal. They are both suffering from severe dehydration. They have not had sufficient water for days. Do you know anything about what happened to them?"

"Nothing."

"The girl was not sexually molested, but she could use some emotional therapy."

She paused. "A few sessions with the therapist wouldn't hurt the boy either. We've notified the police and told them they should question the victims after they're home. They can go home in a couple of hours. We'll give you instructions for their treatment."

After an hour Carl and I went into the emergency room. Fresh bandages covered their faces, and their eyes were closed. After a few minutes Skip's eyes opened, made contact with me, and then closed. Carl and I brought them home later that afternoon.

Skip's father arrived, and after assuring himself that Skip had incurred no permanent damage, Brad said he could only stay overnight. A "huge" business transaction was going to take place in San Francisco, and it was imperative he return.

In the course of a half hour walk with Brad, an unwelcome insight visited me. The barrier between Brad and me was no less impenetrable than the one between Skip and me.

I asked why Brad's business meeting couldn't be postponed. Wasn't it more important that he be with Skip?

"I hear you," Brad said, "but you need to understand. I have momentum now, and if I delay, the whole thing could peter out."

"So it will peter out. Isn't being with your son more important than consummating a deal? He's been seriously hurt, physically and emotionally. He needs you."

"I know, but what I'm doing is for his good. I have to go to the meeting. I know he's in good hands with you."

My voice rose a notch. "Whether he's in good hands with me is not the point. He needs his father to be with him, to talk to him, to show his love for him."

He looked away. "I wish you had applied that advice to yourself forty years ago."

I swallowed hard in the wake of that rebuke. "I'm sorry you feel that way. What did I do that was so terrible?"

"You see?" Brad said. "You still don't understand. You didn't do anything 'terrible.' It's just that you were a . . . *perfunctory* father."

"What in hell does that mean?"

"It means I was just an item on your list of things to attend to. Sure, you took me places, and you played games with me, and you said I should improve my grades. But it was always routine, like washing the dishes or taking out the trash every morning. I was always just one of your annoying obligations."

"You're saying I didn't show interest in your inner life."

"You can put it that way. You took me for granted."

"I didn't show gratitude and enthusiasm for the blessing God had bestowed on me."

"Sarcasm. That's what I need right now."

"What you need right now is to come to grips with your responsibility to your son."

"Don't lecture me, Dad. Those days are gone, like when I rode my bike into the street and you came out of the house screaming like I had committed a crime."

"I was concerned you'd be hit by a car. Was that so terrible?"

"No, but you could have quietly talked to me later instead of embarrassing me in front of my friends."

"As I recall, your mother quietly talked to you later."

"Ah, now we're getting somewhere. It was always Mom who did your clean-up work. You would yell, and Mom would step in and calm us all down."

"Was that so bad, Brad? We're human beings and we compensate for each others' shortcomings. That's how we help each other. That's what I thought Mom and I did."

"Whatever. I'll be off tomorrow. Keep me informed about Skip."

Despite Brad's peremptory termination of our conversation, I might have tried to extend it. Except for "whatever," Skip's favorite and my least favorite word. I knew further conversation would only worsen our relationship.

I also knew the self-lacerating futility of looking back and asking: What did I do wrong? Yet, I occasionally engaged in that unproductive exercise, and each time it came down to the early-on assumption that my parental responsibilities would be properly discharged if I applied the same hands-on good will with Brad that had stood me in good stead everywhere else.

It had never entered my mind that my child needed something more from me. I hadn't been smart enough to figure out that the personality and set of attitudes that had gained me loyal friends and success in business were not going to be enough for Brad.

By conventional standards, I had been a good father. We had played checkers and chess, gone to sports events and rock concerts, and I had provided him every material benefit at my disposal. Somewhere in the process I had missed the boat. There had to have been a period of time - a month, a week, a day, an hour - when he had needed me and I hadn't come through. When I failed to connect with him.

Without thinking about it, I had shifted my psychological responsibilities as a father to Sarah, who had held up her end, spending long, nurturing hours with Brad, talking to him, encouraging him to tell her what made him happy and what made him unhappy, and listening. I would get home, ask how it went that day, joke with him, and go to bed.

Nor did I derive solace from reminding myself that in the history of the world there have been no flawless parents. Maybe this talk, unpleasant as it was, had been a start. Maybe now we'd talk some more and reach some form of détente, and I would be able to put an end to my guilt. But I doubted that would happen. It was probably too late for Brad and me, and for Brad and Skip - and for Skip and me.

I spent the better part of the next day reading and dozing next to Skip's bed. The police called, and asked me questions. I was unable to help them. They asked when they could speak with the victims of the assault. I said Skip and Karen were not yet coherent, and promised to call them in a few days.

By the third day the swelling in Skip's lip had diminished. He was beginning to speak - "How come no Coca Cola in the house?" When he suggested I take a walk, I understood that meant he wanted to smoke some pot. I hadn't touched his room since he left for the dormitory and I assumed he had the stuff stashed away somewhere.

Karen was also on the road to recovery. Except for a thin bandage covering the lower right side of her face, and a few remnants of the black-and-blue under her eyes, the rose was showing signs of a new bloom. She said her hearing was almost back to normal. They spent a lot of time on the phone. The young heal quickly.

I felt as bad about Karen as I did about Skip, and I told that to Carl. When he said it wasn't my fault, I muttered I wasn't so sure. He asked me what I meant, and I let it go.

Neither of them was willing to talk to a therapist. "Out of the question," Karen said.

The police called again and I held them off for a few more days. Then I had the first sustained conversation with Skip since the attack.

"You're going to have to go over everything with the police," I said, "so why don't you take me through it first?"

He hesitated. "All right. Everything was good. My classes were good, Karen was good, the whole scene was cool. One day Karen and me decided to . . ."

"Karen and I."

"Karen and I decide to have lunch at Melons, a cool place near the campus. We get this idea. Why not have a quick smoke in back of the restaurant before we eat? So we go through the kitchen, come out the back door, and walk through the alley. We're about to light up when this dude with a goatee sneaks up behind, puts a vice-like grip on both our elbows, and throws us into a car that pulls up in the street next to the alley.

"Wait a minute, Skip. Bear with me. The quick smoke. You're talking about a joint, right?"

"Yeah."

"Why are you smoking a joint *before* you eat? Isn't it usually the reverse order?"

"Not necessarily. Depends on how you feel. We felt like it then."

"Then why not smoke one on the campus before you left? Nobody on the campus seems to care. Why take the risk of getting caught by the police?"

"What is this, a cross examination?"

"You're going to talk to the police. Your story has to make sense."

His volume went up a notch. "We smoke a joint - *almost* smoke a joint. We get kidnapped and beat up. Why are you ragging on me?"

"I'm sorry to have to say this. I have the feeling you're not telling me everything."

He put the can of Coke on the kitchen table, got up and walked to the door, his back to me. He placed his hands high on the door and stood there. He turned around, sat down and picked up the Coke. He looked like he was about to cry, but he didn't.

"I fucked up. I guess I better tell you what really happened."

"I want to believe you, Skip. This time level with me, give me everything - all the details."

PART THREE

Do not go gentle into that good night,
Old age should burn and rage at close of day;
Rage, rage against the dying of the light.

Dylan Thomas
Do Not Go Gentle into That Good Night
[1952]

Chapter 17

Skip told his story in scattershot fashion - bits and pieces, rambling back in time, and then jumping ahead. When he related the scam that Karen had concocted, he looked straight at me with what I took to be pride in his girlfriend-accomplice. But when he spelled out his willing, indeed, eager participation in the illicit and dangerous scheme, he evaded my eyes. He gave me his best recollections of the e-mails and letters. I gave him my full attention and resolved not to interrupt - a resolution I broke a few times.

*

Skip began by acknowledging my admonitions some months ago. *I want you to cancel the virus, erase the whole thing, pull out, or whatever the hell the terminology is. KILL IT. OK, Grandpa*, he had said. And a few weeks later, *Kill the goddamn virus right now, in front of all of us.* And Skip saying, *Done.*

Skip had lied both times. He had pretended to kill the virus, but left it intact because he was "having too much fun with it." He continued to monitor Hardy's e-mail after he had moved onto the campus, and came up with some more "good stuff" on Hardy's conspiracy. But he couldn't tell me about it because he knew I believed he had closed down the operation.

Karen and Skip had hit it off when they met some four months earlier. She returned to her midwest college after Skip moved into his dorm, but over the next three months she was on Skip's campus almost as often as her own. It appeared to me that she made plans to transfer to Skip's college long before he suggested it.

As their friendship blossomed into romance, Karen assumed the upper hand, and it stayed that way. Skip had fallen under her sway. Their friends were of her choosing, and she selected the courses they took, the TV shows they watched, and the CDs they listened to. She decided when they would study and when they would play. McDonald's or Burger King. Karen called the shots.

Skip was thrilled that an attractive "older woman" found him worthy of her time and attention. Magnetized by her intellectual strength, intrigued with her precocious business acumen, he found her supply of energy to be inexhaustible. But there was more. Avoiding the explicit, he conveyed to me that their lovemaking conferred a level of pleasure and ego-fulfillment he had never experienced. Skip had become her willing captive lover.

What drew this twenty-four-year-old wonder-girl to an eighteen-year-old naif remained to be seen. I speculated that Karen may have had some of the qualities of Skip's mother, Paula. If Karen, like Paula, "got off on" - to use a phrase ubiquitous in Skip's articulations - dominating and controlling men, then with Skip she had a ready-made setup. Like his father Skip was susceptible to an aggressive, sexy woman.

Neither Skip nor Carl, her grandfather, was aware at this time that avarice was at the core of Karen's being. Avarice unencumbered by ethical considerations. As Karen watched Skip demonstrate his remarkable faculty on the computer keyboard, I suspect she felt her main chance would come. All she had to do was wait.

Sitting at the computer together - Skip dazzling her with his prowess, Karen in awe of his proficiency - they read Hardy's e-mail, scoffing at Hardy's arrogance, laughing at his bluster.

When one of the suppliers would complain about Hardy's ten percent fee, as many of them did repeatedly, Karen's eyebrows would rise, and she would say something like, "There's an angle here. I can't put my finger on it, but I smell it. It will come and when it comes I'll know it."

One day, they came upon an e-mail unlike the others. Skip remembered the wording.

Elsie: Sell all the EMA stock immediately. You'll make good money. I have inside word that the company will release a revised financial statement in the next few weeks that will send the stock crashing through the floor. SELL IT NOW.

Chuck

Another e-mail, identical in content, had been sent to "Brandy."

Karen erupted in a paroxysm of joy. "This is what we've been waiting for. This is our ticket to real money. Now we've got ammunition to launch a two-pronged attack. We're almost there, sweetheart."

"I'm sorry," Skip said, "I don't know what you're talking about."

"When I worked at Tallmark they would give assignments to a staff lawyer. Find out what's legit and what's not legit. Price fixing, bid rigging, inside information. Trying to keep their nose clean. I was the assistant and did most of the work. In the space of six months I became an expert. I even got the legal lingo down."

Karen explained that Hardy crossed the line when he "selectively disclosed" nonpublic information, in this case advance warning of earnings reports. If the Securities and Exchange Commission found out about Hardy's disclosure to "Elsie" and "Brandy," whoever they were, Hardy would be subject to a fine and maybe jail.

"I don't see what he did was so terrible," Skip said. "He tipped off a couple of friends, but he didn't hurt anybody."

Karen turned to him, patiently. "Let's say I own some stock and I get word that the company is about to release information that will cause the price of the stock to drop. I sell what I have - fast. You own the same stock, but you don't get the advance word so you sit with what you have. You and I are not on a level playing field. I am getting the tip. You are getting screwed."

"Okay, okay," Skip said. "So how does this help us?"

"We know Elsie Turner owns 500 shares of EMA. Her stock certificate is one of the papers we took from your grandfather's drawer. We're going to send a letter to Mr. Hardy enclosing copies of these e-mails and tell him that if he comes up with $50,000 we won't send this to the government."

"That's blackmail, Karen."

"When did you become a priest?"

"Suppose he tells us to go to hell?"

She smiled broadly. "That brings me to the second prong. Along with the e-mails we send him the Agreement between Hardy and his thirty-five conspirators we found in the drawer and tell him this time it goes to the Justice Department. That would land him in jail for sure."

At this point in Skip's story I broke my resolution not to interrupt. "What are you talking about? *How did she get hold of that Agreement? And the Certificate?*"

"Hold on."

Skip looked at the floor for a long time. Finally, he sighed and began to speak, more slowly than his normal patter.

In the course of the Task Force meetings he had attended, Skip had listened to our conversations, and gathered that I kept what we called the "condo papers" somewhere in my apartment. When Anna and I were in Canada some four months earlier, Skip and Karen entered my apartment, using the key I had given him.

They searched the apartment and found the condo papers in my bottom drawer. They copied everything, including the Agreement and Elsie's stock certificate in Efficiency Management, and returned them to my drawer.

What I had done to Elsie they did to me. I bit my tongue and remained silent. I knew I hadn't heard the worst of it.

Skip continued his story. They rented a Post Office Box in Washington. Then they mailed a typewritten letter to Hardy which Karen had drafted with considerable pride. Skip gave me his rough recollection of the letter.

> Mr. Hardy: Attached are copies of your e-mails to "Elsie" and "Brandy." They show that you are sending stock tips to your friends based on your inside information. Also attached is a copy of your Agreement with 35 suppliers. These documents show that you are engaging in illegal acts. If you mail a certified check for cash in the amount of $50,000 to P.O. Box Number 4978, Post Office at Pennsylvania Avenue and Thirteenth Street, we will destroy the documents and you will never hear from us again.

> Don't try to spot us at the post office. We will know.

Beginning four days after they mailed the letter, they visited the post office at random times every day. Karen would wait outside while Skip would go in and look around. If he saw nothing suspicious he would walk out to the sidewalk, rubbing his right ear. This was always the case. Karen would then go in and check the box.

On the sixth day the reply came to Box 4978.

> Although I have not violated any law, I will oblige you to avoid a complicated situation. I have a severe cash flow problem at this time.
>
> I would like to meet with you and discuss a realistic amount and a schedule of payments.
>
> Chuck Hardy

Their response was prompt.

> Hardy: Under no circumstances will we meet with you. The amount is fifty thou, no less. Borrow it from the bank. You have ten days.

Skip said the students were generally aware of the uniformed campus security force, and were friendly with some of them. During this period, Skip noticed that the security people seemed to be watching him beyond their usual routine

After a few days, he told Karen about the surveillance he had observed. They worked out a system where Skip would go about his business on the campus, and Karen would hang back and observe the uniformed personnel to see if Skip's suspicion was for real.

"They're watching you, and me, too," she said. "Your grandfather has totally lost his mind."

"Tell me about it."

"Pretend we don't know anything. Ignore them," she whispered into his ear.

On the third day, he and Karen had no classes until two. Skip called her in the morning and suggested lunch at Melons, an off-campus restaurant. He'd pick her up in front of her dorm.

"They're on us like glue around here, but they can't follow us when we leave the campus, so I think we'll lose them," Skip said.

As they took the ten-minute walk leisurely, Karen, through adroit window shopping, determined that nobody was following them. They made their way through the crowded restaurant, smiled their way through the kitchen, and came out the service exit onto an alley. Laughing all the way, they walked hand in hand down the alley toward the quiet residential street intersecting with the alley.

Vaguely, they heard somebody behind them, talking. Skip looked around and saw, some distance away, a tall man in a suit speaking rapidly into his cell phone.

When they reached the street they stopped to look around, still laughing. The cell-phone man, now wearing a mask, had caught up to them. Tough looking and beefy, he placed a numbing lock on both their forearms. He said, "Do what I tell you." Karen looked at Skip, a pleading look on her face.

"We stood completely still," Skip said. "I was scared as hell. I asked the guy what this was all about."

The cell-phone man said, "Shut up." They waited for perhaps half a minute, until a dark blue Buick Le Sabre drove up. "I looked at the windows to see who was inside, but they had been coated. The cell-phone man told us to get in."

Skip and Karen turned, resisting, and as they began to protest, the man punched Skip hard just above his belt with his left fist, and, almost simultaneously, landed a roundhouse slap to Karen's right ear with his right hand. Later she told Skip she heard loud ringing and nothing else. A thin man sitting next to the driver got out of the car and helped the cell-phone man drag and push Karen and Skip into the car. All of them wore masks. Nobody else was on the street to hear their cries for help.

"They blindfolded us and drove for a while."

"How long?" I asked.

"Maybe half an hour. Whenever I started to say something, somebody told me to shut up. So the drive was silent. I had a hunch this was connected to the e-mail stuff. I was never so scared in my life. I couldn't stop trembling."

After they arrived at their destination Skip was led up a flight of stairs. A voice said, "Give me your wallet." Skip reached for the wallet and held it in his hand. Somebody snatched it away. The voice said, "Now, yours, li'l darlin'."

I sat there listening impassively, but a frisson ran through my body as I recalled No-shave in San Juan gently admonishing Airhead. *Now calm down, li'l darlin', Dolly's just doing her job.* How many people in the world used that phrase? Hardy had dispatched No-shave - Gus - to do the dirty work.

Skip said the amount of cash in both their wallets was negligible. He was made to sit on a straight back chair. The blindfold remained in place, his ankles and wrists were tied to the chair, and a gag was taped across his mouth. A long silence ensued and Skip assumed the thugs were not in their immediate area.

He wondered if Karen was in the same room. Feet flat on the floor, he rose with considerable effort, carrying the chair with him, and banged onto the floor twice. A few second later he heard two answering bangs.

They remained bound to the chairs, blindfolded and gagged with what felt like industrial tape. Except for the occasional sound of a passing car, the room was silent. Skip developed a dryness in his mouth, and a growing thirst.

After the "endless" passage of time, a voice said, "I'm going to take the gag off and give you water. You say ONE WORD, the gag goes back You have to piss or shit, bang your chair twice like you did when you thought nobody was in the room. Somebody will be in the bathroom with you."

The tape was stripped away from Skip's mouth, producing a painful sting in his lips. The voice said, "Open up," and Skip opened his mouth wide. A stream of water was squirted into his mouth, faster than he could ingest. He swallowed as much as possible. As the remaining water fell onto his neck and down his shirt, the tape was replaced on his mouth.

Skip next heard the voice say, "You heard what I told him. Same goes for you, li'l darlin'."

Skip imagined water being poured into Karen's mouth. He heard a slight choking sound from her. This was followed by "hours and hours of silence." The blindfold was thick, and Skip was unable to discern lightness or darkness. He slept intermittently and fitfully.

He was having a tortured dream when he woke up to the sound of people talking. The dry thirst had returned with a vengeance. He wasn't hungry, but he felt the thirst could be his undoing. In desperation he rustled around in his chair.

"Sit still, asshole," a new voice said. "I know what you want. You'll get water when I think you're ready." Skip ceased his movements. He began to retch through the gag and thought he was about to pass out.

"All right, asshole, the gag comes off. ONE WORD and the gag goes back." The gag was stripped away. Skip's burning need for water was so all-consuming that he hardly noticed the stinging pain in his lips this time. The watery cascade resumed and Skip drank in huge gulps causing him to choke, but through the chokes he continued to swallow the water.

The new voice said, "I'm taking your gag off, li'l darlin.' You going to say anything?" Skip imagined Karen shaking her head from side to side. He knew her thirst must have equaled his.

The regimen continued for what Skip guessed was more than twenty-four hours. Deadening thirst, agitated bouts of sleep torn by nightmares, and the stench of urine forced by fear.

"Now for the fun. Who goes first, you or li'l darlin'?"

Skip banged his chair twice, clinging to the hope that if he could buy some time for Karen, somehow she might be spared. He was wrong.

Somebody untied his wrists and ankles, grabbed hold of a tuft of his long hair, and lifted him to a standing position, producing a piercing burning sensation through his scalp. The blindfold and tape were left in place.

The following minutes - maybe hours - lived in Skip's memory as a kaleidoscope of blows, grunts, cries, and above all, pain surpassing his limited experience. When they finished, he lay in a motionless state hovering between conscious and unconscious. He vaguely discerned that numbness had replaced pain in most of his face, but his left arm broadcast its torment to the rest of his body. He assumed it was broken, and it turned out he was right.

The worst was yet to come. Through the fog now imprisoning his mind, he heard screaming. He thought the eerie sounds must be coming from some other place. Then he realized they were from Karen. He understood why they had removed Karen's gag after leaving his in place. They wanted him to hear her screams.

An hour later, the first voice addressed them again. "Now, listen up, assholes. We've got a message for you to give to Grandpa."

Skip was alternately retching and dozing, and could barely keep his head up straight. A sharp slap crossed his face.

The first voice said, "Are you with me, asshole? Do you hear me?"

Skip tried to nod yes.

"You tell Silva we know the bitch gave him the e-mail and some other shit after she sold the stock. Then he sics the two of you onto the extortion. He is to destroy all the paper, drop the investigation, and call off the lawyers. He doesn't do all that, what happened here is NOTHING compared to what he'll get. It's OVER. Tell him the bitch is next. Now repeat the message."

For the third time the tape was stripped from Skip's mouth. Skip was unable to speak.

"You going to give me the message?"

Skip began to repeat the message as best he could remember it through the pain and thirst. "They know that Elsie gave the e-mail to my grandfather. They know that my grandfather told us to . . ."

"After she sold the stock, asshole."

"After she sold the stock. They know my grandfather told us to try the extortion and . . . but listen, please, that's just not true. You've got to hear me. My grandfather didn't know anything about . . . ."

This time there was no slap. Instead, a steel-hard object struck Skip's jaw with the force of a sledgehammer. When he regained consciousness he could only hear the sound of Karen - it had to be Karen - retching and choking.

Water was thrown at his face and voice number one said, "Last chance, asshole. Give me the message for your grandfather."

"They know everything. They know Elsie gave you the e-mail after she sold the stock. They know you got Karen and me to extort money from Hardy. We drop everything. No more investigation, no more lawyers, no more nothing. Otherwise, they'll hurt you more than they hurt us. And Elsie is next."

Eventually, he was lifted up and led to the sound of a car engine.

"Duck your head, asshole," the second voice said, pushing Skip into the car. "You, too, li'l darlin', we don't want nothing bad to happen to you." Skip smelled, or imagined he smelled, a faint whiff of the fragrance Karen had been wearing when they left the dorm.

They drove for a half hour or so, and Skip could hear hard rain falling. Only one exchange occurred in the car.

"You remember the message? Or we go back and try again."

Skip nodded.

As the car slowed down, the second voice said, "Out."

The car came to a halt, and Skip was led onto the sidewalk. The first voice whispered, "One full minute before you take off the gag and blindfold. *With* me?"

Skip nodded vigorously. He heard the car drive off, waited a few seconds, and pulled off his blindfold and gag. Although it was still raining, Skip had the impression of a sharp light stunning him for a moment. He turned to Karen, who was sitting on the curb, quivering, and relieved her of the blindfold and gag. He looked around and realized they had been deposited on Connecticut Avenue in front of the Oasis.

The wet street was empty. Skip, half carrying Karen, staggered toward the building. He worked the key I had given him into the front door. The lobby, elevator and corridor were empty, and after the third attempt Skip unlocked my door.

They plunked themselves onto my sofa, unable to move about or even speak. Skip estimated it was twenty minutes later when I got home and found them.

*

By the time Skip had finished his narrative, I was drained. Perhaps unnaturally, my disgust was focused as much on Skip and Karen as it was on Hardy. But to sound off now would likely wreck what little was left of our relationship.

Anna's concern for Skip's well-being was justified, but not for the reasons she had supposed. Skip and Karen had not suffered their nightmare because the Board had retained counsel or because I had by-passed the lowest bidder. Hardy had other ways to act out his reaction to those events. He unleashed his fury on Skip and Karen because of their attempt to extort money from him. They had brought this on themselves.

The first priority was for Skip to get well. I tried to do all the things on the hospital instruction sheet, but my efforts were clumsy, and Anna and Sheila took over. They brought light food and juice. They administered the prescribed drugs, applied dressing to the wounds, changed bandages, and performed tasks I wouldn't have thought of.

Anna was especially good with Skip. The friendship and mutual affection they had been developing came to the fore, and without a doubt, Anna's presence made a difference in the progress of Skip's recovery. The two of them had conversations out of my presence, and my hunch was that Skip gave her the entire story.

Coordinating with Anna and Sheila some days later, Lars brought pizza and beer for everybody, action movies on DVD for Skip, and, for me, a case of Absolut. Lars said he was sorry he hadn't insisted on a campus surveillance team. I held back on telling them Skip's story, and they didn't press me.

My son called every day from California. After speaking with Skip, Brad would speak with me. He told me he was urging Skip to transfer back to the west coast.

We moved Skip's super-computer from the dorm to my place, and Mickey, who by this time had heard everything - from Maria who had received it from Anna - resumed his e-mail exchanges with Skip. He mailed three new advanced computer books to Skip. I told Skip that if I had the least glimmer that he was using the computer to intercept anybody's e-mail, the computer would be removed immediately.

"That crap is out of my life," he said. We'll see, I thought.

I spoke with Carl on the phone, and he told me Karen was "coming along." He pressed me for more information, but I stuck to Skip's story as modified.

A few days after Skip's return, I brought a box of chocolates and flowers to Carl in his apartment. Sitting up in the living room, Karen was no longer the emaciated skeleton I had seen on my sofa in that awful moment. She was clear- eyed, the ringing in her ear from that first slap was beginning to dissipate, and her other injuries were fading.

Carl, who had been attending Karen day and night, took advantage of my visit, and went out for a walk and fresh air. I was left alone with Karen.

Watching her crunch a cherry-filled Godiva, I gave it a try. "Skip has told me the whole story from the time you came to my apartment while I was in Canada. The exchange of letters with Hardy, the abduction, the beatings, the message. I would like to see what you can add."

"I can't talk about it. I'm sorry, Mr. Silva, I really can't." Tears were in her eyes.

After Carl returned from his walk, Karen went into the bedroom. Through the closed thin door, I could hear the sound of her voice on the phone. I knew that she and Skip called each other several times a day.

Carl and I split a beer, and, again, he pressed me for information. I remembered what he had told me - that Bunny would have to "think about" their relationship. Knowing Carl, I assumed there was little he wouldn't do to remain in her good graces. Whatever I had told Carl in the past had gone to Bunny and then to Hardy.

Not a person of strong character, Carl might be so desperate to mend his fences with Bunny, so dependent on her, that when she put the question to him - "What have you learned?"- he might just blurt out everything. So I kept quiet. Hardy knew, of course, that I knew he was behind what happened to Skip and Karen, but I didn't want Bunny to know about it.

Maurice had the entire matter in his care, and I would not interfere with him. I had reported everything to him, of course, including Skip's story, unedited.

"That kid could use some straightening out," Maurice had said.

"No shit, Sherlock," I had replied.

Two days after Skip's return, I told the police he was able to talk to them. Maurice arrived a couple of hours before the police, and listened to Skip's story, this time directly from Skip. Maurice advised Skip in strong terms to tell the police everything. Maurice and I sat in on the interview, and interjected no comments or questions.

The two plainclothes detectives, a man and a woman, were courteous and professional, but seemed to be going through just enough motions to cover themselves and leave. Skip related his story, omitting the extortion attempt and the "message" he had been told to deliver. He made these deletions in the absence of any suggestion from me that he leave out anything, and contrary to Maurice's admonition to tell them everything.

When they finished the questioning, they surprised me by discussing their tentative conclusions in front of us. The woman, the older of the two and apparently of a higher rank, sipped on her coffee, turned to her colleague, and said, "I think these perps are crazies. They took the wallets and decided to have some fun. After the fun, they said, screw it, let them go."

The man said, "Yeah, but the hospital report says the woman was not sexually molested, just severely beaten. That's not my idea of fun."

"Your idea of fun is rape?"

"I didn't say that."

Neither detective inquired about the reason the perps dropped off Skip and Karen in front of my building. After they left, Maurice asked Skip why he had left out the extortion and the "message."

"I figure Sid's situation is complicated enough without me adding to it," Skip said.

Maurice looked at the carpet and shook his head.

I asked Skip if there was any reason to believe that Hardy was present. Skip had the feeling that Hardy was nowhere near them, but he believed that everything said and done had come from Hardy.

"One thing I don't understand," Skip said. "We went to the post office at odd times when the place was empty. How did they spot us?"

Maurice said, "My guess is they got to the clerks who work there. Gave them a hundred dollars each and cameras. Watch Box 4978. When somebody opens it up, take their picture. Hardy had his own surveillance people on the campus, and they had already snapped you and Karen many times. They compared the photographs."

"How come campus security didn't spot Hardy's surveillance people?" Skip asked.

Maurice looked at me, and I said, "I don't know. I suppose they weren't interested in anybody who didn't make any threatening moves on you."

"Okay," Skip said. "Last question. Part of the message was about Elsie Turner. What's that all about?"

I hesitated, and gave him a half-true answer. "Hardy believes that after Elsie sold the stock, she decided to stick it to him by giving the e-mail and Agreement to me. And then I got you and Karen to squeeze money out of him. I have to warn Elsie. I've been putting it off, but I have to talk to her."

I made an on-the-spot decision. I would tell everything to Anna, Sheila, Lars, and Carl. Especially Carl. He had a right to know exactly what his granddaughter did.

I would review the formation of the task force, the bugged phone conversations, the e-mail interceptions, the break-ins, the surveillance, my theft of the documents from Elsie's desk, and Skip's story as he told it to me, not as he told it to the police. If all this went from Carl to Bunny to Hardy, so be it. If the story made the rounds of the gossip mill, the hell with it. I decided, as they say, to let it all hang out.

Once and for all, my role was finished. The chips would fall however they fell, but I was no longer a player.

Skip had been wanting to see Karen, and I had been urging him to wait. I thought a little distance from each other was in order. But now I needed him out of the place. I suggested that maybe the time had come for him to visit with Karen. He took off for Carl's place in five minutes, still wobbly. I called Carl, Lars, Anna and Sheila, and asked them to be at my apartment in fifteen minutes.

I told them everything I knew. When I finished, a long silence ensued, finally broken by Lars' exclamation, "Shit."

Carl said, "I think Skip put her up to this."

Another silence was broken by Sheila. "Carl, sometimes your stupidity is dazzling."

Carl looked like he was about to launch an attack on Sheila. Apparently, he thought better of it, and said, "Well, you should know, the police came and talked to Karen, and I sat in on the interview. She told them the exact same story Skip told them as Sid just related."

Anna urged me to walk away and leave everything in Maurice's hands. Sheila glared at me and said, "You know she's right."

I said it was all over for me except for one thing. I needed to warn Elsie. I would take her out that night for a bite and tell her what I had just told them. They agreed that was appropriate. They left and for the first time in days I was alone in my apartment.

Chapter 18

I called Elsie three times and left messages. Later that day, half asleep, I was watching the 5 p.m. local news. I was roused from my semi-stupor as the anchor said:

> The latest tragic event in our recent rash of hit-and-run incidents occurred last night at ten-thirty. While crossing Massachusetts Avenue just west of Dupont Circle, a woman identified as Elsie Turner was struck by a vehicle.
>
> Witnesses said a tan SUV with out of state license plates, moving at an excessive rate of speed, struck the victim. One witness, who withheld his name, said, "That SUV was heading right for her, like he wanted to hit her." Other details were not available. Ms. Turner was pronounced dead at George Washington Hospital.

I went into the kitchen and poured Absolut, neat, into a water glass. I walked around the apartment in a daze. I poured the vodka from the water glass into a rhododendron Elsie had given me. Then I went back to the kitchen and poured more Absolut into the glass. I swallowed some, poured the rest into the rhododendron I had bought as a companion to Elsie's plant, sat down, refilled the glass, and stared at it.

I went outside and began to walk at a fast pace. Sarah popped into my mind. Following her death I had experienced grief. Pure, unadulterated grief. What I felt now was different. A mix of anger, remorse, fear, and guilt. Above all, guilt.

The rapid walk did little to calm me down, but I kept at it, picking up the tempo. I must have walked a mile up Connecticut Avenue and into the park. I found a grassy strip, and tried pushups for a few minutes. I watched the squirrels and school kids playing soccer. I smiled wanly at the teachers and mothers supervising them. They smiled back.

Returning to the Oasis I went into my kitchen, and sat with my Absolut. I was responsible for the death of Elsie Turner. I folded my arms on the table in front of me, lowered my head, and for the first time since I lost Sarah five years earlier, I cried.

When Skip got back just after seven, he found me in that same position. "What's the matter, Sid?"

Before I could answer, the phone rang. Sheila asked, "Did you listen to the news?"

"Yes."

"Then you heard what happened to Elsie."

"Yes."

"Do we go to the cops?"

"What are we going to tell them? Hardy was behind this? Where's our proof? We'll end up implicating ourselves and do nothing to hurt Hardy or vindicate Elsie."

I was aware that I had been acting, to say the least, erratically. I'd been running around like a dog with a full bladder hunting for a fire hydrant. Involvement, non-involvement, involvement, non-involvement. The events in my life over the past months, especially the past weeks, were a far cry from the placid retirement I had envisioned.

Exhausted, I got into bed at ten o'clock. In the course of that sleepless night, my non-involvement came to a grinding halt as I formed the nucleus of a two-stage plan. First, I would humiliate him. Then I would turn him over to the justice system.

At 9:30 the next morning, I looked in on Skip. He was still sleeping. I went to the nearby Staples, bought a pack of envelopes, and made copies of Hardy's e-mails to Brandy Buffington and Elsie Turner. At the post office I bought thirty-five stamps.

I got out my vintage Royal typewriter and, referring to the bottom of the Agreement, typed the names and addresses of Hardy's thirty-five co-conspirators on the envelopes. I placed the e-mail copies in the thirty-five envelopes, affixed the stamps, and dropped them in the nearest mailbox. No cover explanation was necessary.

Each of Hardy's thirty-five co-conspirators held at least a thousand shares of EMA stock. The question remained, why had Hardy apparently failed to tip them off about the impending decline in the value of that stock, and at the same time disclose this information to Elsie and Brandy? My best answer was that he followed the principle of "selective disclosure," as Karen had used the term. The more people you tell, the greater the risk.

But what, in the first place, accounted for Hardy's largesse toward Elsie and Brandy? Elsie had withheld the Agreement from me because her possession of that confidential document was her leverage with Hardy. Elsie, God bless her, had been extorting money and stock from Hardy. Brandy presumably had her own form of leverage.

Hardy had mistreated both women, and in returning the favor they had upped the stakes. Hardy knew that each of them was in a position to wreck him and his career, and he complied with their demands.

Why had he not done to them what he had done to Skip and Karen? My guess was Elsie and Brandy had let him know their lawyers had copies of the documents together with explanations in a vault, with instructions to release the papers to the appropriate authorities if they were harmed. If Hardy knew this why did he order Elsie's murder? My only answer was his wrath had overcome his caution and common sense.

I went back to Carl's apartment and questioned Karen again, gently and low-key. Her resolve not to talk about what had happened was stronger than ever. I didn't push her.

While Karen was in the bedroom talking on the phone, presumably to Skip, Carl and I talked again.

"You said you told us everything," he said. "What's next?"

"Nothing. It's all in the hands of the lawyers."

"Why do I have trouble believing you?"

We asked Skip to join us in the kitchen for some of Anna's grilled chicken, but he declined, remaining in his room, apparently in one of his sullen moods. We heard a knock on the outside door. It was Karen, arriving unexpectedly, and looking pale.

"Just in time for supper," Anna said.

Unsmiling, Karen threw her a brusque "No thank you," and continued on her way to Skip's room, closing the door behind her.

"What is that all about?" I asked.

"That is all about Karen's swan song to Skip," said Anna.

"How do you know that?"

"You'll see."

When the chicken was ready, I tapped on Skip's door, and said, "Chow time for whoever's ready."

Two voices in unison said, "No thanks, not now."

We began to eat, and after a few minutes, Karen came out of Skip's room, said "Goodbye" without looking at us, and left the apartment.

Anna leaned toward me. "I think she told him it's over. We should help him understand this is the best thing that could have happened."

Skip came out and sat down with us at the kitchen table. He said he wasn't hungry and didn't want to talk. After Anna and I silently cleared the table, I put on a CD of Peggy Lee. *You let other women make a fool of you.* Standing behind Skip, Anna glared at me, and I quickly substituted Fats Waller singing "Ain't Misbehavin'."

Sitting down opposite Skip, I said, "Let me guess. She told you it's not working out, so a little distance between the two of you might be worth a try."

"I've made a decision," he said, ignoring my words, staring into his empty plate.

Anna smiled. "Can I guess? You're going back to the west coast."

Skip looked at her with a blank face and a slight nod.

"Good luck to you," Anna said.

"It adds up, Skip," I said. "I think you're showing good sense. Get into a school out there near your father, make a fresh start."

"She's going back to Kansas."

"This is the best thing that could have happened," I said. "You may not know that now, but in time you will. If I were you, I'd forget about her."

"That's for me to decide."

The decision was obviously Karen's to make, and she had made it.

I called Lars, our Treasurer, and told him that Oasis reserves had been augmented by the amount of $150,000. "You are really something," he said.

I dropped into Nikki's office, poured some coffee into a plastic cup, and sat down opposite her at her desk. On her face was a sad smile.

"I'm afraid this is goodbye, Sid."

"What are you talking about?"

"Hardy called early this morning. As of 5 o'clock I'm fired. Out of here."

"WHAT?"

"I haven't shown the loyalty he expects from high level employees. I asked him what that means. He said if I didn't know, I was more stupid than he had thought. He was getting rid of me for incompetence. His secretary was fired, too. He figured out how you knew he was going to be at the Ritz-Carlton in San Juan."

"I'm going to call him."

"Don't call him. It may have worked out for the best."

Nikki explained that Joe Fowler's hardware store was busier than ever, largely because the customers loved Joe. He had just taken over the lease for the store next to him, and was planning an expansion. For some time Joe had been after Nikki to quit her job at the Oasis and work part time in the store. She'd be terrific there, he had told her.

"After we're married I'll give it a try. The wedding's one month from now and you and Anna better be there."

"Nikki, I'm so sorry. You're a terrific asset for the Oasis, but more important, I've come to regard you as a good friend. I'll miss you."

"I'll tell you something, Sid. I know you better than you think I do. I know you shoot from the hip. I know you tell fibs. I know you can be evasive. I also know you're the kindest, most considerate, most generous man I've ever known."

"I love it, Nikki, but don't pile it on too much."

"I've worked for five condo presidents. You're the only one who helped my self-esteem. You're the father, brother, friend, lover I never had."

"What's this lover stuff?"

"Wishful thinking. Besides, you don't have to go to bed with somebody to love him. You went to bat for me and didn't ask for anything in return."

"I asked you for information about Hardy."

"I would have given you that for free."

Travail called later that afternoon. "I would like to meet with you, Sid. It's important to me."

"Fine. We can have lunch, but no Broth-L."

"I never want to see the Broth-L again."

"Buona Sera, noon tomorrow. I'll meet you outside the Oasis at eleven."

I got to Maurice's office at quarter to seven the next morning. He had mobilized his team of lawyers and paralegals. Within twenty-four hours they would begin to interview people from the properties that Efficiency managed, and would obtain affidavits from the more promising of these potential witnesses.

When the initial stage of the investigation had been completed, Maurice would communicate with the Antitrust Division of the Justice Department. At the same time, working with attorneys for the other properties, he would begin to prepare a class action suit for triple damages. He estimated three to four months for this phase.

Maurice took up the question of Elsie. Even if we were to push it with the police, he said, there would be insufficient evidence for them to believe she was murdered. One witness who thought an unidentified car was targeting her was not enough. I disagreed, arguing that we should go to the police, and at least talk them into an investigation.

Even if the witness were enough to establish police suspicion, Maurice said, how could the police tie it to Hardy? Would they believe that Elsie gave Sid her abusive ex-husband's e-mail so that Sid could use it to cause trouble for Hardy? Not credible.

Maurice discussed Skip and Karen. Assuming we could persuade Skip to go back and tell the police everything this time, where would that leave us? *I tried to extort money. I committed a felony.* Skip could tell them about the "message" from Hardy, and Hardy would, of course, tell the police he didn't know what they were talking about. Skip's assailants, including Gus, were out of sight, and there was no way to tie anything to Hardy.

"Now," Maurice said, "the big question. We'll ask that the interviews be treated confidentially, but there'll be leaks getting back to Hardy. He could very well come after you. I think you should get out of town for six months. With your friend, Anna."

"I like it here."

The weather continued to be moderate, and Travail and I took our time walking to Buona Sera. We exchanged a few platitudes, but avoided anything of substance. The lunch crowd was out in force, and I welcomed the semi-private table Maria had reserved.

"Some wine, Francis?" I asked after we were seated.

"Diet Coke, please."

Travail's physical earmarks were in place. His face was florid as always, and the drops of perspiration were perched on his forehead as always. But something was different. Gone was the imperial-imperious manner, and in its place was deference bordering on contrition. Every so often he would lightly touch his fingers to his throat.

From the outset, it was clear to me that he wanted to talk, and it turned out that he was groping toward the catharsis of something resembling a confession. While we were waiting for our shrimp salads, Travail spoke first. "I know you're going after Hardy. I think I can help you. Tell me what you want me to do and I'll do it. Anything."

"All right, Francis, I will. But first, why this change of heart?"

"I did some foolish things with Chuck Hardy, but violence was never part of any arrangement I had with him. Never. My life is pretty screwed up, but maybe I can do something right for a change. I remember saying . . . "

"Why don't you begin at the beginning?"

"The *very* beginning?"

"Why not?"

*

Francis Travail grew up during World War II in the sedate section of Northwest Washington called Cleveland Park. His father, Donald, was a successful banker, relying, Travail implied, on questionable wartime practices to expand his initial fortune. Donald was one of the major benefactors and a member of the Board of the Washington Cathedral, a leading contributor to the National Symphony Orchestra, and an active participant in the affairs of the Chamber of Commerce and the Board of Trade. A valued civic leader.

Hardly a month went by when The Washington Post did not report Donald's activities on behalf of such institutions as the United Way and the Boy Scouts of America. Local supplements ran features about Donald. His was a name to be reckoned with.

To Francis's mother, Eleanor, Donald was the charismatic center of social intercourse among their circle of prestigious friends. They moved easily within Washington's old society and diplomatic circles, including dinners at the White House. Eleanor knew one thing with implacable certitude. Donald's judgment was infallible.

Donald gave his only child every privilege, every opportunity to replicate and, indeed, exceed his father's financial accomplishments and social status. From a cultured English nanny to early acceptance at St. Albans School for Boys, Francis received all the advantages his father's position, means, and largesse could confer.

Consumed by his dream that Francis would one day be his successor, Donald had little tolerance for signs of imperfection in his son. He berated the boy when his grades were found wanting, excoriated him when his teachers reported misconduct, and upbraided him in front of his friends for whatever peccadillo Donald perceived to be inappropriate. By the time Francis was ten, he would cower if his father so much as frowned in his direction.

As a result of the unrelenting criticism from the one person he most respected and most feared, Francis arrived at the onset of his teenage years with his sense of self-worth sorely damaged. He would not be able to identify the source of this impediment to maturity until many years had passed.

When Donald died prematurely, Francis was in his senior year at the University of Pennsylvania and had applied for admission to the Wharton School of Business. Upon his father's death, he left school and never returned. Francis took over Donald's investment "portfolio," and provided for Eleanor during her remaining five years. By dint of luck and perhaps a modicum of skill, the portfolio grew, and his investments appreciated substantially. It appeared that Francis would never have to worry about money.

By the time he moved into the Oasis in the late eighties, Francis, now in the dawn of middle age, had taken to drink and had slithered his way through a couple of bad marriages, expensive divorces, and a series of dubious dalliances. The combination of alcohol and ill-advised romances had cost him. His roller coaster life took its toll on his emotional well being, and this, in turn, impaired his business judgment.

He began to make imprudent investments, resulting in a severe reduction of the value of his portfolio. Francis began to visit Atlantic City and try his luck - poker, blackjack, whatever was available.

The more his fortune shrunk, the more he gambled, and the more he gambled the more money he lost, and the more money he lost the more he drank, and the more he drank, the more frequently he attached himself to duplicitous women. Aware that his behavior was self-destructive, Francis launched himself into a succession of Alcoholics Anonymous, psychoanalysis, Buddhist meditation, Scientology, and Gamblers Anonymous. Nothing he attempted arrested the downward spiral of his life.

After a month at the Oasis, he met Bunny Slack to whom he was attracted, but who had other fish to fry at the time. A year later, Bunny's amorous life was between acts, and she let Francis know she might be willing to test the waters with him.

In one respect, Bunny resembled the other women in Francis's adult life. She was a scheming hustler with an insatiable appetite for money - the possession of money, the trappings of money, and the prospects of more money.

In other ways, Bunny was unlike Francis's women. She constantly sought social approval. Although she was sometimes vociferous in expressing her strongly-held views, she was adamant that the social niceties be observed and that her friends and peers regard her as "a person of breeding and responsibility." She wasted no time in letting Travail know that if he was to be her "escort" he would have to quit, or at least curb, his drinking. With a will he had thought he lacked, Francis did this.

"I tamed my habit," he said to me, "and became a social drinker."

A key element in Bunny's definition of "social responsibility" was to "give back" to the community some of the benefits it had bestowed upon her. Bunny's version of repaying her debt to society was to serve on the Board of the Oasis. In this capacity she could prevent the feckless expenditure of condo funds, a pattern, she believed, that had characterized previous Oasis Board practice.

Most of Bunny's friends lived in other opulent condos and served on their boards. An informal "network" had evolved in which these friends would meet over brunch and exchange condo information, including financial strategies. The opportunity to rub shoulders with these people of affluence and influence nourished Bunny's self-pride.

During their period of incubation, Francis learned that Bunny was probing her friends to find out as much as she could about Francis Travail. Francis knew that some of what she learned was accurate, but much of it was more myth than fact. Bedazzled by the grandeur of Francis's aristocratic provenance as well as the pile of money she now believed he had amassed, she invited him into her bed.

Francis's interest in Bunny ripened into ardor, and before long he was, if not subservient to her every desire, cautiously respectful of her needs. One of those needs was the accumulation of jewelry.

When Bunny showed him her hoard, Francis was incredulous - every shape, size, material, and function of gemstone her taste and imagination could embrace. Her drawers overflowed with broaches, clasps, pins, pendants, earrings, bracelets, necklaces, and rings. Bunny took him through everything, supplying a running commentary on the esoteric qualities of each of the sapphire, ruby, topaz, garnet, amethyst, emerald, onyx, pearl, jade, gold, and silver pieces. An entire armoire was dedicated to diamonds.

The heaven-on-earth into which Bunny had admitted Francis eclipsed his most cherished experiences, and following a month of erotic rapture, Francis said he would like to take her on a visit to Cartier. Bunny feigned hesitation, and after his insistent importuning, she obliged him.

With Francis urging her on, Bunny selected an assortment of gems, mostly diamonds, the cost of which brought Francis's dwindling portfolio to its lowest level. He revealed not an iota of discomfort. He did the reverse. He suggested they pay a monthly visit to one or another of Bunny's favorite jewelry stores. She could barely contain the surge of euphoria flowing through her body. She was now able to appreciate that this man didn't just have money. He had *real* money.

Francis's burst of generosity propelled Bunny into broaching a certain subject sooner than she had planned. Francis should run for the Oasis Board after which she would manipulate the Board members into electing him President. She told Francis this was his chance to "give back to the community." He readily assented.

Bunny had another, more pressing, motive. After the election, Bunny would attend the network brunches with the new President of the Oasis at her side. When the members would learn, as Bunny would ensure they would learn, that the father of her companion was Donald Travail - *the* Donald Travail - and that Bunny's relationship with Francis was something more than collegial, their attention and respect would no longer be perfunctorily polite. She would finally be accepted as an equal.

Bunny's plan worked smoothly. Francis was elected to the Board for a four-year term, and in the three days preceding the "organization meeting," Bunny lobbied skillfully among the Board members. The Board elected Francis President.

Francis did not delude himself that the glory and power he now enjoyed would have arrived without the help of Bunny. On the contrary, his gratitude to her merited a return trip to Cartier.

On the very next day, Francis received his monthly financial statement. For the first time the value of his portfolio had fallen below the six-figure mark. It was imperative that he find a way to supplement the meager dividends he was now receiving.

Serendipity was with him. Even as Francis was digesting the grim financial information, Chuck Hardy called to congratulate him on assuming the Presidency of the Oasis, the "crown jewel" in Hardy's panoply of properties. Hardy said he would like to take Francis to lunch at Hardy's favorite restaurant, the Broth-L.

They met in front of the restaurant, and as they were led to their table, Francis reveled at the slit in the skirt of the buxom hostess, and the cowboy hats and fringed mini-skirts and boots-up-to-the-knees on the waitresses. And their flirtatious banter.

Francis' suppressed fantasies sprang to life. Sipping his Dewars, he began to perceive Chuck as his kind of guy. This man had his priorities straight. Hardy spoke freely about the ebbs and tides of his business, and Francis felt sufficiently comfortable to mention how poorly his investments had been doing.

Francis sized up Hardy as a man who was maybe fifty, and looked you straight in the eye. What once might have once been corpulence had been honed to a slight paunch behind which, Francis suspected, was a hard strength. Hardy, he believed, would uncoil like a snake if somebody provoked him. But provoking people was not what Francis did.

At this point in reciting his narrative, Travail went to the restroom, and I reflected on Hardy and Travail sitting across from each other in the Broth-L. Surely, Hardy found himself looking at a weak, fat, sweaty boozer with a perpetual hard-on who needed money. He had found his man.

Travail returned and resumed his story.

After more Scotch, Hardy said, "Congratulations on your new job. You're going to be the best they've ever had."

"Thanks. Pain in the neck, but somebody's got to do it. Ha, ha."

Hardy dug out two cigars from inside his jacket, and offered one to Francis, who shook his head no. Shrugging, Hardy lit up and exhaled in the general direction of Francis, who sniffed in the smoke, trying to recapture a piece of the pleasure he had once enjoyed.

They talked about the Redskins' chances under the new coach. Not good. And the Wizards' chances under the old coach. Not good.

Mostly, they watched the waitresses at work, and speculated about which of the sexy beasts would be the most fun.

Francis, grinning, said, "The blonde holding the tray, two tables over. That would be some kind of a weekend in Atlantic City."

"She'd kill you the first hour," said Hardy. "You want somebody who'll take her time. The slinky one with the black hair, that's what the doctor ordered. Slinky would make every minute count. You wouldn't just pay her, you'd thank her."

Francis sat back in his chair and sipped his Scotch. He hadn't felt this contented in a long time.

It was apparent that Slinky had spotted the two geezers looking her over. As she passed Francis's chair, she trickled her fingers down his back. She kept on walking, slowly, wiggling her rear-end, knowing Francis would be taking it all in. Watching Francis leering at Slinky, Hardy gave Francis a wink and a nod, and Francis's previous spark of insight was confirmed: this man spoke his language.

After the second round of drinks, Hardy suggested they order food. Francis picked up the wooden-slab menu shaped in the profile of a nude woman with exaggerated buttocks and busts. Taking hold of the outsized nipple to open the page, he giggled, and said, "How'd you find this place?"

Hardy winked again. "Stick with me. It only gets better."

They had the special, "beef broth," a salad, and another round of drinks. They ate quickly, and when they were finished, Francis said, "Dee-lish-us."

"Yeah," said Hardy, peering into Francis' eyes as if he were looking for the solution to a puzzle. "Let me run through a little scenario, see how it grabs you."

"Shoot."

"You've got something I need and I've got something you might want. Maybe we can do business."

"I'm listening."

"It's pretty simple," Hardy said. "Your new job, you're going to come into a lot of information. You send it my way, I pay you. End of story. But, and this is a big but, it has to be between you and me. Word gets out, it screws up my system."

"I don't want to be part of anything that will get me in trouble."

"No way," said Hardy. "You'd just be giving me advance notice on things that will become public anyway. Help me organize more efficiently, save people money."

"What do you mean, organize more efficiently?"

Hardy's face registered impatience. "The market is messy. I try to bring a little order out of chaos, help people get into line. Follow?"

Francis wasn't following. "What would I have to do?"

"Easy. Keep your eyes and ears open, stay on top of jobs coming up. Roof, elevator, plumbing, electricity, drain repair, whatever. Your condo, other condos you hear about. Small jobs, big jobs, whatever. What is the Board thinking? Who has the inside track? Strictly information. Call me or e-mail me. You have e-mail?"

"Yes."

"Okay, send me e-mail. Anyway, we'll have lunch like every couple of weeks and get up to date with each other. You like this place?"

Francis smiled. "You know I do." He ran his fingers around the nipple on the menu. "You say you'd pay me. What kind of money are we talking about?"

Hardy told him the amount. "We'll call it a stipend, paid monthly. And when you come up with really good info, we'll get out of town. You like to try your luck, you said something about Atlantic City."

"I've been to the tables a few times."

"We'll go there. You'll be my guest, of course."

Francis hesitated. "One thing. You said you try to bring people into line. That means?"

"No rough stuff," Hardy said. He paused. "I understand you're hooked up with a group that meets for brunch."

"You mean the condo network. We swap info back and forth."

"We'd make that part of our package."

"Sounds good to me."

Francis was delighted. This wouldn't restore the portfolio to its earlier level, but it would ease a few burdens. All he had to do was listen and feed the stuff to Chuck.

Over the four years he was President, Francis stayed in constant contact with Hardy. By telephone, e-mail, and lunches at the Broth-L,

Francis supplied accurate, up-to-date accounts of Board deliberations concerning vendors and service providers. These accounts covered Oasis Board meetings and inside information of a dozen other condos which Francis learned about at the brunches.

The stipend, always in cash, arrived on time every month, and for especially useful information Francis earned a bonus. This occurred two or three times a year, and Hardy, true to his word, would treat Francis to a weekend in Atlantic City. The priorities Francis had admired during that first discussion at the Broth-L never varied. Accommodating women, booze, and casinos.

Francis came to understand that Hardy was happy to have him as a companion on these sojourns because Hardy could control him. When and with whom to have sex, when to gamble, when and where to eat. Whatever Hardy wanted was fine with him. And Hardy grinned when Francis regaled him with stories about Bunny's jewelry fetish.

From time to time, Francis would let Bunny know he was "cooperating closely" with management. She would shrug, and change the subject. Once, in the repose following sex, he told her what "cooperating closely" meant, and disclosed his clandestine activities with Hardy. She yawned, and said, "Whatever turns you on."

Although their fire came to burn less intensively over the four years, Bunny and Francis found it mutually advantageous to continue seeing each other. Francis was not able to host the Cartier excursions as often as Bunny would have liked. Nor was she unaware that their sexual zeal had cooled. She chalked it up to the inexorable erosion of fervor time wreaks, and it didn't bother her. As for Francis, a pittance was better than nothing.

The crunch came when Francis's term on the Board expired after four years. He was not eligible to run for reelection under Oasis rules, and a relatively new resident, Sid Silva, was elected to succeed him. Hardy asked Francis to check this new guy out. Take him to the Broth-L, he said, on me.

After the lunch, Francis reported to Hardy that Silva was a mixed bag. When Francis told Silva not to put too much stock in the always-complaining Lars Rehnberg and Anna Carroll, Silva seemed to go along with the don't-look-for-trouble advice. Silva then expressed concern about previous condo costs. Francis gave him some more leave-well-enough-alone counsel, but Silva did not seem satisfied.

Hardy said, "We'll have to keep a close eye on this guy."

Hardy told Francis he owed him one more "big weekend fling," but it would have to wait a while. He asked Francis to flag a Board member who could take over the job Francis had been doing for Hardy.

Francis didn't hesitate. "Bunny Slack," he said. "She'd be perfect. She stays on top of what the Board is doing, and she still has her network connections."

Hardy approached Bunny, and gave her the proposition he had given Francis four years earlier. Bunny was delighted, and Hardy immediately put her on his payroll. Stripped of power and extra money, Francis resumed serious drinking, and after a few weeks, Bunny said, "The time has come for you and me to call it quits."

With no leverage left to resist this fiat, Francis slunk away like a dog whose master has grown tired of his pet and no longer feeds him. Later, Francis heard that Bunny had taken up with Carl Harrison, one of his poker rivals. Francis resolved not to allow his hurt to show. He was partially successful.

Eight months later, as promised, Hardy hosted Travail's final bonus payoff in Puerto Rico.

"That's my story," Travail said, gesturing the waitress for a diet Coke refill. "Not pretty, but every word is true."

"I appreciate your coming forward like this," I said. "Would you be willing to give my lawyer an affidavit?"

"I guess so, but I could be in trouble, myself. My confidential information helped Hardy squeeze more money out of the properties he managed. Can your lawyer help me?"

"If he thinks you need a lawyer, he'll recommend one. I'm not a lawyer, but I've had business experience. I can't see a prosecutor breathing hard over somebody disclosing the maintenance plans of a nonprofit condo."

"Tell me where and when to meet your lawyer and I'll be there."

Chapter 19

Nikki's replacement was a thin-lipped sour lemon of few words who seemed to have abandoned all pretense of social grace. During our initial conversations, she was punctilious in taking notes. Hardy had presumably instructed her to commit to paper every word I said.

Toward the end of our first meeting, I said, as an experiment, "Looks like we're in for rain this afternoon." Sure enough, without so much as a nod, she dutifully recorded my comment onto her yellow pad, and didn't seem to care whether I noticed or not. At our first two meetings, Mrs. Crowe, as she wanted to be called, never once smiled.

In the course of our second meeting, Mrs. Crowe asked, "Does the Oasis have a lawyer?"

"Why do you ask?"

"There is a new law that requires us to submit a form in order to keep our non-profit status. It's complicated and I think we need advice on what to say."

Nikki had told me about this and said she would have no trouble filling out the form. She was discharged before she could get to it.

"Ask Mr. Hardy to recommend a lawyer."

In late August Anna and I drove Skip to the airport, nobody saying much. He was leaving as he had arrived - backpack, portable CD player, cell phone, and bottled water.

Inside the airport, we walked slowly toward his gate, and I said, "Well, Skip, lots of water over the dam."

His eyes glued to the floor, he mumbled, "Whatever."

Anna looked at him sharply. "When your grandfather speaks, I think you should answer him respectfully."

Eyes still on the floor, Skip said, "If he hadn't brought me here in the first place I wouldn't have . . ."

"Listen to me, Skip. Sid didn't bring you here. You wanted to come here. Sid was kind enough to give you a place to stay. He may have made a mistake inviting you to play a part in our foolishness, but you weren't forced into it."

"You would have been mad if I took off when you talked about it."

"Please." Anna's tone became harsh. "And what about Karen? Do you accept responsibility for what you did with her? Or did we force you into that, too? You may think of yourself as a kid, but you're not. You're a young adult. It's time you grew up and stopped blaming other people for your dumb mistakes."

Skip's eyes finally came up from the floor, and he looked at Anna with hurt on his face. I had never heard Anna speak to him - or anybody - this way. I was pleased. With less guilt and more gumption I would have said what she said.

When we got to the gate, he gave me a shallow embrace, and Anna, a warmer one. There may have been a tear in his eye, but I might have imagined that.

On the way home, Anna said, "I know this is tough for you. But he'll come around. I told him he's a young adult. He's not. He's an overgrown kid. When he grows up, he'll come to understand how lucky he is to have you as his grandfather."

"Promise?"

"Promise."

Maurice called and said he had a preliminary report ready for me. He was only free at 6 p.m. I settled back in the one easy chair in his office and listened closely as he recited the progress he had made, the present status of the investigation, and the prognosis. His tone was upbeat.

Maurice had put together an informal group of eight lawyers representing the properties injured by the conspiracy, and they had elected him their leader. He now had forty-three affidavits from these properties, setting forth the details of their purchases of goods and services over the period in which, the lawyers believed, the conspiracy existed. The affidavit from Francis Travail was particularly valuable, Maurice said. It provided insight into the connection between the conspiracy and its victims.

Fifteen of the thirty-five co-conspirators had furnished affidavits, and Maurice expected an additional six, shortly. This was unusual. Ordinarily, the lawyers for the co-conspirators would counsel their clients not to cooperate with a non-government investigation in which no complaint had yet been filed and in which the plaintiffs' attorneys had no subpoena power.

This was Maurice's only experience where potential defendants *wanted* to cooperate, even contrary to their lawyers' advice. They were outraged after receiving the anonymous e-mails, and were willing to place themselves in potential jeopardy to nail down a case against Hardy.

When I had told Maurice about my mailings he had frowned in disapproval. Now, he said, "You scored on that one, Sidney."

Maurice's legal team would be in touch with the Justice Department in about a month. The pace of the government's investigation would determine the timing of civil complaints to be filed by the team.

"What's your best estimate on our eventual recovery?" I asked.

"It's premature, Sid, to speculate when we haven't even filed a complaint."

"Best estimate. I won't hold you to it."

"Six figures. Near the top, near the bottom, or in the middle - too soon to say."

Hardy's personal lawyers had filed complaints with the State's Attorney for Montgomery County, Maryland, alleging that Lars, Sheila, Anna, and I had conspired to, and Lars and I did, break and enter and wiretap the property of Efficiency Management in Wheaton, Maryland. Maurice didn't know whether these complaints were filed with the consent, or even the knowledge, of the parent company, EMA.

After speaking with the State's Attorney's office, Maurice's understanding was that the prosecutors would accept misdemeanor pleas from Lars and me. We would pay fines on the order of $5,000, and serve ninety days of community service to be prescribed by the judge. The State's Attorney had no interest in proceeding against Sheila and Anna.

Hardy's lawyers were unlikely to file civil suits against Lars and me. Such a case, Maurice said, would be questionable, resulting, at most, in damages of a few thousand dollars. After subtracting his lawyers' fees, Hardy's recovery would be insignificant.

Maurice had tapped his law enforcement sources in Washington and Maryland, and it appeared that no complaints had been filed against Skip and Karen for attempted extortion. Hardy's lawyers would have to convince California and Kansas to extradite an eighteen-year-old and a twenty-four-year-old who had been severely beaten. Maurice was confident that his lawyers had told him to forget it.

"More important," Maurice said, "the U. S. Attorney's office would want to know the basis for the attempted extortion. Hardy was not about to tell them it was a bid rigging conspiracy and inside trading in which he was heavily involved."

Maurice looked at his watch - it was 10 past 7. He put the documents spread out on his desk back into their folders. Then he got up, went to the inconspicuous cabinet tucked away in the back of the office, and took out a bottle of Chivas Regal and a bottle of Absolut.

Pouring the two drinks, he said, "The next part will be of special interest, and I will ask that this be between you and me."

Maurice said that the national corporation, Efficiency Management of America, Inc., EMA, had found out about Maurice's investigation. No surprise - hundreds of interviews could not be kept secret. EMA had discharged Hardy's lawyers in connection with any matter relating to the corporation. Hardy could hold onto them for his personal use. EMA's regular law firm was now fully engaged on behalf of EMA.

"The lead attorney is a man named Leonard Lister. Leonard and I go way back," Maurice said. "We fight like hell, but we trust each other. All of this is off the record."

Hardy was asked to resign and was given twenty-four hours to clear his office. He refused. He was handed a letter from the CEO of EMA discharging him, effective immediately. Security personnel escorted him out of the building, and he was told if he set foot on EMA property he would be arrested for trespassing.

Spotting the sparkle in my eyes, Maurice said EMA had cancelled Hardy's pension and stock options based on his "illicit conduct."

"The word on the street is that he left his wife and grand-kid, went to California, took up with his ex-wife, and is working on construction projects out there. He's a washed-up case. Nobody will touch him for any position of authority."

I asked if Hardy's departure from Efficiency would weaken our case against the company. EMA would argue, Maurice said, that they had no knowledge of the conspiracy, and that they promptly discharged the perpetrator when they learned about it. No matter how truthful this argument, it would not exonerate them for the wrongdoing. Hardy's actions were legally deemed to be in furtherance of his company's goals. In the eyes of the law, Hardy's acts were the acts of his company.

"Let me back up a minute," Maurice said. "After EMA heard about our investigation, but before they fired Hardy, I asked Leonard Lister to meet with me informally. Just him and me. I showed him five of the affidavits from the conspirators and five from the victims, with the names blacked out. He kept a straight face, but he turned pale. I think I made a believer out of him."

"What does that mean?"

"It means we might have a shot at a good settlement without going to court. I think his seeing those affidavits led to Hardy's firing."

"It kills me to tell you this, but you're not a bad lawyer."

"Just remember that when my third comes off the top."

"Tell me," I said, "which came first? Hardy's lawyers complaining to Maryland about the breaking and entering, or Hardy's discharge from the company?"

Maurice thought briefly. "The complaint came first, then the firing of Hardy."

"Maybe we've seen the last of Hardy," I said.

"I doubt it. I still think you should get out of town for a while."

No sooner did I get home than the phone rang. It was Hardy, cheery and helpful.

"You doing okay, Mr. President?"

"Fine, Chuck. How about you?"

"Great. I'm taking a little vacation from work. Time I smelled the roses. Follow?"

"Yeah. Where are you doing that?"

"Doing what?"

"Smelling the roses."

"What do you care?"

"Find out where the roses smell good."

"Very funny. I thought I'd check in with you, let you know you're in good hands with Stane as Acting Manager and Mrs. Crowe."

"I think it will work out."

"Should have got rid of Nikki years ago. How'd you get it out of her, where I was? Just between us girls, you were banging her, right?"

"Please, Chuck. How long will you be away?"

"As long as the spirit hits me . . . You ready to return my money?"

"We've been through that, I never saw your money."

He laughed. "Thought I'd give it one more shot."

"You broke our deal, Chuck. Your lawyers complained to Maryland about Lars and me."

Then it happened again. His ebullient congeniality vanished abruptly behind a cloud of rancor. "You sonofabitch. You have to know I got canned. You think that happened out of the blue? Your lawyer's been spreading shit around, and the smell got to EMA, so I decided to throw some shit your way, too."

The order had been reversed, as Maurice had said. Hardy's complaint first, then his discharge. Not that it mattered.

I said, "I don't know anything about that."

"You'll be hearing from me. You know that, don't you?"

"If you say so."

Morton Moody, Jane Fountain, and Bunny Slack had called to inquire about the status of our legal matter, and I scheduled an executive session of the Board to bring them up to date. I then arranged a meeting with Mrs. Crowe so I could get a better handle on the state of the Oasis financial position in preparation for the executive session.

The sour lemon had turned into a sweet plum. Gone were the gaunt visage and the squinting eyes. Her lips seemed fuller, and there was a touch of color in her face. When I first walked into her office, she smiled and said, "Good morning, Mr. Silva."

We discussed income, expenses, operating reserves, and replacement reserves, and not once did she jot down notes on anything I was saying. Mrs. Crowe was helpful, forthcoming, and agreeable. Her demeanor and appearance were distinctly different.

When our financial discussion was over, she said, "Oh, by the way, I looked over that form again. On our nonprofit status? I don't think we need a lawyer. I can do it."

"That's great, Mrs. Crowe. Any savings are welcome."

The jury was still out, but maybe I could develop, if not the mutual trust I had with Nikki, a productive working relationship.

I continued the subject. "Did you ever get to ask Mr. Hardy to recommend a lawyer? I'm just curious about the name he might have come up with."

"Oh, Mr. Hardy's gone. Didn't you know?"

"Gone?"

"Left the company. Somebody said he's in California."

"Really. Who took his place?"

"Mr. Stane is acting manager."

"Is that a welcome change?"

Her smile faded and she looked at me for a few seconds. "You may or may not know that Mr. Hardy was not an easy man to work for, even in the short time I knew him. Yes, it's a welcome change."

"Well, that's good, Mrs. Crowe."

"We're going to be working together. You might call me Ruth."

At the executive session the next day, I summarized what Maurice had told me and said the situation on our recovery looked promising.

Bunny Slack led off. "What kind of money are we talking about?"

Four months earlier, Jane Fountain had asked the same question.

"It's still speculative," I said. "It could be in six figures, but I can't tell you if it will be near the bottom, or the middle, or the top of the range."

Bunny could not contain her excitement. "This is a historical moment. Instead of raising condo fees we'll be lowering them."

They all began to talk at once. The din was broken by Jane Fountain. "I feel compelled to remind you all that the vote to retain an attorney was four to three. It sounds to me like four of us showed good judgment, especially Sid who led the way."

Bunny Slack, Morton Moody, and Audrey Weeks glared at Fountain, and to break the tension, I said, "Let's wait and see what we end up with and what our needs are at the time. Now, there are a couple of other matters You've all met Ruth Crowe, I'm sure. She strikes me as competent and professional."

Bunny said, "If she'd only loosen up."

"She's coming along," I said. "Give her time."

Moody asked, "By the way, what happened with Nikki? I still don't understand why she left."

I said, "She told me she's going to work in her fiancé's store."

"She left pretty abruptly," Moody said.

I shrugged. "The other thing is that Mrs. Crowe's boss is now William Stane. Hardy has left the company."

I tried to avoid eye contact with Bunny, wondering what she might say. But she said nothing. When I couldn't resist a quick glance, she was twirling the pearl necklace around her neck, staring at me. Did she know I knew about Hardy and the stipend? Hardy would have had no reason to tell her he had talked to me. Nor would Travail.

Her eyes fluttering, Audrey Weeks spoke for the first time. "Why did Mr. Hardy leave the company?"

Anna, Lars, and I shrugged as if on cue.

In an uncharacteristically condescending tone, Fountain looked at Audrey, and said, "Because, my dear, it came to their attention that he's a thief, and keeping a thief on the payroll would not be in the best interest of their company."

Audrey persisted. "Will Mr. Stane be a good manager?"

"We'll find out," I said.

Morton Moody spoke again. "Getting back to the legal thing, have you kept your eye on your friend, Maurice Ruffin? Is he ripping us off on the Xerox stuff?"

"It costs a dollar to Xerox a page," I said. "He bills us a dollar."

I would have to ask Maurice if I was right.

One morning in early July, Nikki called, out of the blue. "How are you, Sid?"

"I'm fine. How is it going? How's the hardware store?"

"I love it. I want to tell you something so you won't be surprised. I've invited Mr. Travail to my wedding. I have the impression he may not be your favorite person."

"He's okay."

"Well, I got to know him while he was President. He was a little stand-offish, but he meant well. Whenever Hardy's name came up, he would stiffen up. So maybe I feel sorry for him. Anyway, he's coming. Just wanted you to know."

"No problem. I'm sure we'll have a wonderful time."

The wedding was my first occasion since Sarah died to drag out my navy blue suit. The pants button could not quite make it to the button-hole, and I hid the gap with a belt. The jacket was tight and here again, the button fell short of the buttonhole. Nor did the top button of my white shirt make it around my neck. I left it unbuttoned, hidden by the knot of my tie. It had not occurred to me that ten-year old clothes were no longer wearable.

I climbed the stairs to pick up Anna, cursing as the strain of my corset-like clothes took their toll. When Anna opened the door, she looked me over, not missing the tie holding the collar together, the belt hiding the pants problem, and the jacket hanging open. She smiled and wound her arms around my neck, and my heart sang.

I took a step back, and looked at her tailored rust-colored skirt fall-ing just to her knees, with the matching gold necklace and earrings I had bought for her in Florence. I had a vague recollection that her black, mid-calf boots were called "chunky shoes" - thick soles and sturdy, broadly bottomed heels.

"You look wonderful," I said. "And I really love the boots."

"They turn you on?"

"More than you know."

"You'll have to deal with that. I'm not taking them off."

"Are you aware," I asked, "of the difference you've made in my life?"

"Of course I am. It works both ways."

Nikki and Joe Fowler were married in a small Catholic church in Silver Spring, Maryland. About a hundred guests attended the late afternoon ceremony, and then retired to a neighborhood Italian restaurant Joe had taken over for dinner and dancing.

It appeared that most of the guests were family, friends, and a contingent of Joe's favorite customers. Nikki had arranged for the Oasis people to be seated together. Sheila and her friend, Clarence, sat next to each other, and I was flanked by Anna and Francis Travail. I missed the presence of Lars, but I was aware that Nikki never had occasion to know him. Father Murphy, who had performed the marriage rites, was also at our table.

The ambience of the restaurant was plain and pleasant. The meal was enjoyable, and the conversation was convivial. A five-piece band - piano, bass, drums, sax, and girl singer - played quietly as we ate. They began with some light rock, and to my surprise, they resurrected a few hoary standards from the thirties and forties.

As coffee and dessert were served, four people, one after another, had something to say to me. The first was Father Murphy. He walked around to my seat, crouched beside me, and shook off my offer of my chair.

"I haven't had the pleasure of meeting you," he said, "but Nikki has given me chapter and verse about you."

"Then I'm in trouble, Father."

He laughed. "On the contrary, you are a person of moral fiber and empathy. But I didn't come to tell you that. Nikki would appreciate your saying a few words to honor the occasion - whenever the spirit hits you."

"Thank you for the message, Father. The honor will be mine."

A few minutes later, Joe Fowler pulled up a chair between Anna and me, and introduced himself. I had noticed in the church that Nikki had two or three inches on him. I gave Joe about five-five. He introduced himself and we had a delightful exchange. He was a bright, plain-spoken guy without artifice, and he wore his good will so naturally, you believed he was born with it. No wonder his customers loved him.

The third person was Travail. Nursing his diet Coke, he turned to me after I had asked the waiter to bring me another Absolut on the rocks.

"This is a lovely affair, Sid, don't you agree?"

"Completely."

"I'm glad Nikki invited me. I don't have your knack for being at ease with everybody, but I think she understood I tried to be fair with her. I'm sure she knew I was regularly in touch with Hardy, but she never mentioned it. She lived in fear of that man. But she's a person of such loyalty that she would never say a bad word about him. He was her boss. Period. She's what I call a class act."

"Speaking of Hardy," I said, "I appreciate your cooperation with Maurice Ruffin. He told me your affidavit will make a difference."

"Anything else I can do, say the word. I'm trying to put my life together, and helping you is a good starting point . . . Now, there's something else."

Lowering his voice, Travail told me that Hardy, adopting a friendly tone, had called him on what Travail later learned was - unbeknownst to Hardy - his next-to-last day with EMA. Making light of "our little flap down there in sunny San Juan," Hardy asked if any lawyer had contacted Travail about their "business relationship." Travail said no one had contacted him, and if they did, he didn't know anything.

Pleased at Travail's response, Hardy asked him to take "that sonofabitch Silva" to the Broth-L for lunch and find out "what he's up to," including any contact with lawyers. Hardy told Travail to send him the bill for the lunch. "And don't forget," Hardy added, "we have another San Juan coming."

Travail looked hard at me. "He sounded worried as hell."

"With good reason. Thanks for filling me in, Francis."

The fourth visit I received was a double one - Nikki and her son, Steven. She must have prepped him well because when she introduced the stocky eleven-year-old boy to me, he said, with poise, "I'm very pleased to meet you, Mr. Silva."

"I'm pleased to meet you, Steven. I've heard a lot of good things about you, including your wrestling ability. You want to try me right now on the dance floor?"

His eyes opened wide, and he said, "Are you serious?"

Nikki, possibly believing that I *was* serious, said, "Steven, he's pulling your leg. That's the way Mr. Silva operates."

His eyes fixed on me, Steven asked, "What does that mean?"

"I'll tell you later," Nikki said. "Now let's let Mr. Silva enjoy himself."

"Okay," said Steven. He shook hands with me, and he and his mother began to walk away. Steven turned after a few steps, and said, "Any place, any time, Mr. Silva."

The band leader announced that the first dance would be for the newlyweds, Nikki and Joe, all by themselves on the dance floor. Nikki, lowering her head in an effort to obscure her height advantage, and Joe, clearly not caring one whit about who was taller than whom, proved to be good dancers. The band launched into "Someone to Watch Over Me," and as they reached the halfway point, I spoke to the leader quietly, and he nodded.

When they finished the first song, they segued directly into "Happiness is a Thing Called Joe," and the girl singer came up front, giving it her all. *It seems like happiness is just a thing called Joe. He's got a smile that makes the lilacs want to grow. He's got a way that makes the angels heave a sigh, when they know - little Joe's -- passing by.*

A tear creeping down her cheek, Nikki blew me a kiss. I wasn't surprised to see Anna, too, with a moist face, but I was flabbergasted to see Sheila staring at the couple on the floor, obviously trying to hold back emotion.

When the song was finished, I made a short speech about Nikki's special qualities, and how fortunate Joe was. I concluded by saying, "Francis Travail worked with Nikki before I did. He said to me tonight, Nikki is a class act. It's hard to put it better than that, but let me try. Nikki and Joe are a class act."

*

The Indian Summer heat was hellish, and I developed a yen for poker in a cold room. Sheila's place was the answer, and she made the calls. Francis Travail was hesitant, Sheila said, but finally agreed to play.

I ran into Travail on the way to the game. He said, "I almost didn't come. I'm trying to put gambling behind me, but I guess a friendly game for small stakes won't hurt."

If he were serious, I thought, he should quit cold, but I said nothing.

I won the first three hands with one "set" - three of a kind - and two straights, and before we were fifteen minutes into the game, I was "in the zone." I lost the next two hands holding low-card flushes, and just like that I was out of the zone.

Halfway through the game, we were playing a modification of five-card stud where the first and fifth cards are "down," and the middle three cards are "up." The betting on the three open rounds was heavy.

When the last up card was dealt, Travail, relaxed and focused, had a pair of nines and a king showing, Lars a pair of aces and a four, Sheila an ace, a king, and a five, Carl a pair of threes and a jack, and Ron a six and a pair of jacks. I had a deuce and a pair of queens showing, and a third queen in the hole.

After the fifth card was dealt down, Francis bet, Lars called, I raised, and Sheila, Carl and Ron folded. Three of a kind in five-card stud is respectable, and I was sanguine. But Lars could have been holding three aces over my three queens. I was less worried about Francis. I figured him for two pair or three nines against my three queens. Either way I had him.

I bet, Travail raised me, and Lars called again, telling me he held two pair rather than three aces. But why did Francis raise? He knew my three of a kind would beat his three of a kind unless he had an unlikely pair of kings in the hole, giving him three kings. He must have assumed I had two pair, queens over, and he probably was holding two pair, kings over nines. My three queens would dispatch any two pair he had.

I raised Francis, and Lars dropped out. Travail raised me again, and I called. Francis spread out three nines next to his pair of kings. He had a full house, a very rare bird in five-card stud. I was stunned.

On the way home, Travail asked if we could sit down on the greenspace bench. It was humid and warm, but I obliged him.

"Sorry about that full house," he said. "I had to play the hand I was dealt."

I smiled, remembering Hardy using that expression in the El Convento. "Actually, you played that hand well. Sucked me in, spit me out. But it's only money, Francis."

"Well, the subject of money came up last night. Hardy called me from California. Have I seen Silva? I told him no. Have I talked to you? No. Why haven't I taken you to the Broth-L? Haven't had a chance. If you get in touch with me will I call him? Yes. Why are you asking me these questions, I asked. He received subpoenas from the Securities and Exchange Commission and from the Justice Department. He thinks you had something to do with it."

"Thanks again for filling me in. Everything is proceeding on course."

"He added something. He said, 'I'm not out of this yet. I know Silva's playing games, and he'll find out I can play games, too.'"

Chapter 20

When Maurice asked me to come to his office, I wondered if I was in for still more good news. I had no sooner sat down with my coffee, when he launched into a briefing on the status of the various federal investigations into Hardy's business dealings.

The SEC had released its "findings." Because Hardy had occupied a high level management position within EMA, he received confidential information concerning projected earnings reports. Hardy used this information to purchase and sell EMA common stock for his own account, and had disseminated advice to friends and business acquaintances regarding EMA common stock based on the confidential information.

These activities violated EMA policy and the U.S. Code. The SEC ordered Hardy to return his "ill-gained profits" from his illegal trading activities in the amount of $770,000, and to pay a fine of $100,000.

Two days later, an indictment had been returned by a Grand Jury sitting in Washington, D.C. The first count charged Hardy with organizing and participating in an illegal conspiracy to rig bids and fix prices. Maurice said he'd been told that if Hardy were found guilty, the Justice Department would ask the District Court to impose a jail sentence of three years, and assess a fine of $250,000.

The second count, flowing from the SEC order, charged Hardy with insider trading. Maurice understood that Justice would ask the District Court to impose a five-year jail sentence, to run consecutively after the first-count sentence expired. Hardy was free upon posting a bond in the amount of $500,000.

"What happens now?" I asked.

Hardy's lawyers could appeal the SEC order to the courts. And they could litigate the indictment. Maurice doubted this would happen.

"My sources tell me Hardy is out of money. I think his lawyers will tell him he's got to plead, try to reduce the fines, and get a minimum sentence with no jail time. All this, of course, will be subject to the assignment the case gets."

"I don't understand."

"The luck of the draw, the judge who gets the case. Some judges lean toward the prosecution and some toward the defense."

"That could make a difference in the outcome."

"Absolutely."

"This whole thing has gone faster than you thought it would."

"Yes. I'm sure EMA wanted the publicity to be over with as soon as possible. Their lawyers probably pressured Justice and the SEC to get the lead out of their ass. And that brings me to the main point. I'm going to ask you again. Get lost for a couple of months, you and Anna."

"I'm beginning to think seriously about it."

Maurice got me at home the next morning at 8:30. The judge assigned to the Hardy criminal case was Sylvester Dudley, who had a track record of bias against the prosecution in white collar matters. Dudley's speeches outside the courtroom suggested he was reluctant to send somebody to jail who had not committed a crime of violence. Around the court house, they called him second counsel for the defense.

"If Hardy pleads, and I expect him to," Maurice said, "we're probably going to see a mild sentence with a short stay in jail - or no jail."

Anna and I were sitting in her kitchen, and gazing into my coffee mug, I did some thinking aloud. When Maurice first said we should get out of town for a while, I brushed it off. When Hardy called me and said I'd be hearing from him, I felt the first tingle of alarm. When Travail told me Hardy had been asking him questions about me, I felt that Anna and I had better actively consider a leave of absence.

Looking up at Anna, I said, "Maurice's last report was the wake-up call. I talked to Maria yesterday. They have a place in Bethany Beach, Delaware, they use in the summer when they can get away from the restaurant for a few days. Right now, it's vacant and will be as long as we want. Suppose you and I go up there for a couple of months. Even Hardy can't know about that place."

"I've been wondering when you're going to get in touch with reality. Yes, I'll go."

She messed around with the coffee filter, dumping out the grounds, and washing the filter holder twice. Something was bothering her.

"When do you have in mind to leave?" Anna asked.

"Tomorrow? The next day?"

She stared at her coffee cup.

"What's the matter, kid?"

"I'll have to betray a confidence," she said with a thin smile. "The Board is throwing a surprise party for you at your favorite restaurant. Jane Fountain was the instigator. She called all the members and said that thanks to you the Oasis will shortly be flush with money. The least we can do is show our appreciation for what you have done."

Anna said that Moody and, naturally, she and Lars, were enthusiastic. Bunny was reluctant at first, but finally went along. Audrey said it would be "sinful" to celebrate the act of gambling, but she, too, eventually said she would attend.

They had reserved a table at Buona Sera, and had initially invited Sheila and her friend, Clarence, and Mickey. "I took the liberty of inviting Carl Harrison," she said. "I know he has irritated you, but I thought it was appropriate."

"Fine."

Anna wasn't finished. "Then, Francis Travail. We're aware of what he's done, but you've said he's trying to straighten himself out. And he has been useful to Maurice. Then we thought of Maurice and his wife, Valerie. And, of course, Nikki and Joe."

"You've gone overboard," I said, "and I thank you from the bottom of my heart."

I paused. "Bunny took a lot of notes at the Board meeting. I could be wrong, but I have a hunch she may still be in touch with Hardy. I'd rather Hardy didn't know about it, but there's nothing we can do about that so we'll just have to have a good time."

"When is this big bash supposed to be?" I asked.

"One week from today."

"We'll do it. Bethany Beach can wait a few days."

Maurice gave me another report on the day before my surprise party. Upon receiving his assignment, Judge Dudley had set a trial date, and told counsel, routinely, if they wanted to work out a plea agreement, he would look at it.

Over the next ten days, the judge had received letters attesting to Hardy's high moral character from two priests at Hardy's church and the principal of the high school Hardy's granddaughter attended.

On the morning of Maurice's report to me, Judge Dudley announced that he had carefully reviewed the plea agreement, the report of the pre-sentence investigation, and the communications he had received. On Count One, the plea agreement recommended that Hardy be sentenced to pay a fine of $10,000 and serve one year in prison. On Count Two, it recommended a fine of $20,000 and a jail term of two years.

Judge Dudley adopted the recommendations, except that he suspended the jail terms under both Counts.

"Hardy is a free man," Maurice said.

"Can't the prosecution appeal the sentence?" I asked.

"No."

Earlier in the week, I had bought myself a blue blazer, gray pants, and a red-striped shirt. The least I could do was not show up at my surprise party looking like a trussed-up mannequin. When I finished dressing, I looked in the full-length mirror. Not bad for an old guy. There was still a vestige of Burt Lancaster somewhere in there.

Earlier that day, I had packed clothes for a two-month stay in Bethany Beach, and Anna had done the same thing. When we woke up the next morning, we'd have a quick breakfast, and take off on the three-hour drive to Maria's hideaway cottage.

I walked up to Anna's apartment. She was wearing an all-black suit, a rust-colored blouse, and the jade necklace I had bought her in

Venice. Her pants were just short of her ankles, and her stylish black shoes featured thin straps across her instep.

I hesitated. "You look wonderful."

"But?"

"But what?"

"I detect an unspoken 'but' there somewhere."

"I was just wondering about those boots you wore to Nikki's wedding."

"You mean my chunky boots with the solid toes."

"Yes."

"What about them?"

"Well . . ."

"You want me to wear them tonight?"

"If you wouldn't mind."

"I put them away for the summer . . . but if they turn you on . . . you have a chunky boot fetish. Right?"

She went into the bedroom and came back in a few minutes. I looked at the boots, and Anna said, "Down, boy."

As a result of my nonsense with Anna's boots, we arrived late. We circled the poorly lit outside parking lot next to Buona Sera twice before coming upon a car pulling out. After locking the car, we walked across the now-deserted lot to the booth for the ticket that would be validated in the restaurant.

I detected a blur of motion behind a van, and two spectral figures began to emerge. At that moment a large green SUV, oversized head-lights beaming, pulled into the lot searching for a space, and as the lights swept over the area, the figures disappeared.

We approached the restaurant, and I said, "I could have sworn I saw Hardy behind that van."

Anna looked straight ahead. "Maybe one vodka tonight will be enough for you."

When we entered the restaurant, our friends were already there, and I followed the script Anna had urged on me. This was supposed to be a quiet dinner for the two of us, and I was flabbergasted by the party. I went through the motions of surprise, delight, and humility, and they all seemed pleased.

Maria had arranged a long rectangular table against the wall next to the service bar, catty-corner from the entrance-exit doors on the other side of the room. Although we were not closed off, and could see and hear the other patrons, we enjoyed semi-privacy.

I sat at one end, my back to the swinging kitchen door, Anna on my right, Sheila on my left, Clarence next to her. Jane, Bunny, Audrey, Carl, Lars, Dr. Moody and his wife, Mickey, Nikki, Joe Fowler, Travail, and Maurice and his wife filled the remaining chairs. All told, there were seventeen of us. Maria would have been the eighteenth, but she insisted on serving.

The restaurant was at capacity, and the festive mood at our table seemed to infect the eighty-or-so other customers. Different kinds of merriment filled the air, from lilting laughter to seductive smiles to buoyant braggadocio to mellifluous mockery.

Our group was in top form, and during any lapses in our repartee, which were infrequent, Sheila could be counted on to fill the gap. "Maurice," she yelled over to him in the middle of a rare few seconds of silence, "you're a big-time lawyer. Let's see if you can answer this question. How many lawyers does it take to change a light bulb?"

Maurice looked up the heavens. "I give up."

"Three. One to change the bulb and bill the client, one to watch the first guy and bill the client, and one to supervise the billing and bill the client."

Groans and hisses came from every corner of the table.

"All right, all right," Sheila said, "I was on the line with that one."

"On the line?" Lars said. "You crossed the line years ago."

Nikki and Joe walked around to shake my hand. "Steven asked me to give you a message," Nikki said. "He's willing to take you on, one hand tied behind his back."

"I like him, he's a good boy. You tell him I said he should never forget what a wonderful family he's part of."

Maria brought us red and white wine and bruschetta, followed, after a few minutes, by calamari. She placed a bottle of Absolut and a glass with ice in front of me.

Maurice got to his feet, and held out his glass. "I want to make a toast." They picked up their glasses. "This is to Sid - off-the-wall, unpredictable, stubborn, reckless. Also the most gutsy, decent man I've ever known. Here's to you, my friend."

After we drank the toast, "Speech, speech," was thrown at me.

I grinned, and said, "I will, but later."

We had finished the bruschetta and calamari, and were waiting for the pasta, listening to Sheila's bag of gags. Smiling broadly, I happened to glance toward the entrance of the restaurant. Walking through the door was Chuck Hardy in black shirt, black jeans, and black leather jacket, bald dome glistening. Following him was No-shave Gus, this time wearing what appeared to be a black, tight fitting suit with white shirt and the same wide, flowered tie I had seen before.

They spotted us and negotiated their way toward us through the tables. As Anna began to turn her head around to see what I was staring at, Hardy came up behind her, placed his left arm around her neck, and yanked her out of her chair. He reached under his jacket with his right hand, pulled a small revolver from his belt, pressed it against Anna's right temple, and bellowed, "Nobody move."

Gus stood at Hardy's side, watching everybody, especially me. All conversation in the restaurant ceased, and silence descended over the room. Nobody moved.

My world was falling apart in front of me. "Chuck," I said softly, "we can talk. Just let her go. Tell me what you want."

He tightened his hold around Anna's throat. "I want you to be miserable, motherfucker. I want to see you sweat. I'm taking your whore with me and we'll find out how fast you'll come up with $500,000 in cash. While I'm waiting, she's going to get a taste of what you've put me through. Does that answer your question?"

Hardy made a quick survey of our table. When he spotted Mickey, he said with a sneer, "Oh, Mr. Delano, how nice to see you. You want to come after me? I'd love that."

Mickey sat motionless.

Hardy's eyes lit on Travail. "You wimpy souse. Whose ass are you sucking now?" Next came Nikki. "Ah, there's my ex-secretary. Who's that midget next to you? Does he know Silva's been into your pants?"

After Nikki, Sheila. "What do you know? The foul-mouthed bitch is here, too."

And Lars. "Still looking for shit in my office, you prying prick?"

He tightened his grip on Anna's throat, and pressed the gun harder into her flesh. At no time did Anna struggle. Her eyes were pools of resignation.

As Gus began to explore the swiftest exit route through the crowded tables, Hardy whispered something into Anna's ear. Looking straight ahead, Anna formed a soundless word on her lips. I couldn't make it out. Hardy slowly turned her around until they were facing the exit door on the other side of the room. I sensed some stirring from Mickey and Lars, and without catching their eyes, I shook my head from side to side, fearing that Hardy would pull the trigger at the first sign of resistance.

The next twenty seconds played out in slow motion choreography. As Hardy, Gus, and Anna took their first steps in the direction of the front door, Maria came out of the kitchen through the silent swinging door. She was behind them, carrying a large bowl of hot, steaming pasta. They didn't see her.

In one swift glance, Maria took in the entire scene - utter silence, bald stranger's arm around Anna's throat, his gun pressed to Anna's temple. She followed them quietly, slowly catching up. When she was almost upon them, she shrieked, "*Figlio di puttana*," piercing the soundless room like a firecracker going off in the middle of a meditation group. Hardy jerked his head around, and Maria shoved the bowl of pasta into his face.

Releasing his hold on Anna's throat, Hardy reflexively brought his hands up to his stinging, smarting eyes. His finger twitched repeatedly, yanking the trigger of the gun, and it fired three times. The first bullet struck Carl Harrison who slumped over onto the table. The second bullet went into a wall, and the third struck Gus who fell to the floor.

Now clear of Hardy whose hands were still at his agonized face, Anna stepped back on her left leg, lifted her right foot, and brought it crashing into Hardy's groin. The chunky boot made contact with the target. Hardy fell to his knees, writhing and moaning, one hand on his face, the other clutching his groin.

If those twenty seconds were in slow motion, the next few minutes were in fast forward. Mickey and Lars sprang out of their chairs, yanked the gun from Hardy's fingers, and stood over him. I followed them and as I arrived, Hardy lifted his head, and made out the prone body of Gus. His head shook from side to side, and in a choking voice he said, "I told the stupid bastard to come alone."

Were the tears rolling down his face from Maria's hot pasta in his face? From Anna's boot into his testicles? From grief or guilt? From all combined? Something gnawed at me, but this was not the time or place to sort it out.

Maria called the police, who arrived in five minutes, and an ambulance which showed up in ten minutes. Two of the patrons in the restaurant were physicians. One examined Gus, and said he was dead. The other examined Carl, and said he was alive, but had been severely wounded and had lost considerable blood. The medics took Carl and Hardy to a nearby hospital. Hardy would be under police guard.

One of the physicians examined Anna, and said she had no serious injuries, but her throat might be sore for a day or two. Sipping on my Absolut, Anna was calm and controlled.

On the heels of the police came a cavalcade of newspaper, radio, and television reporters and camera crews. The police put up yellow crime scene tape, and kept the media outside. They set up cameras and congregated on the sidewalk and in the parking lot, interviewing the customers when the police subsequently released them after questioning.

The police were in the restaurant for hours, taking statements from all the customers. When they asked why Hardy had done this, Maurice gave them an explanation. Hardy had committed serious crimes which my lawyer had reported to the authorities, and he was angry.

As the police were finishing up, Maria announced that no customers would be billed for food and wine on this night. If they would print their names and phone numbers in the book near the exit, she would invite them back for a dinner on the house. In the months that followed, Maria was swamped with requests for reservations.

It was midnight by the time the place was cleared out. Only the people at our table remained, and Maria pulled up a chair between Anna and me. We sat there, drained, saying nothing. A waitress set out cups and two large coffee pots.

Travail asked if he could have a double Scotch. Over the next hour he went through three more double Scotches, and Maria later called a cab to take him home.

After our coffee was poured, Sheila, looking at Anna, said, "Remember that first night we were together? Sid, you and me? The next day I told you this guy will bring excitement to our lives? Get us off our lazy asses?"

"Yes."

"Was I right or was I right?"

Anna gave me a kiss on the cheek, and, looking at Sheila, said, "Ask him not to do us any more favors."

"Maurice," I said, "what will happen to Hardy?"

"With eighty witnesses, he'll be away for a long time."

"Maria," I said, "before you came out of the kitchen, did you know something was wrong?"

"Not really. I thought it seemed unusually quiet, but that happens sometimes. For no reason, a crowded restaurant will become silent out of the blue."

"It took guts to do what you did."

"No more so than Anna's. I hope she never kicks me like that."

After a silence, I said. "I could swear I saw them lurking outside. The SUV headlights must have scared them off. But why would he do this? And why in front of eighty witnesses?"

Another pause, and Anna hazarded a theory. This thing has been stewing in his mind for months, she said, and when he heard about this affair, that was the trigger. He was not able to contain his rage, and decided to come after us in the parking lot.

"He got there early and when we didn't show up, he was frustrated and confused. When he finally saw us, the headlights were about to expose him, and he hid, instinctively. It gnawed at him that he had missed us, and he said, the hell with it, and did his thing."

"He sends somebody to do his bad stuff," I said. "Why did he come with Gus?"

Nobody knew the answer.

"But how did he know we'd be here tonight?" Lars asked.

"My hunch is we'll find out when we see Carl Harrison in the hospital," I said.

Lars asked "How did he know Anna was your . . . friend?"

"There isn't much he *doesn't* know about me." I glanced at Travail who was staring at his Scotch.

Mickey relieved the tension. "What kind of pasta was it, Maria?"

"Linguini in a white sauce. I know Sid likes hot pepper mixed in, and I had Stefano add some. The pepper got in his eyes. That was worse than the heat of the pasta."

"One question for me, Maria?" asked Maurice.

"Go."

"What was it you said to him?"

"Figlio di puttana."

"What does that mean?"

"You don't want to know."

It was three in the morning when Anna and I got back to the Oasis. Before going to sleep, I called the hospital. They would only say Carl's condition was serious.

Still exhausted, Anna and I drove to the hospital early the next morning. We found Carl's room and walked in. The nurse asked us to leave, but Carl waved her off, pointing to the door. After she left Carl motioned for us to come close, removing the oxygen mask.

His breathing labored, Carl talked. After Travail had left the Board, Hardy cut Bunny's stipend to "a pittance." Aware that Travail had been receiving more money, Bunny was furious, and cut back the information she fed Hardy to match the "pittance." After Hardy was fired by EMA, the stipend ended, and Bunny gave him nothing more. When the Board had voted to retain Maurice, Bunny withheld this item from Hardy.

When Hardy arrived in California, and moved in with his former wife, Brandy Buffington, he happened onto some jewelry hidden in an alcove in Brandy's walk-in closet. He knew this jewelry to be valuable. Travail had told Carl that while he, Travail, was Board President, he had entertained Hardy with tales of Bunny's avarice for jewelry.

Hardy sent Bunny pieces of Brandy's jewelry, "one piece at a time," in return for whatever information she would dole out to him. After

Bunny had received a bracelet - a "stunning bijou," she told Carl - she called Hardy and told him the Board had previously retained an attorney. A few days later, Bunny received a pair of Brandy's earrings - "knock-outs," she said to Carl. Bunny then gave Hardy her last item - the "big bash" to be held at Buona Sera to honor me.

We talked to the nurse outside Carl's room. She told us the bullet had pierced Carl's aorta, and the prognosis was poor. "The doctor says maybe twenty-four hours." Carl fooled them. He hung on a week before he died.

Chapter 21

The media had a feeding frenzy, playing it as an example of "Golden-Oldie" heroism and courage. Local TV news program included discussions and interviews about the Buona Sera story, as they called it. Newspaper headlines highlighted the event above the fold, below the fold, and in the op-ed and feature sections. The New York tabloids grabbed hold of the story and wouldn't let go.

FEMALE SENIORS FOIL THUG

PASTA LA VISTA, GRINGO

KILLER GETS THE BOOT

HOOD GETS KICK OUT OF PASTA

LINGUINI, MEANY?

LADIES LAND LOLLAPALOOZA, HAVE A BALL

Pictures of Anna and Maria saturated the local television channels. Maria consented to a TV interview, and was asked such questions as "Were you frightened?" and "What were you thinking when you dumped the pasta into his face?" After that, she said, "No more interviews - ever."

As for Anna, she would sooner have subjected herself to the medieval rack than to an interview. Camera crews encamped outside the

Oasis, and Anna remained secluded in my apartment until they gave up and left. She considered writing an article about her experience, but when she realized this would trigger even more requests for interviews, she dropped the idea. She wanted nothing to do with reporters.

The local TV channels sought out Sheila who, after all, had witnessed everything sitting a few feet from the assault and was a close friend of the victim, Anna. Sheila's first few TV appearances were limited. As the station managers began to appreciate the special magnetism she projected, they asked her back for more, lengthier interviews.

Sheila knew when to cry, when to laugh, when to be reflective, and when to be light-hearted. In rendering Anna's valor, Sheila struck a balance of admiration, gusto, and sensitivity. She recounted Anna's bold lashing out at Hardy seconds after the hot pasta struck his face, and followed up with, "She knew what to do and when to do it." And then, after a measured pause, "It will go down as the most famous kick in history."

Newspapers in the city ran feature stories the day after Sheila's first TV interview, two coming up with the same heading: **THE MOST FAMOUS KICK IN HISTORY.**

Sheila painted a verbal picture of Maria's quick reaction. "This woman showed us what guts are all about," said Sheila with feeling. "Anna went for his you-know-what, and Maria *had* you-know-what." This time she grinned. She delivered her "testimony," as one interviewer characterized it, with a blend of objectivity and wit.

As the local channels asked her for more appearances, the TV networks ran thirty-second excerpts of her interviews on their evening news shows. Sheila and the camera took to each other like lost soul mates who, after years of searching, finally come together. After all her wanting and waiting for this moment in the sun, she thrived on the attention. Viewers began to contact the TV stations, expressing admiration for Sheila.

In the course of her television interviews, Sheila had become friendly with the station personnel, and kept Anna and me posted on what she was hearing. One of the local TV stations had been running a live twice-a-week, late-afternoon talk show called "Crime in the Streets." People of note - politicians, professors, clergy - alternated each week as hosts, interviewing victims and near-victims of crime, and after the interview, viewers phoned in questions and comments.

The station manager suggested to the producer of the show, an up-and-coming young man named Norman, that Sheila, currently in the limelight, might deliver a shot in the arm to the faltering fortunes of "Crime in the Streets." They asked her to host the show for two weeks at a modest fee that was flattering to Sheila.

By the end of the first week, she was connecting with her guests and forming a rapport with her audience. The trickle of letters, e-mail, and phone calls turned into a torrent. Viewers wanted to see Sheila. Several said, "Keep Sheila or lose me."

Norman asked the station owners for authority to offer Sheila a three-month contract with a hefty increase in her fee. By the end of the first week, she had already demonstrated her special talent. She cast a wide net to attract colorful guests with diversified experiences, talking about their harrowing confrontations with criminals.

Sheila knew, instinctively it seemed, how to extract interesting stories. With uncanny skill, she was able to manipulate the guests into including detailed accounts of the lurid and lascivious aspects of their experiences. Nor was Sheila concerned whether these accounts were accurate or embroidered so long as they *sounded* authentic.

According to the area Nielsen ratings, the audience for "Crime in the Streets" had doubled during Sheila's two weeks as host. More important, she drew viewers from a broad spectrum of socio-economic-age demographics. The seniors identified with her, the teens and sub-teens thought her raucous way with words was "cool," and the middle-aged viewers found her to be sensible and down to earth. The owners signaled a green light.

The show would now be taped in the early morning for telecast at 4 p.m. the same day, and Norman, the producer, with Sheila at his side, would view the tape at noon. After watching the first tape, Norman said, "The camera loves you."

"It's mutual," Sheila replied.

She looked at the camera the same way she looked at her guests, the same way she looked at Clarence and Anna and Lars and me. Her grimaces and grins, her gestures, her body language, and her manner of speaking were no different in the studio than they were in her living room. She was naturalness incarnate.

Sheila was not intimidated by the "suits" - the station executives. "They're always pontificating," she said to Anna and me. "Everything with them is a goddamn *immutable truth*. The suits are full of themselves, but guess what? They piss and shit just like the rest of us."

As her self confidence grew in the studio, Sheila began to employ the four-letter words punctuating her speech from her childhood. These were words as inherently a part of Sheila's mode of expression as track suits and sneakers were to her attire. From the moment I met her, Sheila relied on language that was, to say the least, coarse. She had once said to me, "Words ain't never gonna fuck you up, Sid, it's the people who use them to hurt you that'll fuck you up."

Increasingly uncomfortable with Sheila's use of obscenity, Norman asked her to clean up her act. She believed Norman's aversion to what she called "plain-spoken language" stemmed more from his prudish sensibility than from legal considerations.

At the noon viewing of the tapes, Norman removed material courting danger with the government. But he didn't stop there. He would also "bleep out" words and phrases he thought were inappropriate if not in poor taste - such as "it sucks" and "shove it' and "get a life" and my favorite, "whatever." Norman felt such language was not in keeping with the sober tone the show, as he conceived it, was supposed to project.

Sheila described to us how she resisted the bleeping. Squarely facing Norman, hands on her hips, she had said, "The bad-ass words are what they want to hear. Coming out of an intelligent, mature woman of substance and dignity, it turns them on. Let them hear what I say and how I say it. They'll love it, I'll be satisfied, and you'll be happy as a pig in shit because the Nielsens will soar into the wild blue yonder."

Sheila, Anna, Lars, and I - and sometimes Clarence, when he could get away - watched the 4 p.m. shows on my twenty-five-inch screen, and Sheila would fill us in on what was happening in the studio. She also supplied for our edification the missing words that had been "bleeped out" at what she called the noon "censorship sessions."

One of Sheila's guests was a history professor from the faculty of the college Skip had attended. With Sheila leading the way, he related his near-disastrous brush with three pre-teenagers who he estimated were eleven or twelve years old. As the professor approached his car in downtown Washington at 11:30 one night, the three of them surrounded him, and, in menacing tones, said, "Give us your money!"

On the tape, Sheila then said, "You should have told those [bleep] to take a hike." To us, she said, "*Assholes -* or was it *fuckers*? You should have told those *fuckers* to take a hike."

Sheila was relentless in urging Norman to stop deleting the words he didn't like. "The show is taking off now," she said. "Imagine what it would do if the audience could see, and *hear*, the show the same way we tape it."

Norman shook his head. "If we left those words in, we'd lose our license before you could say . . . ."

"Up your ass."

"God in heaven."

"We could go to court, argue the First Amendment."

"Forget it," Norman said. "We'd lose our license in a flash. Besides, I have to tell you, the obscenity you use is personally offensive to me."

Despite their disagreement, neither Norman nor Sheila wanted to walk away from the other. Sheila devoured the enthusiastic support from her growing fans, and Norman's superiors were gleeful every time a Nielsen report was released. In television parlance, the program was showing signs of having legs. But the Sheila-Norman tensions continued.

Late one afternoon in my living room, after watching a show with four bleeps, Anna said, "Why can't you just cut out the bad language?"

"I could live with two bleeps per show," Sheila said.

"Sheila,' I said, "let me ask you a question. Do you like being on the show?"

"I love it."

"Then swallow your pride and tell Norman no more dirty words."

"No, I don't throw in the fucking sponge that fast."

"What do *you* think, Clarence?" I asked.

He looked directly at Sheila. "I think they're right. You've had your fun, it's time to dispense with the smut."

My surprise of the week was her reply. "All right."

After Sheila eliminated the obscenity, her relationship with Norman took a positive turn, and Norman asked if she might color her hair to hide the gray. Sheila told us she felt like saying, *My hair is my hair, and if you don't like it look the other fucking way.* Instead, she thanked him. The suggestion was well taken, but she would hold off.

Toward the end of Sheila's three-month contract, the station owners were facing decision time. Did it make business sense to offer Sheila a long-term contract? Although they were jubilant over the rising Nielsens, the owners were puzzled. It was received wisdom in the television community that America adored, revered, cherished, and craved youth, especially female youth. The anomalies - Barbara Walters, Diane Sawyer - were no more than exceptions to prove the rule.

Norman overheard the station manager breaking in his new assistant. "Even old farts don't watch old farts on TV. Anyway, old farts don't buy. The buyers are eighteen to forty-five, my friend. That's where it's at. There's one immutable truth: age don't sell."

Selecting a woman in her forties for a key role on any program was questionable, and a woman in her fifties was downright risky. Going up front with a gray-haired, boorish-mannered, vulgar-spoken, sassy-brassy, headstrong, crude, lewd loudmouth in her sixties who insisted on showing up at her taping sessions dressed like a hippie, was a sure-fire recipe for ratings disaster. And no amount of coaching, coaxing or cajoling from the station "pros" was going to change her. What you saw was what you got.

Still, "Crime in the Streets" had been floundering before Sheila arrived. Ratings had been slipping and advertising revenue had been in free fall. The owners could not ignore that with Sheila at the helm, this tottering tub of a show had become a swift clipper. The size of the audience had soared and advertising had kept pace.

Despite all the immutable truths of the trade, the owners had to confront the vexing question: Why had this happened?

Some of the owners opposed to extending Sheila's contract had an answer. "She's riding high right now," they said, "but it's an aberration. Once the public grows tired of her act, the ratings will plummet. There's one immutable truth in this business: Plan for disaster. We say keep her on a short lease, ninety-day commitments, tops."

Other owners argued that Sheila was articulate, funny, adept at drawing out the guests, and, albeit in a geriatric kind of way, appealing. They pointed to the demographics demonstrating that the show's growing audience resembled a cross section of America. The station had on its hands a once-in-a-lifetime phenomenon. A member of the pro-Sheila group told Norman who told Sheila who told us in my living room, "There's an immutable truth in our industry: When you've got a good thing going, hold onto it."

The two factions of owners argued back and forth for weeks. Their procrastination cost them Sheila.

The major networks could no longer ignore the unprecedented success of the program. While the station owners were trying to resolve their differences, a twenty-four- hour bidding contest ensued to determine which network would pick up Sheila and Norman, who owned the rights to the show, now called "Crime in the Streets with Sheila Marcuse." NBC won and promptly decided to telecast the show nationally every weekday afternoon, and to increase Sheila's compensation fivefold.

Dispensing audacity mixed with charm, "Sheila Marcuse Talks Street Crime," the show's new name, broke daytime records. Sheila's nagging dream of fame and fortune had been transformed into reality. She was a nationwide star, and for years to come her clipper would ride high on the waves of performance in a sea of adulation.

But she never forgot who she was. When Norman refused to allow her two [bleeps]-per-program, Sheila appealed to NBC's President. He obliged her.

*

In the midst of Sheila's adventures with the media, I had called Bunny Slack and asked her to meet me in my office.

"What's this all about?" she said.

"Just be here tomorrow morning at ten, okay?" I gently placed the phone down. I was resolved to be calm and unemotional when I met with Bunny. But resolve doesn't always carry the day.

Bunny showed up at 10:30 the next morning with a frown. "Why are we having this mystery-meeting? " she asked, the frown deepening.

I looked at her without expression. "Sit down. I'll get to the point. You are a destructive force on the Board. I'd like you to resign."

"What the hell are you talking about?"

"You've been disloyal to the condo association and our residents."

"Oh, for God's sake, speak plain English."

"You leaked proprietary information to help an illegal conspiracy which victimized the Oasis and other properties to the tune of millions of dollars Your actions have been unethical. I don't know if you're legally liable, but one thing I do know. You have to go."

She stared at me, fondling her ruby bracelet. Her words came out in a snarl. "This confirms what I've been saying right along. You're irresponsible and you think you're the dictator of the Oasis. You go off half-cocked, inventing plots and stirring up trouble. *You* should resign from the Board. Who's been telling you this cocka-mamie story? That drunken slob, Travail, who can't even get it up any more?"

"Let's talk about Travail. You knew what he was doing because he told you. As a member of the Board you had an obligation to inform the Board. You didn't. So long as he was satisfying your weird lust for jewelry, you saw no evil, heard no evil."

Her head began to execute a slight up-and-down tremble, and her voice took on a tremulous sound. "Let me be clear. I was elected to the Board, and your paranoia is not a reason for me to resign. You want me off the Board, you get a vote of two thirds of the Board to remove me like the By-laws say. In the meantime, leave me the hell alone."

"When Travail's term was over," I said, "you stepped into his shoes. Now it was no longer a question of failing to tell the Board what you knew. Now you were an active player in the sleazy business."

She got to her feet, and said, "I don't have to listen to this . . . *craziness* of yours."

"And you were responsible for the death of Carl. You told Hardy about the party at Buona Sera, and Hardy killed Carl. I want you off the Board - now."

"I'm afraid of you. You've lost it." She walked toward the door.

I got up from my chair. "**SIT DOWN,** I'm not done."

She turned around, and I saw that the slight vein next to her left eyebrow was now inflamed and prominent. She came back, but remained standing, her arms folded.

A knock sounded, and I said "Come in."

Ruth Crowe peaked her head in. "Is everything all right in here?"

"Fine, thank you, Ruth." I smiled, and she left, closing the door.

Switching off the smile, I said, "If you won't quit voluntarily, I'll pursue your removal by two thirds of the Board."

She glared at me. "Two can play that game. I'll also have a few things to tell the Board. Like you and Lars breaking into offices in the dead of night, and illegally wire tapping telephones."

Hardy had told her everything.

"You do what you have to do. But there's something else I'll do. I'll talk to those fancy friends of yours you see at the breakfast meetings - I know who they are - and tell them how you abused their trust and extracted confidential information from them. I'll tell them how you betrayed them."

"That would be . . . blackmail. You wouldn't dare."

"Try me."

"Can I go now?"

"My pleasure. I assume I'll hear from you today."

For a short time in my little office, I thought she was afraid of me. As distasteful as the meeting was, I confessed to myself that I had derived a small satisfaction.

Carl's memorial service was held at an Episcopal church a few blocks from the Oasis. Anna, who had only known Carl slightly, asked if I wanted her to accompany me, and I said I did. Sheila, who had known Carl mostly through the poker games, joined us.

Before the service started, I looked around. There were twenty to thirty people present. I saw the other poker players, including Lars and Travail, and I spotted Carl's granddaughter, Karen, sitting in the first row with an older woman, presumably her mother, Carl's daughter.

After the minister began to speak, Anna turned around in her seat, and whispered to me that Bunny Slack had just arrived and was sitting in the back row. When the minister finished his remarks, he asked if anybody wanted to speak. Nobody came forward, and after a few seconds I walked to the podium.

"Carl was my first friend at the Oasis, and he helped me adjust when I arrived. Carl and I played poker, sipped a little vodka, and had dinner together once a week. We enjoyed each other."

I looked over the heads of the group, and fastened onto Bunny's eyes. "Carl and I also trusted each other. He had a wonderful quality of trusting people and he in turn gave people the benefit of the doubt in believing they trusted him. Carl's foremost desire was for people to help one another enjoy whatever fruits of life were available to them."

I then told them about Carl's persistent desire to build a recreation center at the Oasis where the residents could play games, watch big-screen television together, and get to know new people and enjoy one another's company.

"Carl and I were at ease with each other, and he enhanced my life with his sense of irony, his humor, and, especially, his good will. I hope I gave him some moments of comfort and satisfaction. He was a good man."

No one else spoke, and the minister made some concluding re-marks. A few people, including Bunny, left, but most of them remained, mulling around and chatting softly.

Karen came up to Anna, Sheila, and me and introduced us to her mother, a woman of deliberate manner with eyes hard as steel. They thanked me for my "comforting words," and after a few minutes Karen asked if she could speak with me alone. We excused ourselves and went into the small antechamber adjoining the chapel.

"I know," Karen said, "how much my granddad valued your friend-ship. You gave him a lot of pleasure."

I nodded.

She turned on a smile. "I've been talking to Skip long distance. He's doing good with the computers, and he's a really, really nice guy. He thinks the world of you."

I nodded again.

"I can understand his feeling that way. You were nice to me when I was in trouble. You came to see me, and you were so thoughtful in bringing me chocolates and all that."

Third nod.

"I'd like to do something nice for you in return. Skip tells me you're an investor."

"Oh?"

"You know, like buying stocks."

This time I didn't nod, and only looked at her.

"Something came up about a month ago. It's confidential. I'm not supposed to know about it, but, you know, I get wind of these things in my office, and I can't go around wearing blindfolds and earplugs."

She told me about a "leveraged buyout" in the final stage of planning. According to Karen, anybody holding common stock in the company to be bought out, would realize a tenfold increase in the value of the stock following the public announcement to be made in ten days.

"If I ever saw a win-win situation," she said, "this is the one. These people are the real thing. They're players, you know what I mean? Talk about a deal! I mean, you can go a lifetime and never have an opportunity like this. Interested?"

I remained expressionless.

"I'll give you all the info - who's doing it, who's bankrolling it, who's brokering it, but there's a couple of conditions. Minimum investment is fifty thousand."

I didn't respond.

"Second thing is this has got to be confidential. You have to promise me nobody will hear about it from you."

I couldn't take anymore. "Thanks, Karen, but right now I'm fully invested. I have no cash to spare."

I didn't mind her hustling me. My irritation came from her assumption that I wouldn't recognize the ineptness of the hustle.

We rejoined her mother, Anna, and Sheila, and after we traded banalities for a few minutes, Karen and her mother excused themselves. As Anna and Sheila headed toward the restroom, I said I'd meet them at the exit. When I got there, Travail approached me.

"Join me for a drink, my friend?"

"I don't think so, Francis. I'm waiting for Anna and Sheila and then we're going home. I'm a bit tired."

He looked disappointed, but didn't leave. When Anna and Sheila came back, Travail shook hands with them, and said, "I asked Sid to have a drink with me, but he said he's too tired. Think you can talk him into it?"

They both looked at me, and there was no mistaking their compassion for this lost soul. Misplaced compassion, I thought. "All right," I said, "one drink."

We went to a nearby bar. Anna and Sheila ordered club soda, I ordered diet Coke, and Travail had a double Scotch. We talked about Carl, Travail and I reciting innocuous anecdotes, and Sheila commenting on his uneven poker game.

Motioning to the waitress for a refill, Travail said, "You know, something I never mentioned. Funny thing, it just hit me. After Sid was elected to the Board, it was my job as outgoing President to schedule an organization meeting where the Board members would elect officers. Bunny wanted to be President so bad she could taste it."

Holding his glass in front of him, he said, "Bunny knew Sheila was campaigning among the Board members to elect you President. She knew Sheila was telling them you were the second coming, the greatest thing that ever happened to the Oasis."

Travail smiled, gulped down some Scotch, and told us how Bunny had urged him to delay the organization meeting to give her time to lobby the members on her own behalf. She also wanted Travail to lobby for her.

"She knew, of course, that Lars and Anna were backing Sid. But she thought I still had clout with Fountain and Moody and Audrey, and their votes plus her own would give her the four votes to put her over. I did lobby the three of them, for what it was worth."

Now well into the Scotch, Travail paused and looked at each of us in turn. "Here's the spicy part of the story."

Bunny could see that Sheila was making headway with the three uncommitted votes, and it began to look like I would be elected President, six to one. Travail told Bunny he couldn't delay the meeting more than another two or three days, and Bunny was desperate.

"She says if I want our relationship to continue I have to go to Moody and Fountain and Weeks and tell them that just before Sid moved into the Oasis, he beat up his wife and she died from the beating. He was arrested, but there were no witnesses and they had to release him. I tell her I won't do that and she throws me out."

Anna tapped the watch on her wrist. The compassion factor was no longer operative. I paid the bill and the four of us took a taxi the few short blocks back to the Oasis. Over the next few months I would run into Travail in the lobby, but we didn't have a lot to talk about.

Chapter 22

I called another executive session of the Board to bring them up to date. I opened up with, "I want to tell you what's been going on. You all saw the tragedy at the restaurant, of course. I can't tell you how proud we are of Anna."

Expressing the condolences of our community over the passing of Carl Harrison, I asked for a minute of silence. At about the half way point, I lifted my eyes to Bunny who, massaging her watchband studded with tiny diamonds, was staring at me.

I told the Board that Chuck Hardy, the former Manager of our management company, had been indicted that morning for first degree murder. The U.S. Attorney was seeking a sentence of life without parole. Hardy's lawyer, according to Maurice, believed that if a jury found Hardy guilty of first degree murder, the judge - no longer Dudley - was prepared to adopt the prosecution's recommendation.

I did not tell the Board that Maurice believed that with seventy to eighty eyewitnesses, the odds were overwhelming that Hardy would be convicted. Surely, Maurice had said, the lawyer was urging his client to plead, arguing that thirty years with a third off for good behavior could mean his release in twenty years.

"Want to know what I'm thinking?" I asked, nursing my Absolut.
"Do I have a choice?" Anna asked, taking a sip from my glass.
"I'm thinking we're due for a second shot at Italy."

"You've been reading my mind. This morning, for some reason, I started thinking about that phone call we got in the hotel in Florence. Mickey telling us Skip was gone."

I poured some more vodka. "That will be with me for a long time, too, but we had a good time before that call. Milan, Florence, Parma, Bologna. Two wonderful days."

"I cherish the memory.."

"Suppose we pick up where we left off," I said. "A day or two in Florence. Then on to Venice. September in Venice - we could do worse."

We consulted with Maria once again, telling her we had a week in mind - two more days in Florence, five days in Venice, and home. She laid out an itinerary for us, and we flew to Milan in late September. During the flight I brushed up on the Italian my mother used to speak when I was growing up. My father would insist it was more appropriate for his native Spanish to be spoken in the house. As in most things, my mother prevailed, but that was another story.

We rented a car and drove to Florence. It was even lovelier than it had been in May, and we stayed at the same hotel on the Arno near the Ponte Vecchio .

"Tomorrow," I said, "I'd like us to go back to the Uffizi Gallery."

"Fine," Anna said, "but we were there in May. Why again?"

"They just acquired something special we should see."

"What?"

"Just wait."

We slept nine hours, got up early, and were in line for the Uffizi before ten. As we walked to Room 29, I explained to Anna what we were about to see.

"It's a painting by Titian called 'The Danae.' One of many he did. This one is on loan from the Hermitage in St. Petersburg. When you see it tell me what you think."

We arrived at Room 29 and Anna gazed at the Titian for a couple of minutes. "The woman lying there under the man has a pained look. She's distressed."

I gave her a smug look.

"What?" Anna said.

"This is the oldest painting in the world of a female orgasm."

"Come on."

"Titian explains it in his diary in 1527. *Il primo orgasmo della principessa.* The first orgasm of the princess. Jupiter, King of the Gods, is making love to the Danae who is a Princess. They're doing it under the shower of gold you see there."

"He's not taking her by force?"

"No. A God, especially Jupiter, makes love to you, that's an honor, a privilege."

"That's the way you see our relationship?"

"Ha, ha."

"I think Titian is putting me on. You, too."

The drive to Venice was pleasant, and, like everybody else, we parked our car outside the city. No cars in Venice.

We took the *vaporetto* crowded with tourists and blue-collar and white-collar locals, and as the waterbus wound its way through the canals, we tracked the lines on the buildings marking the high-water and low-water levels of the unpredictable flooding that dominated and often threatened the life of the city.

A couple who I guessed were approaching their eighties came onto the boat and sat opposite us, speaking Italian softly to each other, and we covertly observed them. His clipped black-gray mustache trimmed neatly, the man was wearing a black suit, white shirt, and gray foulard tie. He was holding a handsome cherry wood cane between his legs. The woman's olive eyes and skin were as clear as they must have been fifty years earlier. Both of them had full, thick black hair flecked with gray.

From time to time one or the other of them would register a barely discernible negative gesture, and they may have been having some disagreement. On the other hand, their mutual warmth and attentiveness reflected a level of affection and respect consistent with a discussion about which restaurant they might favor that night.

At the landing of the Luna, two attendants took our bags off the *vaporetto*, and led us up to the hotel. We looked around the lobby, and, once again, we were struck by the Italian genius for beauty. Anna pointed out the small, unobtrusive chandelier which served as the esthetic polestar for the paintings, furniture and rugs adorning the lobby. Everywhere we looked, the scene was dazzling, but never offensive to the taste. *Semplice,* the Italians call it, but simple it's not.

Exploring the city, mostly walking, we sometimes picked up a *vaporetto.* We gorged ourselves on Tintoretto, Bellini, Veronese, and lost count after a few hours. We visited museums and galleries and palaces, and, on successive days, went to the Island of Murano to watch the glass work artisans, and to Burano, the celebrated center of lace-making. Anna selected three exquisite wrap-around shawls, a gray one for Maria, a yellow one for Sheila, and an amber one for herself.

No matter how much distance we had covered, no matter how tired we were, in the late afternoon we headed for the *passeggiata* - the stroll - in the *Piazza San Marco.* Selecting a table at random in the square, we marveled at the variety of tourists from all over the world, walking and talking and eating and gazing, and all of them smiling.

We would order mineral water or coffee or *grappa* - vodka is not their thing - and listen to one of the two bands spelling each other with old Broadway music from opposite sides of the square. The bands competed on the basis of which one could play more out of tune.

For Anna and me, the special moment in St. Marks Square was the 4 p.m. feeding of the pigeons. At the striking of the campanile in the bell tower, the pigeons would fly to one end of the square and squabble for the grain a government-employed attendant threw down to them.

On our next-to-last night we boarded a gondola for a two-hour ride. Our baritone gondolier sang his way through a half dozen arias, and Anna said, "You know, this is a corny cliché, and I love it."

We returned to our room just after midnight, and Anna, preparing an article tentatively to be called, "Florence and Venice: The Best of the Best," got out her pad and began to enter notes of the day that she made every night. I snuggled under the covers and closed my eyes, enveloped by a warmth of joy. I slept for what seemed like an hour, but turned out to be a minute or two, when the phone rang.

"Oh, please God, no," Anna said.

I made a calming gesture, but my hands were trembling when I picked up the phone. I said, "Yes?"

"Sidney, you lecherous old bastard, did they lock up all the virgins when you arrived? I know one thing - Italy will never be the same."

The jocular tone of Maurice's voice was the most reassuring sound I'd heard in years. I covered the mouthpiece and whispered, "It's Maurice Ruffin. Everything's okay."

"Maurice," I said. "I know you're a big-time lawyer, but do you know what time it is here?"

"I know, I know. When I give you my news, you'll tell me I can call you any time, day or night."

"What's your news?"

"We settled with EMA. Better than I had imagined. I thought you should know."

"How much?"

"Guess."

"Maurice, cut the shit."

"We got the biggest slice of the pie. The other plaintiffs got proportionately lower amounts. Ours was $1, 400,000. Deduct my third, and we're talking something over $933,000 for the Oasis."

"You told me you were shooting for six figures, not seven, before your cut."

"I lied. I didn't want to build your hopes too high."

"What was your starting point?" I asked.

"Four million. We knew that was going nowhere, but if I say so myself, the strategy was effective. They came back with $250,000, and I said all of us are wasting our time, we'll see you in court."

He cackled like a satisfied hen. "They said, what do you consider reasonable, and don't say four million. I said three point eight. They said three hundred thou. I said three point five mil. They came back with three-fifty. I said three point three. They said three-eighty. I said three point one They said four hundred. I said two point eight. They said four fifty. I threw two point five at them, and said that was it. No more back and forth."

Maurice said that at that point they broke off the negotiation. They called Maurice a week later. "They said, We're tired of this hassle We'll give you one point four, and that's it for real. You say no, and we'll see *you* in court. I said, Done."

324

"You were shooting for over a million, and didn't tell me."

"Don't worry about it, Sid, you're way ahead of the game. We figured from the start their goal was to keep it below two mil. And we figured they figured our goal was to get it above a mil."

"Maurice, it kills me to say this. You're not a bad lawyer."

"You've told me that before, and you were right both times. Mind you, I'm just giving you the quick-and-dirty. All this took place over months of intensive effort. meticulous, detailed planning. Round-the-clock, tension-ridden sessions. Times I got to bed at three a.m. Ten-hour meetings when I drank fifteen cups of coffee and no food."

"Please. Spare me the melodrama."

"One thing more. I'm getting the word that the SEC and Justice are bearing down on Hardy's lawyers. Call me when you get back. By the way, when I spoke to your friend, Sheila, to find out how to reach you, she asked me to give you and Anna a message. Remember your age, don't overdo it on the sex."

For our last night in Venice, we went to the restaurant Maria had recommended, Corte Sconta. A "very unfancy place" she had said, that is "seafood heaven" in a city renowned for its sea food. Furthermore, Maria had said, it passes the litmus test: on any given night you will find as many locals as tourists savoring the briny delicacies.

Anna and I were seated opposite each other at a simple wooden table in an open courtyard. Three other couples, French, English, and German, were at our table. The French couple next to us were paying their bill as we sat down, and after a few minutes the hostess seated our new neighbors. I did a double take. It was the elderly Italian couple from the *vaporetto.*

The man carefully hung his cane on the back of his chair, and turned around slowly to face me. Fingering his mustache, he smiled and said, "Buona sera." Anna and I said, "Buona sera," and it appeared we would have pleasant dinner companions.

They turned out to be more than that. They were engaging and simpatico, with a sophisticated wit, and over our three-hour dinner, strangers became friends. And as sometimes happens with strangers, we opened up to one another.

The woman, Elena, spoke a heavily-accented, but fluent English. She told us she had earned a degree after three years at Harvard Medical School. Her husband, Antonio, spoke and understood English, approximating my crude competence in Italian. We learned in short order that Antonio, sitting next to Anna, was a retired judge, and Elena, next to me, was a retired psychiatrist.

Elena explained that if we were cautious we could order our meal from the menu. Or, like Antonio and her, we could place ourselves at the mercy of the restaurant, and eat whatever they served and drink the small glass of wine selected for each dish. We followed their lead.

Between our first course, cuttlefish-ink pasta with scallops and zucchini, and our second course, clams sautéed in ginger, Elena told us about their twice-divorced daughter, Olga, who lived in Boston, juggling her stockbroker responsibilities with those of a single mother of a teenage girl. I had the impression that Olga was not an unmixed blessing. But then, I thought, whose child is? Elena and Antonio went to Boston twice a year.

I spoke briefly about Sarah and Brad and Skip, and Anna even gave them a synopsis of her long-ago, short-lived marriage that had us all laughing. Antonio, in his halting English, described their apartment overlooking the Grand Canal. It was at this point that I began to flirt with the idea of telling them the highlights of the Hardy-Oasis story. What could we lose? They might even provide some insight we'd missed.

I said, "I'd like to run something by you, get your reaction."

Anna leaned toward me. "I can't believe you're going to do this."

Before I could reply, Elena said, "Like in America, be my guest."

I gave them an account, with Anna - now on board - filling in my gaps, and Elena supplying a running translation to Antonio. By the time our *cernia* - grouper grilled in olive oil and lemon - arrived, I had painstakingly taken them through our discovery of the Hardy conspiracy, Nikki's help, Travail's torturous odyssey, Bunny's nefarious role, Elsie's dubious "accident," Skip and Karen's misguided venture, Hardy's background as uncovered by Lars, and the tragic night at Buona Sera.

After the salads came dessert. Over a warm zabaglione with Venetian cookies and sweet Piedmont wine, I filled them in on the legal developments.

Antonio, for the first time, addressed words to his wife. Elena smiled. "Antonio says, with no disrespect, that Americans are still living in the wild West. He wants to know if your lawyer believes this man will go to prison."

"Yes. For twenty to thirty years."

Elena was quiet and seemed to be preoccupied for a few minutes, and then asked, "Would you like my jargon-opinion, for what it's worth, or my lay-opinion?"

"Jargon," I said. Anna gave me a quick, questioning glance.

Given Hardy's behavioral pattern as we had described it, Elena believed he may have been suffering from what she called "intermittent explosive disorder." She said this disorder suggested a "borderline personality" characterized by feelings of rejection and abandonment, and resulting in uncommonly poor judgment.

"Central to this syndrome," Elena said, "are discrete episodes of failure to resist aggressive impulses that result in serious assaultive acts. The degree of aggressiveness is grossly out of proportion to the provocation."

"How about your lay opinion?" Anna asked.

Elena smiled. Hardy, she believed, had an unquenchable need to act out violence under certain circumstances. Most people who feel insulted or offended will have nothing more to do with the perceived offender, or might direct abrasive verbal remarks at the person. In Hardy's case, violence is the likely option. This violence could be directed at anybody, she said, but here, I was the "primo candidate." To the extent that Hardy knew how close Anna and I were, she would be his "secondo candidate."

Anna asked, "If he had been successful in abducting me, what do you think would have happened?"

"From what you have told me, if Sid met his demands I think he would have released you, undamaged at least physically. If Sid had not met his demands I think he would have beaten and possibly killed you. If you will permit some unsolicited advice, I think it would be in both your interests to try to forget about him."

Elena paused. "Please understand, we psychiatrists depend on jargon no less than our patients depend on therapy. In lay terms, this man cannot control himself. Sometimes his rage governs his behavior. But he is no longer a threat to you. Forget about him."

At the end of our dinner, we exchanged street and e-mail addresses and phone numbers, and after I insisted on paying the bill - "our quid pro quo for your patience" - they embraced us. They would let us know when they were coming to Boston. We would try to get together.

On the sidewalk outside, Elena had a sudden thought. Would we be their guests at a nearby coffee café, one of their favorites? After a five-minute walk, we ensconced ourselves in upholstered chairs, and Antonio ordered espresso for the four of us.

"Something bothers me," Elena said. "If I understand correctly, this man has been successful in his business pursuits. Is that right?"

"Very successful," I said.

"I know of very few instances where a successful businessman commits violence. He may hire someone to do the dirty work, but rarely does he *physically participate*."

It was true, I thought, that so far as we knew, Hardy was not near the scene of Elsie's death - accidental or homicidal. Nor to our knowledge was Hardy present at the brutality committed on Skip and Karen. He may have been responsible for these events, but he did not show up at the scenes of the crimes.

"Why was he physically present in Anna's case?" Elena asked. "His bodyguard, this man Gus, was with him. Why was Hardy there at all? Why didn't he dispatch Gus to carry out Anna's abduction? Why did he make an exception this time?"

*

Within a day after our return from Italy, I called a hurried executive meeting of the Board. "I'm happy to inform you," I said, "that the Oasis will receive a check for $1,400,000 in settlement of our cause of action against EMA. A third will go to our attorney, leaving us with something more than $933,000."

They broke into applause, and for the first time since I was President, all the Board members were smiling at the same time. Even Audrey Weeks had forced a vapid grin. I noticed that Bunny Slack hurriedly wrote something on the yellow pad in front of her. Presumably, "one point four - nine-thirty-three."

I distributed the papers Maurice had given me for each member to sign - to make it a "done deal," Maurice had said. Audrey looked around the table with that faux-innocence of hers. "I would like to know why Mr. Hardy left. I asked last time and I didn't get much of an answer."

Fountain exhaled a large sigh. "You still don't get it, Audrey. The guy is a crook. He put together an illegal conspiracy to rip off the properties he manages. As far as we know, EMA knew nothing about it. It cost them millions of dollars to find out what Hardy has been up to. What would you do? Give him a medal?"

"Oh, I see," Audrey said.

Bunny was still writing notes on the pad.

Lars asked, "Should we continue to retain EMA as our management company?"

I said, "That's a good question. EMA has now paid fines amounting to $4 million. It's hard to believe they knew what Hardy was doing. The Stane-Crowe team seems to be working. Before we begin the long process of looking for another management company, let me talk to Stane, and I'll report that conversation to the Board."

They all nodded. I knew that if he hadn't been an active participant in the conspiracy, Stane at least had knowledge of it. I would have to sit down with him and determine whether he stays.

Dr. Moody asked, "May I say something?"

"Yes," I said.

"I checked the bills from that lawyer friend of yours. You were wrong. When he Xeroxed something that cost him a dollar, he billed us $1.10, not a dollar. He made a profit of ten cents on every page."

Jane Fountain said, "Get a life, Morton."

Bunny Slack said, "You have a knack for the big issues, Doctor."

Even Audrey Weeks spoke out. "Aren't you making a molehill out of a mountain?"

Dr. Moody said, "You mean a mountain out of a . . . never mind."

"The next item of business," I said, "concerns Elsie Turner. Some of you may recall that Elsie actively supported and regularly volunteered to help battered women. I would like the Board to make a gesture. May I hear a motion that the Oasis contribute $50,000 to the Network of Battered Women in Elsie's memory?"

Lars said, "I so move."

Bunny said, "Not so fast. A gesture is one thing - you want to give away the farm. She was a good woman, but we don't have go crazy. It seems to me that $500 says very nicely how we feel. There'll come a time when we'll need that extra money."

Anna said, "I think we should contribute $100,000, and I move we amend the motion to that end."

Lars and I nodded affirmatively, and Bunny threw her hands in the air. "You people have lost your bearings."

I called for a vote, and the motion as amended carried six to one.

I then told them how Carl Harrison had been after me to get a recreation hall built. Carl felt, I said, that a comfortable room with a big-screen TV, where we could play bingo and bridge, and even poker, and have guest lecturers, art shows, potluck dinners, and musical evenings, would help bring us together as a community.

"I had construction people come over, and they estimated we could build a suitable extension from the office for $250,000. If the Board approves this project, I propose that we call it The Carl Harrison Social Center. May I hear a motion that we proceed?"

Anna made the motion, and murmurs of approval came from everybody except Bunny. "This is insanity," she said. "We get a once-in-a-lifetime windfall . . ."

"Thanks to Sid," Jane Fountain said.

Bunny was on the verge of losing control of herself. "Oh, shut up," she said to Jane. "We have this windfall, and you want to squander it. Look, I knew Carl. He was a nice guy, but he wasn't the Messiah. We can put up a goddamn plaque for him, for Christ's sake. We're going to need that money for a rainy day. *Do you know what you're doing?*"

Lars, the Treasurer, spoke up. "I think we do know what we're doing. We received a very large check this morning. Subtract the $100,000 contribution to Elsie's project and the $250,000 contribution to Carl's project, and we have more money in our reserves than we ever dreamed. We will be in excellent shape for a rainy day."

Jane said, "My turn. According to our understanding with Sid, Lars will give him a check for the $50,000 he advanced to cover the lawyer's costs."

They nodded, and Jane continued. "I think we should also reimburse Sid for the $100,000 he contributed so we could have Security install the new roof. I so move."

Before the inevitable clamor began, Lars seconded the motion.

Moody spoke first. "Now we are courting madness. We get a bonanza from out of the sky, and you want to piss it away."

"I *never* expected to hear that kind of language from *you*, Dr. Moody," Audrey said.

"You have a point, Audrey," Moody said. "Allow me to revise my statement. We get a bonanza from out of the sky, and you want to urinate it away."

The next few minutes were nothing short of bedlam. Everybody was angry at everybody. Lars spoke up in tone and volume uncharacteristic of him. "Let's all calm down and look at what we have. We begin with $933,000. We subtract $100,000 for the contribution to Elsie's fund, $250,000 for Carl's memorial, and $150,000 in reimbursement to Sid. By my calculation that comes to $500,000, leaving us with approximately $433,000. That will cover any rainy day I can foresee. I say we vote."

There was no further discussion, and to no one's surprise the vote was four to three to adopt the motion.

"There are two more items," I said. "The first concerns the provision in our By-laws requiring a two-thirds vote of the Board to remove a Board member. I'll come back to that. The second item is a committee I'm going to establish to contact a group of Board members from a number of upscale condos who meet regularly at breakfast. This committee will tell these people about . . ."

Bunny scooped up her papers, stood up, and said, "I'm bored with this Board, and I've had it with you people. You sit around like stupid little children and find nothing better to do than squander our resources. I don't want to be part of this anymore."

She looked at me, said, "You have my resignation," and stomped out of the room.

Jane Fountain raised her eyebrows. "What was that all about?"

Anna said, "I think she's miffed over the generous contributions.'

Lars looked at Anna. "When things don't go her way, she over-reacts."

Audrey said, "She'll be missed."

All of us looked at Audrey, and Dr. Moody said, "Let's get back to the subject at hand. You were saying, Mr. President, you're going to establish a committee and the By-laws require two thirds . . ."

"That's okay, Morton," I said. "Both subjects have become moot."

"How can a subject be mute?" Audrey asked. "Only a person can be mute."

I made an appointment with Stane, and drove out to the EM office. The gum chewer was gone. The murmur of businesslike conversations had replaced the hush pervading the office when I first met Hardy. And Stane's vapid manner had disappeared. He was responsive and, as far as I could tell, candid.

We sat down in Hardy's old office which Stane now occupied. He had coffee for us, nothing else.

"I'm here, Mr. Stane, to help the Board decide whether or not the Oasis should stay with EM or find another management company."

"Ill try to answer your questions."

"Thank you. First, were you aware of what Hardy was doing?"

"Yes."

"Did you participate in these activities?"

Stane looked directly at me. "No."

"Did Hardy ask you to help?"

"Constantly."

"And?"

"Not a week went by when I didn't try to get him to stop. I kept telling him it was wrong, and he laughed at me. I told him that sooner or later he would get caught."

"We know he has a temper. Did he say he would fire you if you didn't help him?"

"No. He knew I was a first-rate accountant, and replacing me would be hard."

"After Hardy left, did EMA question you? Did they ask if you knew about the conspiracy?"

"Yes. I told them I knew nothing. I was scared and I lied. They believed me."

"Did you consider going to the police?"

"I thought about it, but I needed the job, and Chuck did a lot for me."

Stane said that in the sixties and early seventies he and Hardy worked together in the construction business in New York, and became friends. Around the time Hardy went to Washington, Stane was "messed up on booze" and was fired from his job. Hardy sent for him to come to Washington and take this job.

"You could say he saved me. I haven't had a drink in twelve years."

"So you owed him," I said.

"No question. But that doesn't mean I didn't tell him he was stupid to be messing around with the suppliers." He looked up from his coffee. "That's just not my style."

"Tell me about Gus. Where did he come from? How did Hardy recruit him?"

Stane sat quietly for a long few seconds. "I guess it doesn't matter now. Gus is dead and Hardy will be away for a long time. Gus was Chuck Hardy's brother."

He looked at me to see my reaction. I kept a poker face.

"His original name was Guy Hardy. When they were young, there was some kind of trouble in the family. Something to do with the father. Anyway, Guy picked up a limp that's still with him. Hardy looked after his mother and brother. When Hardy got out of the army in '68 he went back to construction, and he got Guy a job with the same company."

Stane said that Guy "was always trying to find himself," and was going through his life "in a daze." Chuck continued to send him money - Stane made out the personal checks - but Guy, moving from site to site, was "not with it."

"When Chuck sent for me in '76 he told me to take Guy with me. Chuck had a job for Guy with EM. Administrative Assistant - bodyguard. Chuck asked me for a favor. Would I help Guy change his name, legally, to Gus Hadley? Confidential. If they knew Gus was Chuck's brother, the company would call it nepotism. Which it was. Until now nobody has known."

I absorbed this information. "When did you last speak to Hardy?" I asked.

"On the morning of your party at the restaurant. Chuck had called me from California. Could he and Gus camp out at my house? They got here two days before the party. Chuck wanted Gus to go alone to your party and kidnap your girlfriend. Gus said he was finished with the rough stuff. Past tense, he said. Chuck could go by *himself*."

Stane said they argued back and forth over who should go. "What do you think I pay you for?" Chuck would ask. "Kidnapping a bitch ain't the same as being your bodyguard," Gus would answer.

Finally, Chuck said they would both go. Gus wasn't happy, but he agreed.

"Weren't they bothered that you were listening to this running argument over who should do a kidnapping?"

"No. They trusted me."

"So Chuck Hardy killed his brother because Gus was finished with the rough stuff."

"That's about it."

"You've been open and frank with me and I appreciate it," I said after a pause. "I'm not a lawyer, but I can tell you that your knowledge of the conspiracy could be a problem for you. With the government or with EMA or with both. The Oasis will have to find a new management company if you stay on this job."

"Why am I not surprised?"

"I have a friend, a good lawyer. If you want me to ask him to talk to you I will."

On the drive back I thought about Elena's questions in Venice. *Why was he physically present in Anna's case? His bodyguard, this man Gus, was with him. Why was Hardy there at all? Why didn't he dispatch Gus to carry out Anna's abduction? Why did he make an exception this time?*

Now I knew the answer.

At my request, Maurice spoke with Stane. He advised Stane to resign immediately from EM, and sit tight. Stane did this, and EMA promptly replaced him. As it happened, the Justice Department had closed the file on this case, and never questioned Stane. I later heard that Stane found a job with a management company in another city.

I recommended to the Board we stay with EM on a month-to-month basis, watch them closely, and decide later whether to enter into a long-term contract. They concurred.

I had asked Anna to stay away from the courthouse when the judge came down with his sentence for Lars and me. Although Maurice had given us assurances that the sentence would be "acceptable," we were nervous, and wanted no audience.

We stood when the judge entered, Maurice on one side of us, and the local criminal lawyer Maurice had brought in, on the other. The judge asked each of us how he pleaded on the misdemeanor, and we said, in turn, "Guilty," as Maurice had instructed.

The judge asked us a few questions about our career backgrounds, shuffled through some papers in front of him, and came down with our sentences. After he dismissed us, I thanked the two lawyers, told Lars I'd see him soon, grabbed a cab back to the Oasis, and ran up to Anna's apartment.

"What happened?" she asked.

"We pleaded guilty to a misdemeanor, and were fined five thou each plus two hundred hours of community service. Maurice said it could have been a lot worse."

"What do you have to do for the community service?"

"Guess."

"Clean up dog droppings on public streets."

"Nope."

"Teach senior citizens how to use a cell phone."

"Nope.

"I give up."

"This judge showed imagination. Instead of the usual Red Cross work, he took into account my construction background. Lars, my new assistant, and I will be working with Habitat for Humanity, helping them build houses, shelters, and churches.

"Can I stand on the sidelines and cheer you on?"

"Only if you wear your boots."

The first snow of the season was on us, and we were propped up on our pillows, watching it fall through the dusk. My hand was resting on Anna's arm, and her hand was on top of mine.

In the middle of an embrace, a half hour earlier, Anna had asked, "How long do you think this will last?"

"Ten, fifteen minutes," I had replied.

She had burst out laughing. "I mean us, silly, you and me, our relationship."

"Can you deal with twenty years?"

"Easily."

Now, we rested in the calm following our first intimacy since "the incident."

I said, "Remember, I told you Travail was putting his apartment up for sale a few weeks ago? Well, this morning I heard it sold and he'll be moving out in three weeks. Nobody knows where he's going and I don't think anybody cares."

"I wish him well," Anna said. She meant it.

There was a comfortable pause. Something was on my mind. I turned toward her "Do you mind talking about that night?"

"No."

"I know we're going to try to forget about it, but I have one last question. What did Hardy whisper to you just before Maria came out of the kitchen?"

"He said, and I quote, 'You were getting tired of that slimy bastard anyway, right?'"

"Then a word formed on your lips I couldn't get. What was it?"

"Never."

About the Author

Dick Lavine is an attorney who specialized in antitrust law in Washington, D.C. When he retired about ten years ago, Dick pursued a long-suppressed ambition to write novels. "The Condo Papers" emerged from the process. Dick's four-year tenure as President of his condo in Bethesda, Maryland. gave him the experience and ideas he needed to write this book, although he hastens to say, EVERYTHING in the book is fiction.

Dick is also a classical and jazz musician, playing clarinet and sax. He produces musical shows in his condo celebrating the giant Broadway composers. He and his wife, Eileen, travel extensively. They visit New York frequently where their two children live. Dick is presently working on his second novel, "Perfect Pitch."

LaVergne, TN USA
12 March 2010
175879LV00001B/105/A